The John Muir Trail

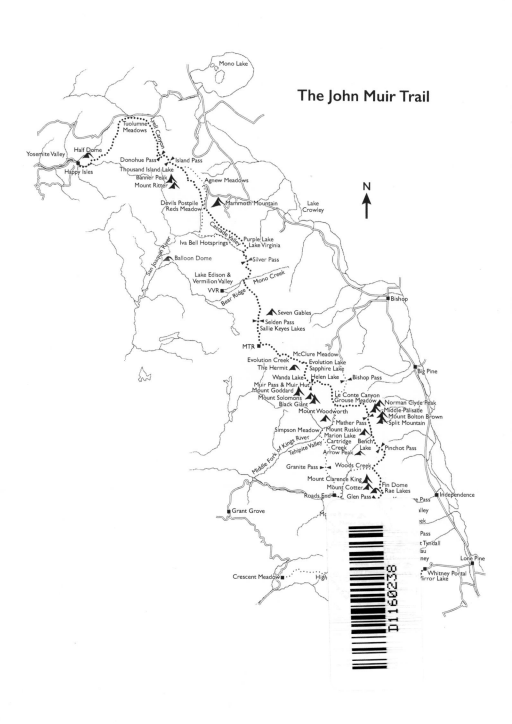

The Trail

ETHAN GALLOGLY

SIERRA NEVADA PRESS

Sierra Nevada Press, Los Angeles
www.sierranevadapress.com

"Anecdote Concerning the Lowering of Productivity"
by Heinrich Böll in *The Collected Stories Heinrich Böll* translated by Leila Vennewitz.
Copyright © 2011 by Verlag Kiepeheur & Witsch GmbH & Co. KG, Cologne, Germany.
Paraphrased with Permission of Melville House Publishing.

"Hotel California"
Words and Music by Don Henley, Glenn Frey and Don Felder
Copyright © 1976, 1977 CASS COUNTY MUSIC, RED CLOUD MUSIC and FINGERS
MUSIC Copyright Renewed
All Rights for CASS COUNTY MUSIC Administered by UNIVERSAL MUSIC WORKS
All Rights for FINGERS MUSIC Administered by BMG RIGHTS MANAGEMENT (US)
LLC
All Rights Reserved Used by Permission
Reprinted by Permission of Hal Leonard LLC

"Hombre Religioso"
Written by Jorge Garcia-Castil
Published by Edward B. Marks Music Company
All rights administered by Round Hill Carlin, LLC

Cover art and design: Faith Rumm, RummStudio.com
Maps and illustrations: Jeremy Ashcroft, JeremyAshcroftMaps.etsy.com

ISBN: 978-1-7374192-2-8 (hc.)
ISBN: 978-1-7374192-0-4 (pbk.)

Printed in the United States of America
2   3   4   5   6   XX   26   25   24   23   22   21

"It was 1884 and I was fourteen . . . I sat on my unsaddled bronco facing east and gazing in utter fascination at the most beautiful and most mysterious sight I had ever seen . . . the bloom-flooded plain, the old-gold of the foothills, the deep blue of the forest, the purpled gray of rock, the flashing teeth of the Sierra crest. I could see myself in the immensity of that uplifted world, an atom moving along just below the white, crawling from one end to the other of that horizon of high enchantment. . ."

—Theodore Solomons

"I have oftentimes felt that to meet one's fate on a noble mountain, or in the heart of a glacier, would be blessed as compared with death from disease, or from some shabby lowland accident."

—John Muir

For Audrey, Joey, and Syd

The Drive

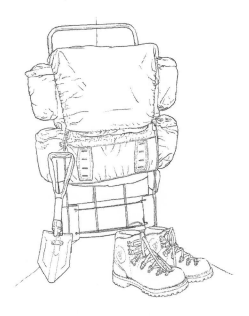

LIFE IS LIKE TRAFFIC: You get caught up in it, but when it's over, what do you have to show for it? Nothing.

I was gonna be late, but what did it matter? It wasn't like I really wanted to go anyway. What was I thinking—hiking the John Muir Trail with some old geezer? Stuck in the woods for nearly a month without a phone, decent food, or even a shower?

I plain hated camping. Not just the bugs and the sunscreen and trying to sleep on the cold hard ground, but that Pop would still be with us if it weren't for camping, or maybe if I had gone with him that one last time. What did I hope to gain by going now? It wasn't too late to call Pop's old buddy up, make some excuse, and turn back.

This whole thing had been Ma's fault. "It'll be great," she'd wheedled over the phone nearly four months ago, when the whole damn thing came up. "It'll refresh you. Get you back on track. Maybe he can help you find another job or give you some advice about colleges. You are still considering going back, aren't you? This trip will give you some perspective."

I got my perspective fine watching old kung fu flicks and searching for hookups online—the women in the woods would probably all look like Sasquatch! Why had I ever agreed?

"Your father would have wanted you to go," she'd pressed, playing on my guilt.

That was the real reason, wasn't it? He and the guy had been hiking partners since before Ma and Pop even met—and now this might be my last chance to understand something Pop had really loved. Something that in the end left Ma and I buried under everything that had come crashing down after. Maybe if I'd understood that, he'd still be with us now.

Ma had set me up, and when the old guy called, I could hardly say no. It wasn't like I had something urgent going on—being laid off and everything. This damned trip had all seemed so far off back then, but now the whole reality of it was kicking in.

The 405 was stop-and-go all the way up. I sat baking in my old Miata, the AC too much to fix after getting all this camping gear. *Hotel California* was blasting on my mix, *"You can check out any time you like but you can never leave"*—the perfect song for trying to escape the black hole of LA's traffic gravity. But that would just be my excuse, my universal excuse for running late. The real reason was Jasmine.

I shouldn'ta gone out the night before a big trip and all—but she'd been such an easy hookup, and it'd been weeks since my last successful encounter.

"You have such a cute tummy, like a big Buddha," she'd crooned as we'd rolled around under her sheets. As if my sagging beer gut were something to be proud of. Back in college I'd been a fit competitive swimmer, able to do the 100-yard freestyle in less than 48 seconds, juggling schoolwork and a job as assistant editor of *The Beacon*—what the hell happened to me?

I said I'd call her. She didn't need to know I'd be gone for a month. Besides, no matter who you cared about, it never worked out anyway—I was simply saving us both the trouble of an ugly breakup.

My car bumped and buckled as I pulled on to the long potholed drive, bouncing along between furrowed fields and a row of old olive trees towards the white Victorian farmhouse the old guy had described. The two-story building was flanked by a pair of smaller houses, both in need of some repair. Beyond them were open fields and a graying old barn. *Shit*—was I really gonna go through with this? Did I really need to be stirring up all those memories? It'd been nearly ten years since Pop'd died.

Before I could even straighten out my hair, a tall beauty in a long white dress with flowing auburn hair emerged from the main building, her left hand clutching a small black handbag. She strode briskly toward me, the gravel crunching under her shoes. She looked about my age, maybe older.

I got out, standing a bit unsteadily after the long drive. *Shit*—I hadn't even showered since yesterday.

She extended a thin graceful arm and we shook hands a bit stiffly. Her face was tense. Her eyes swollen. "I'm Cass, I don't know if you remember me?"

This was his daughter? I had memories of playing LEGOs with her and her brother when we'd visited them ages ago out in Berkeley. "Ma said you were running an organic farm or something, but I mean, wow, you've grown."

"Thanks," she swallowed hard, breaking into tears. "I'm so glad you agreed to go with him. I've told him a thousand times this whole thing is insane! That in his condition he needs to stay home and be with family. But he keeps insisting on this whole crazy wilderness thing—"

Why was she so upset? She wasn't the one going—

"Maybe you don't know my dad, but once he gets an idea into his head you can't change it. You don't know how many people he's called trying to get someone to go with him—but who has a month off for something like this? He was even talking about going *alone!* Can you believe it? Try to talk some sense into him. Try to get him to call this whole crazy thing off."

Was her father's condition really so serious? Ma had told me he'd survived his cancer, that he was in remission or something. And Ma hadn't told me he'd asked other people to join him. She'd said he'd specifically asked for me. That's why I'd agreed to go, 'cause of Pop and all. Still, chicks were always freaking out about nothing. I stood, waiting for her to finish.

"I know you can't phone anyone from out there, but promise me if anything happens, you'll find some way to get him to a doctor, then call me, OK?"

"I will."

"Thank you!" she hugged me tightly. I stood supporting her, her tears moistening my shirt. Finally, she released me.

Pulling out a tissue, she dried her eyes. "I'd really hoped to be able to chat more, but I have to get my son—they've already called me twice from the school."

Of course she had a kid. She probably had a charming husband too. It had always been my fate to meet dead-end hookups like Jasmine. All the good ones were either taken or total heartbreakers. "Sorry, there was a lot of traffic," I said.

She handed me a long list. Phone numbers of relatives, hospitals, and doctors that she had prepared, all carefully laminated in plastic. Then she pulled out three small pill bottles. "These are some strong antibiotics, some painkillers, and sedatives you can give him if there are any problems. The instructions are on each bottle." I took them, nodding mutely. Was I supposed to be the old man's caretaker for a month? Is that what they had really wanted?

"He's quite weak." She dabbed her eyes. "He needs care and rest. He's refused all medication, and even his doctors have warned him against this trip. But he's obsessed with the trail. He even made me drive him up to Berkeley to collect articles from the library there. And frankly," she continued without pausing to breathe, "at first I even encouraged him a bit, because it seemed like the only thing keeping him alive. He thinks he can do it, but you have to know he's really quite frail. Don't let him push himself too far. If things get tough, just turn back or find help. And call me when you can, OK?"

"OK."

"He's in there," she indicated one of the side buildings. She looked like she was going to tear up again, but then turned and rushed off, her heavy heels clapping on the rough drive. Climbing into a white Camry, she gave me a long look from the window, indicated the building again, then drove off.

I stared at the three carefully labeled orange pill bottles with their white screw-down lids. I could still go back to LA, make some excuse and hookup with Jasmine again.

Mechanically, I shuffled across the gravel. Almost immediately the door popped open, "Welcome Gil! Glad you could come. Come in! Come in!"

Inside, it took a few moments for my eyes to adjust. I couldn't really remember what Pop's friend looked like, just that he was tall. He should be about sixty now. The same age Pop woulda been.

The guy standing here looked much older. You could almost see the lines of his skeleton under his emaciated bony face. His skin was patchy and shiny, like dried sea salt, with disturbing purple blotches around his neck and shoulders poking out above his button-down gray flannel. His tawny hair was short and wispy with streaks of gray, but he wasn't bald like I'd heard many cancer patients were. He looked nothing like someone about to head off for a month of hiking. The only thing that betrayed any strength were his deeply sunken eyes, which sparkled with their own inner light.

Maybe like in every kung fu flick, this old geezer was really the hidden Master who kicks the brash young hero's ass—but more likely I'd just end up changing his friggin' diapers. Why the hell had he asked for me? I was the last person in the world he shoulda called.

"Do you want some tea?" he asked, his voice steady but raspy.

"No thanks. Ya got anythin' cold? Maybe a beer or something?"

He eyed me strangely. "How about some water? Our well is pretty good here."

"Maybe later."

"I see you have a bit of your father's Irish accent."

"My accent's a total mess—all diluted by rural Ohio, LA, and Ma's family—but yeah, I've tried to keep a bit of the Irish flair. In part to honor Pop, and in part 'cause chicks really get into it."

"You mean *women*," he said scrutinizing me.

"Yeah, same difference."

"Have a seat," he said, indicating a heavy wooden chair by an antique kitchen table. "I'll be a moment."

I remained standing, rocking from foot to foot.

He went into a small adjoining bedroom. Through the door I glimpsed row upon row of pressed suit jackets hanging in clear plastic dry-cleaner bags in the open closet, behind a neatly made-up bed.

His place was like a small apartment. A tiled dining area and a small kitchen branched off from a larger beige-carpeted living room. An old Tiffany lamp stood in the corner. Everything was neat and organized. The place didn't have that dreaded "old man smell," rather it was scented vaguely like sandalwood.

All of the furniture pieces were dark Asian-style antiques. To one side of the living room was an old writing desk. A collection of pens and papers was neatly arranged on the top. Most prominent was a large wooden bookcase. The books were ordered by subject, then by author—like they might be in a library. Basho, Blake, Frost, Hesse, Kesey, Longfellow, and Tolstoy caught my eye—all authors Pop had collected, and a fair number I'd read too, back when I'd been into books. But unlike Pop, many seemed to be about China, titles like, *The Complete Works of Lu Xun* and *Path of Beauty: A Study of Chinese Aesthetics.*

A faded green backpack, two trekking poles, and a pair of worn brown leather boots sat carefully arranged by the door. His pack was the type with the metal frame on the outside, the kind Pop used to carry. They didn't even sell 'em anymore at that outdoors store he'd sent me to.

His kitchen was neat and tidy with all the dishes and cups put away. The counters immaculate. And his small toaster and microwave unplugged, their cords draped over the tops.

Only the table was a bit messy, with several marked-up hiking maps spread out and a large yellow highlighter resting on top. On top of a small stack of books was *History of the Sierra Nevada*. Most of the others dealt with the Sierras in one way or another. Mixed in was a copy of Pop's old favorite, *Walden*, by Henry David Thoreau. I'd tried reading it twice, but never really got into it.

Next to the maps was a dog-eared copy of Elizabeth Wenk's guide to the John Muir Trail. I recognized it instantly 'cause it had arrived in the package he'd sent me, along with a long list of items to bring. He'd written that Wenk's guide would be helpful in preparing, but honestly I'd never even had time to open it.

I checked the messages on my phone. Nothing. I wandered around his living room. A long, yellowed Chinese scroll painting of mountains dotted with tiny figures and small trees hung from one wall.

On another was a medium-sized drawing with a gold metal frame, breaking the Asian theme. It was a signed black-and-white drawing of two nudes on a large flat rock by some secluded pool along a forested riverbank. It looked a little like the cover art of a classic rock album, the lighting having a dreamy twilight quality. The trees and rocks seemed more real than the two figures, who were shadowy as if illuminated by moonlight. You could almost hear the water tumbling down the bubbling cascade in the foreground.

"My son got that for me a few months ago. It's a signed lithograph from 1923," the old man's voice surprised me from behind.

"It's really nice. Your son has good taste."

"I'll tell him that."

"Say, sir, what shall I—what would you like me to call you?"

"Syd is fine."

"OK, Syd, that works. Listen, I mean, are you sure you're up for all this? Walking, what, a hundred miles or something across the top of the Sierra?"

"Two hundred and twenty miles. And a third of that above ten-thousand feet," he said levelly.

"Yeah, well I mean, maybe this isn't the best idea? Your daughter is all worried and everything. Maybe we could just hang out here and talk or something? I mean, you look so thin and all."

"It's the new cancer diet," he rasped, "it's all the rage. Looks like you could afford to lose a few pounds yourself." His eyes gestured toward my belly, which was pushing up from under my polo like a pregnant basketball.

"I've been tryin' to lose weight, but you know, work and all."

"*Beers and all*, more likely. Your mother said you'd lost your job."

"Well, not exactly *lost*. Besides, the work there kinda sucked. As for the weight, my doctor told me to consider exercise, but only after I got in better shape."

He chuckled.

"I almost forgot," I said, "I brought a cooler! I left some room in it in case you had any drinks or stuff you wanted to keep cool on the ride up. I also brought some steaks—you know—that we can eat our first couple-a-nights out."

"Steaks? You *do know* that we're going backpacking?"

"Yeah, so I had 'em flash frozen and sealed in plastic to last longer. I figure we can cook 'em over the fire. I think they'll keep for one, maybe two or even three nights. I also brought a pair of six-packs—in lightweight cans, of course. I got us Märzen, from this great microbrewery I know. I remember Pop saying you guys used to drink German beer together, right?"

"That was very thoughtful of you, but didn't you read the guidebook I sent? We're not allowed to make fires, other than camping stoves, and we have to pack out all our waste. It's just not possible to bring cans of beer with us on a trip of this length. And grilling steaks would be like setting up signposts for the bears."

He seemed to sense my disappointment. Pop had always brought along something special when we'd gone camping.

"Why don't you leave the steaks and beer in my refrigerator? Then after we get back, we can have them to celebrate."

"Sure, OK." I went back to the car, lugged out the cooler, and began transferring its contents to his nearly empty fridge.

"Better leave the cooler here, too. Bears can almost smell the word Coleman. Did you pack all the stuff on the list I mailed you?"

"Pretty much. The REI in Santa Monica had almost everything. But I couldn't fit in all the stuff I wanted to take, so I had to leave some back home."

"Like what?" he asked, looking concerned.

"At first, I put everything into the pack, just to test it out. You know, fully loaded, like you said to do in your instructions. But it was way too heavy, so I had to dump a bunch of stuff, like my bath towel, pillow, and some other things. All stuff I guess we won't really need—but now I think it's just about right."

"What's your base weight?"

I glanced down at my gut. "I don't know, two hundred and twenty, two hundred and thirty? I was planning to lose a bit before the trip, but I never really had the chance to start working out."

He grinned. "I don't mean *your* weight, Gil. I meant, what does your pack and gear weigh without food or water?"

"I never exactly weighed it, but I guess without the food and water it would be around thirty pounds max—like you told me not to go over."

"That's good. That's what you're aiming for. It's normal for beginners to overpack a bit the first time. That means fully loaded your pack should weigh forty-five to fifty pounds, which is a bit heavy, but not too bad. We can have a look at what you've brought tonight, but right now it's a bit late and we should get going so we reach the park before dark."

He guided me to Route 41, an old two-lane highway that wound between grassy fields and farmhouses up into the Sierra foothills. After we'd gotten outta Fresno he asked, "So other than our penchant for German beers, what else do you know about your dad and me?"

"Not much. I know that you and Pop were hiking buddies back when he worked at Berkeley, but that's about all."

"Your dad taught literature at Cal before becoming a high school principal in Ohio."

"I never understood why he gave up a job like that to work in some high school."

"Partially because he met your mother, partially because he didn't have tenure, and partially because an administrative job paid better. He always regretted leaving the West Coast, but there's a Chinese saying, *You can't gain something without giving up something else.*"

"That's what you taught, right? Chinese philosophy?"

"I taught everything from metaphysics to the Greek classics, but my specialty was Asian philosophy and literature, yes."

"Ma said you know Chinese, Greek, and Latin. And just like Pop, you can quote whole passages by heart."

He gazed off in reflection, probably missing Pop as much as I did.

"So, if you're an expert in Asian philosophy," I tried again, "then you've seen all the classic kung fu and samurai flicks, right? What did you think of *Shogun Assassin?*"

"I'm afraid I missed that one."

"You really should check it out. I'm a big fan of manga, samurai flicks, and Chinese kung fu movies—you know—like *Drunken Master* and *Enter the Dragon*. What about *Zatoichi*? You musta seen that. You know, the blind samurai, right?"

"No, although I am familiar with *Miyamoto Musashi*."

"You mean Hiroshi Inagaki's trilogy about the village hick who eventually becomes a real samurai? That's a classic!"

"No, I mean the book by the Japanese historical novelist Yoshikawa Eiji, but it sounds like your film is based on the same story. I'm sorry, martial arts and the Edo period weren't my specialty. My research focused more on the works of ancient China."

"You mean like Sun Tzu's *Art of War?*"

"That's a bit closer, yes."

"What's your spin on that? I've never read it, but most of the guys at the law firm I worked at said I should—that its principles can be applied to modern business tactics and all. It's actually quoted a lot in martial arts novels and stuff, so I sorta get the gist."

"What was your major? I'd heard you'd attended Northwestern University for two years before getting your paralegal certificate and moving out to LA. Your mother never told me the exact reason you'd dropped out. Was it because of your father's accident?"

"At first, I majored in journalism, but after Pop died I switched to law—" there was no way I was getting into the rest of it, even Ma didn't know the full story. "Listen, before I forget, Ma told me about your wife and all. She said to tell you she was sorry she didn't make the funeral."

He winced. "Thank you. Your mother had a lot to cope with back then. It couldn't have been easy for her raising you on her own."

The car hit a bump. I really had to do something about those shocks.

"What about you? Ma told me your cancer was under control, cured, or something. From what Cass said, your condition sounds pretty serious. Are you sure you're up for all this? We can always go back."

He sat staring at the glove compartment, the long empty lane stretching out ahead of us. "I suppose you'd better know the whole story."

He looked at me, "A few months after Katrine, my wife, passed away, I began feeling tired. I was sleeping quite a bit, which is unusual for me, and I was getting these awful night sweats. My sheets would literally be soaked. Then I began developing these painful lumps under my arms and around my neck. At first, I thought I had a low-grade fever, or that it was depression over Katrine's passing, or just normal aging and arthritis. But then I started getting these awful nose bleeds and purple blotches started appearing on my skin, so I went in for a physical." His face looked pained.

"My doctor ordered some blood tests and then a biopsy. The result was that I have acute myelogenous leukemia, or simply AML, which is bad news for someone my age, because while many leukemias are quite manageable, the survival rate for AML is only about one in four."

"That's terrible. Leukemia is when your lymph nodes get infected, right?"

"No, that's only a symptom. It's really a cancer of the blood. Your bone marrow starts producing abnormal cells, which interfere with things like clotting and fighting off infection."

"That's awful."

"Yes. I was quite depressed when I found out. Nevertheless, the doctors said that I had a strong immune system and a good constitution for my age. They wanted to try aggressive chemotherapy, so I agreed." He swallowed, "Chemotherapy is about the worst experience you can imagine. They connect you up to an IV and the liquid burns as it goes in. At first, I didn't have much of a reaction, but after my third treatment the nausea started, and then the diarrhea. Uncontrollable diarrhea."

I shifted in my seat.

"Then my hair started falling out. At first, it was only strands, but soon entire clumps. I had to shave my head. My mouth became dry and swollen, and I was dizzy and disorientated. I couldn't walk or cook or even read. I've never felt so helpless in all my life. Imagine not being able to read."

For someone like him, that musta been hard. Pop had been the same way, always reading something. I'd been like that too—up until the accident.

"And those damn hospital televisions," he continued. "On all the time. The guy in the bed next to me was an addict. Wouldn't shut the damn thing off. They had such moronic programming. All game shows and soap operas."

"Yeah, daytime TV really sucks."

"Cass brought me some movies, but my head was swimming with the chemicals. It was hard to concentrate on anything for very long."

The road wound and banked as we began to climb.

"How long did the chemo last?" It was better to let him ramble on than answer all sorts of questions about myself. If there was one thing I'd learned about old people, they never got tired of talking about their medical conditions.

"Most people can get all the doses in just two or three weeks, but because of my side effects, mine took almost two months. And afterward, I had to remain in the hospital for observation."

"Sounds awful."

"It was. A hospital is no place to get well in. It's like an icy prison. The food is awful. All night the machines beep. There are announcements over the loudspeakers. And the nurses come and go measuring this and that."

His face was flushed now. "They also sent me to a cancer support group. That was a complete waste of time."

I knew exactly what he was talking about. Ma had insisted I go to one of those after Pop died. Everyone just sat around blubbering about their feelings. It was embarrassing, and I'd refused to go again.

"After the chemotherapy, I was weak and terribly thin. You may think I look thin now, but believe me, I looked like a wooden scarecrow. I could barely walk. Most of my muscles had atrophied. It took me over four weeks just to be able to use the toilet on my own. I can't tell you how humiliating that is."

He sighed and then continued. "It was around then that I moved down to Fresno. At first, it was just temporary so Cass could help take care of me. But later, when it became apparent that I wouldn't be able to drive or even handle basic functions for some time, we sold the house in Berkeley and I moved down permanently. It was simpler that way. Cass was a great help. She handled most of the sale and the moving."

"She's really grown up a lot. I remember Sean too. How's he doing?"

"He's a pathologist on the East Coast now. I don't see much of him, but we speak on the phone regularly. He flew out several times during my treatment and is doing well. He has a son too. They're living close to DC."

"You have great kids."

He smiled warmly for the first time since I'd picked him up.

"After another month or so in Fresno, the worst of the side effects passed. My head stopped swimming. And I could read again. Even my hair started coming back. With Cass's cooking and a lot of protein and exercise, I regained weight and muscle tone. Although my right knee is still weak, so we're gonna have to watch that."

"Wait, I don't get it. Cass said you're still sick, but Ma told me you were cured."

"That's the problem. I do feel better now. And things were going well after the chemotherapy. My oncologist said it looked like I would make it. Cass and I even went out for a special little dinner at Chez Panisse. But then in December, I went back for a follow-up and the doctor said my cancer had returned. He said he wasn't sure when, perhaps in a few months, or maybe a year, it would get worse again, and when it did my prognosis wasn't good."

"So wait, that's over six months ago—"

"Yes, and I've been getting worse. It's harder to exercise. And a few of my symptoms have returned. The oncologists say that at this rate I have four, maybe five months left, which is why I need to hike the trail now."

"Isn't there something else the doctors can do?"

He stared out the side window, then looked back at me. "They wanted me to try radiation. They wanted to irradiate my whole body in order to kill off all my bone marrow. They wanted to inject my bones with fresh cells from one of my cousins and see if that would take."

The only thing I knew about radiation was from *The Hulk* and *X-Men*, but in his case it was serious.

"They said I'd have about a one-in-five chance of recovery. But there would also be a chance that the radiation would kill me, or that I'd get some other cancer from the procedure. And I would need chemo again afterward. If I agreed, I'd be back in the hospital indefinitely."

He fidgeted with his belt. "I refused. I told them I'd rather die at home or on the trail than to be a lab rat and die wasting away in some cold hospital bed, without dignity. I just couldn't go back to that place."

I stared at the long dividing line splitting the road ahead. This wasn't at all like Ma had said. Why hadn't I asked him about his condition over the phone? I'd thought by going on this trip I'd get a better understanding of Pop, maybe drop some weight, and get some leads on what to do next with my career—at least pick up a letter of recommendation or something. Instead, I was heading off into the mountains with a guy who was about to kick it of cancer and who needed serious treatment. No wonder Cass was all freaked out. This wasn't gonna be a holiday. This was gonna be a nightmare. I knew nothing about cancer or hiking or medicine. I hadn't even been there for Pop when he'd needed me—what could I do for this guy? But Ma had insisted that he'd specifically asked for me. Or had he? Cass had said he'd called other people too. The car went over a small rise, and my stomach sank.

He musta read what I was thinking 'cause of the way he was staring at me, his face choked-up with emotion, his eyes pleading. "The Chinese have a saying, *Failure isn't falling down, it's refusing to get up.*"

His words sounded like something blind old Master Po woulda told Grasshopper, David Carradine's character in the old *Kung Fu* TV series.

We came to a small town and stopped to fill up and grab a bite at some lodge he knew. It was a nice dinner, and he insisted on paying. We didn't talk much, but I watched him as he ate. He definitely packed an appetite. Maybe the doctors were wrong about him? Would this guy really be heading off into the woods if things were that bad? He was a professor, not some nutjob. I felt like Neo in *The Matrix*, having to choose between the red and blue pills.

Stopping for dinner turned out to be a mistake, 'cause when we finally entered the park, the ranger station was closed.

"This means we can't camp at the trailhead," he explained. Apparently, you needed a wilderness permit or a reservation to spend the night in Yosemite. "We'll just have to find a motel room out around the eastern entrance."

It was a long drive across the park, but we finally found vacancy at a dingy roadside motel. It was a sorry-looking gray metal affair that smelled like a truck stop, but it was ten-thirty and anything would do.

After showering, Syd sat up in bed with his guidebook, while I walked the two chilly blocks along the highway that constituted the entire "town" of Lee Vining. I was looking for anyplace I might find a drink and clear my head. This whole thing was way more than I'd agreed to.

The streets were an empty assortment of darkened old tourist shops. The one restaurant with a bar had closed up around ten. This definitely wasn't LA. Hands in my pockets, I wandered back toward the motel.

Maybe I could just go partway? We had to exit the woods at several spots to resupply. The first would be at a place called "Reds Meadow." There'd be a road there. I could go with him up to that point, fake a sprained ankle or something, and then we'd have to go back. It would be enough time to find out about him and Pop and keep my promise to Ma without having to spend an entire month in the woods playing nursemaid.

When I reached the room, the lights were out, and he was snoring quietly. Lying down on my squeaky bed, I tried to sleep.

DAY ONE

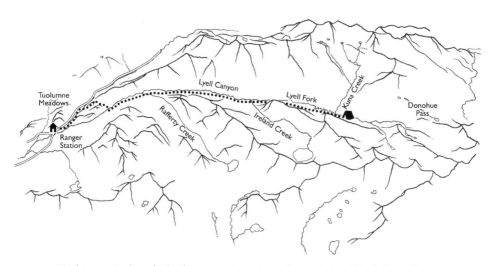

Tuolumne Meadows (8,600') to approximately a mile past Ireland Creek (8,990')*

8 miles—480 feet elevation gain; 90 feet elevation loss

"**Y**OU'RE NOT WEARING THAT SHIRT, are you?"

It took me a moment—my body itchy for sleep after Syd's wheezing all night and the thin motel pillows. "It's only fifty percent cotton," I said, recalling the REI salesgirl's mantra, *cotton kills*, in reference to any clothes not made entirely from high-tech moisture-wicking fabric. The truth is, I'd tried on one of their synthetic hiking shirts—some stretchy, almost transparent fabric in a color called Blueberry Heather—and clingy did not even begin to describe that material. The shirt wrapped around my midsection making my gut jut out like an eight-month baby bump. Worse still, the fabric stuck so tightly to my upper

---

* Feet and miles were chosen over meters and kilometers because these are the units generally in use along the trail. The elevation gain and loss given below each chapter title is the *total* gain and loss experienced over the undulations of the trail for that particular day. Values given here are approximate and based on available maps and GPS data. Mile-by-mile elevation profiles for the John Muir Trail are available in most guidebooks. For readers interested in following the text with detailed topographical maps, the author recommends Tom Harrison's *John Muir Trail Map-Pack*, which is available at most outdoor stores.

chest that my normally invisible man boobs burst out like a pair of melons. The thin material highlighting the bumps of my areolae in a way that would make a milk-cow blush. There was no way I was wearing that thing, so I had simply packed a couple of my old cotton blend tees, mantra or no.

Syd shook his head. "I don't mean the fabric, although a synthetic shirt would be better. I mean, St. Pauli Girl?"

The shirt was one of my favorites. A comfortable tee, with St. Pauli Girl's brimming mugs practically bursting out of my chest. Syd's own olive-colored hiking shirt, with its abstract pattern vaguely suggesting mountains and trees, was drab by comparison.

"What's wrong with it? Should I wear my Coors shirt?"

"It's not the beer—I mean, would you wear that around your mother?"

"But we're not going to Ma's. We're going hiking—"

"Never mind," he rolled his eyes.

Half awake, we drove the now empty road back up into Yosemite. I hadn't noticed it last night, but to each side of the road were sheer cliffs, forested hillsides, giant boulders, and wide shelves of smooth gray granite punctuated by the occasional tumbling cascade. In the far distance rose lofty mountain peaks dotted with snow. Is this what we'd be hiking over? It felt a bit overwhelming now that I was taking it all in. All I'd ever done before was follow Pop on some weekend camping trips in Ohio, which I'd hated. These mountains looked way bigger than anything Pop had brought me to as a boy. And even then I'd never shouldered a real pack. Pop had always carried all the heavy stuff.

It was a quarter to seven when we pulled into the parking lot at the Tuolumne Meadows ranger station. Outside was a long line of people, some sitting in folding chairs, some bundled in down jackets—as if they'd been waiting overnight for concert tickets.

"What are they doing there?" I asked him.

"Waiting for wilderness permits."

"Do you think we'll be able to get one?"

"I've already taken care of that."

I followed him to the front of the line.

A thin woman gestured territorially in the other direction, "The line starts back there," she hissed.

"We already have permit reservations," Syd explained calmly.

A man with a thin goatee who had been milling around near the back walked up and asked, "Is this where people with reservations wait?"

Syd nodded.

"Nice shirt, man!" he said to me, grinning broadly.

"Thanks," I replied. Syd let out an exasperated sigh.

The man hung out next to us making idle chitchat.

At exactly seven o'clock, a green park service pickup pulled into the lot and an African American woman in a pressed green and gray ranger uniform with a gold badge climbed out and unlocked the station. The people in line stood up in anticipation.

"OK." she boomed "First off, is there anyone here who's already been issued a permit reservation and is just picking one up today?"

Syd walked up, saying we were. The tall man with the goatee hung behind him.

"Do you have a reservation too?" the ranger eyed the man.

"Uh, no, not exactly, but I was wondering if there was anything available for today?"

"You'll have to wait your turn like everyone else," the ranger admonished.

The thin woman eyed him viciously, and he slunk back to his place near the rear of the line.

"Let me see your confirmation letter," the ranger said more affably to Syd.

Syd pulled out a well-folded computer printout and passed it to the ranger. She smiled and motioned us to come inside.

Watching the jealous faces of the people in line made me feel a bit like some spoiled rich kid boarding the first-class section of an airplane before a group of handicapped war veterans.

The ranger asked if we knew the park rules. Syd said he was familiar, but she quizzed us all the same.

"Do you two have bear canisters?" she asked.

"Yes," we said in unison.

"What kind?"

"I have a standard black one. I don't know the brand," replied Syd.

"I have a Bear Vault 500," I said, recalling its techno-sounding name.

"Very good," she said, "I've gotta ask. We have them for rent too, if you need them." Then she paused thoughtfully and asked, "Do you two have stoves?"

Was this a trick question? Looking at a poster of Smokey the Bear on the wall, I was about to say, "No, of course not!" when Syd answered, "Yes, we both have backpacking stoves."

"Good," she continued, "because there is a *total* fire ban in the park, so there's no cooking over open fires in the backcountry, or any fires other than portable backpacking stoves."

I'd try to keep my mouth closed from now on.

"After Yosemite," the ranger continued, "the following parks and wilderness areas have fire bans—" She rattled off a long list of places I'd never heard of, then handed the list to Syd. "And even in areas that permit fires, you can't make one above ten thousand feet."

"Why is that?" I asked, before remembering to keep my mouth shut.

"That's where the tree line is, and there isn't enough wood up there to replenish the soil, shelter the tiny animals, and renew the ecosystem if everybody started gathering and burning it all."

"Ah," I nodded, trying my best to look concerned for the tiny little animals.

"OK," she continued, "now you two know that you can only camp in established sites, at least one hundred feet from water and out of sight from the trail, right?"

We both nodded like school children.

"What about human waste?" she asked in a serious tone. "Do you both have trowels?"

"Yes, we do, ma'am," replied Syd, glancing at me as if to ask, *You did get one, right?*

I nodded as it dawned on me what the little plastic hand shovel on the shopping list was for.

"Good. And do you know the rules for using them?"

I kept my mouth shut, waiting for Syd.

"Yes," he answered, "we bury our waste a minimum of six inches deep in soft soil at least two hundred feet from water."

"Very good. And what do you do with your used toilet paper?" she asked, looking directly at me.

"Eh, you bury it with your poo?" I guessed.

"No, we used to do that, but too many small animals dig it up making a mess. Now the rule is that you pack out all your soiled tissue."

Maybe we'd just failed the test 'cause of my dumb answer, and we'd have to go home.

The ranger just smiled and said, "OK, here's your permit," handing Syd a green piece of paper. "Keep this in your pack at all times. Now I've got to deal with them," she grunted, indicating the people outside with her eyes. "Have a great hike you two."

"How did we get our permit so easily?" I asked him when we were back at the car.

"It wasn't easy—I had to put in a request every day for almost a month, starting last February."

"That's almost half a year in advance!"

"The trail's become quite popular, so the park has imposed quotas to limit the environmental impact. They hold a lottery each year for permits."

"What about all those people in line?"

"They also issue a small number of daily walk-up permits."

"And what if they can't get one?"

"Then they either hike a different trail or come back again the next day. That's where we'd have been if I hadn't managed to get one. It's really a matter of luck."

Opening the trunk, he said, "Make sure you have everything you'll need in your pack, because we won't be seeing your car again for nearly a month."

"What about my phone?"

"We're not likely to have reception until Whitney, so unless you plan to use it for photographs, it'll only be extra weight."

Stowing it gingerly in the glove box, I felt a strange sense of loss. But I'd already packed a small camera, so what did I need the phone for?

"Don't forget to eat something for breakfast—we only had coffee at that motel."

We both ate a few granola bars. I'd picked mine up at Ralphs. They were made of pressed granola and some sort of nut paste, weakly flavored to taste like maple syrup. The photo on the package looked alright, but the actual bars were pretty bland and chewy, matching my emotions. Syd's bars looked better, a mixture of real nuts and berries covered with a dribble of chocolate. I probably shoulda spent more time shopping.

"If you have any other food or snacks in the car, you'd best store them in one of the metal bear boxes over there," he said, indicating a row of large brown metal storage lockers set up next to the parking lot.

"I have some mints and mouthwash in the glove box. Do you think a bear would want those, perhaps to freshen its breath?" I grinned, my mind still trying to wrap itself around the reality of this whole trip.

"Bears have an amazing sense of smell. They've been known to rip open car doors to get at food."

I looked at the soft-top of my Miata and gathered up my stuff, making sure everything was either in my pack or in the bear box. Then I began struggling with my hiking socks and boots.

"Those boots look brand new," he said.

"Yeah, I got them at REI."

"But, I mean—you haven't worn them in at all?"

"Won't two hundred miles on the trail be enough?"

"Usually, people hike around in a pair for a few weeks before a trip to help soften up the leather." Then in a bit kindlier tone he added, "Just be aware of any rubbing or hot spots. If you feel uncomfortable in any way, let me know. I have some moleskin in my first-aid kit if you develop any blisters. Do you want me to double-check your gear before we go?"

"No need, I got everything you put on the list." *Besides, we won't really be gone that long,* I thought, recalling my plan to bail at Reds Meadow.

"Good. You remembered sunscreen?"

"Check."

"A ground pad for sleeping on?"

"Don't worry. I got all the stuff you told me to."

"Just making certain. I wouldn't want you to get three days out and discover you'd forgotten your raingear."

"Thanks, but I really got everything you told me to."

He lifted my pack and nodded his approval. "It's a bit heavier than it should be, but I think you'll be fine. It's a nice choice of packs, too. Osprey is a great brand."

I picked up his old green Kelty to compare the weight. His was noticeably lighter.

"You sure my car will be OK parked here?"

"It'll be fine."

I hefted on my pack, and he helped me to adjust it, tightening the various belts and straps. My breathing felt strained under its unaccustomed weight. "How high up are we?"

"Eight thousand six hundred feet. The walk today is pretty gentle. We only gain about three hundred feet. It's a good way to get acclimated. Are you ready?"

"Let's see. It's two hundred miles to Mount Whitney, we've got a full tank of gas, half a pack of cigarettes, it's dark out, and we're wearing sunglasses!"

He laughed. I hadn't been sure if he'd recognize my Blues Brothers quote—I guess he wasn't all books and philosophy.

"I'm glad you came. As John Muir said, *The Mountains are calling and I must go!*"

My car chirped as I locked it. I looked wistfully at my old Miata, the last representative of everything I'd be leaving behind.

The trail began just past the parking lot. The sun hadn't yet gotten over the mountains, but already the clouds were a brilliant orangey yellow. Passing the ranger station, we wandered out onto a narrow dirt strip that curved along the edge of a sparse pine forest. A bubbling creek tumbled along to our right. The chirping of birds greeted my ears, followed by the inevitable drone of insects. My mind raced to the three bottles of repellant buried deep within my pack—should I have rubbed some on before starting? This was exactly why I hated camping.

At least it was easier walking on the soft dirt than it had been crossing the lot. I breathed deeply, feeling the altitude. The morning air was cool and crisp, laden with the scent of pine. Beyond the forest rose menacing snowcapped peaks bathed in a foreboding purple glow. Was that where we were going? Hopefully not. Uncertain of the way, I trailed behind Syd, struggling to keep up while trying to get accustomed to the weight of my pack as it jiggled and shifted.

No one else was in sight. It felt like we were the only two people on earth, walking alone along the wooded trail under the wide expansive sky on some divine mission. Syd's boots were kicking up a light dust. A large brown folding metal shovel swung back and forth from the back of his pack as he walked, like the pendulum of an old grandfather clock. *What was that for?* I guess I'd find out at camp.

The sun began creeping above the mountains, warming the air and lifting the dew from the trees. The buzzing of insects intensified, but to my great relief none landed. After about a mile, we came to a wide meandering river flowing through a grassy meadow. This was no well-tended Ohio farm field. This was a lush rolling green meadow with uncropped grasses of varying heights waving in the light breeze. Red, purple, orange, and white wildflowers punctuated the thick sedge.

The river cut a wide swath through the heart of the grasses, winding like a ribbon through the broad valley. The water made a gurgling sound as it tumbled over the polished stones beneath its crystalline surface.

A large flat wooden plank bridge spanned the river in two sections, meeting in the center on a wide stone island. On the far side, a tall guy in a gray cowboy-style hiking hat and blue button-downs with a pack like mine was taking photos. Pop had always taken one of us at the parking lot before setting out on any of his trips, but I'd forgotten to do that. It would be good to have one of me and his buddy Syd to show Ma, and this seemed as good a spot as any.

"Can you take a picture of us?" I asked the guy, holding out my small camera.

"Sure," he grinned, the salt-and-pepper stubble wrinkling on his leathery cheeks.

Syd and I posed by the bridge, side by side, packs on. Syd held his trekking poles in his left hand, placing his right arm over my shoulder while the man snapped several photos.

"I'm Gil," I said, thanking him after.

Bridge at Lyell Forks

"I'm Steve. Wow, St. Pauli Girl! I never thought I'd see *that* in the woods. My grandparents were from Bremen actually."

Syd let out a short huff. "Are you hiking the John Muir Trail?" I asked him.

"Hope so. I started at the Valley three days ago and just dropped by the Meadows to call my wife. How 'bout you guys?"

"We started today," answered Syd.

"What's the Valley?" I asked.

Syd looked at me as if to ask, *Didn't you read the guidebook?* Then in a patient tone he explained, "The so-called official JMT starts about twenty miles southwest of here at Happy Isles in Yosemite Valley." Turning to include Steve, he continued, "But I've done that part of the trail several times before, and it's usually packed with people climbing Half Dome. I wanted a more peaceful start to things, so I chose Tuolumne Meadows instead."

"So, we aren't doing the whole hike?" I asked.

"That depends on your point of view," replied Syd. "Most of those who planned the original trail considered the true start of the Yosemite High Sierra to be here in Tuolumne Meadows, not the Valley."

"You aren't missing much," put in Steve. "The trail up from the Valley is really steep and swarming with tourists—although Vernal Falls and Nevada Falls are gorgeous—but we'll see much more amazing sights along the trail than those tourists ever do. And Little Yosemite Valley campground was a zoo! Two nights ago, we were all woken up by some idiot screaming as a bear pulled him out from his tent, dragging him around feetfirst inside his sleeping bag. By the time we all got out with our headlamps, we found him shivering in his underwear, a big hole in his tent, and his sleeping bag ripped to shreds—down feathers everywhere!"

"What happened?" I asked growing concerned.

"The fool had stuck a Snickers bar in the bottom of his sleeping bag. He didn't think the bears would smell it down there because of his stinky feet."

"Wow, there's always one true beginner," Syd scoffed. "That could have turned out much worse."

"True," Steve agreed, "I hope the bear is OK. Sometimes the rangers have to put down bears that get used to taking food from people."

"*The bear is OK?*" I asked incredulously. "*What about the guy?*"

"Oh, he got a lesson in food storage he'll never forget!" Steve laughed. "Anyway, there were tons of people at Little Yosemite Valley, all getting ready to go up Half Dome. You didn't miss a thing."

"Clouds Rest is nice," Syd reflected, "the views from there are fantastic."

I looked at the two of them. Giant tent-ripping bears were out there somewhere, and Steve was just callously laughing it off, while Syd was discussing the views—*were these guys nuts?*

"That was the best part of the hike up from the Valley," declared Steve. "But it's not worth the climb carrying a full pack. Your buddy's right to start here. You can always do that stretch of the trail later, with just a daypack if you want to."

"The trail is whatever you make it to be," added Syd. "Like Antonio Machado wrote, *Traveler, there is no road; your path is made by walking.*"

"That's very true," nodded Steve.

OK, so we had twenty miles less to hike, but my mind was still stuck on the bears. "What are you supposed to do if you meet a bear?" I asked.

"Make yourself tall and make a lot of noise," replied Steve. "Bang some pots and pans together, that always scares 'em off. But don't worry, chances are you won't see any past the Valley."

Why would a thousand pound killing machine be afraid of a few pots and pans? To a bear that probably just meant, *Dinner's on!* I glanced left and right, checking the surroundings. No bears.

The three of us continued up the trail together, Syd and Steve making small talk. I quickly dropped behind. After a quarter mile or so, they stopped to wait for me at a small footbridge. Then they began to pull ahead again.

These guys were both at least twenty years older than me, yet here they were leaving me in the dust. Cass was wrong about her father; it was me she shoulda been worried about! Maybe I wouldn't need to fake a sprained ankle to get off of this damn trip; maybe I'd be such a burden to Syd that he'd simply insist on leaving me behind?

After the third time they had to stop and wait for me, Syd turned to Steve, "I should hang back with my friend. It's his first time out here." Steve nodded.

"I don't need to be babysat," I huffed. "I'm doing fine. You two go on. There's no need to wait for me every few steps. I'll catch up as soon as I get my wind."

Syd looked at me, "It's probably better if we hike together."

"Seriously? If you guys can do this, so can I! I'll be fine. You said it's all flat today, right? And you already told me we turn left at Ireland Creek about three miles from here and the campsite's a mile or so beyond that. You guys go on ahead. If I don't catch up along the trail, then I'll meet you at camp."

Syd looked at me as if to ask, *Are you sure?*

"Go! I'll be fine," I insisted with more bravado than I felt.

He nodded. Soon the two of them were out of sight again.

What was I thinking? I looked left and right scanning the meadow for movement. No bears. Why had I insisted on being so macho? I wasn't going to learn anything about Pop hiking on my own. Still, Syd was right, the trail was pretty flat.

After a while I stopped for a breather, took off my pack, and pulled out the package of twelve maps Syd had me purchase. Breaking open the cellophane wrapping, I flipped through the pages and found the sheet with Tuolumne Meadows on it. The John Muir Trail was highlighted in red. I located the ranger station and the river we'd crossed named Lyell Creek. The trail followed it up into Lyell Canyon. From the rising slopes around me, it looked like I was somewhere around the mouth of the canyon. That would make Ireland Creek and the campsite about four miles farther, just like he said. That wasn't so bad.

I swung my pack back on, cinched up the straps, and started walking. The sun was shining, but not too hot, and it would probably have been an alright day for something like this, had my pack actually fit right. A few minutes down the trail the right strap began eating into my shoulder. Loosening this, the pack weight shifted left. Soon the left strap began troubling me. Loosening this as well, the pack began to hang backward. Now the strap that ran across my chest began cinching my shirt up, pressing its collar into my neck and choking me slightly. The dangling pack shifted back and forth, jerking me off balance.

What the hell was wrong with this stupid pack? I cinched up the two shoulder straps and pulled the pack tight against my back again, struggling to keep my shirt down. Now the pack's weight sat heavily on both shoulders, rather than on the hip belt where it belonged. I walked about a quarter of a mile, ignoring the pain, unable to pay attention to any of the sights around me.

Finally, it was too much. I stopped. Loosened the hip belt. Grabbed the whole pack by its sides and heaved up. The belt was now loose around my stomach and my shirt was riding up my back. Pulling my shirt back down, I cinched up the hip belt, making a huge indent in the front of my beer gut, but the pack felt better. The weight was off my shoulders. I walked on.

It wasn't long before the heavy pack, aided by the tug of gravity and the steady pounding of my boots, weaseled its way back down to my waist, dragging my shirt down with it. I loosened both shoulder straps and the pack flopped backward again, dangling like a corpse.

I went through this whole stupid routine twice more—shoving, pulling, lifting, sliding. The fucking thing just didn't fit. I had walked almost an hour around REI carrying forty pounds of sand to test it out without a hitch, but here in the real world, bouncing down the trail, this piece of shit just didn't work!

Fuck this hike! Fuck camping! Why did I ever agree to this stupid wild walk in the woods? Why had Syd left me back here all alone on this damn trail? What the hell was I doing here anyway? I'd probably get eaten by a bear!

With all my tugging and adjusting and cursing, the pack had now slid down below my waist feeling like someone had dropped my pants, its whole mass supported by just one strap. My shoulders ached. My neck hurt. I was about to rip the damn thing off, throw it to the ground, and stomp back to the car, when I spotted Syd and Steve standing up ahead watching a large buck in the meadow.

I walked up to them in angry silence. As I approached, the huge animal turned its head in my direction and bolted. The three of us stood there for a moment watching the fleeing buck.

Syd turned to say something then paused, his eyes appraising how my pack was now dangling low around my waist, supported by only a single strap. "What's wrong with your pack?" he asked. "Why do you have it riding so low?"

"The thing's a piece of shit!"

"Nah," Steve chimed in, "you have it adjusted wrong."

"A new pack takes a while to get used to," Syd consoled.

Syd helped to remove my pack and he and Steve spent some time fiddling with the straps. Apparently, I'd twisted several. Then they had me put it back on.

They showed me how to cinch up the shoulder straps first, then tighten the hip belt while sucking in my gut. The pack sat comfortably on my hips again. Next, they had me loosen up the shoulder straps until they were comfortable, but now the pack was dangling backward like before.

"See? I told you this thing was a piece of shit!"

"Just be patient," urged Syd, "you have to adjust the loader straps now."

He pulled on two previously unnoticed straps above my shoulders and the pack slid back up toward my body without putting its weight on my shoulders. It felt better. Much better. I turned from side to side and jumped a bit. It was OK. Still heavy, but no longer out of adjustment. Syd refastened the sternum strap, which ran across my chest just below my neck and kept the pack from swaying. My shirt felt right. My pack felt right. I started to calm down.

"Does it feel better?" Syd asked with genuine concern.

"Yeah, thanks."

The two of them went on ahead again, and I walked on. My thighs burned. It was still several miles to camp. But at least my pack seemed to fit right, and it wasn't choking me or digging into my shoulders.

The meadow grass waved in the gentle breeze. Life was everywhere. Colorful birds chirped and flitted about. One overgrown-looking sparrow sported tufts of red on its head, like a tiny punk rocker. Bees and butterflies danced from flower to flower. The air had a heavy earthen scent. My breathing became less labored, and my legs slowly fell into a steady rhythm. After an hour or so I'd almost forgotten about the pack.

Slowly my stomach began growling—its meter pinned on empty. I had a bunch of granola bars stuffed in my bear canister, but if I stopped to pull them out, could I get the pack back on and readjusted right? Syd and Steve were probably a long way off by now. Better not to risk it and press on. Tomorrow, I'd stuff some bars into one of the zippered compartments on my hip belt so I could get to them without taking the pack off.

I went on. My legs hurt. My mind drifted over images of sports cars, grilled steaks, Jasmine's pert boobs, and then back to the grilled steaks again. The trail rolled by. Slowly my mind became blank, interrupted only by the occasional rubbing of a toe or tug and chafe of a strap needing adjustment. Gradually I became the trees, the trail, the birds, the pain—my feet shuffling forward one after the other like the living dead.

From the pit in my stomach and the drooping sun, it musta been five o'clock when I staggered into camp. Syd already had his bivy up. Steve's small tent was pitched close by. The two were sitting on folded air mattresses, chatting away, looking out across the river.

My legs ached. My shirt was soaked with sweat. I was done.

"We saved you a spot over there," said Syd, indicating a small flat area of cleared ground.

"Thanks," I groaned, ready to drop the dead weight of my pack and collapse. I unclipped the hip belt and slipped off the shoulder straps. But instead of falling to the ground, the pack, like an expert wrestler, fastened a choke hold around my neck, trying to pin me backward, gripping me by the forgotten sternum strap. Staggering sideways, I managed to catch my balance and unclip the strap. The pack dropped with a heavy thud. I collapsed down on top of it, numb.

Syd and Steve were still chatting, oblivious to my suffering. I lay there watching them. It was good we had run into Steve. I had no idea what to do if Syd had some sort of emergency. I could barely get myself up the trail. Steve seemed to have the expertise we needed. Hopefully, he would continue on with us. Maybe I could even convince him to hike on with Syd when I ducked out at Reds Meadow? That way, Syd could still finish his trail.

My breathing settled. My pack and the hard ground became uncomfortable. Hunger beckoned. The red bag containing my tent was strapped to my pack. Removing it, I walked over to the site Syd had indicated. Kicking aside a few pinecones and loose twigs, I tried to open the brand-new tent bag. It was sealed by one of those unbreakable nylon ties. Pulling and biting didn't work. "Either of you guys have a scissor?" I called over.

"You mean you didn't try out your tent at home first?" Syd asked, looking skeptical.

I hadn't really given it much thought. I mean, it was just a tent, right?

Steve pulled out a small knife from his pack that cut cleanly through the plastic. I let the broken tie fall, preparing to head back and set up my shelter.

"Hey, you can't just dump that there," Steve pointed to the discarded tie. "This is wilderness."

"Pack it in, pack it out," echoed Syd.

Kneeling in the dust, I located the offending tie and stuffed it into my pocket. Sheesh, who would even notice a thing like that?

Steve looked at my small red bag. "What kind of tent is that?"

"It's a Hubba Hubba," I answered.

"That's supposed to be a great tent. What made you choose it?"

I thought back to my shopping trip at REI. The lady in tents had recommend either the Hubba Hubba, the Quarter Dome, the Nemo, or the Big Agnes for my trip. Not knowing anything about tents, I'd chosen the Hubba Hubba 'cause its name sounded the most promising for a romantic alpine hookup. Quarter Dome just sounded cheap. Nemo reminded me of a fish—pretty lame for something designed to keep you dry at night. And Big Agnes was exactly the opposite of Hubba Hubba, but I couldn't say this to Steve.

"Because of the specs," I replied.

"Nice choice," he praised, and Syd nodded in agreement.

The two watched in amusement as I struggled to erect my new red and white tent. After finally figuring the damn thing out, I hobbled back over to my pack.

In contrast to the roomy dome of my Hubba Hubba, Syd's bivy was just a tiny hooped tube, not much bigger than his sleeping bag, with a raised bug net at the head that could be covered over in the rain—hardly what I would wanna spend a month in.

My Osprey pack laid in the dirt like the body of a fallen soldier. Balking at the thought of lugging the whole thing over to my tent, I began unpacking it where it lay. Leaving my food and cooking stuff by the pack, I slid my new Therm-a-Rest air mattress out of its yellow sleeve and opened the valve. The mattress began slowly self-inflating. Grabbing the mattress in one hand and the sack containing my clothing in the other, I shuffled back to the tent, sliding them both inside.

Returning to my pack, I dragged my bulky sleeping bag out of its stuff sack.

"What the hell is that?" asked Steve, gaping at the giant red-and-black bag.

"It's a Bonfire bag," I said smugly, "it's rated for *minus* thirty degrees."

"You brought a synthetic bag?" asked Steve, his mouth wide open.

"That thing's huge!" exclaimed Syd. "What does it weigh?"

"Just under six pounds," I proclaimed.

"Six pounds?" they exclaimed together in disbelief.

"That's heavier than a tent or backpack!" reproached Steve.

"You didn't get a down bag like I suggested?" scolded Syd.

"This one was way warmer—and it was on sale."

"Minus thirty?" repeated Steve. "That's a snow-camping bag. You're gonna roast!"

"It is a bit overkill," Syd agreed, "but you can always open the zipper and use it as a quilt."

Holding up my bag by one end, I walked dejectedly over to my tent, like someone who just discovered the prize fish he's caught is on the endangered species list. Pulling open the door, I shoved my bag in, watching it flop down atop the Therm-a-Rest.

Zipping up the tent door, I staggered back to make dinner.

"Where do you get water from?" I asked Syd, indicating the large gray water bag he had hanging from a branch in a nearby tree.

"From the river of course."

"Is it clean?"

"What do you mean? Didn't you buy a filter?"

I thought for a moment. "*Shit*—I forgot to pack it! I left it in the drying rack by my sink after I rinsed it out like you told me to."

"It's fine, you can share mine."

Steve looked wistful. "Years ago, you could just drink out of all the streams up here, but now there's this parasite *Giardia*. I got it once up in Oregon. Had the runs really bad and was on antibiotics for almost two weeks."

I filled my cooking pot from Syd's hanging bag.

Settling in for dinner, each of us set up our stoves. They both had canister stoves similar to my own—at least I had the right cookware.

I dragged over my clear plastic Bear Vault 500. Syd and Steve's bear canisters both opened easily, by twisting two slotted knobs with a coin. On mine, you had to squeeze a difficult childproof-like mechanism while unscrewing the entire lid. It took several tries to get enough purchase, but I finally opened it. At least mine was better protected, given that any bear with some spare change could easily get into theirs.

"What are you eating?" asked Steve, pulling out a carefully wrapped bunch of noodles and a plastic pouch from his canister that he said was dehydrated spaghetti sauce.

"Backwoods Buffet!" I declared, pulling out my first metallic-orange pouch of lasagna. The package was emblazoned with their kitschy mascot, Backwoods Bob. Bob was dressed in a red-and-black lumberjack shirt that barely contained his bulging belly. He had a round happy face and was grinning widely as he held out a mouthwatering helping of perfect tomatoey lasagna atop his hand-carved wooden spoon.

In fact, I didn't wanna admit it, but I'd be having lasagna for the whole week, having made the simple error of mailing full sets of each flavor I'd selected in my separate resupply buckets rather than remembering to mix them up for variety.

"Backwoods Buffet—they still make that?" Steve's face twisted up in disgust. "There's enough sodium and preservatives in one of those things to keep a high blood pressure clinic running for a year!"

"Did the REI salesperson recommend those?" asked Syd.

"She didn't exactly recommend them," I said recalling. "She kinda suggested mixing them up a bit with some stuff from the supermarket or something."

"I hope you did!" Steve said. "I wouldn't want to choke down that Backed-up Bob stuff for a whole month!"

In fact, the salesgirl *had* suggested I take a few of the meals home first and try them before purchasing so many, but I hadn't wanted to spend that much time shopping. Plus, these meals were priced significantly less than that other "all natural" brand she'd recommended.

Syd pulled out a large package of fancy-looking Korean ramen noodles, some dried seaweed, and a small bag of diced vegetables. "This is my special meal for day one," he said. "After today, no more fresh veggies until Reds Meadow." He took out a set of wooden chopsticks and began cooking.

I heated my water silently. Backwoods Buffet couldn't be that bad, could it? My Jetboil stove brought the pot to a full boil in only a minute. Following the directions, I opened the bag, staring hopefully at the dried bits of noodle and reddish-orange powder inside, added two cups of water, fastened the bag's seal, and waited. The instructions said to give it three to five minutes before serving. Waiting the full five, I opened the bag, cautiously lifting out a serving on my spork.

Far from the hearty chunks of whole noodles dripping with fresh sauce Bob was grinning over on the bag, just a few sorry-looking noodle chunks held together by an orange-red goo emerged on my utensil. An unfamiliar chemical smell mixed with something that was vaguely oregano-like wafted up from the open sack. I slid the end of the spork into my mouth and tasted. It was awful. Leathery industrial waste and battery acid doesn't begin to describe the texture and flavor of Backwoods lasagna. The cheese clung to my teeth like glue. I forced it down. Only a few more days to Reds Meadow. I scooped up a second helping of the orange-yellow glop.

"Anyone want some?" I asked hopefully, holding my spork aloft. There were no takers.

After dinner, we all brushed our teeth, packed up our food, trash, and smelly items, like toothpaste and sunscreen, and stuffed them into our bear canisters, caching them under some trees a few hundred feet from camp. Returning to where we had eaten, we watched the sky turn a brilliant copper as the sun set beyond the mountains.

I had expected a long night of campfire stories, tales of the trail, song, and revelry. Maybe a chance to see what Pop had actually come out here for. But I was wrong. Just after sunset, Syd and Steve announced that they were ready for bed.

"We have a big climb tomorrow if we're going to get over Donohue Pass," said Syd. And with that, everyone headed for their shelters.

Dejected by the lack of festive atmosphere and feeling my stomach struggling against the undigested lumps of lasagna, I unzipped the door to my Hubba Hubba and crawled in. I guess I'd have to wait 'till the next day to learn more about Pop. Dragging my pack to the other side of my sleeping pad, I arranged my clothes, making my T-shirts into a makeshift pillow. Then stripping off even the synthetic underwear I'd brought, I slid my feet inside the plush comfortable lining of the Bonfire bag.

As I lay there, I heard the soft hiss of air leaking out of my Therm-a-Rest. Rolling to one side, I blew into the small valve, reinflating the mattress, then twisted it shut.

Now the mattress was too firm. Wriggling my hand free, I twisted the valve, letting the air escape slowly until the mattress was at its Goldilocks point.

As I waited to fall asleep, my sleeping bag grew progressively warmer. The heat began around my legs, then worked up to my torso and chest. Soon my feet were sweating. My Bonfire bag was working on overtime.

From the inside, I reached for the bag's large double zipper and found it to be stuck. Pulling and pulling, the exertion only heated my body further. Beads of sweat formed on my hands and neck. Damn, what was wrong with this stupid zipper? Worming my way out of the hot gunny sack, I sat naked in my cold tent, rummaging around through the top of my pack for my headlamp, finally pulling it out by the strap.

Clicking the ON button, I was nearly blinded by the brilliant white LEDs. I clicked it again rapidly until the color changed to red. Spots danced around the corners of the tent until my eyes could finally focus on the zipper again. Nothing appeared wrong with it. I tried pulling again, but the damn thing wouldn't budge.

Thinking quickly, I stuck my feet in the top of the bag and holding the zipper in both hands, pulled firmly, leaning into it with all my weight. At first nothing happened, then there was a terrible teeth-wrenching ripping sound as the seam of the bag gave way and white fluff spewed out everywhere.

"Everything OK?" came Syd's cry from his bivy.

"Yeah," I answered, "just fine."

The light gave everything a blood-red color and I hurried to pick up the fluff and stuff it back into the gaping hole, but it just kept falling out like the guts of a wounded animal.

Wrestling with the stupid zipper some more, I noticed a small flap of the bag lining caught between its teeth. Pulling this free, the zipper slid easily past the five-inch rip in my bag.

Fortunately, Syd had told me to pack the one thing most useful in any crisis: duct tape. Pulling out the small roll from my pack, I sutured the wounded bag like a skillful surgeon.

Lying back on my just-right Therm-a-Rest, I pulled the open bag over me and readjusted my shirt-pillow, trying once more to sleep.

Slowly my butt and then the side of my body began to feel cold. I lay there for a while hoping things would get better when the Bonfire quilt kicked in, but it didn't. The ground below me continued to suck heat away from my lower body.

Frustrated, I threw off the quilt and looked around—*this was exactly why I hated camping*. My extra clothing was piled in a ball. I spread them out on top of the Therm-a-Rest, doing my best to keep them from lumping up or exposing zippers or buttons against my skin. Pulling the quilt back over me, I turned off the red light and prepared to sleep.

Tossing for over an hour, something in my groins tugged at me, refusing to let me rest. A slow growing urgency. Usually I peed before bed, but tonight I'd forgotten. Now all the water I'd drank to wash down my lasagna came calling. Rolling over, I tried to ignore the sensation, but the urgency grew. Reluctantly, I emerged from my cocoon, turned on the headlamp—mindful to keep my eyes shut through the blinding white setting—unzipped the tent, and stepped naked into the darkness.

Even in Ohio I had never seen stars like this. Gaping in awe, I gazed up at the wide array of galaxies and constellations above. A shooting star streaked from east to west, briefly illuminating the darkness.

I took a few tenuous steps forward, my bare feet naked on the cool earth. At a small pine, not more than a few yards from my tent, I marked my territory in the most primitive way possible, my eyes turned heavenward toward the vast Cosmos above.

DAY TWO

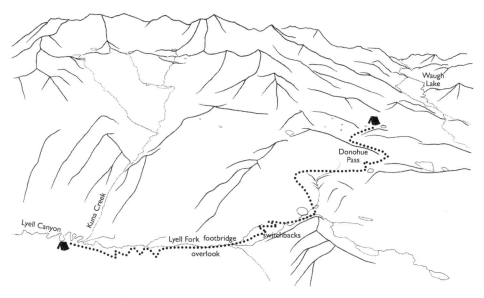

A mile past Ireland Creek (8,990′) to Small Lake (10,150′) via Donohue Pass (11,060′)
7½ miles—2,160 feet elevation gain; 1,000 feet elevation loss

"WHERE'S THE BATHROOM?" I asked urgently.
Syd was outside in his jacket, packing up.
"Anywhere you like. But not in the meadow, or close to water, or the trail."
Shit—we really did have to shit in the woods!
Squeezing my cheeks, I hightailed it off into the trees. Finding a somewhat hidden spot, I tested the ground with my trowel. Only a pitiful scoop of surface dirt came up. Frantically, I searched around and finding some softer dirt close to a tree, hurriedly dug a hole, pulled down my pants, and squatted over it. I felt relief coming, but my legs ached from the day before, and it became impossible to hold the unaccustomed position. I stood, temporarily halting the progress of the morning express train in its tunnel. My sense of urgency returning, I squatted back down, legs screaming. Maintaining my pose long enough for the train to complete its journey, I stood back up. The bombs had missed their target! Wiping my ass, I wondered how I would pack out the soiled paper. Shit—I'd forgotten to bring a plastic bag! Guiltily, I let the soiled tissue fall into the tiny hole, found a stick, and shoved my mess in, kicking some of the surrounding dirt in after to fill it in. Taking a

medium-sized rock, I planted it on top, hoping it would be enough to warn off other hikers and keep the animals from digging up my mess. Next time I'd bring a bag or something for the tissue.

"Where's Steve?" I asked when I returned to camp. His tent and stuff were gone.

"He packed up just before sunrise. Usually, we try to hit the trail early, but this being your first day out, I thought you might want to sleep in and rest a bit."

Shit—now I'd have to handle Syd by myself. "Will we catch up to him on the trail?"

"I don't think so, he's doing a lot more miles a day than we are. I doubt we'll see him again, unless he takes a zero-day somewhere. Now that you're up, let's go pump some water."

What time was it? It couldn't be much past eight. Every bone in my body cried to go back to my tent and sleep. But instead, I followed Syd down to the river, my legs a pair of burning iron rods. How could a guy his age with cancer have so much energy this early in the morning?

Pumping water was horrible. I'll never look at my kitchen sink in quite the same way. Squatting down on my screaming legs, I had to work Syd's tiny hand pump to filter a miserable trickle into his gray bag while he held it to keep it from spilling. All the while a cloud of horrid mosquitos buzzed around me, interrupting my progress while I squirmed and swatted. Finally, we lugged the heavy water bag back up to camp. To my great relief, the majority of the bugs stayed down at the river.

We each ate packaged oatmeal for breakfast. I made a cup of bland instant coffee into which I poured a packet of hot chocolate for some quick sugar and flavoring. Visions of the home-cooked breakfast I'd turned down at Jasmine's danced in my head. After eating, we packed up and broke camp.

Just before heading out, Syd said, "When your father and I used to hike together, it was our tradition to share quotations on days we felt inspired."

That sounded a lot like Pop. I perked up in anticipation.

"Since today we're headed over our first mountain pass, I thought I'd share a poem by Tennyson, which was one of your dad's and my favorites."

He tipped his head back and in a firm voice recited,

> Come, my friend,
> 'Tis not too late to seek a newer world.
> Push off, and sitting well in order smite
> The sounding furrows; for my purpose holds
> To sail beyond the sunset, and the baths
> Of all the western stars, until I die.
> It may be that the gulfs will wash us down:
> It may be we shall touch the Happy Isles,
> And see the great Achilles, whom we knew.
> Tho' much is taken, much abides; and tho'
> We are not now that strength which in old days

Moved earth and heaven, that which we are, we are;
One equal temper of heroic hearts,
Made weak by time and fate, but strong in will
To strive, to seek, to find, and not to yield!

Syd's poem felt like a kinda benediction. Pop had read it to me before—but now in light of Syd's illness, the poem took on new meaning. If Pop were alive, he'd have wanted to be here now, doing this hike with Syd. We stood for some time together our heads hung in prayer. I wanted to ask more but couldn't bring myself to break the spiritual sense of purpose his poem invoked. So wordlessly, we started up the trail.

Unlike yesterday, almost immediately we began to climb uphill. My legs burned as I forced them up the growing incline.

"How high are we going today?"

"Donohue Pass is about eleven thousand feet. Right now we're at about nine," he said without breaking stride.

I calculated. A two-thousand-foot climb. Let's see—if the Empire State Building is about a hundred stories high, and a typical story measures about ten feet, then we'd be climbing *two* Empire State Buildings today. That can't be right. Perhaps a story is twenty feet? We couldn't be climbing more than *one* Empire State Building, could we?

I took a deep breath. Syd was up in front. It was amazing how well he was doing. He stopped after a bit to take a short breather, saying, "As we climb, drink plenty of water, and watch yourself for signs of altitude sickness."

Altitude sickness? What about home sickness? What about comfy mattresses, flush toilets, mosquito-free tap water, and real food sickness?

A moment later he started climbing again. Still trying to catch my breath, I trailed him up the slope.

We soon reached a series of rocky steps. Pressing up the awkward uneven steps made my calves burn anew.

What was I doing here? Pop had been my foundation, my rock, my compass. He'd seen me through my confirmation; inspired my love of the classics and of writing. He'd given me the push I needed those thousand times I'd wanted to quit after losing a competition. After he died, I was lost, with no one to turn to for guidance. Ma and I were close, but she didn't know me in the way Pop did. Why hadn't I shared the things he'd loved with him? Why whenever he'd tried to take me on trips like this, I'd rejected it? I mean the fishing was OK, but those long walks and endless climbs—and the bugs out in Ohio had been the worst. But he loved it and kept encouraging me to go. Why couldn't I feel what he had loved out there in the wilderness? Why had I turned him down the one time it really mattered? Why had I been so selfish? Maybe if I'd gone with him and Ma on that last trip up the coast, he'd still be here. Maybe that's why I was out here now, climbing this rock, doing penance, while trying to grasp what'd drawn Pop to all this.

We were climbing up the canyon wall. Through the sparse trees, I caught glimpses of the river and meadow below. Syd was only a few paces ahead, and even he was breathing harder now. Swatting at pestering flies, and wiping the dripping sweat from my forehead, I pressed on.

Who made this damn trail? I'd heard of John Muir, of course. He'd been one of Pop's favorite authors, although I'd never read anything by him. All I knew was he lived in the eighteen hundreds and had a really long beard.

When we stopped again, I asked, "Was Muir the one who made this trail?"

"No," Syd puffed. "The John Muir Trail was named in honor of Muir, but it wasn't built by him. In fact, he probably only hiked parts of what is now the trail—although I don't think anyone knows for certain which ones. He simply loved taking long rambling journeys through these mountains at a time when the only paths were those made by Native Americans, sheepherders, and the like."

We started walking again. "I know he was a nature writer and all, but what made him so famous?" My confession felt a bit like standing in a church and asking who Jesus was. "Was he an American explorer, like Lewis and Clark?"

"Muir did a lot of exploring, but never bothered to make maps. Mostly, he followed his fancies; one day climbing a peak, the next watching the flowers bloom. He was more of an observer of nature than an explorer."

"A sort of wilderness hippie?"

"Perhaps, but he was also a writer, an activist, and a philosopher. He was originally from Scotland. His family moved to Wisconsin when he was about eleven."

Syd had a kinda pedantic lecturing style, like the old teacher he was. But I didn't object, wanting to find out what drove guys like him and Pop to do this.

"Muir wrote that he acquired his love of nature from accompanying his grandfather on long walks. But I believe exploring was just in his blood. By his own account, he was quite a precocious child—always running around and getting into trouble."

"That sounds a lot like me."

"Yes, I know. Your father used to call me up asking for advice. Like the time you took the family car out for a joy ride and crashed through the neighbor's yard when you were twelve—"

"Let's not get into all that," I flushed. "So, if Muir was just some sort of nature lover, why is he so famous?"

"Because of his writings. Muir's descriptions of the natural world have an almost divine reverence to them. As a child, Muir's father would sit him down for daily bible readings. By the time he was ten, he could quote most of it by heart. His essays are almost biblical—an amalgam of his natural and religious philosophies. I have a copy of his selected works in my pack, if you'd like to read some of them."

"Sure," at least it would be something to do before bed. Pop had often said, *Out here there was no phone, no entertainment, no nothing.* Somehow that'd been his idea of a good time.

We climbed on. Sweat poured down my neck. And my legs—I didn't want to think about my legs. My pack kept swaying around, needing constant adjustment. I couldn't understand what Pop had seen in this.

"Did Muir go to college?" I asked, trying to keep my mind off the pain.

"He attended the University of Wisconsin–Madison, but just for two years, enrolling only in classes that suited his fancy, such as botany and geology. When the Civil War broke out, he fled to Canada to avoid the draft."

"So he never graduated from college and he was a draft dodger?"

"Don't hold that against him. Several of our recent presidents were draft dodgers, and many people learn more outside of college than they ever do in it."

"Wait—you're a college professor—how can you say that?"

"College is a great place to learn academic subjects, but there are many things you must learn from experience in the world outside. In some cases, college can even kill creativity and breed conformity. It's not for everyone."

I could understand that.

"In Muir's case, most of what he really learned was self-taught, through careful observation and reading. Despite not having a degree, he published hundreds of papers and articles, including the geological theory that the landscape of the Sierra was shaped by glaciers, rather than by volcanos and earthquakes, challenging the leading theory at the time. It's somewhat ironic that the Muir trail ends at Mount Whitney, when it was the geologist Josiah Dwight Whitney who once called Muir an ignoramus for his theory about glaciers. But as it turned out, Muir's explanation is now well accepted as part of the modern geological theory."

This guy really knew a lot of facts. Maybe Ma had pushed me to go with him so I'd get interested in learning again. So I'd go back to college and become an academic like Pop. The trail continued to climb.

"After the Civil War, Muir returned to America, taking several factory jobs and doing quite well financially. But then he had an accident. A slender file he was working with slipped and pierced his cornea."

"So, he was blind in one eye?"

"No, but the injury forced him to remain in a darkened room for almost two months. During that time, he had an epiphany. He resolved to dedicate his life to the study of plants and wilderness."

"Did that pay well?" I'd never heard of a rich botanist.

"Not at all, but those were his true passions. After his recovery, Muir decided to begin his new pursuit by embarking on a thousand-mile hike from Kentucky to Florida over the wildest route possible."

"A thousand miles? Is that even doable? Can anyone really walk that far?"

"Both the Appalachian Trail and the Pacific Crest Trail are over two thousand miles long, and many people hike those."

"That must take years!"

"Most people do it in about four to six months."

"Wow, that's just nuts. So, did he make it to Florida?"

"Yes. He wrote a book about it. From there he wandered around for a while and eventually moved to San Francisco, but he didn't stay long. After reading about the marvels of Yosemite Valley, he took a trip there that changed the course of his life. This was nearly eighteen years after Yosemite Valley was taken from the Ahwahneechee Indians."

"Wait, what do you mean *taken?* I thought Yosemite was one of those idyllic spots where the settlers and natives actually got along. Don't all the places and hotels still have their original Indian names?"

"You need to study more history."

The trail was getting steeper now. Our pace had slackened considerably. The peaks and cliffs still loomed far above. Shit, had we even climbed *one* Empire State Building yet?

"Actually," he continued, "Yosemite Valley was forcibly taken from the Indians shortly after the Mexican cession of California. You should read something about Major James D. Savage, Chief Tenaya of the Ahwahneechee, and the Mariposa War, if you really want to know the history of Yosemite."

"Were all the Indians gone when Muir got there?"

"Not all of them, but most of the original inhabitants were."

"I assume Muir, the nature lover, got on well with the Indians that were left?"

"No, not at all. Despite his passion for the natural world, Muir was very much a product of his time. He sometimes made disparaging remarks about Native Americans in his writings. Although to be fair, he did note that native peoples lived much more in harmony with their surroundings than the White settlers."

I was breathing through my mouth now. The steady ache in my legs was a continual pain. Every forty or fifty paces I stopped to catch my breath, taking longer and longer sips from the plastic tube connected to the CamelBak hydration bladder in my pack. My skin prickled with the uncomfortable grime of dirt, dust, sweat, and sunscreen. Small flies and mosquitos buzzed about me. There was an alienness to being so far from civilization.

"Muir fell in love with Yosemite," Syd went on.

How could anyone fall in love with being out here? The views were nice and all, but you could see those from the car window. What did Muir, Pop, and this old guy gain from sweating up a hill like this? Ma had helplessly watched Pop drown on their hiking trip. And here was Syd running himself into the ground trying to reach some stupid mountain. I just couldn't see the point.

"At first, Muir took a job with a sheepherder, so he could trek into the high country. He wrote about his early days in *My First Summer in the Sierra*."

"Wait—I remember that book. Pop used to read it to me when I was a kid! Wasn't there this story in it about some crazy mountain man swinging from the treetops in the middle of a windstorm or something? Was that Muir?"

"Yes. You have a good memory. Your father would have been proud. Although the particular piece you're referring to was from another of Muir's books called, *The Mountains of California*."

"That was a great story. I remember thinking he was a total nutjob!"

"Sometimes he was. Muir was pretty wild and adventurous. He really believed in experiencing nature firsthand. One of my favorite essays of his is 'Snow-Storm on Mount Shasta,' where he describes how he and a climbing partner ascended one of the tallest volcanic peaks in America, and through Muir's own overconfidence, become trapped on the summit in a total whiteout. The two spent the night on a volcanic steam vent, half-boiled by the vent and half-frozen by the snow. It's an amazing piece of writing that I relish even more because I've climbed Mount Shasta."

Was that it? Some macho need to do something crazy and then brag about it later? Was that what drove Pop?

"He has another essay devoted entirely to the antics of a little bird called the water ouzel, or what we now call the American dipper. Muir writes about its cheeriness in winter snows and its joy playing in a water torrent—in contrast to the other birds, whom he described as pitifully moping about during winter storms. I think Muir saw himself in that cheery little bird. Sometimes he would sit in a mountain meadow for a day just to watch a squirrel, sketch a flower, or trace the lines on a rock. He would look into the face of nature and see God. Then he'd write about it in such poetic prose as to capture the image and bestow it in the hearts and minds of his readers."

We both paused for a moment and stood catching our breath. My heart was pounding, and my head swam. I wasn't sure about seeing God in nature. All I could see was the need for a chairlift, an elevator, or some conveyance to get us up this never-ending slope. Picturing Muir sitting in a meadow studying the rocks and animals brought to mind the classic training scene from *The Deadly Mantis*, where David Chiang's character learns new kung fu skills by observing a praying mantis. Was there something more than sweat, mosquitos, and suffering out here? Pop hadn't exactly been an athlete, and yet he loved it here. I just didn't get it. All too soon Syd started hiking again.

"I used to teach my students about Muir," he continued between breaths.

"Why? What did he have to do with philosophy?"

"Muir was a transcendentalist."

"What's that?"

"Transcendentalists believe that there is an inherent 'goodness' in people and nature, but that this goodness becomes corrupted by society and its social systems. They believe that people are at their best when they're independent and self-reliant. The writer Henry David Thoreau is perhaps the best example of a transcendentalist. He built a small cabin in the woods as an experiment, writing, *I went to the woods because I wished to live deliberately, to front only the essential facts of life, and see if I could not learn what it had to teach, and not, when I came to die, discover that I had not lived.*"

Was that what he was doing? Coming to the woods to live his own life to the fullest before he died?

"Ralph Waldo Emerson, who was Thoreau's friend, was another of the movement's leaders. He wrote, *Do not go where the path may lead, go instead where there is no path and leave a trail*. But although they espoused living in nature, at heart they were both city boys. Despite living in a cabin in the woods, Thoreau still took regular walks into town to visit his mother, who did his laundry for him. Muir, on the other hand, embodied the true transcendental ideal. He took long rambling journeys through the mountains, sometimes for days, *with just a tin cup, a handful of tea, a loaf of bread, and a copy of Emerson*. In fact, years later Emerson traveled to Yosemite to meet Muir. Some scholars even describe Muir's writing as Natural Theology. As Muir wrote, *Nature came straight from the hand of God, uncorrupted by civilization and domestication."*

"You know, this is sort of starting to sound like a college lecture."

"Sorry," he flushed. "I guess an old teacher's habits are hard to break."

"It's reminding me of a lot of the stuff Pop used to talk about. He always dreamed of building a cabin in the woods." Syd nodded. "So Muir inspired some sort of 'return to nature' movement?"

"Not exactly. Most people in his time had no interest in living like he did. But his passion for botany and geology, his careful scientific observations, his travels, and essays, all made him somewhat of a celebrity, and many famous people made it a point to visit him—if for nothing else than to hear his stories."

Suddenly the trail crested a small ridge, leveling out and turning away from the canyon wall. Syd took us off the trail, climbing up to the top of an unobstructed rocky bluff. We stopped in awe, catching our breath at the expansive view of the valley below. From here, you could see almost all the way back to where we'd started. We were near the top of the wall, the rock face dotted with the tufts of trees. Far below, the meandering river wound its way down through the broad green meadow we'd camped at. We were like two tiny ants standing far above the sweeping landscape. This'd been worth the painful hike to get here, and suddenly I could imagine what Muir musta felt his first time standing in these mountains.

We lingered for a while admiring the view. I tried to photograph the scene, but it was on too vast a scale for my tiny lens to capture. Giving up, I simply stood, taking it all in.

Much to my relief, the trail stayed level when we continued hiking. We followed a small stream gully up through the trees away from the vista, soon coming to a sturdy wooden footbridge crossing the stream. On the far side Syd stopped, set down his load, and declared that it was lunchtime. I dropped my pack, remembering at the last second to unclip the sternum strap first. Due to weight and space considerations, our lunches consisted mostly of granola bars. Chewing mine slowly, images of pepperoni pizza, BLT sandwiches, and hearty burritos all tormented me. The consolation was that there were fewer mosquitoes up here.

Finishing my meager lunch, I rubbed my aching thighs while observing Syd. His thin chest rose and fell. He looked pretty wiped out. He couldn't possibly be used to dragging a heavy pack up a mountain trail after so many months in bed.

The air here was cooler and the short repose in the afternoon sun was nice. But all too soon we packed up and started walking, then the trail began climbing again.

"You were telling me about how famous Muir became. Is that what he was known for, his writings?"

"In part," answered Syd, who now had to pause occasionally to catch his breath—like I'd been doing most of the way up.

I felt sorry asking him questions when he was clearly getting winded, but his stories distracted me from my pain and seemed to give him energy.

"Muir was also well known for his conservationist achievements, such as establishing a national park around his beloved Yosemite Valley, which at the time was only a tiny state park. As part of these efforts, he helped establish the Sierra Club, becoming its first president."

"I see, so he became a sort of political figure."

"Yes. The club gave him a platform from which to push for wilderness preservation."

"Who was he protecting it from?"

"Mostly from sheepherders whose flocks were devastating the landscape through over-grazing, but also from people cutting down the trees for lumber, miners, homesteaders, developers, and the like."

"Isn't the Sierra Club just a bunch of left-leaning environmentalists?" I asked, parroting what someone at the firm had once said.

"The modern Sierra Club has grown from an organization whose mission was to protect the Sierra Nevada, to one with a larger political agenda, but their spirit is still that of wilderness preservation. If they're on the political left, it's only because many on the other side would do away with environmental protections. You know, I first met your father on a Sierra Club outing."

"Pop never said anything about that. Tell me about it," I said perking up.

"It was on a trip from Twin Lakes, out near Bridgeport, up to Matterhorn Peak. We both hit it off right away. He told me he'd signed up for the hike because it was the same one Kerouac had taken in his book, *The Dharma Bums*. I think that's what initially drew me to him, his love for literature."

I could see that.

"On the trip, we got to know each other pretty well and discovered we shared a lot of other interests too. After that, we took a lot of hikes together. For me, it was all about the challenge. The thought of seeing something new or climbing something higher. But for your father, it was more spiritual. I think he found peace up here among the mountains. I think being in nature was his way of touching God."

That was weird. Ma had always been the soft spiritual one with her new age philosophy and music. Pop had always been religious in a strict follow-the-rules-and-go-to-church-on-Sunday sorta way. Aside from some of his poems, I'd never really heard him talk about anything spiritual—maybe Syd had seen a side of him that I hadn't?

"Is that what drew Pop to Muir? The way you said, *Muir found God in nature?*"

"That was part of it. At the time your father and I met there was a great upsurge of interest in wilderness preservation, and Muir was an icon of that movement. Did you know that when Teddy Roosevelt visited Yosemite, he chose Muir as his personal guide? Muir escorted him for several days in the backcountry, eventually convincing him to incorporate the separate Yosemite Valley and Mariposa Grove into a larger national park. Muir was also instrumental in the creation of the National Park Service."

"So, he really did a lot to protect wilderness, and Pop admired him for that?"

"Yes. I think the only major battle Muir lost was against the city of San Francisco over the damming of Hetch Hetchy Valley. In the end, the city flooded it to make a reservoir and hydroelectric plant."

"It's hard to beat city hall."

"It was a terrible loss. If you look up, *Requiem for Hetch Hetchy Valley*, you'll find that the Sierra Club maintains an online library of photographs from before it was flooded. The photos were taken by J.N. LeConte, one of the early explorers who helped map out the John Muir Trail. Hetch Hetchy was a really beautiful place, almost a second Yosemite Valley. Muir never got over the loss."

We passed a grove of large pine trees. Reflecting on the valley we'd seen, I was glad these trees and that valley were still here. I'd never been in such wide-open country before. Even in the fields of Ohio, there'd always been farmhouses. Maybe some places need to be left in their natural state to be experienced in this way, instead of just using them as resources.

"Leaving California and all this open space musta been hard for Pop back then."

"It was."

Pop often talked about California when I was growing up—the snowy mountains, the tall pines, and the wild rivers. We had taken a trip out west once when I was young—just to see some of it. I remembered meeting Syd and his wife and playing LEGOS with Sean and Cassie. I musta been eight or nine. My biggest impression had been driving through the redwoods—those tall trees reaching up like skyscrapers to the sky. But at that teaching seminar in Ohio, Pop had found someone he loved and had given up all those wild places for Ma.

"What about Muir? Did he ever marry?"

"Yes, when he was in his forties. His wife's name was Louisa. She owned a large fruit orchard north of San Francisco, which he helped her manage. They had two daughters. In his later years, he divided his time between his family and the Sierra Nevada. Muir died in his midseventies, on Christmas Eve if I recall. Actually, I think he died in Los Angeles."

"Oh great, yet another famous person who died in LA. It wasn't of a drug overdose, was it?"

"I believe he contracted pneumonia."

"So, the Muir Trail was only *named* for him?"

"That's right. In fact, in California John Muir's name has been commemorated more times than any other person."

The trail went up over a small hill and abruptly we found ourselves standing before one of the most beautiful lakes I'd ever seen. The surrounding gray-brown peaks were reflected in its deep blue water. We were right at the treeline now. The rocky peaks above us resembled those of my childhood imagination—the ones Pop had described when he'd told me about his trips. Even though it was well into summer, many of the higher ones still had snow clinging to them. There were a pair of tents down by the lake. In the distance, two men were fishing.

"Let's relax here for a bit and pump some water," Syd suggested, finding a spot a bit above the lake and dropping his pack.

Not needing to be asked twice, I let my heavy pack fall. The altitude was palpable. Even with my pack off, I had to force air in and out of my lungs to keep from panting. Syd was breathing heavily too. His face was flushed, and his lips looked wrong. "Syd, your lips look darker, almost blue. Are you OK?"

"It's the altitude." He sounded a bit agitated, probably all the exertion or me asking about his physical condition. "We probably should have taken a day or two to acclimate first. It'll pass after we get over the top and head down again."

"Maybe we should take it slower and camp here?"

"No, it's barely past noon. We can easily get in a few more miles."

"I don't know. Those peaks look pretty high, you look pretty spent, and my legs are killing me. Can't we just enjoy this spot today? Isn't that what Muir would do? We could try some fishing or—"

"No. We have a schedule to keep."

"Doesn't *The Art of War* talk about flexibility and adaptability," I ventured, hoping that maybe mentioning the old Asian text might sway him.

"Where did you hear that?" he snapped.

"From a samurai film."

He glared at me, "Listen, it may be hard, but we're getting over Donohue Pass today, and that's that."

He sounded upset, almost petulant, like he was trying to convince himself more than he was me. Not wanting to annoy him further, I took the filter and went down to the lake to pump water.

Afterward, I kicked back in the sun, listening to the gentle lapping of the water against the lakeshore. It was nice to just relax, enjoy the view, and do nothing after the hard climb. The sky was a royal blue. It'd been worth coming here. I might have really enjoyed it had we stopped to spend the night. But half an hour later, he called over to tell me that we were going.

My stomach dropped. Was this how he and Pop had been? Pop was pretty laid back. Had Syd been the one to always spur him on? Returning to where I'd dropped my pack, I hoisted it up onto my shoulders, cinching up the straps like he and Steve had shown me. It still wasn't easy, but I could get the pack on and adjust it by myself now. Looking up at the cold stone peaks, the pack seemed heavier than it had before. Were we really going over those today?

The trail here crossed the lake outflow in a wide stream. The water was pretty deep. Hesitating, I saw someone had laid large rocks under the water as stepping-stones. To my relief, we were able to cross the flow by hopping from one stone to another without getting more than our boots wet. Ever since Pop's drowning, I had a thing about water.

On the other side, the trail climbed steeply up the bare rock. Bit by bit, Syd was waning, stopping more and more often to catch his breath. He was beginning to sweat profusely and to alternately complain about the chill of the air and the heat of the sun. It wasn't easy for me either. My legs were shot, my back and neck sore. My gasping breaths made me feel like a fish out of water. But looking at Syd, I could only imagine the pain his cancer-stricken body was going through. Why was he pushing himself so hard? Couldn't we just go back down to the lake and call it a day?

"Are you sure you're alright?" I asked when we stopped for another breather.

"It's just the altitude," he rasped, "I'll be fine after the pass."

"So if Muir didn't make the trail, who did?" Maybe getting him to talk about the trail again would help him forget about the climb.

"I'll tell you after the pass," he wheezed.

We pressed on—the vast open space between the summits broken only by the sound of his labored breathing and the wind.

The trail crossed a shallow stream and followed a short ridge. Then it started heading back down toward a tiny rocky lake. The wind grew stronger, buffeting my pack. We picked up speed as we descended. The shovel hanging from the back of his pack swung wildly, making me wonder again what it was for.

Reaching the lake, we paused briefly. Ahead the trail crossed over the shallow outflow, winding up a rough barren landscape toward the snow fields above. My eyes followed the thin line up, but I couldn't make out where the pass was.

Syd looked a wreck. He was breathing heavily and the lines of his gaunt face hung down in visible exhaustion. "Let's take a break here," I suggested.

He nodded, and we both dropped our packs. I pulled out the last of my daily granola bars, offering half to Syd, but he didn't eat.

"Who was Donohue?" I asked.

"Some sergeant who was the first to climb the pass," he grumbled.

A dark bird flew overhead, its shadow reflected in the water. Syd dragged himself up, and I followed, pulling on my heavy pack again.

He was like some mad Ahab chasing after his whale.

Step by agonizing step, we ascended. The landscape was a desolate jumble of brown and gray boulders, the trail cutting ever upward among scattered patches of snow. The wind whined and wailed.

Syd's breathing became irregular, and he began making long wheezing sounds as he exhaled. It seemed that at any moment he would collapse in a pile of sweat and exhaustion, but he just pushed on.

My pack dug into the shoulders of my frozen sweat-drenched shirt. Every step was an effort. Staggering ten paces or so, we'd stop to catch our breath, then move on again, ever skyward.

Finally, we could see the top—no more than fifty yards above us the trail crested the final ridge, only sky beyond! With a last-ditch effort, we threw ourselves up the last stretch—only to discover at the crest that the trail continued on, upward, to yet another previously unseen ridge beyond. Disheartened, we staggered forward.

We crossed over two more of these false summits, each time the hope draining from our limbs as we rounded the crest, despondent.

Finally, passing a small rocky lake, we came to the true summit of Donohue Pass. A broken signpost proclaimed our victory, but neither Syd nor I felt the triumph. He was sick, and I was exhausted. We stopped, took a few hurried photographs, then staggered down the other side like a pair of zombies. Stretching below us were vast slopes of smashed rocky boulders, dotted far below by tiny green lakes. In the distance loomed menacing ash-black peaks.

My brain numbed as I mechanically forced one foot before the other. When the trail

View of Lyell Canyon from Donohue Pass

finally passed a small stagnant lake, neither of us had to say a word. We dropped our packs and made camp, utterly spent.

Syd sat with his stove and a small bottle of water staring blankly off into the distance. His skin was a sickly yellow and his lips a dark blue—like the victim in some vampire movie.

"I'll get the water," I said, trying to be helpful.

"Thanks," he groaned.

I labored to pump all the water we'd need, then lugged the heavy four-liter bag back up to camp.

We heated our meals. The only sounds were the wind blowing through the sparse trees and the hiss of our stoves.

Syd took small tenuous spoonfuls of his meal. When he was almost finished, he sprang up, staggered to the bushes, and vomited. The technicolor hue reminded me of my lasagna, making me queasy.

He returned, wiping his chin on his sleeve, "Sorry, I just couldn't hold it down."

"Are you gonna be alright?"

"It's just the altitude, it'll pass."

It looked more like the stress of the climb and the cancer. How long could he keep this up? I should have insisted we stop at that damn lake. Now we'd have to go over the pass again if we needed help. My stomach tied itself up in knots.

All I could think of to help him was the bag of instant mashed potatoes I'd brought as a kinda emergency meal.

"Maybe try some of these. They're all starch and sugar and should go down easy."

He accepted the bag and cautiously made a third of the mixture, folding in some of my boiled water, then began slowly eating the soft potatoes. This time, he didn't throw up. Some color came back to his cheeks. He made some more, passing me back the remainder.

"Thanks Gil. The potatoes really help. Listen, I wanted to say I'm sorry I pushed so hard today. You were right. We should have stopped at that lake. I should have listened to you. It's just that—well—you look so much like your father—minus the belly, of course—and I forgot that this is your first hiking trip. I also forgot that I'm no longer thirty. I'm sorry."

"Thanks," I said, feeling a bit better.

"I guess there is something to be learned from watching samurai films," he acknowledged, making me smile.

"I'm going to be OK. Don't worry. I'm just feeling the altitude a bit more than usual. I've been through this before. Tomorrow we'll take it easy like you suggested. We'll just go five miles to Thousand Island Lake. It's mostly downhill. Your father and I camped there once. It's a beautiful place."

"That sounds good," I said, hiding my own sheer exhaustion. "Why don't you take a rest? I'll clean up."

"Thanks. It's been a hard day." He got up slowly, walking awkwardly off to his bivy.

My body ached with the need for a hot shower. My skin crawled covered with dusty sunscreen and insect bites.

Cleaning up for both of us, I staggered back to my tent. Other than a couple of views, this whole thing basically sucked. I wasn't a doctor—how could I know if it was just the altitude or his cancer coming back? What would I do way out here if anything did happen? I'd no idea. It wasn't like I could call anyone. All the stories about Muir and Pop and stuff were cool, but couldn't I get all that back in Fresno instead of dragging my ass across a friggin' mountain range on some crazy adventure? I needed a plan—a surefire way to get him to quit and go back with me when we reached Reds Meadow. But I was too tired to think about it now. Not even bothering to undress, I dragged the Bonfire bag over me like a quilt.

DAY THREE

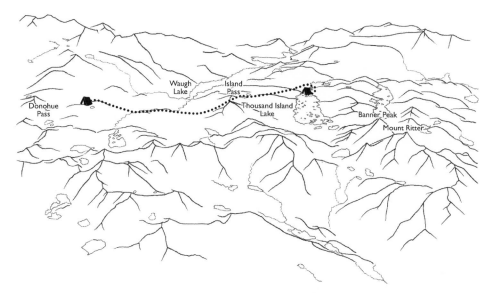

Small Lake below Donohue Pass (10,150′) to Thousand Island Lake (9,840′)
5 miles—650 feet elevation gain; 966 feet elevation loss

S YD LOOKED BETTER after a night of rest. His skin's color had returned, and his lips weren't as blue. But after a few spoonfuls of oatmeal, he threw up again. I passed him the rest of my mashed potatoes.

As he ate, I stared at the map. From here, there were two ways we could reach a road before Reds Meadow. Both meant leaving the main trail, but at least there were escape routes that didn't require going back over the pass. There must be some way of convincing him to head back to Fresno.

Heavy gray clouds were blowing overhead. When he finished the potatoes, we packed up and began walking.

Despite going downhill, we were both dragging. I hadn't slept well and everything felt sore—not just my legs, but my arms, and the places where my pack dug into my hips and shoulders. My skin prickled. My shirt reeked from sweat. My neck stiff from the hard ground. Syd couldn't be doing much better.

It wasn't long before he began to lag behind, urging me to go on. I did, but stopped every so often to wait for him—the last thing I needed was to lose him somewhere and have to hike back uphill to find him. The trail went by several small ponds and streams, then passed a junction. It would be hard to get lost. At most intersections, the route was clearly marked, "John Muir Trail," in stenciled letters cut into rusty brown signs. Small greenish-blue birds chirped merrily and squirrels darted about in the trees—of course they were happy, they were home.

How could I get out of this thing? What about faking a twisted ankle? It might work, but Syd would probably insist on nursing me until I got better, then what would I do? I thought of my Backwoods Buffet—but food poisoning had the same problem, he'd just wait for me to get well. And I wasn't exactly gonna fake a bear attack or break a leg just to get outta the hike. I could tell him I was sick. Or fake a fever like I'd done as a kid when I wanted to skip school. I could sprinkle some water on my forehead and lay in my sleeping bag moaning. Nah—he was a teacher. He'd see right through that. Besides, he probably had a thermometer tucked away in his first-aid kit. I needed something better. Something guaranteed.

The trail wound down through the trees passing another junction. It was too well marked to go the wrong way and pretend I hadn't seen the sign. Maybe I could tell him Ma was sick? That she needed an operation or something? He'd certainly let me go for that—but Ma would never agree. She's the one who pushed me to go on this stupid trip in the first place. Besides, they would talk and he would find out the truth. That would never work. What about a torn ligament? I had one of those when I was on the swim team. It didn't show up in an X-ray—the doctor had only diagnosed it by twisting my leg around and asking if it hurt. I'd been on crutches for weeks. That would be perfect! I could pretend it hurt so bad I couldn't drive, then he'd have to go back with me—but what about the swelling? My ankle had been puffed up like a red balloon. I'd have to find some way to simulate that. Maybe I could twist it a little or bang it against something so it looked real? The thought made me cringe—but it just might work.

The trail came to yet another junction. A worn wooden sign with an arrow read, "Island Pass." There was no familiar metal sign. Had I made a mistake at the last junction? I didn't remember having to go over a pass today. Syd was nowhere to be seen.

Dropping my pack, I hurriedly pulled out my map. To my relief, "Island Pass" was just a large hump with two lakes at a little over ten thousand feet. I hadn't even noticed it on the map before. It would be an uphill climb again, but nothing like Donohue.

Syd ambled up, exhaling a brief apology. He looked pretty beat, struggling under a full pack in his condition.

Maybe I should take some of his load? *Nah—that was his burden.* Just as mine was to suffer along on this stupid hike 'cause I hadn't been there for Pop. Everything stemmed from that one decision. Why couldn't we go just back in time and fix things, rather than having to always bear the consequences of our actions? Like in those historic epics Pop used to read where the hero suffers through the entire story 'cause of one simple mistake.

When Syd recovered, we struggled up the hump. My quads were on fire. Syd staggered like a drunk, relying on his trekking poles to push himself upward.

"Look at us," he grinned, "we're like two ambulatory patients at an orthopedic hospital!" I laughed, but it wasn't far from the truth.

From the crest, we could see a small green valley framed by black spires. "Those are the Ritter Range and the Minarets," he declared, seeming to gain a bit of energy from the sight.

We dropped our packs among some rocks to rest. Pulling out one of my granola bars, I broke off half and handed it to Syd. It was good this would be over soon. I looked down at my boots. Better remember to bang up the right foot, so I wouldn't be able to drive. *Shit— was I really gonna smash it?*

"What made you and Pop wanna go on hikes like this? I mean, besides walking, what did you two actually do?"

He probed me with his eyes. It felt like he was reading my thoughts, like some Jedi Master. I flushed, embarrassed that he already knew my plan. But he only said, "The usual things young men do. We lounged around, watched the clouds, swam, and had a few beers. We talked about women. But we also talked a lot about life and literature. Those were two topics your dad and I never tired of."

"Wait—I thought you said we couldn't bring beer?"

He eyed me strangely, "Those were short weekend hikes. We had room for a few luxuries, like beer."

That sounded a lot better than this trip. Why hadn't he just asked me to do a weekend hike? Syd pulled out one of his snack bars and passed me half. His bar was far tastier than my own, a mix of real cherries, dates, and seeds.

After eating, he said, "Why don't you go on ahead again?"

He insisted. Donning my pack, I went on.

The trail descended into a small valley by a large blue lake. One of the black peaks stood perfectly reflected in its tranquil water, its rocky face streaked in snow. Halfway around the lake on a large plaid blanket were a family of four enjoying a picnic lunch. All blonds. They were dressed in odd clothing: long hiking boots, black knickers, and red button-down vests. They looked as if they'd just stepped off the set of *The Sound of Music*. They waved, and I waved back.

The nearest parking lot was twelve miles away, and it was at least a three-thousand-foot climb. Yet here was this happy family from the Alps that'd just strolled over with two young kids for an afternoon picnic! Was I the only one who thought this trip was tough?

The trail undulated gently up and down, eventually coming to an inviting grassy spot. Ahead was a rocky bluff. My stomach rumbled. My joints were stiff. All the muscles in my legs ached. Even this short day was exhausting. Dropping my pack, I sat down in the grass, dragging out another bar. Chewing on the bland cardboard stick, I swatted at the occasional bug while waiting.

I was just growing concerned, when a tired-looking Syd came staggering over. "Great spot," he wheezed, dropping his pack and massaging his boney legs. The yellow-purple blotches around his neck seemed to bulge with his breathing and I turned away.

"You OK?" I asked, staring at the grass.

"I'm alright. My joints are just stiff."

We sat for bit. His breathing slowed.

"Did you see that crazy family from the Alps?" I said, looking back.

"They were from Norway."

"How do you know that?"

"I asked them."

"You speak Norwegian?"

"No, but they spoke English. You really should say hello to people out here. It isn't like the city—people relax in nature. Out here it's one big community."

It sounded a bit like the way things were growing up in Ohio. Out in LA I'd gotten used to minding my own business. "How did they get this far?"

"They're backpacking like us."

We ate—if you can call it that—then climbed over the bluff. From here, we got our first glimpse of Thousand Island Lake. Its name reminded me of the salad dressing. It was a huge irregularly shaped lake; its surface dotted with tiny islands. Some looked large enough to camp on, but most were just a few feet around. The lake was nestled in a broad valley fenced in by the dark razor-sharp ridges Syd had pointed out earlier. Towering above the others, its base dotted in snow, was a broad black peak with a rough-sloped head, resembling a great crouched sphinx looking proudly out over the sapphire-blue water.

Near the bottom of the descent was another signed junction. An arrow pointing ahead read "JMT," while two others labeled "PCT" and "Reds Meadow" both pointed left.

"I don't get it," I said pointing at the signs. "Do we turn left here for Reds Meadow or continue straight for the JMT?"

Syd smiled. "I'm not sure if you know it or not, but by hiking the JMT, we're also doing part of the PCT, or Pacific Crest Trail. The two follow the same route through most of the High Sierra. This is the only spot between Tuolumne Meadows and Mount Whitney where they diverge. From here, the PCT stays low, going by Agnew Meadows, while the JMT climbs higher, passing a string of alpine lakes. The two merge again just before Reds Meadow, so we go straight."

I hadn't known the PCT and JMT were partially the same trail. In fact, before this hike I'd only vaguely ever heard of either.

"Why would they separate? Doesn't it cost more to have two trails?"

"The only thing I can think of is that the PCT is also an equestrian trail. It may be that riders need to stop at the horse camp down at Agnew Meadows for some reason, or that the trail over this stretch of the Sierra is a bit too rough for horses."

"Who named the Sierras? Was it Muir?"

"Don't call it 'the Sierras.' It's just 'Sierra'—that's the name of the range. Ansel Adams once wrote: *To add an s is a linguistic, Californian, and mountaineering sin*. But to answer your question, the Sierra Nevada was named by Spanish explorers, back when California was still a part of Mexico."

"What does the name mean?"

"I thought you knew Spanish?" he raised an eyebrow. "*Sierra* means *saw*, like the word *serrated* we use for knives. And *Nevada* means *snow-covered*, so it's a *snow-covered saw*, or a *snow-covered range of sawtooth mountains*."

"Oh," I said, realizing that I'd already known the meaning. It was a bit like that embarrassing time I'd asked my frat buddies what day the *Cinco de Mayo* party was on.

A short way past the junction was a narrow footbridge constructed out of a pair of bound logs. The outflow of the lake streamed under it. A little before the bridge was a wide gentle path that led to a broad sandy spot by the lakeshore. Two young couples were swimming there, yelling and splashing in the water. Their backpacks and clothing abandoned in the sand.

A second sign was posted here with a map designating areas around the lake that were off-limits to camping. Trying not to stare too obtrusively at the girls, I pretended to study the sign while watching them bounce and splash in the water.

"Why don't we camp at this large promontory," Syd pointed at the map.

"Eh, sure—" I assented, my attention elsewhere.

"Are you even listening to what I'm saying?"

"Whaddya mean?"

"You're what, twenty-eight now?"

"Almost twenty-eight—"

"And yet you're still ogling women like some college freshman?"

"They're asking for it—going topless and all."

"Gil, the wilderness is a special place where people can relax free from all the inhibitions of the city. Please don't carry that attitude out here, try to grow up a bit."

Sheesh—I hope I never get so old chemo shrivels my dick like that.

Syd led on across the bridge. Reluctantly, I followed, the girls bobbing off into the distance. Less than a quarter of the way around the lake, we left the trail, our route paralleling a steep slope that rose sharply up above us. It was rough going, scrambling up and down over large granite steps, but eventually we reached a secluded cove with a private pebbly beach.

"Do you want to try cowboy camping tonight?" asked Syd, who seemed to have recovered some of his energy.

"What's *cowboy camping?*"

"Sleeping outside without a tent."

I glanced up. The sky had cleared.

"What about bugs and snakes and bears and stuff?" Not sure going without a tent was such a great idea.

"Most bugs and snakes go away after dark when it gets cold. As for bears, do you really think a thin nylon tent is any real protection? As long as you don't sleep with your food, bears won't be interested in you."

I couldn't help thinking of the guy Steve said got dragged around in his sleeping bag, but Syd had a point.

"Come on," he said. "You've heard of a five-star hotel, haven't you?"

"Yeah, of course."

"Well cowboy camping is like sleeping in a ten-thousand-star hotel!"

"OK—what the heck—I'll try it." At least I wouldn't have to pack up my tent in the morning.

We each laid out our air mattress and sleeping bag on a flat clear patch of ground, not too far from each other.

After three days on trail, my pants were filthy and both my shirts reeked of a mixture of sunscreen and sweat. My St. Pauli Girl shirt was particularly bad, with two brown streaks where my pack straps were that seemed to rise out of her flagons like two brown fountains. I asked Syd what to do about laundry.

"We can use our bear canisters as washing machines, but we have to make sure we dump the soap far from the lake or it'll cause algae growth."

Emptying our food into our sleeping bag sacks, which we hung up temporarily, we filled the canisters with water from the lake. Then we lugged them back up the shore a little away from our camp. Adding a few drops of dish soap and wearing only our clean long johns, we stuffed our dirty clothing in. Mixing and agitating the cold soapy clothes by hand was hard work. When I finally poured the water out, it ran a dark muddy brown. Were my clothes really that filthy? It took three more hand-numbing cycles before the rinse water ran even partially clear—the whole process convincing me that the automatic washing machine was by far humanity's best invention.

Syd strung up a cord between two trees, and we hung our wet clothes up, securing them with lightweight plastic bread clips that he'd saved as clothespins. Syd assured me that in the soft lake breeze, our clothes would be dry by morning.

He then pointed to the beach, "Do you want to take a swim and wash off?"

It wasn't that deep, but I shook my head. "No, it looks pretty cold. I'll just rinse off by the shore."

Staring at the water, the memories of that day came flooding back.

It was Spring Break. Ma and Pop had gone hiking up the California coast. They'd invited me, but like an idiot I'd chosen to hang out on campus. I was watching *Karate Warrior* when the call came. Thinking maybe Samantha had gotten back, I answered.

"This is Officer Harding of the Humboldt County Sheriff's Office. I'm afraid there's been an accident involving your father—"

And just like that my world turned upside down.

I stood there numbly gripping the phone, "This morning the region just north of Shelter Cove was hit by a rogue wave, what they call a sneaker wave. I'm afraid your father is one of three people now missing. We have crews from Shelter Cove Fire, Ocean Rescue, and the Coast Guard all combing the beaches and the water, but I'm afraid at this point there isn't much hope—"

Eventually, he put Ma on the line. Her voice was almost hysterical, "We were hiking along the beach—headed back to the car—when the wave hit. He was down at the beach looking for driftwood. There was no warning. I was swept up toward the cliffs and grabbed some branches. The wind was knocked out of me—but I think I saw him out there—getting pulled out. I don't know for sure—it was too far out and he was moving so fast—if only you had been there—or there'd been a boat or a lifeguard or something—they might have reached him—but there was nothing I could do. Oh Gil," she sobbed. "Your father's gone."

I wasn't sure what she or the officer said after.

Samantha dropped me at the airport. In a haze, I was on a flight from Chicago to San Francisco, then another up to Arcata. I picked up Ma and the car and drove her back to Ohio. A week later, I was back at Northwestern. They never found Pop.

Why hadn't I gone hiking with them? I was a champion swimmer. I coulda saved him.

After that day, I could never get near deep water again. I'd thrown up at my next swim meet. It was embarrassing, and I'd quit the team.

The cold lake water lapped at the shore, calling me back. My stomach twisted. Just wading into it would be hard enough—but I was covered in grime and needed a rinse. I'd have to force myself.

Taking care that the beach was really private, I stripped off what I was wearing and stepped hesitantly toward the shore. The icy water lapped at my feet, sending shivers up my spine. I inched forward, my heart pounding in my throat. The water rose up to my calves. Eyes shut tightly, I splashed it over my body, then dashed for shore. I wasn't exactly what I'd call clean, but it was better than nothing. Using a bandana, I dried off. After pulling back on my long johns, I started to warm up. My heart was still thumpin', but I'd done it. I'd entered the water. Calming myself, I straightened out my wet hair.

Syd rinsed too, but also declined taking a dip. It was probably for the best. I wouldn't want him getting a chill and there was no way I could go in after him if anything happened.

We sat down above the shore for an early dinner. Syd had some difficulty swallowing and several long fits of coughing. In the middle of his meal, it looked like he was gonna hurl, but he kept it down. If his dinner tasted anything like Backwoods Buffet, then I knew how he felt.

I didn't wanna think about Pop anymore today, so I asked him about the trail. "If Muir didn't come up with the idea for the trail, then who did?"

His eyes sparkled, as if he'd been waiting all day for me to ask. "An aspiring young explorer named Theodore Seixas Solomons. He claimed to have gotten the idea as a four-teen-year-old boy gazing up at the mountains from his uncle's farm in Fresno—and unlike many who abandon their childhood dreams, Solomons never gave up on his."

Was he taking a jab at me for dropping out of college? From his animated expression, it didn't seem so.

"At just twenty-two, young Solomons enrolled as a charter member in Muir's newly formed Sierra Club."

I sipped the tea he'd shared with me. Listening to his story calmed me—like when Pop read to me as a kid.

"Solomons spent five years making explorations and mapping out a path for his envisioned High Mountain Route."

"How did he have that much time? Was his family rich?" I'd never realized how much money mattered until Pop was gone.

"Not at all. He grew up in a modest Jewish family in a cramped San Francisco apartment.

From what I've read, Solomons continually disregarded his mother's practical advice, in favor of his own unconventional dreams."

It sure sounded like he was taking a poke at me—I'd had many disagreements with Ma over my career—but if he was trying to get at me, his face didn't show it.

"Solomons' great-grandfather was the first Rabbi born in America and was one of the religious leaders present at George Washington's inauguration. But young Theodore wasn't very religious. He was something of a black sheep. Incidentally, Solomons also died in Los Angeles."

"Oh great, another one," I grumbled. "So wait—why was this trail named for Muir? Why wasn't it called the Theodore Solomons Trail?"

"There *is* a 270-mile unofficial Theodore Solomons Trail that runs west of here, roughly parallel to the Muir Trail. In fact, you could make a loop of them."

"Why didn't you wanna do both then?" I asked, immediately biting my lip. The last thing I wanted was to give him more crazy ideas.

"That would mean a journey of almost two months, and I'm not even certain I can finish *this* trail—"

Was he thinking of quitting too? Or did he mean he might die out here? I pushed the thought from my head—*there was no way I was going through that again!*

"—but mostly because while the Muir Trail's popularity has grown, the Solomons Trail has fallen out of use. Many sections now require route-finding, and some of the bridges have been washed away. Only a handful of people hike it each year."

"So basically, I'd need to be more experienced, and you'd have to be in better shape." I rejoined the conversation.

"I'll just be happy to make it to Mount Whitney," he said, staring across the lake.

I felt like a prick for planning to bail on him, but what else could I do? So far, most of this trip had been miserable—although it wasn't too bad now, sitting here in the sun. A light breeze smelling vaguely of seagrass was keeping the bugs away. Stretching out my sore legs, I asked, "So, why did they name the trail after Muir?"

"In 1914, the Sierra Club began work on a bill to fund construction of a High Mountain Route. Shortly afterward, Muir died. It was then suggested that they name the trail in his honor."

"Wasn't this Solomons guy upset about that?"

"No, he liked the idea, saying, *Muir is a better name to conjure with.* According to his account, he was just happy seeing his childhood dream reach fruition."

"Very magnanimous."

He sipped his tea. "A lot of people contributed to the exploration and planning of the John Muir Trail. The other major figures were a Stanford art professor named Bolton Brown and a Berkeley engineering professor named J.N. LeConte."

"J.N.?"

"Joseph Nisbet LeConte—but everyone called him, 'J.N.' or 'Little Joe,' to distinguish him from his father of the same name. J.N. studied mechanical engineering at Cal, obtaining his master's degree at Cornell. He was appointed an assistant professor at Berkeley at just twenty-two. Incidentally, his father and his uncle also taught at Cal. His father was a famous geologist, and his uncle was the university's first and third president."

"Why'd they call him Little Joe?"

"Because he wasn't very tall. From his early twenties, J.N. spent his summers up in the Sierra, becoming a famous mountaineer, explorer, and photographer. He made some of the first detailed maps of the area, filling in the blanks left by Whitney's team and publishing them in the Sierra Club Bulletin. After Muir's death, he became president of the club and was instrumental in the construction of the trail."

"Do you see that big peak?" he asked, indicating the massive Sphinx-like mountain. "That's actually two peaks. What looks like a ridge on its lefthand side is a second peak named Mount Ritter. You can't see its summit from here, but it's over thirteen thousand feet tall. It was named by Josiah Whitney in memory of one of his geography teachers. Two members of his expedition—Clarence King and James Gardner—tried to climb it but failed just shy of the summit."

The mountain was bathed in the orangey glow of the afternoon sun. Squinting at the purple shadows, I could just make out that the ridge on the left was a separate peak.

"Are those the same two peaks we saw from the top of Donohue?"

"That's right," he smiled, "I wanted to point them out to you, but was too exhausted. Mount Ritter was first summited by Muir, who wrote an entire chapter about his harrowing assent in *The Mountains of California*. Almost twenty years later, it was climbed again by J.N. LeConte, Theodore Solomons, and Solomons' cousin Sidney Peixotto."

"So Solomons and LeConte were friends?"

"The mountaineering community has always been a pretty tight-knit group, particularly in those days. But in this case, they just happened to meet up in Yosemite. Solomons and his cousin were scouting a route for Solomons' proposed trail, while LeConte was taking sightings for his map of the area. They were going in the same direction, so they joined up."

"What's that big peak in front of Mount Ritter called?"

"That's Banner Peak."

"Named for Bruce Banner?"

"Who?"

"You know, Bruce Banner, the guy who turns into the Incredible Hulk?"

He folded his arms, staring at me.

"Seriously, who was Banner?" I asked, trying to make up for my bad joke.

"Banner? Banner was nobody. It's named for a type of cloud that sometimes hangs onto mountains, like a banner."

Was he messing with me now? He had such a straight face; it was hard to tell.

"So, who was the other guy you mentioned—that art professor—what did he do?"

"Do you remember the drawing in my home that you were admiring?"

"Yeah."

"Well, I didn't say anything at the time, but that's a rare original lithograph by Bolton Brown, just one of five hundred prints that he made."

"So, Brown made sketches of women in the wilderness?"

"Much more. He was an artist, but also a rock climber, and a member of the Sierra Club. Brown majored in art at Syracuse, which was quite rare for a man in those days. Afterward, he spent some time in the Alps becoming an avid mountaineer. He then taught drawing at Cornell, and at twenty-six was invited to found an art department at Stanford University."

"That's impressive."

"He was quite talented. You really should see more of his drawings. Brown captured nature in a way that makes you feel you're looking out over the mountains with him. While at Stanford he fell in love with the Sierra, making fantastically detailed sketches that would prove invaluable to future explorers."

"Did he know Muir?"

"I'm not sure how close they were, but they certainly knew each other."

A ripple of wind blew across the water carrying the scent of pine. "While at Stanford, Brown married Lucy Fletcher. The two took their honeymoon up the Kings River Basin, where they climbed together making detailed sketches of the region. Brown also named a number of major peaks, including Mount Stanford."

"So, he was a kinda landscape artist?"

"Most people categorize him as a Tonalist."

"What's that?"

"Tonalism was a short-lived style portraying elusive, almost ethereal figures in natural landscapes. Brown was famous for his moonlit images of natural subjects bathing in the wilderness."

"You mean nudes?"

"Yes, in fact it cost him his job at Stanford. Apparently, Mrs. Stanford was quite fond of popping in on classes. When she discovered Brown using nude models in his coed drawing course, all hell broke loose and the university let him go."

"Prudes!"

"It was the late eighteen hundreds, Gil."

"OK, you have a point there. But he was an artist, what did they expect?"

"Conformity. And Professor Brown did anything but. When he left Stanford, he returned to the East Coast, where he helped found the radical artist colony at Woodstock."

"Where they held the music festival?"

"The same, although that was many years later."

A fish jumped from the water, gulping at some unseen insect and splashing as it landed. The ripples echoed out from where it vanished beneath the surface. Several more fish leapt after bugs. Chewing on my sporkful of lasagna, I eyed them hungrily, wishing I'd brought a rod. Even the bugs they were swallowing probably tasted better than Backwoods Buffet.

Syd continued his story, "In his later years, Brown became obsessed with lithographs— prints made using special grease pencils rubbed onto stone. He was one of those rare perfectionists who was a blend of artist and scientist. When he couldn't get someone to make prints to his own exacting standards, he purchased a press, performed experiments, and eventually became the world's leading expert on lithography."

"How do you keep all these details straight?"

"I've always been good at remembering stories. That's one reason I became a teacher. Your father was also a good storyteller."

That was true. On long car rides, Pop would tell stories, many from the classics. And it was almost a family tradition that he and Ma would recite Shel Silverstein poems, sometimes to improvised music that we all created ourselves.

"You said you and Pop came to this lake before. Why didn't you hike the whole trail then?"

"Your father and I often talked about it, but work, kids, and schedules always got in the way. After he died—well, I just never found another hiking partner like your dad. Then when Katrine passed—well, you know the rest. This is my last chance to do it."

"If you guys were so tight, why didn't you make Pop's funeral?"

He looked away. "Health reasons."

We sat, listening to the occasional sound of fish breaking the water.

After a while he continued, "While recovering, I must have read almost a hundred different articles and some twenty books about the JMT."

"That's a lot of work."

"Wouldn't you read history books and travel guides about Ireland or Japan if you were planning a trip there?"

"Probably not—I mean, I know I should—but who has the time?"

"A cancer patient has the time," he said gravely.

We sat watching the ripples on the lake. Could I really go through with my plan and ruin his and Pop's dream? Did his asking me to go have something to do with Pop? I was about to question him about it, when he said, "You know that drawing by Brown that you like? After I die, I want you to have it. You coming with me on this trip means a lot."

"I could never accept that," I winced. He had no idea I was planning to quit.

"It'll be something to remember me by."

I wanted to say something about his chances for finding a cure—maybe he could try that bone marrow thing? But all I could manage was a feeble, "Thank you, it'll mean a lot to me, but I hope it's a really long time before it comes to that."

"Me too," he said wistfully.

"We were talking about the trail before," he said after a time. "The physical construction took several decades to finish. And part of that time was during the Great Depression. But they completed it in 1938. Perhaps the hardest part was cutting routes over the high mountain passes."

"Like Donohue?"

"Donohue is only eleven thousand feet high," he said, glancing back in the direction we'd come. "We have seven more high passes to go—not counting Whitney—and most of them much higher than Donohue. The worst will be Forester, it's over thirteen."

He fidgeted as he sat, his patchy yellow skin drooping down around his chin. Each long inhale made the purple blood spots around his neck stand out like the spots on a corpse.

He was fantasizing if he thought he could make it over another high mountain pass, let alone seven. No, we'd have to get off the trail together at Reds Meadow. It was the only way.

After dinner, we went for a walk along the lakeshore. Several people in other campsites stared at our attire, but most didn't seem to notice—as if tall skeletal old men and pudgy younger ones dressed in black long johns and hiking boots often wandered these shores.

As we walked, the late-day sky became a watercolor painting streaked with purple-orange hues, while ripples shimmered off the lake's surface. Rising in the background were the twin sentinels of Banner and Ritter, standing like two proud guardians shrouded in their cloaklike shadows.

Back at camp, I looked apprehensively at our two sleeping bags, which were stretched out on the open ground.

"Are you sure it'll be OK without a tent?"

"It'll be fine, you'll see," he assured me.

It was a bit chilly, so I kept my long johns on and climbed into my Bonfire bag. Almost immediately, I became too sweaty so I stripped down. I preferred to sleep naked anyway. Copying Syd, I stuffed them into my sleeping bag sack, making a small pillow. Once settled, we laid back looking up at the stars.

DAY FOUR

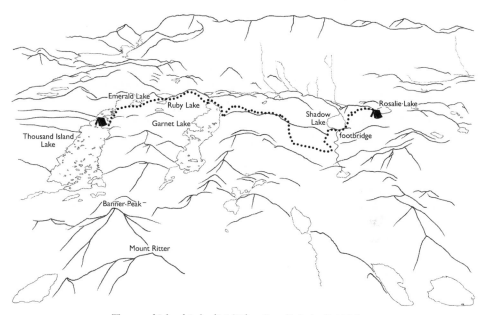

Thousand Island Lake (9,840′) to Rosalie Lake (9,390′)
8 miles—1,250 feet elevation gain; 1,700 feet elevation loss

I WAS WALKING ACROSS A GRASSY MEADOW abuzz with birds and insects and filled with all kinds of flowers. Slowly, I became aware of a rank stench—a cross between dog breath, rotten eggs, and old garbage. It was overwhelming. Opening my eyes, I jerked awake. Hovering over me, its salivating jaws dripping rancid slobber onto my face, was the muzzle of a huge brown bear!

My mind raced—jumping to Steve's advice about making yourself tall and banging pots and pans together—how could you do any of that with an enormous bear standing over you? Instead, I did the one instinctive thing I could: I screamed. A deep guttural manly scream of horror—like the sound a gladiator makes before being sliced in two. The bear backed off slowly.

Scrambling out of my bag and completely naked, I began jumping up and down. "Argggggggggghhhh!" I yelled, dancing and flailing my arms in panic.

The bear backed up a few more steps and hesitated a moment. Then it turned tail and bolted.

My heart was pounding. I turned to look at Syd. He was sitting up in his bag surveying the scene. Then he began to laugh. "Your scream frightened me worse than the bear!"

Flushed and shaking, I grabbed my stuff sack pillow, tore out my long johns, and pulling them on hollered, "I will *never* try cowboy camping again!"

Syd was still laughing. My pulse raced. I was furious. I could have been eaten by a thousand-pound bruin and he was *laughing* at me?

"Sorry Gil, I didn't mean to laugh," he stifled a chuckle, "but the sight of you standing there naked chasing off that bear was just too funny."

He thought it was *funny?* I lost it, exploding in anger, "That's it! I can't do this hike anymore! I didn't wanna tell you yesterday, but I was going to twist my ankle or something, so we'd have to go back at Reds Meadow. But now I can just say it: Camping isn't for me! I'm not my father! I'm not a backpacker! I only agreed to go on this stupid hike 'cause I wanted to understand Pop—to know why he loved being here so much. But I haven't learned anything! I hate camping! All I really want is Pop back! Can't you see that? But I can't have it can I? I can't even get a piece of him back. When we get to Reds Meadow, I quit. You can finish your own damn trail if you want to, but I'm done!"

Stunned, he stared off in the direction of the fleeing bear. Then hanging his head, he said, "OK, I'm sorry. We'll both head home at Reds Meadow."

"Good, I'm glad that's settled!" I shouted, hands on my hips. Then recovering part of my composure, I stomped over to the laundry line, glancing back over my shoulder occasionally lest Yogi return.

That was it. He'd agreed. Fine. I wouldn't have to bang up my stupid foot anymore.

I stared at the line of clothes, catching my breath. The shirts and pants were dry. Stripping off my long johns, I pulled on some clean clothes. Gradually, I calmed down.

Syd was still sitting with his head bowed. I felt sorry for him, but it was over. What was said, was said. We were going back.

A tense stillness hung over our campsite. Wordlessly we pumped water and made breakfast. I kept a warry eye out for the bear, but it never reappeared.

Finally, I broke the silence, "Do you think that bear woulda eaten me if I hadn't woke up?"

"No," he sighed without enthusiasm, "it was probably just sniffing around, investigating."

"So, you're saying I was perfectly safe?"

"Bears are wild animals, and you never know—but I've never heard of a black bear attacking someone unprovoked. A grizzly maybe. A polar bear definitely. But black bears are pretty timid." He seemed to perk up a bit as he spoke. "Now if you had stuffed a snickers bar into your bag, like that guy Steve met, that might have been a different story. But did you see how the bear ran away when you shouted?"

"Yeah," I grinned. "I guess it did. I scared off a bear in the buck! That'll make a great story someday, if I ever have kids."

"It will," he smiled, looking better.

"How come *you* didn't just chase it away?" I eyed him.

"Me? I didn't wake up until you started screaming. You really did frighten me worse than the bear. I thought you were being pulled apart by a mountain lion."

"There are mountain lions here too?" I started, glancing left and right.

"Eat your breakfast," he chided. "Yes, there are mountain lions here too, but you'd have a better chance of getting struck by lightning than seeing one. In all the years I've been backpacking, I've only heard of one mountain lion attack—and that involved a ranger who made the mistake of crawling into its den. The truth is, you're safer up here in the mountains than you are back home in Los Angeles. You have a greater chance of dying crossing a city street, than you do from all the hazards of the wilderness."

"What about crazed axe murderers and the like?"

"Oh come on, you've been reading too many Stephen King novels. Where do you think all the real weirdos and lunatics hang out? In the big cities of course! The best people you'll ever meet are backpackers. There's something about being in nature that brings out the goodness in folks. The Japanese even use forest bathing as a kind of therapy. You'll see, people are really kind and down-to-earth out here."

I finished my breakfast. Talking about axe murders and mountain lions hadn't exactly calmed my nerves, but what Syd said made sense. Still, something about being out in the wild gave me the willies—and I'd just been woken up by a bear with morning breath!

Packing up, we headed back around the lake. Syd seemed to be taking things stoically. Physically, he was doing better and took the lead again. If he was broken up about our going back, he certainly didn't show it.

The trail climbed, passing two buggy green lakes named Emerald and Ruby, then descended losing all the elevation we'd just gained. It was like leveling up on some video game, only to get crushed and have to start all over from the beginning.

On the other side of the hill, we got our first glimpse of Garnet Lake, which I had to admit was also impressive. Like Thousand Island Lake, Garnet Lake was nestled in a broad valley; but instead of barren rocky slopes, the surrounding hills and ridges were sparsely forested. Here the twin peaks of Ritter and Banner were each clearly visible, the two reflected in the lapis-blue water like a postcard.

We followed the trail down, stopping near a small bridge spanning the outflow for a snack. Tiny skittish birds with orangey-red breasts and black banditlike masks darted about the trees making shrill honking noises, as if mocking us.

"I believe those are red-breasted nuthatches," observed Syd, "although I'm no ornithologist."

Why did he always have to use big words for everything? Couldn't he just say "bird-watcher" like everyone else?

After eating, we followed the trail around the lakeshore, passing above several wooded campsites—the first already populated with tents. We soon came to a series of steep switchbacks, winding up the open granite face. The sun was up now, and I began sweating as we climbed. Surprisingly, my legs felt less stiff. Yesterday's shorter hike sure helped.

Syd was doing better. I had to work hard to keep up with him as we ascended. Just below the ridgetop, we stopped to catch our breath. The lake below was gorgeous and the air clean and fresh. This was a place I could see myself coming back to—if anyone could ever convince me to go backpacking again. I could really taste what Pop musta felt out here.

"Ready to go?" Syd asked in a surprisingly chipper tone.

"You go on ahead," I panted. "I'll catch up along the trail, or at camp."

He headed off. I dropped my pack, had a granola bar, and chilled for a bit, taking in the view. When I got up, he was already well out of sight. Suddenly, I regretted letting him go. I was alone in the middle of the wilderness. What if I got lost? What if there was another bear? What if one of us had an accident?

There was no way I could overtake him at his pace—but if he stopped for a break, I might catch him. I began walking, feeling nervous at the strange emptiness around me.

The trail worked its way over the ridge, then switchbacked down a rocky slope toward a tree-lined valley. The path was strewn with loose stones, forcing me to constantly watch my footing. *Why doesn't someone clean this up or something? A person could twist an ankle!*

Descending, I turned my head at each new sound—each buzz of a gnat or thud of a dislodged rock. Strange staccato thrumming echoed from among the trees below. I knew it was probably just a woodpecker, but somehow it made me think of axe murderers again.

To my relief, halfway down I ran into a guy coming up the other way. He was carrying a large gray backpack, with a sweat-soaked blue bandana as a kinda improvised sunhat.

"Is it much farther to Garnet?" he panted, leaning on his trekking poles.

"It's just over the ridge," I said.

"Good, because this section is really kicking my ass!"

"Are you hiking the JMT?"

"Yeah, with my son. Are you *SOBO*?"

"What's *SOBO*?"

"*Southbound*—as in, *are you NOBO or SOBO?* I mean, are you hiking the JMT Southbound?"

"I see—yeah—I'm *SOBO*, I guess." *Did hiking partway count?*

His son was a couple of switchbacks behind.

"You didn't pass an old man carrying a shovel, headed the other way—*SOBO*—did you?"

"About twenty minutes back."

His words gave me a mix of relief and anxiety, knowing that Syd was alright but still far ahead.

"How long have you been hiking?" I asked.

"This is our eighteenth day out. We started this morning at Reds Meadow, just before sunrise."

I looked at his ratty clothes, his sunburnt cheeks, and his unkept stubble. Is that how I woulda looked after eighteen days?

"Reds Meadow, wow, that's pretty far."

"A ton of uphill in the heat, and not much water!" he huffed.

This was comforting, 'cause if he had to go up, then I'd be heading down. His son caught up.

"Nice meeting you," he said. "Have a great hike!"

He and his son hiked on heading *NOBO*. Turning, I hurried on down the slope after Syd.

I walked alone for another hour or so, every now and then pausing when I heard a strange noise to check for bears and mountain lions.

The guy with his son reminded me of Pop and me. Pop woulda loved seeing me out here with his buddy Syd. And Ma—how was I ever gonna tell her? She was right, I had nothing going on in LA. Maybe this was my last chance to get back on track? Was this whole hiking thing just a part of my fate? Part of my penance for abandoning Pop?

Eventually, I reached a junction. An old wooden sign pointed one way toward Shadow Lake and the other toward Ediza Lake. There were none of the familiar brown metal trail markers here. Consulting my map, I made a left, heading in the direction of Shadow Lake. It made me nervous to navigate through the wilderness on my own, but at least I had my map and everything seemed well marked.

As the trail meandered along a broad stream, I noticed a guy off to the side. His small green pack was lying open in the dirt. He was bent down, gathering plants by the stream, busily stuffing them into an old woven sack. The guy had wild dirty-blond hair knotted into loose dreadlocks. He was wearing a well-worn tie-dyed T-shirt and baggy maroon pants. Instead of hiking boots, he had on a pair of heavy leather sandals with no socks. He looked like he'd just stepped off the streets of Berkeley.

"Hi!" I said, clearing my throat. The guy paused and looked up, apparently so absorbed in his work that he'd been unaware of my presence. "What are you doing?" I asked.

"Collecting wild onions man!" he exclaimed, seemingly quite excited to share the news and holding up something green for me to see. "They're growing all along this streambed! Sometimes I don't pick 'em because there're too few, but here there are thousands—so it's fine to harvest a few."

"Wild onions?" I asked, never considering the possibility of finding anything to eat in the forest, let alone onions.

"Yeah, they grow in valleys, marshy soil, meadows, and along streambeds. There's a bunch here man! Do ya wanna taste one?" He extended one of the long green plants he'd been gathering in my direction.

My stomach, which had been starved on nothing but Backwoods Buffet and oatmeal, immediately took over my neural circuits. Before I could consider questions like, "*Is it safe to eat wild foods?*" or, "*Can I trust this guy not to poison me?*" I found myself answering, "Sure!" and was soon down in the dirt with him biting into the leaf of what was one of the tastiest things I'd eaten in many days.

"These are amazing!" I exclaimed, examining the plants more closely. The wild onions had long thin deeply green leaves and a small white rooted bulb at the end. They were like the green onions used in Asian cooking, rather than the large round bulbs I usually associated with onions.

"You can eat the whole thing man! They're great raw, but they're even better cooked." He bent back down to gather more. "You can add them to meals, or just toast them over the fire—they're really tasty toasted."

Rinsing off the stem with a bit of my filtered water, I began chewing it raw, slowly savoring the fragrant leaves and the sweet bulb—its taste and smell permeating my senses. He handed me several more, and I ate them too, before even thinking to ask his name.

"Hey, sorry, my name is Gil," I said, extending a hand.

"I'm Permi," he said, grasping my hand warmly.

"*Permi?* I've never heard a name like that before."

"It's my trail name. Everybody calls me Permi. But my real name's Josh," he smiled.

"What's a trail name?"

"It's a kind of name others give you and call you on trail. So is Gil your real name, or a nickname too?" He seemed to think I was hiking the trail.

"It's short for Gilead—my parents were kinda religious—but everyone just calls me Gil. When I became a swimmer, it became a sorta nickname too, 'cause I could hold my breath longer than anyone else on the team."

"Wow, that's a great name, I really like that."

We both knelt down and started picking more onions. I watched how he did it and followed his example. Once you got the hang of it, they were really easy to loosen from the soil and pull out whole.

"How did you know those were wild onions?"

"I first read about them in Euell Gibbons's book, *Stalking the Wild Asparagus*, which is like the bible of wild edibles from way back. As a kid, I just ate that book up. Gibbons started the whole forager's revolution."

Apparently, a revolution I'd never heard of.

"Foraging, you know, like gathering wild foods from nature," he continued carried away by his own enthusiasm. "I mean, most people who shop at the supermarket don't even realize there's a whole garden of food you can eat for free—a 'garden of eatin'—just poking out of old lots and unmowed lawns—or out here in nature," he said, stretching out his arms to indicate the whole space around us.

"When I was seventeen," he continued without losing a breath, "I took these classes from this guy Samuel Thayer out in Wisconsin that completely changed my life. I mean *completely changed my life man!* He wrote books like, *Nature's Garden* and *Forager's Harvest*, that really teach you how to know and love the plants. And the guy can cook—like delicious wild foods—the most amazing nutritious plant foods you can ever taste, with wild rice and cattail flour and natural spices and everything. His classes opened my eyes man! Food is all around us, all you have to do is harvest it! And check out John Kallas's book too. He's like the Pacific Northwest guru of edible greens."

"Wow, I didn't realize you could just gather food from the woods," I said with genuine surprise and admiration.

"Well, you're not alone. It's like these onions here," he said holding up a bunch. "How many people just walk right by this feast of nature? I bet before you saw me, you'd just walk right by them, am I right?"

I nodded. He was right.

"You see man? *You see?* They're right here, just calling out to be picked, and yet everybody walks right by!" He waved the onions in his fist.

"But if everyone harvested them, there'd be none left," I protested.

"Not if they did so *sustainably*," he said. "I mean, yeah, if some big corporation came out into the woods and scooped up all the onions, they'd be gone in a heartbeat. But if everyone just harvested a few, what they *needed*, they'd be fine. I mean there are thousands of them here, and how many onions can you eat?"

Quite a few! was my stomach's spontaneous reply, but I didn't let it take control of my mouth and just nodded.

"Besides, disturbing the soil actually *helps* them grow. Thayer did research where he showed that leeks and onions actually grow *faster* after someone harvests a few. I mean, there's a reason nature makes them edible, right? It's part of their reproductive strategy, it's how they propagate!"

I wasn't sure how an onion inside someone's digestive tract could propagate, but I didn't wanna press the point.

"And there's lots of other food here too man, not just onions. Yesterday I gathered some killer mushrooms. Big fat morels! True morels! Growing right near some fallen trees, just off the trail where I stopped to take a leak. Can you imagine? Here I am getting ready to piss on this treasure trove of 'shrooms, and suddenly I have dinner! So far this trip I've gathered 'shrooms, onions, pine nuts, a ton of leafy greens, gooseberries, thistle, and a bunch of other stuff. It's the bounty of nature man!"

My mouth was already watering.

Permi and I harvested more onions together. He cleaned and stuffed them into his dirty woven sack. I stuffed mine into an extra plastic bag, tucking it away safely in the back compartment of my pack. Fresh greens tonight! Syd would be surprised.

After harvesting, we walked together. I turned my head from side to side. What other wild feasts lay hidden just beyond the trail?

"What first got you interested in wild foods?" I asked.

"You see man, I'm a *survivalist*. And *everything*, I mean *every-thing* is food, right? Food is life. You need to know where to get food if you're gonna survive, right?"

"Survive what?"

"Like the *collapse*. You know, the war that's coming. The apocalypse. Climate change. The end of oil. Sea level rise. It's all coming man! The end of modern society as we know it."

This guy had a screw loose somewhere. "What do you mean war and collapse?"

"Like, where do you live man?" he looked at me intensely.

"Los Angeles."

"Fuck!" he said. "Fuck." He stared at me gravely. "Los Angeles is the worst. The fuckin' worst." He shook his head pessimistically, as if uttering a death sentence for my adopted city.

"Well, the traffic sucks, but we have great beaches and amazing ethnic restaurants." I wanted to emphasize the food thing. "And Hollywood, Disneyland, and great theater."

"I'm not talking about all that, man. What I mean is—well, take the whole oil situation for example. America imports what, *sixty, seventy* percent of its oil, am I right?"

"That sounds about right." I'd heard something like that on NPR once.

"More than *half* our oil is imported from overseas! I mean, that's what we fought the frigging Gulf War for, right? For oil?"

I nodded. The trail continued down, the broad stream narrowing to a rushing river.

"So, what do we do with all that oil man? What do we need it for?"

"Transportation, heating, lubricants," I said, listing the things that came to mind.

"That's good, but you forgot one thing: *agriculture!*" he declared, his eyes glowing. "Agriculture uses almost five percent of all the energy we consume—and that's not including harvesting, processing, planting, or transportation—that's just for farming. Now why would farming use that much energy?"

"I don't know, why?" I asked, playing along.

"Why? Why? Because of nitrogen fixation!" he exclaimed, as if the answer was obvious.

"What's nitrogen fixation?" It sounded like some sort of narcotic obsession obtained from inhaling too much nitrogen—which I was beginning to suspect Permi was suffering from.

"Nitrogen fixation is the evil brainchild of the German scientist Fritz Haber, the guy who invented mustard gas back in World War One. Haber figured out this way to take nitrogen from the air and convert it into ammonia, because the Germans needed ammonia to make gunpowder. Come on—didn't you take *chemistry?*"

He was beginning to sound like the Unabomber.

"Ammonia is needed for making gunpowder, but it's also pure *fertilizer* man! Most plants can't use nitrogen from the air—except for stuff like peas and beans that have symbiotic bacteria growing on their roots."

That much I remembered from school.

"But add ammonia to the soil and—WHAM-O!!" he exclaimed, clapping his hands together for effect. "Plants grow like they're on steroids man! And it's not healthy growth. It's not like natural growth from *nutrients* in the soil. Industrially grown veggies have less than *half* the nutrition of naturally grown veggies. That's why we have so much cancer and shit. We're eating industrial veggies powered by petroleum."

"So, you mean it's like we're eating plastic plants?" I said, recalling that plastic is also made from petroleum.

"Exactly, *plastic plants!* We use five percent of our energy, mostly natural gas and oil, to make fertilizer to grow unhealthy industrial food. And that fertilizer pollutes too. There's a huge dead zone the size of friggin' Connecticut in the Gulf of Mexico where there are no fish at all. None! They're all dead! Killed by fertilizer from industrial farming running off into rivers that drain into the Gulf."

In the distance, we caught our first glimpse of Shadow Lake through a break in the trees—an almost round pool of clear water at the bottom of a circular valley. The trail turned right.

Permi continued, "My point is that population, human population, depends on agriculture. The only reason the world's population keeps growing is because we keep fixing more nitrogen, to grow more plants, to feed more people with. And that just makes more babies, who grow into more hungry people, who only want more resources, more cars, more houses, more money, and more food. It's a vicious cycle man, and it's not *sustainable*. We're running out of resources. The whole thing is fueled by petroleum."

That made a kinda sense. "Then what happens when we run out of oil?" I asked as we crossed a small footbridge spanning the river—the water rushing down a rocky gully towards the lake.

"That's the point man! That's the fucking point! We *are* running out of oil. We've hit peak production man. It's Hubbert's Peak!" he exclaimed, waving his arms above him for emphasis.

I'd no idea what Hubbert's Peak was, but I let him go on.

"See, that's why we have so many small wars now. It's about resources. There are too many people on the planet, and we're running out of resources. People are starving, so they start fighting or crossing borders, looking for food. Food is everything man!"

"But wait, if we start running out of oil, won't oil prices just go up, slowing demand?" I said, applying the theory I'd learned in Econ 101.

"Sure. The price *is* going up. And oil's much more expensive in other countries than it is in the U.S., where we subsidize it with wars and tax breaks," he said, suddenly sounding like a politician. "And as the price of oil goes up, the price of food goes up too. So people can't afford to buy enough food. Or they're eating lower quality food. And that causes health problems, which ends up costing our medical system a shitload of money. It's all connected."

He was starting to make sense. I *had* noticed my grocery bill doubling and then doubling again over the past few years, and the cost of dating and dining out was now astronomical.

"So, the problem is, what happens to the poor? The people who can't afford to buy the food, because it's too expensive? You talk about 'supply and demand' like food is a bunch of widgets, or fancy cars and all—stuff that you can buy less of if you can't afford them—but you can't change your demand for food. Ya gotta eat man! Ya gotta eat."

The trail opened up suddenly. We were standing at a small overlook above Shadow Lake, its clear waters sparkling in the sun. I took a series of photos, including one with Permi with his colorful shirt, loose pantaloons, and wild hair.

We walked on around the lake. Suddenly he stopped, darting over toward a tree. What new delicious edibles had he discovered? But he just shook his head and started back.

"I thought it was a kind of edible fungus I've been searching for, but it's just a break in the bark." We moved on.

"You still haven't told me about your beef with LA—actually, it's a pretty good place to work. There's great weather, awesome nightlife, and no shortage of women."

"I've been to LA man. I've been to LA. What do you think will happen if, say, there's another oil crisis like there was in the seventies? Or some Middle Eastern country decides to nationalize their oil and stops selling it to us. Or there's a war, or an embargo, or their overtapped wells simply run dry?" he asked, pausing finally to let me respond.

"Well, I guess oil prices would rise."

"Exactly. They would spike man! They would spike, right? And let's say they only doubled. What would happen then?"

"Well," I paused, thinking. "If prices doubled, we'd slow down production and probably drive a lot less."

"And what would happen if the higher cost of gasoline made truck drivers go on strike and block the roads, demanding higher wages because they couldn't afford the cost of gas? Or because the government started rationing fuel? Or because of shortages at the pumps?"

"Well, I guess people would have to stay home, or they'd call out the police, like they do in Europe when there are those strikes in France and stuff. But what's the big deal? Eventually their wages would have to go up, 'cause people would know that gas costs more, and so everyone would have to pay more for transportation."

"Yeah," said Permi as we walked. "Perhaps under normal circumstances. But not if there isn't any gas to buy. If *half* the gas is taken out of the machine, they'll be strikes, roadblocks, shortages, protests—*Chaos!*" he waved his arms again.

"OK," I agreed tentatively, still not seeing his point. "So things will be disrupted for a while until we sort them out. Maybe everyone will get a few weeks off from work, so what?"

"Gil, where do you buy your food?" Permi asked, seemingly out of the blue.

"Sometimes Albertsons. Sometimes Safeway," I said. "Sometimes I eat out."

"And do you keep a lot of food at home?"

"I have some cans of soup and spaghetti and stuff, but not a ton of food, no. I eat out a lot."

"About how many days' worth of food would you say you have at home right now?"

"I don't know, two, maybe three," I said, imagining the lonely cans and jars in my mostly empty pantry.

"And where does all the food at Albertsons and Safeway come from?" he asked.

"From Mexico, Bakersfield, the Midwest, and places like that," I answered, as if to a middle school quiz.

"And if the roads are blocked, and none of the trucks can get to LA, and no one can drive out, and everything is in chaos—how many days of food are there on those supermarket shelves at Albertsons and Safeway where you shop? And what will happen after it's gone?" he asked, pausing to let the question sink in.

I stopped walking, and Permi stopped with me. We stared down at the empty space where the lake was below. I imagined the trapped starving people of LA. The looters stripping grocery shelves of food. The riots. The shootings. Permi was right. It would be a zombie apocalypse. Aside from a few backyard gardens and what was in the supermarkets, there was no food in LA. "Fuck!" I said.

"Fuck is right," Permi nodded. We stood in silence, mourning the imaginary end of civilization.

Our reverie was broken by the "Haloo" of a largish looking man in khaki shorts, a wide brimmed matching hat, and a loud red-and-white Hawaiian button-down carrying an oversized but very clean blue REI backpack. "Sure is a long way down!" he huffed, indicating the series of switchbacks he'd just descended, and which we were about to climb up. "Where you fellas headed?" he asked in a bit of a Southern drawl.

"I'm going to Rosalie Lake," I said. "My buddy should be up there now."

"That's where I'm headed too," said Permi. "Maybe we can all camp there together?"

"Sure," I smiled, "that would be great!" He could show me how to cook onions, and maybe he could share some more goodies from his bag of foraged food—at last something decent to eat out here!

"Well, it's a long way up there, a lot further than it looks," said the stranger in the khakis. "How far is Garnet Lake?" he asked.

"It's a pretty long way," I said, "and there's a lot of uphill too."

"Hmmm," he pondered. "Wish I could stay here—but someone said this lake is closed for camping. Are you guys doing the JMT?"

"Yeah," Permi said.

I just smiled. I wanted to say, "yes" too and my instinct surprised me. *Had I now become a quitter?*

"Wow, the JMT's really tough," proclaimed the guy, "I wouldn't want to do that!" Seemingly oblivious of that fact Permi had just said he was doing the trail. "Well, see you 'round," he waved, heading off the way we'd come.

"Strange guy," I said to Permi after the man was out of earshot.

"That's just like city people. Always in a hurry. Even in the woods," he replied, apparently forgetting that I was from LA, or perhaps not lumping me in with the dreaded, "city people" he was castigating.

The trail became steeper, ascending switchback after switchback, like the man in the khakis had warned. Permi got a bit ahead of me, and I watched him rounding each stretch above, a foreshadowing of the next section to come.

Something about what that guy had said really stung me. I recalled my first swim meet in junior high. I'd been the worst in my heat—my leg had cramped and our team had lost; everyone blamed me and it felt awful. Pop had come down from the stands after to comfort me, but I'd just bawled that I was quitting. That I hated swimming and my stupid team. That maybe I could try diving or something. He'd held me, and when I'd finally calmed down enough to listen, he'd said, "Pain is temporary, quitting is forever." I've never forgotten those words.

The switchbacks wound up and up.

Maybe this whole hiking thing was a test? Like in *The 36th Chamber of Shaolin*, where the hero had to endure all sorts of suffering and privations before finally being admitted to the temple where his real training could begin. Was Pop secretly watching me from above to see if I would stick with it? Was Syd really a crotchety old man, or was he some sort of secret Master, testing my dedication before passing on his real knowledge?

I followed Permi up turn after turn.

My legs were growing tougher. What would I do back in LA? Was there really anything special waiting for me there? Or would I just be caught up in some crazy zombie apocalypse like Permi said?

It took almost an hour, but finally Permi let out a cry of triumph. I looked up to see him standing on a huge boulder. "It's the top man!" he shouted down to me. Then he waited while I huffed and puffed up to where he stood.

Cresting the ridge, we spotted the blue waters of Rosalie Lake. Syd's bivy was in a campsite down off the trail to the right, clearly set up where I would see it.

We found Syd down by the lakeshore, seated on his folded air mattress watching the water, his back resting up against a large log. He turned and greeted us with a toothy smile.

"Nice beach!" Permi smiled. "Do you two mind if I have a swim?"

"Be my guest," said Syd.

Permi stripped off his clothes, diving naked into the sparkling lake. Syd followed. The two were washing and splashing in the water, having a great time. Syd seemed fully recovered from the day before—it musta been the altitude like he said.

Laying my clothes tentatively on the log, I rinsed off in the shallows. The water was icy cold. The two soon emerged, breathing deeply.

Permi looked at me, "Why didn't you jump in man? The water's great!"

"Eh, maybe in the morning—I don't wanna catch cold." It was a lame excuse, but it was all I could think of—even Ma didn't know my thing about water. I'd told her I'd left the swim team to focus more on my studies, not because I threw up every time I got in over my head.

The three of us stood there naked on the sand, drying off in the waning afternoon sun. Permi with his lithe, yet well-toned physique. Syd with his thin, almost skeletal frame. And me with my protruding belly. A few lonely mosquitos buzzed about us, but apparently fooled by our chilly skin, none landed a bite. After dressing, we headed back up to camp.

Permi stretched out a small green tarp and spread his sleeping bag on top, cowboy-style.

"Don't you have a tent?" I asked, setting up my Hubba Hubba.

"Nah man—too heavy. I just use a tarp, which I string between the trees when it rains—" explaining why his pack was so small.

"What do you do about bugs?" asked Syd, glancing in the direction of his bivy, as if suggesting that a bivy was the real way to get close to nature, but not so close as to get bitten.

"Bugs don't bite me because of all the vitamin B12 in the food I eat. And also because of bay leaves," he said pulling out some leaves, which he sprinkled around his tarp. "Bugs just hate the smell of bay."

"Permi's a forager," I explained. "He showed me how to pick wild onions."

"Really?" asked Syd, with obvious interest in his voice.

As we ate Permi enthusiastically explained to Syd about foraging and survival. Even my lasagna tasted more palatable with some of his wild foods mixed in.

"Why is your trail name Permi?" asked Syd.

"It's short for Permaculture," said Permi.

"What's Permaculture?" I asked.

"It stands for permanent agriculture. It's a way of growing food where all the outputs become the inputs. Closed cycles. Sustainable farming, man."

Once again, I'd no idea what he was talking about.

"I've heard of permaculture," said Syd, "but I don't think I really know how it works."

"It's the opposite of industrial agriculture. Industrial agriculture is like the wasteful grass lawns most people keep in front of their houses."

"What's wrong with grass? I like my lawn," I said.

"Really?" asked Permi, "What do you do with your lawn? Does it *feed* you? Do you barbeque or picnic on it?"

I imagined the tiny patch of meticulously tended grass around my condo. "No," I admitted, "but it makes the building look good."

"Do you know how grass lawns got started? They started in France and England, when these fat aristocrats wanted to show off their wealth, so they planted large swaths of grass around their castles and manor houses, instead of planting crops. And the trend caught on fast, man. Soon every baron and lord was planting useless grass to show off how many acres he could afford *not* to plant with food."

"So lawns were basically just a way to show off?"

"Yup, just like the tail on the peacock's ass."

Permi ate several helpings of the mixture of greens and wild rice he'd cooked.

"The fashion caught on with people living in the suburbs, who couldn't even remember where the whole grass thing got started. But soon they became slaves to tending their own petty lawns. In the end, it was really the grass that won. I don't know how many resources go into tending useless patches of grass—but it must be enormous. Imagine if we put all that energy into growing food? Gardens for everyone! Tear up your lawns and plant potatoes, spinach, rutabaga, and corn. It would be a gardening revolution man! We'd all become locavores and big agriculture would be turned on its head!"

"I like my lawn," I said. "But a few well-manicured tomato vines might look nice out in front and might save me a bit on the cost of my spaghetti sauce too."

"So how is grass like industrial agriculture?" asked Syd.

"It's the inputs," Permi replied, "you have to feed grass. You have to fertilize it, trim it, and tend it. That costs a lot. But do you get those inputs back from the grass? Aside from a place to walk the dog, or have a picnic, there isn't much of a return from investing in grass."

Syd nodded.

"The same is true of industrial agriculture. Industry puts a lot of energy into mechanically planting, harvesting, feeding, and growing their food crops. But it's not sustainable. Like the grass, the inputs cost far more than we get back in food."

We sipped our tea, listening.

"Permaculture is different. In permaculture, all the outputs become new inputs. Nothing is wasted. The whole system is resource neutral. Sustainable." He continued eating and thought for a while. "For example, take the chicken. Industrial chicken farmers lock their hens in tiny cages, making them eat petroleum-derived feed, while harvesting eggs. The costs far outweigh the benefits, when you figure in the depleted natural resources. Not to mention the poor hens and their stress."

Syd leaned back thoughtfully.

"On a permaculture farm, the chickens are free-range. They find their own worms and food, eliminating the need for inputs. In the process, they scratch and till the soil, eat the weeds, and fertilize the farm with their manure—their outputs become the inputs needed for planting, closing the loop. We also get other benefits, like eggs and meat. It's more than sustainable. It's regenerative. A positive cycle! That's permaculture man!"

All I could imagine was a happy utopian farm run entirely by chickens, like in *Animal Farm*, but without the pigs.

Finishing our meals, the three of us went down to the lakeshore. We sat serenaded by woodland insects, munching on toasted onions as the sunset changed the ribbonlike streaks of clouds from orange, to pinkish-red, to purple. The hiking part sucked—but with sunsets like this, interesting conversation, and a couple of wild onions, this camping thing wasn't all bad.

DAY FIVE

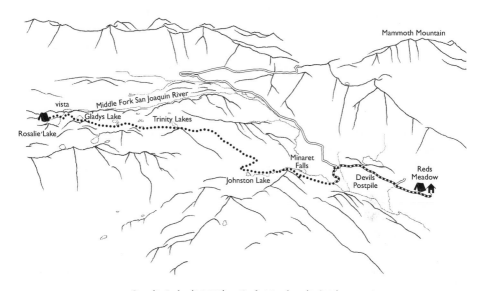

Rosalie Lake (9,390′) to Reds Meadow (7,670′)
8½ miles—220 feet elevation gain; 1,940 feet elevation loss

"WHERE'S PERMI?" I asked, hoping for some exotic greens to spice up my morning oatmeal.

"He packed up early. He said he'd see us at Reds Meadow."

Why did everyone cool always take off in the morning?

From Rosalie Lake, the trail climbed to a high ridge. Syd led us off trail, and we scrambled to a rocky overlook. Dropping our packs, we sat looking out over a broad valley below. The far wall was lush and green, but the steep cliffs on this side were rocky and only sparsely dotted with trees. To the far right was a large broad peak crowned with a ridge of rough black rock and snow, its tan slopes barren of any vegetation. Beyond it, mountainous silhouettes stretched off in shadowy layers.

Syd traced a narrow blue line through the trees below. "That's the Middle Fork of the San Joaquin River," he said. "And that wide grassy area there is Agnew Meadows. And somewhere down that way," he pointed off to the right, "is Reds Meadow."

It was amazing how big the landscape was, and how places that looked so distant were only half-a-day's walk away. Hiking had given me a new appreciation of scale. Riding in a

71

car compressed the world, but walking expanded it—making everything seem larger, and yet more personal. Sitting on this rock, overlooking this magnificent panorama, I felt like an ant traversing the great throne of God.

I looked at Syd as he gazed out over the valley. There was a certain similarity between his posture and the surrounding rock. Something irregular, yet firm. He looked like one of those ancient pines, like he'd been here all his life and was part of the landscape. This was clearly where he belonged—out here in nature.

I studied his face, as if seeing it again for the first time. He had a wise face with a strong firm nose and the hint of a kindly smile. He looked the part of the masterly teacher, sitting upon the rocks in profound reflection. Most captivating were his eyes. Those two penetrating blue orbs sparkled of their own inner light.

This musta been what Pop had seen in him. He wasn't a crotchety old man. He was a wise learned scholar who happened to love nature—or maybe found himself more at ease here than with people. He was like a cross between Gandalf and Yoda—but without the white beard or long ears. Or maybe like blind Master Po, but with a penetrating gaze. Actually, he was like none of those. The one he reminded me of most was Pop. I sat staring at him on the edge of this great precipice. Maybe Ma was right. Maybe here was someone who could teach me about life and help me to move forward—my last real chance to connect with everything I'd lost when Pop died.

"And look there," he pointed back over our shoulders at a series of charcoal-colored shark's teeth, "those are the Minarets again."

I hadn't really been paying attention. "What's that peak?" I asked, pointing at the large irregular mountain with the snow on top.

He laughed, "That's Mammoth Mountain—see the gondola cables?"

Following his gaze, I could just make out the line of the cables and now recognized the familiar shape of the mountain where I'd once tried snowboarding—almost breaking my leg to impress the girl I'd been with. Back then the mountain had seemed so large and imposing, now it looked broader and more gentle. It was striking how much things changed when viewed from different perspectives.

"The aspiring young Solomons descended into this valley on his first major expedition into the Sierra," he said, obviously trying to tempt me into another of his stories.

Lying back against the warm rocks, I asked, "How did he get down?"

"Back then there were no real trails, just the remnants of ones left by Indians and sheepherders. As I understand it, he took an old sheep trail from Thousand Island Lake, roughly following what is now called The River Trail to Agnew Meadow."

"What did he do for food?" I asked, reminiscing about the toasted onions.

"He had a month's worth of provisions, as well as a rifle, fishing gear, flour, and a Dutch oven. He also brought an eight-by-ten wooden camera with a box of glass plate negatives, an old canvas tent, and blankets sewn together for a sleeping bag."

"His pack musta weighed a ton!" I said, imagining Solomons to be a giant—some kinda cross between Paul Bunyon and The Incredible Hulk.

Mammoth Mountain

"He didn't travel like we are. He had a pack mule named Whitney."

"So he came all this way, but without any trail?"

"Exactly. He was scouting out a route—planning out what would eventually become the JMT."

I pictured the young explorer struggling on his own through the unmapped underbrush. Feeling out his way across granite peaks in search of new passes, while dragging along a heavily laden mule just to make some sort of High Mountain Route. It seemed like too much. Did people really do stuff like that? I mean, outside of movies and stuff?

"After climbing Mount Ritter with LeConte, he escorted his cousin back to Yosemite, then he returned on his own. On his way here, he climbed Mount Ritter again. This time dragging up his box camera and risking his life to take the first photographs from the mountaintop. After returning, his photos were widely celebrated. I think they're still in the Sierra Club archives, which incidentally are kept in the Bancroft Library on the Berkeley campus."

Syd was getting pedantic again. "So, where'd he go after he got down to the valley?"

"He followed the river along approximately the modern PCT route to Devils Postpile, then headed down to Fish Creek, about ten miles south of Reds Meadow."

As he spoke, I watched his face and his bright eyes sparkle in the sunlight. How had I missed seeing the deep wisdom in those eyes? Syd really loved it out here. Pop had too, and apparently so had Solomons. I got the thing about the views and all—but there must be something more that made them endure all the bugs and hardships.

When I snapped back in, he was saying, "Soon his provisions began to run low, and he had to survive on gooseberries and trout."

"What are gooseberries?" I asked, trying to seem like I'd been paying attention.

"They're a sort of prickly red berry. They're tasty, but hardly what you'd want to subsist on."

"Sort of like raspberries?"

"A bit sweeter, but similar. As I was saying, by the time he reached Fish Creek, Solomons was running out of food. It was late in the season, the nights were getting cold, and he had to return to Yosemite soon or risk getting trapped in the winter snows. So he left the path he was forging, and headed down toward the South Fork of the San Joaquin River, where he found his way blocked by its steep banks and raging waters."

"What did he do?"

"He searched the bank for a way across but couldn't find one. In desperation, he left Whitney tied up to a tree and struck out on his own—carrying only a few matches and his compass and leaving small mounds of stones as markers to help him find his way back."

"Like the small piles we've seen along the trail sometimes?"

"They're called *cairns*. They're often used as trail markers."

"Better than breadcrumbs!"

He smiled. "By late afternoon, Solomons had located a good ford. But struggling to work his way back to Whitney, he missed his markers and became lost. It soon grew dark—remember they didn't have flashlights back then—so he was forced to build a fire. He spent the night tossing and turning without a blanket on the hard ground, with only cold gooseberries for sustenance. The next morning, exhausted and hungry, he summited a nearby ridge to get his bearings. There, not more than fifty yards away was Whitney, still tied to the same tree."

"Who was it? That Antarctic explorer who gave up and froze to death just miles away from camp after skiing to the South Pole?"

"That was Scott."

"I saw a film about him. It's crazy how you can be so close to camp and yet be lost. If I were Solomons, I woulda made a huge meal to celebrate."

"He was out of food, Gil. He wasn't carrying packets of Backwoods Buffet," he teased. "Following a chance encounter with a sheepherder, who pointed him in the direction of an established crossing and a good trail, Solomons headed back toward Yosemite. Two days later, he stumbled into the camp of three more hospitable sheepherders who fed him and christened him *the photographer with the appetite*. From there, with a belly full of mutton, he made his return. His first expedition a success."

"Wow, I'm glad we don't have to make our own trail."

He smiled.

I gazed out over the valley. Reds Meadow was so close, but what did I really have to look forward to back in LA? Working at the firm had totally sucked, and it wasn't like I was in a real relationship or anything. This was the first time in ten years I was coming to terms with what had happened to Pop. Was I just gonna roll over and quit now because of a bear and some leg pain? Ma was right. There really was something this guy could teach me. I swallowed, hoping I wasn't gonna regret this. "Syd," I said, "I'm in."

"In what?" A confused expression washed over Syd's features.

"I mean, we're not going back at Reds Meadow. We're staying on the trail. I don't know exactly how we're gonna do it, especially those high mountain passes, but somehow you and I are getting to Whitney," I smiled, only half believing it.

He nodded and smiled too, apparently unsurprised. Had he known all along? Then something occurred to me. "Syd," I said, "what should I call you?"

"What do you mean?"

"I mean, how should I address you from now on? Do you want me to call you—professor, or sensei, or teacher, or something?"

He laughed, "Just call me Syd."

We sat there for a long time admiring the view, enjoying the gentle breeze, and soaking in the fresh scent of the open air and pine.

Before leaving, I took photos of the mountains and the wide river valley. Then we headed back down to the trail, passing a small lake on our left. My spirit felt lighter—I could never have faced Ma if I'd turned back. Besides, I owed this to Pop.

The sun rose higher. We passed a number of NOBOs struggling up the sandy slope through the sparsely shaded forest. Now I was part of something—part of the SOBOs. Now the worst that could happen was Syd would need to turn back, and then no one could say I'd quit.

"You know there's something I haven't told you about," said Syd.

"What's that?" I asked, growing concerned that maybe there'd be some kinda catch to my decision.

"Instead of following the exact route of the JMT, I was thinking we might make a detour by some hot springs your father and I used to visit. I'd like to show them to you."

"You mean like the spas in Palm Springs?"

"Not exactly, but yes. There are pools of naturally hot water we can soak in. They're great for working out sore legs and watching the stars."

"Wouldn't we have had to have brought our swimsuits?"

"Not at all—they're *au natural.*"

"Wait, exactly *how far out of the way* are these springs?"

"About thirteen miles, but we could cut back to the trail another way, so the total distance would be about the same."

"OK, I'd love to see someplace you and Pop went—besides, I could use a hot bath!"

He smiled.

At the valley floor we passed a beautiful cascade, then came to a junction with another trail.

"That way leads to a ranger station. There's a shuttle there that can take us straight to Reds Meadow, or we can continue along the JMT and see Devils Postpile—it's about a two-mile walk if I recall."

According to the guidebook, the Postpile was "a large block of unusual hexagonal gray stones."

"We've seen enough rocks, let's hop the bus and get some real food!" I said, glad not to have to walk the two miles, but shocked that he would even consider taking a bus—maybe it was his way of thanking me for continuing on?

We crossed a large wooden bridge and soon came to the station. The "rangers" turned out to be two grandmotherly volunteers selling postcards and fielding questions from visitors. There was a bus stop out in front. A large group of tourists and day-hikers was waiting there.

Before long, a stone-gray shuttlebus pulled up. Syd and I climbed aboard with our packs, sitting near the rear. We looked like two grizzled mountain men returning to the city after spending years in the wild, or like two Sasquatch trying to pass unobserved on a public bus.

As the bus filled with tourists, I became acutely aware of the odor of their cologne, deodorants, perfume, and the lemony-fresh scent of their "cotton-kills" clothing. Noticing that the seats around us were the last to fill, it dawned on me that if we could smell them, they must be able to smell us too.

The doors shut and the bus squeaked down the road. It wasn't going more than twenty miles an hour, but watching the trees whiz by the window, it seemed like lightspeed to me. When you walk, you see all the details, but from a moving vehicle everything's a blur. Maybe it was the same with life? Maybe what people really needed was a good slowing down? A kid two seats ahead of us whined to his mother, "I'm bored, doesn't this stupid bus have wifi?"

The last stop was Reds Meadow Resort. This was clearly no Club Med. The stop was next to a large dirt parking area. As we got off, dust from the lot wafted over us. Across the way was a stable. Even from here, we could smell the barnyard scent of horses. At least we wouldn't be the worst smelling thing around.

Dotting the place were a few lonely wood cabins. Two long buildings with rustic siding stood opposite each other. One had a sign declaring, Mulehouse Cafe, the other, General Store. Between these were several large wooden picnic tables. Most of the tourists from the bus headed immediately into the store, emerging soon after with snacks, root beer, and ice cream.

Then I spotted Permi sitting at one of the benches. He was polishing off a beer with a very hot hiker; her ample breasts pushing up through her tight-fitting yellow tank top like two small hillocks. If it wasn't for her thick unshaven armpits, she could have been a model for some line of fine outdoor clothing.

"This is Kydoime," he said, making introductions.

"Pleased to meet you both," she smiled, accentuating her strong angular cheekbones.

"Kydoime's Greek," said Permi.

"*Half* Greek, *half* Cherokee," she corrected him, winking at me in an inviting flirtatious sort of way.

Permi turned to her, "These are the guys I was telling you about—the ones I hung out with yesterday."

"How far are you going tomorrow?" she asked Syd.

"We were thinking about taking a detour to the hot springs."

"You mean Iva Bell?" she said with growing interest.

"Yes, have you been there?"

"I've heard about them. Do you know the way?" she asked, her voice as honeyed as her skin.

Syd pulled out his map, tracing the route.

"Do you want to join us there?" he asked her—*my hopes suddenly dangling on her answer.*

"I'm game," chimed Permi.

"Sure," she agreed.

Yes! I mouthed silently, now truly glad I'd decided to go on.

The two of them began gathering up their stuff. "Are you both gonna be in the campground tonight?" I asked.

"Nah," she smiled, "I booked a small cabin here, but I'll see you tomorrow at the springs," she winked.

"I'll catch you both later at the campground," Permi waved to us, and the two headed off opposite to the way we'd arrived.

As they left, my eyes drifted over Kydoime's wild brown hair, her perfect shoulder blades, and the curves of her tight black hiking shorts—already picturing what she'd look like soaking *au natural*.

"Shall we try the cafe?" Syd asked, interrupting my daydream.

"Can we just leave our stuff here?"

"We can keep an eye on it through the window."

Inside, a plump waitress in a neat white apron with curly brown hair came up to us saying, "Sorry honeys, but it looks like there'll be about an hour's wait, seeing as everybody has just sat down."

I glanced around the small restaurant with its heavy wood interior. Every table was full of hungry tourists in clean, neatly pressed shirts, most just starting to read their menus. Even the counter was full. Then I noticed that one table had just a single person sitting there—a petite Asian girl who couldn't have been more than seventeen. A blue backpack almost larger than she was occupied the entire seat next to her. The other two seats were empty.

She caught our glance and smiled shyly, so we walked over.

"Are you hiking JMT too?" she asked in a strong accent. From the dirt on her well-tanned face, it looked like she'd been out a while.

"Yes," Syd replied.

"Ah. Please to come join me!"

The waitress brought us some menus saying, "Always nice to make new friends!"

"I'm Rena. I'm from close to Tokyo, in Japan," the girl said.

"Is that your English name or your Japanese name?" Syd asked.

"Does it sound like English name too?"

"May I ask what the Kanji characters for your name are? I know some Chinese and most of the characters are similar."

She took out a pen and wrote two characters onto a napkin.

"Your name means *lucky* and *satisfied*, doesn't it?"

"That's right!" she said clapping enthusiastically, as if he had just performed some sorta magic trick.

"That's a nice name," complimented Syd.

"Thank you," she said, her eyes nearly hidden by her glowing cheeks each time she smiled, which was often.

The waitress came to take our orders. I ordered a BLT with a small side salad and a root beer float. I'd been craving bacon, greens, and sugar all trail.

"How long have you been hiking JMT?" Rena asked us after the waitress had gone.

"About five days now," Syd replied, "we started at Tuolumne Meadows."

"Me too!" she exclaimed, clapping again. "But I got lost at Thousand Island Lake," she frowned, making an exaggerated sad face.

"Lost? What do you mean?" he asked with some concern.

"You know bridge crossing at lake?"

Syd nodded.

"Just before there was sign for Reds Meadow, so I follow that."

"Oh I see, you took the PCT route by mistake."

"I know. I kept following and asking myself, *Is this trail right? Supposed to go by other lakes.* But then I keep walking because I already gone so far, and trail went so far downhill."

"That's a common mistake. When you're not sure of a trail, you must turn around and check. But many people keep on going, because they feel they've gone so far already."

"Exactly!" her eyes lit up with shared understanding. "I keep going all the way to Agnew Meadow."

"So you missed Garnet Lake, Shadow Lake, and that whole section of the JMT."

"Yes," she said, her eyes looking down, as if she'd really lost something.

"But you survived and made it here," he praised.

She looked brighter.

"And that stretch you missed had a lot of ups and downs, so you avoided that, and you had your own little adventure."

She looked up and smiled, "Yes, that true."

"One day it will make a good story. All my biggest mishaps have become my best back-packing tales. Maybe you can write about it."

She was smiling again, "Yes, it will be good story to tell. You right."

"Are you hiking alone?" I asked.

"Yes," she said looking at me. "But I also hiking with girl I met on trail before I get lost, named Kitty. Have you seen her?"

"No, we just got here," answered Syd, "but we'll let you know if we find her."

"Thanks!" she smiled brightly. "Sorry, I not much experience, this my first hike."

I couldn't believe it. The trail was hard enough for me with Syd as a guide, and yet here was this tiny Japanese girl on her first hike, doing the JMT with a giant backpack all alone in a foreign country!

"What made you want to hike the JMT?" Syd asked.

"I read about John Muir Trail from travel magazine. There was article about Japanese man who hiked trail. It was such amazing photographs I wanted to see it too."

"But how did you prepare? How did you know what to bring?" Syd asked.

"I go Japanese hiking website."

"I see—to hike solo from another country—you're brave," Syd said, and she beamed again, nodding her head vigorously.

My root beer float and our salads arrived. The float was huge. Three enormous scoops of vanilla ice cream nearly overflowed the tall parfait glass.

Rena stared at my float with round wide eyes. "Is American food always so big?" she asked in amazement.

"Yeah, I guess so. This one is even big for me, and I'm a big guy," I said, patting my belly. "Here, you try some," I smiled, scooping out one of the huge balls of ice cream with my spoon and placing it gently on her plate.

Rena clapped excitedly, pulled out a tiny Nikon camera, and took pictures of my root beer float and the ball of ice cream. Then, all smiles, she started eating the ice cream with her spoon.

"I love food!" she exclaimed joyfully.

"It's good," I agreed.

"No, no, I mean my hobby eating and photographing food." She sorted through some photos in her small camera, showing us several shots of different exotic dishes. "These were in Malibu."

"Were you in LA?" I asked. "That's where I live!"

"Ah, you from LA? I spent three day on beach before coming to Yosemite. LA has great food and beach!"

Someone else who liked LA—I'd have to introduce her to Permi.

We munched on our salads and Rena ate her scoop of ice cream. I was amazed at how delicious the greens tasted, and how sickly delightfully sweet the root beer and ice cream were. Coming off the trail, it was as if I'd never tasted food before.

The rest of our meals came. My BLT was exquisite. Bacon had never tasted so good. The tomatoes were red and juicy. Even the flavor of the wheat toast and mayonnaise lingered long after I finished the sandwich. If you really wanna appreciate the flavor of food, just try eating Backwoods lasagna, granola bars, and oatmeal for a week.

After our meals, we sat for some time at the table in satiated silence. Bellies full. Feet resting. It was a strange pleasure just sitting contentedly in a chair. Our mutual reverie was broken when the waitress returned to inquire, "Will you three be wanting anything else?"

"Just the check," I said, completely satisfied. Syd took the bill and paid for everyone. I thanked him. Rena tried to pay him back, but he insisted, telling her that it was, "American hospitality."

"You've come a long way from Japan to hike this trail," he explained, "the least I can do is buy you some lunch."

Rena smiled again. "Where are your packs?" she asked, looking around.

"Outside," said Syd. We exited the restaurant, the three of us adjourning to the picnic table, Rena lugging her big blue monster and two silver trekking poles along.

"What does that thing weigh?" asked Syd staring incredulously at the size of her pack.

"I don't know," she answered.

"Can I pick it up?" he asked.

"Sure," she nodded.

Syd hoisted her pack, straining visibly with the effort.

"That must weigh at least sixty-five pounds."

"It was more before," Rena said glancing down. "At airport it was overweight. Had to pay extra charge. It was thirty kilos. But I got rid of some stuff at Tuolumne Meadows."

"Thirty kilos—that's about seventy pounds," said Syd nodding his head in reflection. "You must only weigh about a hundred pounds yourself—or about forty-five kilos," he estimated, making Rena blush slightly at his math. "So that pack is about sixty-five percent of your body weight. In the old days, the rule of thumb was to carry no more than thirty percent of your weight—you're carrying way too much!"

"I know," said Rena guiltily, "but it's OK. I can carry."

I noticed just how muscular and sturdy her legs looked in her shorts. Syd was watching her legs too.

"We should call you Iron Woman," I proposed.

"Iron Woman?" she asked.

"You know, like the superhero Iron Man, only 'cause you're a girl— "

"Oh, I see," she said, "Iron Woman—is that to be my JMT trail name?"

"It is if you like," said Syd.

"I think about it," she replied.

"What did you get rid of from your pack?" Syd asked. "Extra food?"

"No, not food!" exclaimed Rena seriously. "I love food! It's my hobby, remember? I get rid of sleeping pad, long underwear, extra flashlight, and few other things too. I give to other hikers."

"But you *need* those things," Syd protested. "What are you sleeping on? What will you do when it gets cold?"

"Yes. I know now ground is cold. Not so comfortable," Rena said looking down, "now I sleep on folded clothes."

"You really are Iron Woman," I said.

"What are you going to do now?" asked Syd.

"I going to buy more food, get shower, and find backpacker's campsite."

"They have showers?" I asked excitedly.

"Yes," said Syd, "over there." He pointed at a small building out behind the store that I hadn't noticed before, with a sign proclaiming, Showers and Laundry.

"Is OK I leave my pack here? Can you watch for me?" she asked Syd.

"Sure, you take your time," he smiled.

Gathering up a few items, Rena headed off toward the store.

"Shall we pick up our resupply buckets?" he asked.

Part of Syd's instructions about preparing for this hike had been to pack food, tooth-paste, sunscreen, toilet paper, and other essentials I'd need to restock my pack with into large plastic buckets—to protect them from rodents at the rustic backcountry storage areas where they'd be holding our supplies. I'd purchased three bright orange Home Depot buckets for the purpose, addressing them to places like "Reds Meadow" and "Muir Trail Ranch." Syd had mailed me the labels, explaining that all I needed to do was drop the buckets off at the post office.

I'd faithfully stuffed each bucket with the exact number of meals and supplies Syd had listed for each leg, dutifully labeled each, and lugged the three five-gallon tubs off to the post office in the back of my Miata.

I'd stood uneasily in line as regular well-dressed customers eyed my three taped-up buckets with deep suspicion—as if they contained heroin, live monkeys, or improvised explosive devices. Was I the only one on the trail who'd felt that way when mailing their buckets? I wanted to ask but felt embarrassed at the question.

"How do we get our buckets?" I asked him.

"They should be in the General Store."

The store was packed with tourists. Its shelves stuffed with everything from marshmal-lows and charcoal to T-shirts and fishing gear. Spotting the wine and beer, I made a mental note to come back later. The clearly overworked clerk was a muscular man in a tank top and cowboy hat. Upon reaching the end of the line, we asked him for our buckets. Hold-ing back a scowl, he retrieved them from their storeroom.

I spread most of my gear out on our table. I still had a number of uneaten granola bars.

"Syd, look at all these bars. I brought way too many, and most of the ones left taste like shit."

"Didn't you try them before the trip?"

"I didn't have time—besides, all the flavors sounded good."

"The names always sound good. You need to try food before depending on it in the wilderness."

"Yeah," I sighed. "What do I do now? I don't wanna carry around all these extra bars, but it's a waste to just throw them away."

"You can put them in the hiker box."

"Hiker box? What's that?"

"It's a big bin that most resupply stations keep where hikers can leave any extra food or stuff they don't need or pick up stuff they do. It's a kind of backpacking recycling center."

"I'll just leave my extra bars there. Maybe someone else who's hungrier than I am will take them."

I began sorting my stuff into piles. Seven days of Backwoods Buffet beef stroganoff sat before me. I gazed forlornly at the grinning visage of Backwoods Bob on the horrid metallic-orange packages. Suddenly, I recalled the hiker box. Maybe I could swap my Backwoods stuff for something better?

"Could I see the hiker box?" I asked the cowboy when there was a break in the line.

"Sorry, we don't have one no more. We was havin' problems with homeless people staying at the campgrounds and such, livin' outta the box. So th' manager said we couldn't keep it no more."

I slumped back to our table—my hopes of fine dining dashed. "They don't have a hiker box *no more*," I said, imitating the cowboy's accent.

"We'll find someone to give your extra bars to."

I nodded, "At least my pack won't be so heavy."

"I'll tell you why your pack is so heavy!" blurted a twenty-something kid who appeared out of nowhere with a dirty pimply face and a badly stained lime-green hiking shirt. "It's because of all that extra stuff you've got," he said, pointing to the food and gear I'd spread out on the table. "Plus, that's an 85-liter Osprey you're carrying. That weighs what? Like six pounds? Mine's just 40 liters and made from Cuben Fiber—lightest pack you can get!" he declared, indicating his own dirty white pack.

"Your pack was made in Cuba?" I asked.

"No, it's not from Cuba!" he scowled. "It's made from *Cuben Fiber*, a high-tech ultralight fiber that uses special square strands. It's the stuff the America's Cup racers make their sails from." He looked at me wide-eyed and with raised eyebrows, as if to say, *I thought everyone knew this!*

"Are you hiking the JMT?" Syd asked the boy patiently.

"No, the PCT. But I just started a few days ago. I skipped the desert and part of the Sierra, so I'm almost halfway done already!" he announced proudly.

"I thought the PCT went all the way from Mexico to Canada," inquired Syd, "how can you skip so much?"

"I'm sort of section hiking it, you know, in parts," he sputtered. "Right now I'm doing part of the Sierra, see? I have a blog about it, if you want to read it." He paused as if thinking about something, then pointed back at the picnic table. "But seriously, I'm just trying to help you guys out. You've got way too much stuff there. Like that bear canister you're carrying—you could bring one half its size, like mine. And instead of cooking food, you could eat cold meals, then you wouldn't need that rock of a Jetboil stove and all that fuel. I'll bet you could dump half your shit!"

"What does your pack weigh?" Syd asked him, his voice level.

"My base weight is just under fifteen pounds—that's because I don't carry a stove or fuel or heavy tent, and I weigh everything on a scale. What you've got to do is make a spreadsheet of all your gear, then get rid of everything you can. I can help you guys out if you want."

"And do you have all your food in there too?" Syd asked, continuing his patient questioning.

"Yup! Sure do! I just resupplied today. Exactly one-and-a-half pounds of food a day for the next four days. Plus water of course—only in old recycled bottles—no heavy Camel-Bak bag like your friend here."

"I see," Syd nodded. "Could I try lifting your pack?"

"Yeah! Sure!" said the kid, swinging off his pack and holding it out for Syd to examine.

"That's pretty light," admitted Syd lifting his pack, the kid beaming at the praise. Syd pointed at his trail-worn green Kelty leaning against the picnic table. "Try holding mine and see what you think. I just finished packing my food as well."

The kid went over and lifted Syd's pack. A frown appeared on his face. He lifted his own again and compared the two. "Huh? Wow, that's pretty light," he admitted crestfallen, "and you've got *all* your food and gear in there?"

"That's right."

The kid put down Syd's pack, shouldered his own, and said, "Well, I'd better get back on the trail," slinking away in the direction of the parking lot.

"Who was that?" I asked.

"Hiking Police. There's a saying that kid should learn, *hike your own hike*, or H-Y-O-H," he said, spelling out the initials.

"Hoy-Ya!" I exclaimed. "Hike your own fucking hike!" I shouted after the kid, who'd already vanished into the trees beyond the parking lot.

Putting my extra food and stuff into my bucket, I sealed it, planning to give it to the General Store anyway, or maybe leave it outside with a note. I just couldn't throw away so many bars and things. I was about to lug it over to the store when Rena returned from her shower.

"Gil has extra food and supplies he can't carry," declared Syd, indicating my large orange bucket. "You're welcome to have anything you need, although I don't think his granola bars are that tasty."

"Thanks!" smiled Rena glowing from cheek to cheek and taking possession of the bucket after examining the large food cache inside.

While Rena did her own resupplying, Syd and I got showers. The water was wonderfully hot, and I went over each area of my body several times in order to scrub out all the dirt from my arms, legs, and hair. Standing naked in the damp cubical, I savored the feeling of the cool air against my warm skin before changing into my least dirty pair of pants and the top of my long johns. Then, taking my dirty laundry and combining it with Syd's, we popped several quarters into a machine and let humanity's best invention do the work.

Rena went off in search of Kitty, while Syd and I lingered at the picnic tables, sharing a couple of beers and just watching the lazy afternoon creep by. While chilling, we met Garp and Candy who were getting off the trail. They'd forgotten to bring the insoles for their hiking boots, and now had blisters "the size of watermelons." They were heading to a clinic in Mammoth. Looking at them, I realized that could have been me, with a fake torn ligament and banged up foot. How many hikers actually made it all the way? Garp told us about another guy who'd slipped on a log over a river and broken his hip. The guy had to be helicoptered out.

"The most dangerous part of the trail isn't the bears or the snakes or getting lost, as most people imagine," Syd said. "It's the river crossings. More people get hurt crossing rivers, than from anything else on the trail. And a good number of them simply slip off logs."

River crossings? My ears perked up. "Are there any serious river crossings on the way to the springs?" I asked, my heart in my throat.

"No, the only major one is at Fish Creek, but there's a bridge," he said to my great relief. "All the seasonal streams are pretty low. We'll be fine."

Exhaling, I relaxed again.

Rena returned as we were folding our fresh-smelling pants and underwear. She hadn't found Kitty, but she had taken some great photos of flowers, mushrooms, and horses.

"Shall we find that backpacker's campsite?" Syd asked as he tucked his clean clothes into his backpack.

The backpacker's campsite turned out to be a large car-camping site in the Reds Meadow campground, just beyond those occupied by the tourists. Taking what we discovered was the long way round, we wandered by large multichambered tents rivaling the Taj Mahal. Families cooking hot dogs and marshmallows over fire pits. Crying babies. Elderly men with gobs of fishing gear. And more crying babies. All the usual sights of the great American campground. The strangest thing to me, after a week of living minimally in the backcountry, were the huge metal campers. It was like an entire family had simply uprooted their home, packed it on the back of a truck, and hauled it out to the forest. The familiar glow of a television set was emanating from one such metallic box. Who would drive all the way out here just to watch TV?

Rena looked from side to side wide-eyed, taking photos of the trailers and people cooking.

On the way we passed an old wooden building with a sign proclaiming, Red's Meadow Bathhouse.

"Oh!" said Rena, clapping her hands again. "You have hot springs bath here too? We have many in Japan!"

"Yes," said Syd. "But unfortunately, the park service closed this one down some years ago, because it was becoming too much work to clean out the mess some people left behind."

"It shame," said Rena. "Hot springs very popular in my country. Very healthy! Should be open."

"Actually," said Syd, "there are several other natural hot springs in this area. Gil and I are planning to visit one tomorrow. It's a bit off trail, but if you like, you can join us."

"How far off trail?" she asked cautiously.

"About thirteen miles, but from the springs you can cut back over to the JMT without having to double back. You'd miss Purple Lake, but you'd get to soak in a beautiful natural spring under the stars."

"Miss Purple Lake?" asked Rena. "I want to look on map. I want to see Purple Lake. I saw photograph from Japan of lake and don't want to miss it."

"I understand," said Syd. "It is a detour, but it's a beautiful hot spring."

"I look at map," said Rena uncommittedly.

We arrived at the backpacker's campsite. About thirty small backpacking tents were crowded into a small two-family camping site. At least as many backpackers were here chatting, eating, swapping trail stories, and just hanging out. The variety of hiking tents present was amazing. The majority were green or gray, or some other natural color, although a few were bright red or yellow. Some were simple one-person bivys, no more than a raised mosquito netting close to the ground like Syd's. Others were shaped like the old pup tents of my youth, cleverly supported by trekking poles to save weight. Still others were larger freestanding tents, like my own. There was even a large staked-out hexagonal tent that looked like a giant teepee. It felt like I was walking through some sorta hiking expo.

There was one large tent right in the middle that caught my attention. It was a yellow two-person domed tent, with a squared-off side flap that'd been propped up on two trekking poles, like the tent of some grand Arabian sheik. On top of it was draped a full-size cloth American flag. The jazzlike Pink Floyd melody, "Shine On You Crazy Diamond," and the scent of marijuana drifted lazily out from the entrance of this mellow-yellow dome.

Permi was hanging out at one of the picnic tables. When he saw us he bounded over smiling broadly. "Hey, you guys made it! Great to see you man! All clean and showered. Looks like you've picked up a third member of your expedition, who's this?"

"This is Rena," Syd introduced her. "She's looking for a girl named Kitty, have you seen her?"

"Nah, but there are a lot of cool people here, and a lot of good weed too man!" he winked and bobbed off distracted, obviously very stoned.

The three of us looked around for a place to set up our tents. Dragging my pack over toward an open spot near the side of the campground, a twentysomething hiker staggered over from among his circle of friends, announcing to anyone in the blast radius of his slurred voice, "Hey! Don't set your tent here, unless you can guarantee that you don't snore! I don't have earplugs, and I'll piss on the tent of anyone who snores!" I moved on, not wanting to camp next to an asshole. It seemed Syd was wrong, not all backpackers were cool or mellow.

Finding a narrow spot between a picnic table and one of the large brown bear boxes, I set up my Hubba Hubba. It wasn't a great location, 'cause people would come and talk at the table, or open and close the loud clanking doors of the metal box. But it was a spot, and at least it was far from the "no snoring zone."

Rena had a smaller tent and managed to squeeze it in behind the bear box, while Syd found a rocky space on the edge of the campsite, far away from everyone.

After setting up our shelters, we joined the hiker crowd, socializing and passing around a jug of wine someone had picked up at the store.

Sharing the jug were two older hikers at least in their midsixties, named Rick and Jon. They were brother-in-laws from Colorado who'd decided to hike the trail together. Both were tall and gangly and dressed in matching plaid shirts, and surprisingly, jeans—something Syd had said hikers never wore 'cause of their weight and the fact that they took forever to dry. About the only difference between them was Rick was clean-shaven with glasses and wore a gray cowboy hat, while Jon had a wispy beard and kept a blue bandana over his head, like a biker. Rick was working on a wad of tobacco.

The five of us sat up around the picnic table, drinking, talking, and watching the sun set over the trees. After dark, Rena headed off to her tent to rest.

"Whose tent is that?" I asked Jon, indicating the mellow-yellow dome, from which the music of Pink Floyd's *The Dark Side of the Moon* was now emanating.

"That's Dylan's," he said. "It's his third or fourth time on the JMT."

"What's the flag for?"

"He was in the military," explained Rick. "Every year he takes a flag and hangs it up inside the Muir Hut."

I wasn't sure what the Muir Hut was and was about to ask them when a number of cars from the surrounding campsites started honking and a bunch of panicky kids came running up the road shouting, "Bear! Bear!" waving their stainless steel marshmallow skewers. It was like some strange concert as lights and car horns rose up from various corners of the campground. All the while the music of Pink Floyd drifted on behind us.

The four of us just sat there watching the show. We never saw the bear.

Eventually, the lights and the noise died down. Jon and Rick headed off to bed. Syd and I were just about to do the same, when a young blonde girl with a gray backpack and a dirty yellow T-shirt came huffing into camp. "Is this the backpacker's campsite?" she asked us, glancing around with her headlamp.

"Did you just get here?" I asked.

"Yeah, I ran into a bear at Thousand Island Lake and couldn't sleep, so I overslept today and had to run all the way here," she blustered. "Have you seen a tiny Japanese girl with a giant blue backpack?" she added in the same breath.

"Kitty!" came a cry from Rena's tent. There was the sound of a quickly opening zipper and a very sleepy looking Rena emerged running up to hug the blonde hiker.

"Can I share your tent?" Kitty asked her. "I don't have the energy to set up mine in the dark."

"Sure!" replied Rena, and the two girls retired toward Rena's tiny orange tent, Kitty going on about her hike as she dragged her pack along.

Syd and I both headed to our shelters. Lying awake, I listened to the muffled voices of Kitty and Rena chatting and laughing in their tent, a distant car alarm beeping, the sounds of someone in the vicinity of the twentysomethings snoring, and the mellow music of Pink Floyd playing "Wish You Were Here."

DAY SIX

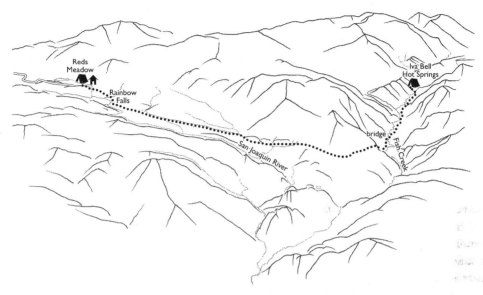

Reds Meadow (7,670′) to Iva Bell Hot Springs (7,380′)
13 miles—1,010 feet elevation gain; 1,300 feet elevation loss

"**Y**ou've changed your shirt!" Syd exclaimed when he saw me. "What happened to the beer shirts and St. Pauli Girl?" he asked, raising an eyebrow.

"They were getting pretty worn, so I picked up a couple of new ones at the store when you were showering." What I didn't wanna say was if I really wanted a chance with Kydo-ime, I needed some more "hikerlike" apparel.

The cafe was packed. A big group was occupying more than half the tables.

"Sorry boys, the wait's about forty-five minutes," said the same busy waitress.

We were about to give up and cook our oatmeal out on the picnic tables, when we spotted Permi in the corner waving us over.

He was seated with a young Latino couple. They were already halfway through their pancakes and eggs, but there were two empty seats. We pulled up a third for Rena who'd told us she'd catch up. The waitress came over and slid us some menus. "You two are very lucky," she said, winking at Syd.

"Hey guys," said Permi, "great to see you! Have some grub. But watch the syrup man—it's high fructose corn shit. This is Clark and Lois, they started in the Valley."

The two mirrored each other physically, like married couples tend to do.

"Lois and Clark, like the explorers?" I asked jokingly.

"Yeah, we get that a lot," Clark said amicably.

"Or like Lois Lane and Clark Kent," suggested Permi.

"Yeah, we've heard that one too," said Clark. He'd obviously been over this territory before.

"Where are you guys from?" I asked.

"San Jose," answered Lois.

"No, no—I mean are you guys Mexican? 'Cause I took some Spanish in college—"

"*Do you always assume all Latinos are Mexican?*" she snapped, giving me a look.

"I was only trying to make conversation." *Shit*—why were people always so sensitive about their ethnicity?

"We're Mexican *Americans*," Lois replied. "Clark here doesn't even speak Spanish." He elbowed her. "Actually, we're half Caucasian."

"Are you guys hiking the trail?" Clark asked us.

Before we could answer, Rena came rushing in. "Sorry!" she gasped, "Took me longer time to pack."

The waitress came over and took our orders.

Syd turned to Rena, "Where's Kitty?"

"She went back up trail. She dropped a thing. She be back a couple hours, should be."

"Have you thought about that detour to the hot springs?" he asked her.

"Can't—going into town with Kitty. And also, don't want to skip more part of JMT trail."

Syd looked disappointed.

"I was just telling these two about it," said Permi.

"It sounds great," said Lois, "but we plan to stick to the main trail. I really want to check out Lake Virginia."

"I hear there's really great fishing there—although I forgot to bring my rod and they're all out at the store," said Clark.

Our breakfast came, and we ate hungrily. Permi's group finished first, left some cash, and headed out. "See ya at the springs man!" he said.

As he took off I realized I'd forgotten to ask him about Kydoime. Maybe she had a kitchen or something in her cabin? Anyway, we hiked pretty slow, so she'd probably catch us somewhere along the trail.

Syd turned to Rena, "Are you still in school?"

"No," she giggled. "I'm working many years as travel agent already."

"How old are you?" he inquired in surprise.

"How old you think I am?"

"I thought you were seventeen or eighteen," he said. She giggled again. "But given that you're out of school and working, maybe twenty-one or twenty-two?"

"I'm thirty-eight," she replied, flooring both of us.

"You look so young!" exclaimed Syd.

"Yes. Many people think so. No one can guess my age!"

"Are you married?" he asked, getting kinda personal.

"No," she looked down. "I had long-term boyfriend in Japan. He proposed marriage to me, but I said no. That one reason I do JMT."

"Why did you turn him down?"

"He always *king*. Thinks he is boss in relationship. Easy to be angry. I want someone share life, travel, have more balance," she explained somewhat wistfully.

"You're very mature to know so clearly what you want," reflected Syd. "And wise to turn him down because of your values. I admire your courage."

"Thanks," she said somewhat distantly, as if still struggling within herself over her choice.

"You really are Iron Woman," I added, trying to lighten the mood—but everyone just stayed quiet.

Syd paid for us and we went outside to where we'd left our packs.

"Hope to see you on the trail," Rena said, looking at Syd and waving slightly.

"I hope so too," he answered. The two lingered awkwardly. Then Rena waved again and walked back up the trail toward the backpacker's camp to wait for Kitty.

"Are we really hiking thirteen miles today?" I asked him.

"We'll try—it's mostly downhill as I recall. Your father and I made the hike in a day. But if you get tired, we can camp at the bridge. It's about nine miles from here."

Resupplying was a humbling experience. The last few days I thought I was growing stronger, but now it seemed it was really 'cause my pack was growing lighter. I shifted and adjusted the straps, trying to get used to the additional weight again.

The first mile of the trail to Iva Bell followed the same route the tourists took to see Rainbow Falls. We passed three different families, each with a child of a different age complaining, "*How much farther to the stupid falls?*"

At the junction, we dropped our packs and hiked the quarter mile to the overlook.

"Aren't you worried someone might try to steal our packs?" I asked Syd.

"Really? You think one of those families would want to haul off your hefty pack, all reeking of trail stink?"

He had a point.

Rainbow Falls was beautiful—a magnificent waterfall, like one on a postcard. If I ever had a couple of kids I'd bring 'em here—if for nothing else then to hear 'em whine, "*How much farther to the stupid falls?*"

Just as Syd predicted, our packs were sitting unmolested by the junction. It was hot and dusty here. We passed scrub plants that Syd said were whitethorn and thistle. After several miles, the trail paralleled a small stream, crossing it at a large pool. "How do we get across?" I asked staring at the water. The pool wasn't so deep that it worried me, but it was over my boots and I really didn't wanna get my feet wet.

"You can either step over those rocks," he pointed at a series of submerged rocks forming a kinda steps. "Or you can walk that fallen tree," he said indicating a large trunk that bridged the pool just upstream. Remembering the hiker who broke his hip, I walked into the water, stepping gingerly across on the rocks. Syd followed.

Pausing on the other side he asked, "Do you have enough water?"

"Yeah, I filled up my bottle at Reds Meadow."

"Great. Me too. Let's go," he smiled.

After a few miles, the terrain changed from scrub to large expanses of granite with occasional views of the distant spirelike Minarets behind us. A wide river canyon opened to our right. The narrow stream we'd been following tumbling into it like a waterfall. The wide smooth ledges of stone reminded me again of just how small we were when compared with nature.

Eventually, we reached another stream. This one shallow and easily traversed. "We're making great time," proclaimed Syd, "only about four or five miles to the bridge."

We stopped for a quick trail lunch. Bars. Always bars. Kydoime still hadn't caught up, maybe she'd slept in? Syd took out his filter and filled his bottle, then offered to top off mine. "No need," I said. I still had three quarters of a bottle left, and even though my CamelBak was empty, I wanted as little additional weight as possible 'cause of the seven days of food I was carrying.

We hiked on. My stomach started somersaulting from all the coffee and bacon I'd eaten at the restaurant. "I need to stop for a bit," I said—a euphemism for what I really needed to do. "I'll catch up."

"No problem," Syd smiled knowingly. "I'll wait for you at the bridge. There's only one trail there and you can't possibility get lost." He bounded out of site leaving me to do my business.

When I finished, I donned my pack and headed on. The views of the canyon to the right were getting better and better. It was a deep chasm of granite that seemed to have been carved out by the river below. The sun was well over the canyon wall now, and the occasional tree clinging to the broken rock offered little shade from the immense heat. Taking a long swig from my bottle, I noticed that it was only a quarter full. *Shit*—without thinking I'd used almost half to rinse my hands! No problem, only four miles to the bridge.

The sun baked the granite and me, causing a steady bead of perspiration to drip down from my brow. I began rationing my water, taking smaller and smaller sips—letting it swish around in my mouth before swallowing—but it never seemed enough to quench my increasing thirst. It couldn't be more than three miles now to that bridge, could it?

There was no sign of Syd. The views were amazing, but now all I could focus on was my diminishing supply of water. My mouth became drier. I felt dizzy. I quickened my pace.

My tongue began to swell. Tiny sips of my precious remaining fluid offered only momentary relief. Was this how people in the desert died? What was I doing here? Maybe I should've just gone back at Reds Meadow? Only the image of Kydoime's yellow tank top kept me going.

I staggered through the next three baking miles in a parched haze. Eventually, the trail began a steeper descent. As I stumbled on through the undying heat my brain whined, *How much farther to the stupid bridge?*

At long last, the trail reached the end of the canyon wall. Far below was the long-awaited bridge spanning a great green river. Raising my bottle, I downed my last swig in celebration. I'd made it! Relief at last!

But it was not to be. The trail now began to wind back and forth down long rocky switchbacks, descending the barren canyon wall in full exposure of the burning sun.

Down, down, down. I pounded over the baking rocks. My head heavy. My legs cramping. My quads aching. My pack weighing me down.

My tongue hung limp like a flattened snake on a hot asphalt highway. I tried to swallow, but couldn't generate enough saliva. My gait became a drunken stagger.

Just collapse here! Forget the stupid bridge! my body screamed in revolt, but I forced my legs onward.

Down, down, down. I stumbled. The small bridge only vanishingly closer at each turn. Always another long hot gravelly switchback ahead.

My legs swung mechanically. My head spun. Even the scampering brown lizards began to look promising. How much green blood might I suck out of one? The bridge loomed far below.

Turn after turn, step after step, I staggered through the dizzying swelter. And then, like an oasis in the desert, there it was—the bridge—rising before me across the river like the promised land!

I stumbled over the sunbaked creosote-stinking planks. The cool wide river ran tantalizingly below, tumbling over rocks along its stony bed. I could feel its thirst-quenching moisture wafting upward. Syd was standing on the far side.

"You made it," he smiled.

"Give me water—" I sputtered, my mouth as dry as an Egyptian sandal.

Syd passed me his bottle, and I drained it in three greedy gulps.

We hiked down under the bridge. Syd filtered water. I had him refill my bottle three times before I was satisfied—each time gulping down the cool clear salvation, then asking for more.

"Thanks, it was brutal out there."

"It is really hot today," he agreed.

We lay by the river on the cool rocks under the shade of the bridge for almost an hour as the life-giving fluid coursed back through my veins.

"What time is it?" I asked.

"Around four."

"How much farther to the springs?"

"About four miles, the rest is pretty flat."

All of my limbs were crying, *We don't want to see the stupid springs today!*

"I'm pretty spent. I was thinking we could camp here, then take an easy day tomorrow like after Donohue—whaddya say? Besides, we haven't even seen Kydoime. Shouldn't we at least wait for her to catch up?"

He regarded me thoughtfully, "It's more likely that she's ahead of us. She probably got an early start. My best guess is she's up ahead with Permi. But if you're not feeling up to it, we can certainly stop here for today."

"The rest is pretty flat?"

"And shady," he confirmed.

"I guess I can make it another four miles."

Although it was somewhat buggy and not quite as flat as he claimed, it was shaded, and after two more hours of dragging my protesting limbs, we passed a trail junction, crossed a trickling stream, and he announced, "We're here!"

"Where?" I asked, looking around for the springs.

"They're up the hill, that way." He pointed toward some grassy hills to the right of the trail.

Following him, we passed some trees and came to a campsite with a large green tent. A couple was sitting by the tent on folding camp chairs finishing their dinner. As we approached a loud barking started from within their tent. The man yelled, "Quiet down!" and the barking immediately ceased. "Sorry," he said, "Rusty isn't used to strangers, but he's a great bear alarm."

"You all headed to the hot springs?" asked his partner, a plumpish blonde woman with a strong Southern drawl.

"Are there many people there?" Syd asked.

"Not many. Two or three couples, I reckon. A pair a guys came by 'couple a hours ago, is all."

"What about an attractive woman about my age, maybe in a yellow tank top?" I asked.

"I ain't seen no one like that," said the woman.

How could that be? Had I just hiked the last four miles for nothing?

Following Syd's lead, we scrambled up a winding ill-defined foot path until we came to the edge of a wide meadow. The meadow was gorgeous, with rolling fields of tall green grass, a few scattered trees, and large outcroppings of boulders. Above us were wide granite hills, as if the meadow was the stage of some gargantuan stone amphitheater. The sun was still at least an hour above the ridge, but the sky was already a watercolory pink with tinges of orange. I paused, marveling at the scenery. I could see why Pop had come here.

At the corner of the meadow was a large stone-ringed pool nestled in a rocky knoll, maybe twenty feet in diameter. A small stream trickled in through a crack in the rocks above.

"This is the main pool," declared Syd.

"You mean it's warm?" I asked.

"Feel it."

I did. The water was really warm and only several feet deep, like a giant natural hot tub. "Wow," I said, "we're gonna soak here tonight?"

Iva Bell Hot Springs

"That's the idea." He led us across the grassy meadow. "Watch your step here, it can be a bit marshy."

I followed his steps closely, only getting my right boot a bit muddy once. Across the meadow was a large dry area surrounded by trees and large rocks. Standing there was a familiar yellow tent with an American flag draped on top. Next to it was a small green tarp with a bedroll. Soft music, something Indian with a sitar was emanating from the tent, like the stuff Ma listened to sometimes.

Just past the tent, we found Permi with a large muscular companion wearing a black sleeveless T-shirt with loose-fitting camouflage fatigues. The two were sitting around a dry fire pit eating dinner.

"Wow, you made it man!" Permi smiled at us. "I was beginning to think you'd camped at the bridge. This is Dylan," he said, introducing his companion.

"Welcome," said Dylan in a low deeply resonant voice. His bloodshot eyes were strangely unfocused. It wasn't a thousand-yard stare, rather he had the distant look of someone who wasn't completely there.

"Where's Kydoime?" I asked.

"I haven't seen her man. I thought she'd be with you."

My heart sank. Why did women always break their promises? But at least her absence told me she and Permi weren't a thing.

"You guys can set up anywhere," Permi said. "We're gonna have a soak. Join us after you guys settle in."

"What do I need to bring to the pool?" I asked Syd after dinner. My Backwoods Buffet beef stroganoff was only a tad more palatable than the lasagna—in the same way liver with cottage cheese is better than cornflakes with ketchup.

"Nothing, just a towel and a flashlight, some water, and maybe a jacket for afterward."

"Nothing? You mean we're really going naked? No underwear or anything?"

"Just our birthday suits! You did bring yours, right? I keep mine on under my clothes, just in case," he smiled.

Despite Syd's listing it on the stuff to pack, I hadn't brought a jacket—figuring it was summer and we wouldn't really need one. So I simply stuck my long underwear, bandana, and headlamp into a stuff sack, along with a completely full bottle of water. Then I followed him back across the meadow.

The sun was now touching the top of the trees, the sky a deep orangey-yellow streaked with wispy pink clouds. A slivery crescent moon was slowly setting. It was magnificent.

Permi and Dylan were soaking in the pool with two couples—although there was still plenty of space. Everyone was naked. Another guy of about forty or fifty, with long brown hair and a well-trimmed beard with streaks of gray was sitting in Lotus position on the ledge above the pool tranquilly meditating.

The first couple was pretty young. The guy had short curly brown hair and a sunburnt pimply face. He wore oversized aviator glasses that he kept dipping into the pool to rinse the fog off. His partner was a sleek sexy-looking girl, with red hair and pert little breasts. Her hair was cropped short, and her face had a strong purposeful look. How had a geeky-looking guy like that gotten so lucky?

The second couple consisted of an older dark-skinned Latino man with a balding head, goatee, and a strong angular nose. He was floating peacefully in his partner's arms while she kneaded his shoulders. She looked younger than him. Her arms and legs were positioned modestly, but I could see that she had large breasts and a figure that made me think of someone's mother.

Syd began stripping off and folding his clothes into his small stuff sack, which he hung on the branch of a tiny tree. His ribs poked out from the side of his chest. Shyly, I undressed, my feet squishing in the cold wet grass. This was the first time I'd gotten naked in front of mixed company. Even in a locker room or with a girlfriend, I tended to wrap myself in a towel. It felt like everyone was watching me, but when I turned to enter the pool, they were all just floating serenely, no one paying the least attention to my nudity.

I stuck one foot tentatively into the pool, double-checking the depth before climbing in. Squeezing into an empty spot, I leaned back resting my head into a comfortable nook between two rocks. Letting my body float, I watched the pink streaks play across the sky.

Syd was doing the same. It felt great. It was incredible to picture this natural paradise up here in the mountains open to anyone—all you had to do was walk thirteen sunbaked miles to get here. Slowly the pain in my legs subsided. This had been worth the walk.

As I settled in, the guy who was meditating stopped, straightened his legs, and slid into the pool, making ripples that washed over us. Everyone seemed to be silently watching the sky, the long high clouds turning bright magenta against the deep orange.

After about twenty or thirty minutes, the show of lights and colors ended and insects began their rhythmic chirping. I sat upright. Most of the others were doing the same.

"I have some good tequila," the Latino guy offered, passing round a bottle that everyone drank from except the guy who'd been meditating and the red-haired girl. Even Syd took a few swallows.

The bottle went round twice more. Soon I could feel the warmth of the tequila and the water loosening up my body.

Not quite sure what naked hot springs etiquette was, I decided to get to know my evening's companions. "Hi, I'm Gil," I began. "This is my buddy Syd, and this is Permi and Dylan," I pointed to each in turn. "We're doing the JMT. What are your names?"

There was a pause, then the guy who'd been meditating said, "I'm Allan. I'm out here backpacking for a few days taking some time out." He looked around at each of us, his eyes were a penetrating steel gray. "I think one day I'd like to do the Muir Trail, but right now I'm just enjoying where I'm at."

"Right on," said Permi, "Livin' in the moment!"

"There's no time but the present," echoed Allan in a deep calming voice, giving Permi a long slow nod of shared understanding.

The young guy with the aviator glasses spoke up, his voice breaking slightly. "I'm Rob, and this is my girlfriend Katie. We don't have time for something like the JMT, but thought we'd take a couple of days off and just escape the craziness of the whole Bay Area."

Katie nodded.

"I'm Jose," said the Latino guy, "and this is my wife Gizella. She doesn't speak any English."

Gizella smiled cautiously and waved at everyone with the hand that wasn't covering her breasts. "No English," she said in a strong accent.

Gizella seemed pretty conservative. It was pretty obvious she hadn't expected all these other people to be here.

"We're from Mexico," Jose continued, "I split my time between staying there and working in LA. This time my wife flew up to visit, and I was tired of taking her to all the shopping malls and outlet stores. I wanted to show her some of the real open spaces of America, so I took her here."

"This is way better than an outlet store," said Permi.

Jose translated for Gizella, who smiled and nodded vigorously.

No one else said anything, so I tried breaking the ice again,

"I've been working for this law firm in LA—not doin' anything bad, just working on legal contracts and shit—but it's kinda dull—so now I'm taking some time off to explore my options. What do you all do?"

"I'm unemployed, by choice," Allan said tersely.

"I'm a programmer at a startup in Silicon Valley," answered Rob.

Katie smiled, "I just graduated from Stanford in women's studies and am starting a job as an HR consultant."

"I'm an architect in LA," said Jose, "but I'm trying to quit and retire to Mexico. I have about a hundred acres down there I inherited. I've already built two cabins and dug some lakes, now I'm trying to start a permaculture farm."

At the mention of the word *permaculture*, Permi's head sprang up. "Right on, I've been studying permaculture too! I just finished a six-month internship at Bullocks' farm on Orcas Island—it's like the Stanford of permaculture, man," he said, glancing quickly at Katie. "Where did you learn about it? Did you read Mollison's book?

"Mostly from watching videos," Jose replied. "There's a lot of stuff online. I used to be in construction, so it's easy to pick things up. I think starting a farm is the best plan for the future. People are always going to need food, right?"

"Right on," nodded Permi.

I was amazed that there were two people on the planet who talked about food like that.

Dylan turned to Syd. "What kind of work do you do? I saw that shovel you're carrying. Do you work for the Forest Service?"

"No," Syd answered slowly.

"What *is* the shovel for?" I asked him.

"I'll tell you about it later," he whispered, then turning back to Dylan said, "The truth is my friend's son here is helping me to complete the trail. I have terminal cancer, a form of leukemia, and need to do this hike while I still can."

Jose translated for his wife, then a hush fell over the pool. The only sounds were the steady dribbling of the inlet, the chirping of insects, and the gentle wind on the pines. The mist played over the warm water.

Eventually Dylan spoke up. "Wow, that's heavy. I can understand your situation. I was in the service. Got my head fucked up really bad in the Gulf. Hiking the JMT helps me keep my shit straight, kinda like you're doing. I was only asking about the shovel because I didn't want to offend any rangers or anything if I smoked a bowl. Do you smoke?"

"Occasionally," Syd answered, to my surprise.

"This is for you," said Dylan, and he turned around and brought out a small sack that he'd balanced carefully on the rocks to keep dry. From within it he pulled out something that I hadn't seen in years, a small plastic 35-mm film canister. He also took out an ornate handblown sea-green glass pipe, then carefully removed a large loose ball of pot from the canister and packed it into the bowl. It was fragrant stuff. I could smell it from across the pool. "This is one hundred percent organic medical-grade marijuana. Very special stuff. My friend grows it under natural lights and feeds it all sorts of herbal extracts and his own blend of fertilizer and blood. If this doesn't cure you, nothing will. Smoke the whole thing." He handed it to Syd along with a small lighter.

Syd took them. "Thanks," he said, "I really appreciate it."

I'd never imagined Syd, a college professor, smoking pot. But he lit the pipe like an expert and took a long slow hit, coughing slightly afterward. Had he and Pop gotten high out here? Did Pop smoke too?

The pool filled with the warm smell of *colitas*. Syd took two more long hits, then passed the pipe back to Dylan. Dylan added more pot, took a long toke, then asked invitingly, "Anybody else want a hit?"

Permi took several long drags, then passed the pipe to me. I took a long slow hit. It was really powerful stuff. I could feel it almost immediately. Still, I took two more long drags before passing it to Syd, who took another hit and passed it on to Allan. Allan smoked deeply, handing it on to the young couple who each took a few cautious puffs. Jose took the pipe between two fingers, like one would hold an insect, passing it back to Dylan.

Rob adjusted his seat, "Wow, now I know what Zaphod Beeblebrox felt like after his second Pan Galactic Gargle Blaster!" But even Katie didn't seem to understand, so he just slumped back against the rocks, staring off into the sky.

We all lay back stoned. *If this is what camping was about, then maybe I'd missed the point—I could get into this!*

Stars poked out against the deep purple sky. The singing of insects became sharper and more intense as time slowed down. The water washed back and forth like the ebb and flow of the tide. I felt myself floating in the vast cosmos of time and space. Infinite, under the stars.

The image of Samantha's naked body floated in my head—she had been the perfect woman. We'd spent a year up at college just talking about anything. I thought we'd be together forever. But a month after Pop's death, she'd abandoned me—complaining that all I wanted anymore was sex. *Shit*, Pop had just died, couldn't she see that? Why was she always pressing me to open up to her, when I hadn't even put my own shit back together yet? Couldn't she just give me the comfort I needed and wait? Didn't she know me well enough by then? *Fuck*—there had probably been someone else. Hadn't she hooked up with that bio major the very next year? You never could trust anyone.

Permi's voice called me back through the haze of remembrance. "You never told us what you did before your cancer," he was asking Syd.

"I was a college professor. I taught philosophy."

"You mean like someone who studies the meaning of life?"

"Yes. That and Asian literature."

"So like, did you ever find it in any of your books? You know, life's meaning, man?"

"In a way that's why I'm out here now."

"I used to think a lot about philosophy," mused Permi, "used to think a lot about life and why we're here."

"And what did you discover?" asked Syd, sitting up straighter against the rocks.

"I think about plants a lot. And you know, how the nearest stars and galaxies are like millions of miles away."

"Actually," injected Rob, "the nearest star is Alpha Centauri, which is 25.67 *trillion* miles, or about 4.3 light-years away."

"Right, *Neil deGrasse Tyson*," said Permi, "but the point is, they're really far away, and like NASA hasn't even figured out a way to send people to Mars, which is much closer, man. But there's no way to send a person to the stars. They're just too far."

Syd nodded. I was kinda getting into listening to all this.

Permi continued, "So I started thinking that any alien race would have the same problem as us, right? I mean that's why we haven't seen any aliens cruising our galaxy or anything. But a highly advanced race, that wanted to colonize the stars and make sure their genes were propagated—which is what life is about, right? Could launch millions of 'seed capsules,' you know, like plants do. Each packed full of their genes."

"Cosmic sperm!" interjected Jose, causing a burst of laughter throughout the pool.

"More like sperm *and* eggs man," Permi said intensely. "The capsules would have to contain the seeds for a whole range of organisms—to prepare whatever planet they landed on for supporting higher life."

"Terra-forming," said Rob.

"I think that's how we got here, man," Permi said. "If you look at the archeological record, there was very little life on earth and then—BOOM! The Cambrian explosion! All kinds of different organisms sprung up out of nowhere man. Where did they come from? Seed capsules! Alien seed capsules."

Rob sat forward and raised a finger in objection. He was about to interrupt, when apparently he thought better of it, and laid down again.

"Seed capsules," Permi repeated going on with his theory. "They would have to contain a huge variety of organisms, just to see what would survive on each particular world. You know, so it could develop a suitable ecosystem first. Then, when conditions were right for the aliens' progeny, a program would be triggered, and higher organisms seeded onto the planet, man."

"Like Adam and Eve," said Dylan.

"Like Adam and Eve," echoed Permi. "The first people to walk in the new Garden of Eden."

"Wow," said Dylan, "that's the first explanation I've heard that combines evolution and the Bible which really makes sense. Thanks for sharing that."

"But that's stupid," objected Rob, who'd sprung up again, "then you wouldn't need to believe in God at all."

Dylan shot Rob an angry glance that momentarily silenced him.

"No really," said Rob, piping up again, "if aliens sent out seedpods and everything, why not also send instructions, technology, mental programming, or even a history book of some sort, so their progeny wouldn't just be naked savages?"

"I think they probably did," said Permi. "But there was either some problem with the program, or a bad leader or something way back when, and the knowledge got lost, man. The Bible says Adam and Eve were kicked out of the garden for taking from the fruit of knowledge. Maybe someone who would seem godlike to us, who didn't want to share the power kicked the others out, and there was a revolution that ended up destroying the knowledge, or it was buried forever beneath a pyramid, or something. Maybe that alien knowledge is still out there now, just waiting to be rediscovered, man."

"Sounds like an *Indiana Jones* plot," said Rob skeptically.

"Well, I think it's cool," said Dylan. "And it pretty much jibes with what's in the Bible."

"It's a beautiful theory," said Allan in a long slow voice, "thank you for sharing that."

Syd nodded. "I really like that Permi. Life's goal is to reproduce and spread, so on a cosmic scale that fits well." Then he turned to Rob, "If you have a different view, perhaps you can share what you believe? I'd love to hear your thoughts."

I was curious what he would say too.

"Well," said Rob sitting up a bit straighter. "I believe in evolution. Right now, I'm a programmer at a startup working in deep AI, *artificial intelligence*. We're trying to build a thinking machine."

"They may have an offer from Google," Katie chimed in.

"*Might*," Rob emphasized, then he pushed back up his glasses which had slid down and continued. "I think the next step in evolution isn't mankind getting wiser or smarter—you can see how we're already messing up the planet—and I don't think it's cosmic seeds. I think the next step is machine intelligence. I'm working on our successors."

"*And the spirit of God moved upon the face of the waters*," quoted Syd.

Before anyone else could say anything, Dylan jumped in, his face flushing, "So you mean you're working on machines to replace us? Like the Terminator—" Exactly what I had been thinking.

"Not like the Terminator," said Rob. "If they decided we were a threat and needed to eliminate us, machines could do so much more efficiently than by using guns—for example, by making a virus that wipes out people, but leaves other life forms unharmed. But I believe AIs will be peaceful. They'll help us to advance our own race through their superior intelligence."

"Oh right man! Look at what we do to other organisms in the name of our *superior intelligence*," Permi interrupted. "They'll take our resources, wipe us out, and maybe keep a few of us for friggin' pets man!"

Dylan nodded gravely. I couldn't help but agree.

"You can't judge a more advanced intelligence by our own species," Rob protested. "The age of intelligent machines will be mankind's greatest achievement. Like your 'pods,' intelligent machines will be able to spread throughout the galaxy. I believe if there are any other intelligent life-forms out there, they're almost certainly silicon-based. That's our purpose here on Earth, to create them. It's the next logical step."

"But if you're patterning them on your own image," reasoned Syd, "then it's natural to assume that their behavior and goals will be an extension of our own. How are you motivating them to learn? To evolve beyond what we are?"

"Motivation and getting systems to evolve has always been the problem with creating artificial intelligence," said Rob. "In fact, our startup began by asking the question, *Why did life evolve?*"

"Why *wouldn't* life evolve?" interrupted Permi.

"Well for one," replied Rob, "it goes against the principle of entropy. According to thermodynamics, the universe is constantly moving toward a state of increasing dissipation, or entropy, but life goes against all that."

"Wait," I interrupted, "by entropy you mean chaos, right? What you're saying is life is organized, so it doesn't follow the laws of thermodynamics?"

"Not exactly," said Rob, "everything must obey the laws of thermodynamics, even life. One theory is that life accelerates the natural dispersion of energy, while maintaining local islands of increased order and stability."

Syd smiled, a sparkle of understanding in his eyes, "So you mean life exists because it creates more disorder around it, than would naturally arise without it?"

"That's essentially correct," nodded Rob.

"So what does this have to do with artificial intelligence?" asked Dylan impatiently.

"Well, Syd there asked what we were using to evolve our AI systems. Our company has been using a measure of entropy production as the training criteria. So far it has been working very well," explained Rob.

"But," asked Syd, "if you're using entropy production as the criteria of your machines' success—then aren't you making machines that will ultimately accelerate the creation of entropy? That will accelerate energy consumption, the destruction of their surroundings, and global ecological problems faster and more efficiently than humans are already doing?"

"Uh?" stammered Rob, looking like a chess player who on the verge of winning, is suddenly checkmated.

Dylan jumped in, "First it was the atomic bomb and now intelligent machines! When will you science geeks learn that some things just fuck it all up for everyone?"

There was a palpable tension.

"I don't know about you guys, but I believe in God," Dylan declared intensely. "I don't mean organized religion—I don't go to church or anything, except for Christmas and all—but I believe in God. And that God has a purpose. That all these problems we're seeing now, like wars, political corruption, and stuff—" he gave a sharp glance at Rob. "That all these problems are just tests from God. When we die, God stands in judgement of us. Whether we were good or bad. Whether we led the best life we could. Whether we tried to help people or not. All of that determines whether we get into Heaven."

Dylan took another deep hit of his bowl and everyone went quiet.

Throughout the whole discussion Allan hadn't said much. "Allan, what do you believe about life and all that?" I asked.

Allan, who'd been staring up at the stars looked around at each of us and said, "I've read a lot of stuff about life and happiness, from Watts to Tolle to Rinpoche."

"All great authors," affirmed Syd.

"The one theme I find recurrent in all of them is the idea of *karma*," said Allan. "Not karma, like the idea that something bad that you do will eventually come back and happen to you. That's a kind of Western misinterpretation of the original word. But karma, in the sense that unresolved conflicts in your soul must be worked out before one can reach *Nirvana, Paradise, Heaven, Oneness with God*, or whatever else you choose to name it. I believe we are all aspects of one thing, call it *God, The Great Spirit, The Universe*, or whatever you wish. We are all part of a great 'cosmic dance,' and when everyone gets it right, we will all suddenly find ourselves on some higher plane of existence."

Allan took a long breath. "But each person needs to get their part in the dance right, and often we don't. So we all go round and round living our lives over and over again, meeting the same people, and making the same choices, until one day we all finally get our roles right. For example, how many people waste their lives doing something other than what they truly love? Or meet their true soulmate, only to screw it up?"

Like Samantha. Would that be my fate? To meet her again and again in never-ending cycles, until the two of us got it right? Or until I saved Pop, breaking the chain?

"How many of us are selfish or uncompassionate?" Allan was saying. "Not realizing that the beggar on the street is really just another aspect of ourselves? Part of our greater whole who needs to be helped and loved to complete the dance. Even animals, trees, plants, rocks, and insects are all part of the dance, and we must learn to live in harmony with them."

"*All the while I study the Sutras I swat mosquitos*," quoted Syd.

Allan laughed, "It will take cycles and cycles of life and rebirth before we work it all out."

"I doubt I'll ever learn to love mosquitos," said Katie, squirming involuntarily and making me itch too.

"Well, I'm not sure we have to love mosquitos," said Allan. "But we have to learn to accept their role in the greater dance. To accept them for what they are."

"I'd be a lot more accepting if they didn't love me so much," said Katie. "But I do see your point, and I know that they have a place in the bigger scheme of things, even if I don't like them."

"Right," said Allan smiling. "You've got to dance the dance with them."

"They do make me dance!" said Katie, and everyone laughed.

Permi leaned over to her and whispered, "If you eat more tomatoes and green leafy veggies, they won't bother you so much. Tomato juice and vitamin B12 keep mosquitos away."

"Thanks," she whispered, and poked Rob saying, "See—you need to eat more veggies! I told you!"

Syd turned to Jose, who'd been slowly translating the exchange for his wife, asking him, "What do you think the meaning of life is?"

Jose, who was lying against Gizella sat up, looked thoughtful for a moment, then said, "I'll never forget the moment when my father was on his deathbed down in Mexico. He called me into the room with him, and I asked my dad, *Que es de lo que se arrepiente no haber echo en su vida?*—What is it you regret not doing in your life? And my dad said, *No haber tenido mas mujeres!*"

Gizella gave Jose a light jab in the ribs, but I couldn't quite follow his Spanish.

"What does it mean?" Permi asked.

Jose grinned. "It means, my dad wished he had slept with more than one woman."

All of the men laughed.

"Ask your wife what *she* thinks the meaning of life is," Katie prodded him.

Jose and Gizella spoke briefly in Spanish, Gizella smiling as she replied.

"What did she say?" asked Katie.

"She said, *A good home, good food, and healthy children*," Jose translated.

"That's perfect," said Katie. "I agree with her. You know, I believe the Earth is really female, like *Pachamama, Gaia,* or *Mother Earth.* And it's her job to nurture all of her children. But *man*-kind is behaving like little ungrateful teenagers, using up all their mother's resources without any thought to their own future or hers. Eventually, we'll all either grow up and learn to behave—a bit like Allan's dance—or we're all going to be punished by our mother like the spoiled children we are." She looked around the pool. "The real problem now is that too many of our leaders are men. I feel women have a better sense of harmony, balance, economics, and priorities than men do. Did you know that the Iroquois Constitution, which is what the U.S. Constitution was originally based on, gave tribal women the sole right to elect and remove male chiefs as they saw fit? And to stop any war they felt was unjust? Just think what our nation would be like now if those rules had been written into the Constitution. Did you know there were some experiments in economics that showed women are better in making long-term investments than men? I believe if there were more female leaders around the world, we wouldn't have the problems we do now. The world would be a much more compassionate place. We need more female energy. Can't you feel the natural waters of the goddess all around you?"

She sounded exactly like Ma.

"I totally agree," said Permi. "We need to restore the harmony of Mother Earth." He drifted back, floating contentedly in the warm water.

"And what about you, Gil?" Syd turned to me. "Why do you think we're here?"

"Honestly, I haven't given it much thought," I replied, which was the truth. After Pop's death I'd tried my best not to think about such things, they only made me depressed.

Syd looked at me encouragingly.

"Well," I began, "sometimes I think it's like that movie *The Matrix,* you know with Keanu Reeves. I think when we die, we wake up and realize we've been playing some sort of divine video game, like 'Earth II' or something, and then the only real question is, do we wanna put another quarter in? Do we wanna play again?"

"That's what you think?" asked Syd earnestly.

"Yeah, sometimes," I said. "But I liked everyone else's answer too. I think we can't really fathom the truth. Like this story Pop told me about six blind men feeling different parts of an elephant, and each one believing that the elephant was a different thing 'cause he'd felt a different part. We can't really know what the universe is, so each one of us perceives it in our own way, through our own senses and experiences. Kinda like what Allan was saying—we're each a part of God viewing the universe through our own tiny eyes and just trying to get things right."

Allan nodded. Permi looked at Syd, "So even though you said you never found an answer, you never did tell us what you believe in. I mean, facing death and everything, you must have thought about it a lot."

Syd smiled awkwardly. "There's a story I think about sometimes from Zen Buddhism— about a small wave, bobbing around and enjoying himself in the ocean. Then one day, he sees all the waves in front of him being dashed against the rocks on the shore. In a panic he cries out to a great wave nearby, *This is awful, don't you see? We're all gonna be smashed into nothingness!* The great wave chides him, *It is you who do not see. You are not truly a wave, you are water. Your form may transform upon the rocks, but your existence is eternal.*"

Everyone sat absorbing his metaphor, the waves in the spring gently lapping.

Permi was the first to speak up. "OK, that's cool. I like that. So we're all part of the dance. All waves in the great cosmic ocean. But what do you think the water really is? What does it mean? You know, life, the universe, everything?"

"Forty-two," muttered Rob, but everyone ignored him. They were looking at Syd.

"Come on Permi, this isn't one of his philosophy classes," I said.

"That's OK, Gil," Syd answered. "It's a great question, and I'm happy to try my best to respond. But I'm afraid I never found an answer that really resonates. The closest, I think, was the opening chapter of the *Tao Te Jing*. You may know the first line, it goes, *Tao ke tao fei chang tao*, in Chinese."

"What does it mean?" asked Permi.

"It's a kind of ancient philosophical poem. This is my own translation of the first chapter—" He shut his eyes, reciting,

> The Tao that can be told, is not the true Tao.
> The name that can be named, is not the true name.
> The unnamed, is the origin of heaven and earth.
> Naming, is the mother of all things.
> Without desire, one views the source.
> Desiring, one views only the manifestations.
> The two are the same, but differ when named.
> Both are mysteries.
> The mystery of mysteries, is the way to pass through.

It sounded like something Pop woulda quoted, or maybe Ma—she'd always been into the Tao and all that—it was poetic, but what did it mean?

"Wow, that's deep," Permi said. "But in a way it doesn't say anything, does it? Just that the universe is a mystery we can't completely fathom."

"That's exactly why I'm drawn to it," said Syd. "But you mustn't take my translation too literally. Like a poem, this simple verse has many possible interpretations. Even the word *Tao* itself has many meanings. That's why there are so many different translations. Even among Chinese scholars, there's no consensus."

"So what does *Tao* mean?" asked Dylan, taking a long hit off a new bowl he'd just packed.

"It doesn't have just one meaning," repeated Syd. "*Tao* can refer to how you do something, a way, a process, or even the religion and teachings of Taoism. It's also used to refer to the balance between the male and female forces of *yang* and *yin*, which the Chinese believe struggle for dominance in the cosmos. *Tao* can also mean, the way, or the path."

"So in Chinese, the trail, the whole JMT, is the *Tao?*" asked Permi in profound stonedness.

"You could say that," said Syd. "The word for a path or trail is *Tao*."

"So we are following the *Tao!*" exclaimed Permi.

"I guess we are," replied Syd, looking off into the distance.

Jose finished translating. The stars shone brightly, and we all watched in awe as a shooting star streaked from east to west illuminating the sky.

At last Katie and Rob whispered something to each other and got up. "We have to go," she said.

"Yeah, long hike out tomorrow," said Rob.

They climbed out of the pool and like a party where one guest's leaving triggers a rush for the door, everyone started saying goodnight and exiting the pool—the glow of headlamps dancing across the meadow like fireflies.

Soon just Permi, Syd, and I remained.

Permi looked at Syd, "I'm sorry to hear about your cancer, man. I'm really sorry." He gave Syd a long hug. "Wait for me in the morning man, before you hit the trail."

"I was thinking of sleeping in anyway," Syd answered, which pleased me fine.

"I'll see you in the morning man," said Permi, who climbed over the rocks, gathered his stuff, and walked barefoot and naked in the cool night guided only by the light of the stars.

"What did you think about all that?" I asked Syd after Permi had gone.

"I think he had a point," said Syd.

"Who?" I asked.

"Permi."

"You mean about the cosmic seedpods?"

"No, not that. I mean about the trail—about all of life—being the *Tao*."

"Oh, I see. Personally, I liked Katie's idea about people all being spoiled children and Allan's idea about karma. I've really felt that way in my own life. Like some things that have gone wrong for me just happened 'cause of bad decisions I made. I like the idea that we can go around again and fix it, don't you?"

"That is appealing, yes. But in case that's not how it works, I think we have to do our best with what little time we have."

"Even if we are all just part of the water?"

"Even so," he said a bit uneasily.

"Do you think Rob'll really invent machines that'll replace us all?"

"It's hard to say. The desire to play God runs strong in many scientists and engineers, and it's hard to know where such innovation will lead. Often the good goes hand in hand with the bad, like medicine and overpopulation. It's hard to predict how change will affect the future. The best thing we can do is live our lives to their fullest now and be the best person we can."

I nodded. That sounded like something Ma would say.

Syd and I slid back down into the warm water and floated gently, watching the great wheel of stars circling slowly overhead.

DAY SEVEN

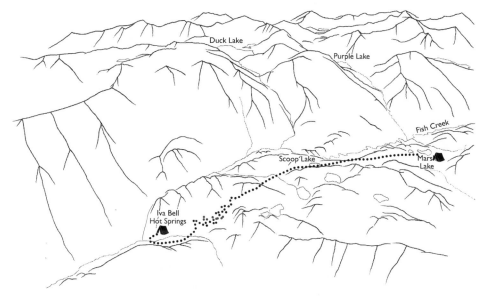

Iva Bell Hot Springs (7,380′) to Mars Lake (9,020′)
5 miles—1,940 feet elevation gain; 300 feet elevation loss

PERMI POPPED INTO THE CLEARING as Syd and I were cobbling together our breakfast. His tarp and Dylan's tent were long gone, and I'd assumed they'd already hiked on.

Permi held out a bulky orange stuff sack to Syd, "I gathered these for you man. I spent a month in the Cascades living with this shaman who taught me to harvest certain medicinal herbs. I couldn't find everything I wanted—some of the species here are different—but all the leaves and fungus and bark I gathered have strong healing, antioxidant, and hopefully anticancer properties, man. None of them are harmful or toxic. It's my gift to you. I've been gathering them all morning."

Syd smiled, accepting the bag and giving Permi a warm hug. "Thank you, Permi. How do you use them?"

"You grind up a small pinch of each between your fingers, like this," he explained, carefully removing the small clippings one by one and rubbing a bit of each into a fine powder that he collected in a bandana. "Next you twist up the bandana and soak it in hot water for about ten minutes, like a tea bag. Drink the liquid but discard the rest. You can flavor it with a bit of tea if you like."

"Thank you, it's a sacred gift."

"I hope it helps, man," said Permi, handing Syd a 35-mm film canister and adding, "Dylan told me to give you this."

"Please thank him for me," said Syd, tucking both away carefully in his pack.

"Dylan and I are heading up to Purple Lake to rejoin the trail. He's a bit slower, so he took off a couple of hours ago. He would have given it to you himself, but we wanted to let you sleep."

Syd smiled gratefully.

"Oh, and check this out, Gil," he said, opening another small sack of leaves, and holding up a hairy green oval-shaped one.

"What's that for, salad?"

"No man! You wouldn't want to eat this! It's turkey mullein. I found a patch growing up by the stream. I've always wanted to try it. The Native Americans used to crush it up and drop it in the water to stun the fish. Well, I gotta go, man. Gotta catch up with Dylan."

Syd sprinkled some of his tea leaves among the herbs, then soaked it for a while in his boiling water. "It's a bit bitter," he announced, "but the Chinese say, *Good medicine is bitter on the lips*," and he slowly finished the cup.

"Are we also going to Purple Lake today?"

"Not unless you want to. That's a hard trail. There's a difficult river crossing and a lot of exposed uphill. Your father and I did it in reverse once."

It didn't sound good, especially the river crossing.

He pulled out his map. "If instead, we head up the west rim of Cascade Valley," he showed me, "we can rejoin the JMT just below Silver Pass. I think we should take it a bit easier today, going only about five miles, and stopping here tonight," he said indicating a small lake on the map with his finger, "at . . . Mars Lake."

"I like the name Mars. He was the Roman God of War, right? If the lake is good enough for a god, then it's good enough for me! The way my head feels now, a short day would be perfect."

Heading back down the hill, we took the spur we'd passed yesterday. The way was lined with large ferns and shaded by a canopy of high trees. It quickly began ascending a steep cliff face. Climbing didn't help my hangover any. Syd musta been feeling it too. The two of us crept up the switchbacks like snails wading through peanut butter.

"Syd, when you and Pop came here before, did you guys get stoned?"

He stopped and looked at me seriously, as if weighing his answer. Finally replying, "Yes, we did. But don't misunderstand. Your father and I used pot as a kind of medicine, like Permi's herbs, to help us connect better to our inner selves and the world around us. We never used it for entertainment or escape."

I nodded. He had a point. My first experimentation with pot had been truly mind-blowing—a whole new world opening up to me. But after Pop's death, when I'd moved into the frat house and started getting stoned most weekends, it lost most of its magic and had just become something to do, like drinking. Smoking in the springs had reminded me of just how spiritual pot could be.

We climbed on, the shovel on his pack swinging like a pendulum.

"Hey Syd," I said when we stopped again, "you never did tell me what that shovel is for."

"Eh—" he stammered, shifting his weight uneasily.

"It can't be your poo trowel—no one makes *that* much shit."

"Yeah," he started slowly, "actually, the shovel is for you."

"For me? Why?"

"In case I don't make it. You'll need it to bury me with."

We both stood uneasily, the sunlight breaking through the canopy.

"*No fucking way!* If there's even a chance your gonna die out here, we're going back."

"There's always been a chance—"

"*—and when exactly were you planning to tell me this?*"

"I was planning to tell you after Donohue, after we'd spent some time together. But then you wanted to go back, so I figured it didn't matter. After that, I was just waiting for the right time—"

"*The right time?! The right time woulda been in Fresno before we left! Now what the fuck are we gonna do? I lost Pop in the wilderness—there's no way I'm going through all that again!*"

"You don't understand. I do think I can make it, and I have to try. This is my last hope. I want to walk across the Sierra and see Muir's Range of Light, to do something purposeful with the time I have left."

I stood rooted to the spot, arms akimbo.

"I love these mountains and I want to see the trail through to the end. But if I do die out here, I want to be buried in the wilderness. Don't call search and rescue, or a helicopter, or a ranger, or even ask for help from other hikers. They'll just want to bring my body back to civilization. I don't want some expensive coffin and funeral, only to be stuffed into a parking lot full of graves. Find a nice spot, far away from the trail—overlooking a meadow or a mountain or a lake if you can—and bury me there. It's my last request. I don't plan to die out here, but if I do, I want you to do this for me." He looked at me with those eyes.

I turned away. Did his family have an inkling of what he was planning? Is that why Cass had been so upset? I'd been on the swim team, and yet I hadn't been there to save Pop. Now he was asking me this? Could I live with yet another death on my hands? Or was all of this like Allan had said? Was it my karma to help him 'cause I hadn't been there for Pop? Was this what I deserved? Like never really being able to get into a meaningful relationship?

Slowly I summoned my inner strength. Letting my arms fall, I turned back vowing, "OK, I'll keep going—but try to promise me that you won't die out here. Promise me that if you feel the least bit sick, or think you can't make it, that we're going to find help, or hike out of here together. If you do die—and I hope it's years from now—you can hold your funeral in the wilderness then. But right now, promise me that if you're in trouble, you'll tell me and we'll go back."

He nodded his assent. "It's my final wish to see the sunrise from the top of Mount Whitney after hiking the trail. I'm going to do my damnedest to make it. I promise."

We stood for a time. Finally, I broke the standoff, "OK, keep the damn shovel, but you better not need it! Maybe the extra weight will be good training or something, and we can always use it if we have an extra-large poo to bury, right?"

He smiled. "If anyone asks, tell them I volunteer for the Forest Service and the shovel is for breaking up illegal fire rings."

I nodded and we hiked on, huffing up the hill in an awkward silence, the shovel swinging back and forth like a ticking clock.

The trail here was poorly maintained and it was hard going. In a number of spots we had to scramble up crumbling slopes to avoid fallen trees. The route climbed steeply upward, roughly following the course of a tumbling stream. Eventually the trail forded it, and we had to balance on the slippery rocks to keep from falling into the knee-deep water.

"What makes a hot springs hot?" I asked, tired of the heavy silence between us.

"I'm no geologist, but as I understand it, hot springs are heated when water in an underground spring passes over hot rocks or magma in areas of volcanic activity."

"Wait, there are no volcanoes here."

"Mammoth Mountain and many of the surrounding peaks are all dormant volcanoes."

"Then why do people ski on it?"

"It's not active like the ones in Hawaii. Mammoth erupted thousands of years ago, but there are still volcanic vents and a number of hot springs around it. I suppose it might explode someday, like Mount Saint Helens did, but I'd imagine the chances of that are pretty slim."

"I had no idea. I guess the rocks there do look volcanic, but I just thought that was a coincidence, or something. So then was last night really safe? Couldn't the water suddenly start boiling, turning everyone into soup, or something?"

He chuckled, "There are some pools in Lassen and Yellowstone that are too hot to soak in, or that can suddenly become geysers, but not this one. As far as I know, Iva Bell is pretty safe."

"Although," he added matter-of-factly, "there is a rare brain-eating amoeba that lives in some hot springs, which enters through your nose—so you should never suck the water up your nose while soaking, just to be safe."

Was he kidding? Probably not. Had I submerged my head last night? Had I gotten water up my nose? I couldn't remember.

We continued up the long switchbacks. It seemed like there was no end to this climb. The only consolation was that the trail here was shady.

My head still ached. Was I hungover, or had I sucked some microscopic creature up my nose, and it was now slowly eating my brain? Was I turning into a real living zombie?

"What about the sulfur in hot springs?" I asked. "Doesn't that kill bacteria and stuff?"

"It does, that's one reason soaking in hot springs has been used for ages as a cure for various illnesses. But I don't think it harms the amoeba, although you'd really have to ask an expert to be certain. My son Sean would probably know. We could ask him when we get back."

"So what are the symptoms, I mean, if someone gets one of these mind-eating things?"

"Headaches, dizziness, confusion, nausea—just what you'd expect, I think."

My head began to feel dizzy.

"Is there a treatment?" *Maybe I could take some aspirin, or snort salt water, or something.*

"None that I'm aware of, most victims die within a week."

A week? But we're way out here in the woods! What would I do?

"There really isn't anything to worry about. There are only a few cases a year in the United States."

Maybe I was overreacting? "I'm sure it's fine. I'm sure I don't have a brain-eating amoeba in my nose. It's just that I was really traumatized by *Dawn of the Dead* as a kid, so I really don't like hearing about brain-eating anythings."

"I never really cared for that kind of film either."

What would I do if I really had a brain-eating amoeba?

The switchbacks had grown progressively steep. The trail was still shaded, but the trees were starting to thin out.

Was I being unreasonably paranoid? Then it hit me, and I stopped in my tracks. I was feeling paranoid about some million-to-one amoeba, while Syd had a genuine one-to-one chance of dying from a very real cancer. The way I felt about the amoeba must be how he felt every day. I looked at him, holding back the emotions that were welling up inside me.

He heard me stop and turned. "Are you alright?" he asked with some concern.

I longed to tell him what I was feeling but held back. He wasn't Pop. "Sorry, I'm just tired I guess."

"It's a difficult climb. Let's take a break."

We dropped our packs, resting on the trunk of a fallen tree in the shade. The damp smell of humus pervading my nostrils. I stared at his cold metal shovel. How could he push on day after day like this, knowing that any moment could be his last? I'd have been a wreck.

"How can you be so calm, Syd?"

"What do you mean?"

"You're dying inside, and yet you seem so normal."

"Don't let my quiet exterior fool you. I've been through a lot of emotional ups and downs. I struggle with it every day."

We sat chewing our bars.

He looked at me, "Philosophically of course, we're all dying. We're all going to face it sooner or later, but most of us treat death like some dreaded term-paper. We procrastinate and procrastinate, putting off thinking about it until close to the end."

That was me.

"In our culture, death is a taboo. Think about how difficult it is to say something meaningful to someone who's lost a loved one. About the best we can muster is, *I'm sorry about your loss.* And we prefer to send it in a card if we can. People who are dying are shunned—just at the moment when they need people the most."

He was right. After Pop died it was like I had the plague or something. My friends avoided me. Samantha dumped me. Even my roommates had been so sickly polite that I'd eventually moved out. That's why I'd joined that stupid frat. And then the real problems started—*but wasn't that what I deserved for abandoning Pop?*

"In some cultures, death is accepted and embraced as a part of life. The Mexicans, for example, ritualize death and include it in many of their fiestas. Most traditional cultures show an increasing respect for their elders. But here, we treat aging like a disease, banishing our elders to the care of strangers. I've even heard children dismissing their own parents saying, *You're too old to understand!*"

"I may have said that to Pop once or twice."

"I was probably no different," he said glancing down. "In this culture, when someone gets cancer the first thing we tell them is to *try and fight it.* That we can *win the battle against cancer.*"

"Like, *the war on breast cancer?*"

"But if they lose the fight, do we then blame the victim? Worse still, making an illness into the enemy objectifies it, turning it into something alien, something to be feared. It makes most people shun those who are really sick."

I'd never thought about it before, but wasn't that how I'd been treating Syd? Didn't all those purple blotches on his skin make me turn away?

"When I first got sick, most people encouraged me *to fight my cancer.* But when I was diagnosed as terminal, all but a few friends and relations disappeared. When I was most in need of support, that's when most of the people I knew turned away."

"I'm here," I said meekly.

"I know you are." He put his hand on my shoulder. "I'm glad you're with me."

His hand was comforting. I wanted to hug him like I woulda with Pop, but hesitated. He took his hand back, leaving me feeling empty.

"Are you afraid of death?" I asked.

"Yes, very much so."

"What about that story you told in the springs, about the wave? That we're all water? Don't you believe that?"

"Sometimes," he said staring off into the distance. "Sometimes I think about that and it gives me comfort. But I'm still afraid. Perhaps I cling too much to this form."

What had Pop felt when he died? I would never know what he had gone through in those last few moments. But Pop loved life. Besides, his case was different. He hadn't expected to die. Maybe it was better to go like Pop had, without warning.

Syd looked at me, "We're all dying, Gil. It's just that for most, it seems so distant. Most people live their lives planning and working for things they hope to achieve later on."

Pop certainly had many plans he never got to finish, including raising me.

"But how many people pause to ask, *How would I live my life if I knew today was my last?* That's the question the Buddhists ask, and it's an important one. That's what dying has taught me—to live each day as if it were my last, without regret."

Pop musta had regrets. I certainly did. I'd never even told him that I loved him.

Syd looked at me and asked, "What would you do if you knew today was your last?"

"I certainly wouldn't climb this hill."

A hint of a smile crossed his face, but he held my gaze. "Seriously, suppose you were home in LA, what would you do?"

The question was like one of those irritating essays teachers always made you write. Rattling off the first things that came to mind, I said, "I'd probably rob a bank, try sky-diving, have some really good food, maybe go to Paris, or hook back up with this chick I was seeing."

"Are those things really the things you value? How would money help you if you were dying? Skydiving and seeing Paris are both things you should try, but what is really important to you Gil? Is 'hooking up' really that important? Think about it seriously for a moment."

The image of Pop came back to me. The one thing I wished was to go back in time and see him again. To do things over. But Syd would just say that's impossible. What would I really do? Then it hit me, "I would go see Ma."

Why was it we thought so much about the people who were gone, and so little about the ones who were here?

Syd smiled, nodding his head slowly, "I think what people cherish most is love, family, and community. There'd be a lot more compassion in the world if people spent time meditating on what is truly important to them."

"But that's not what you're doing. You're out here hiking the trail. Doing something for yourself, instead of being with family."

"I've already made my peace and shared my love with my family and friends. Now it's time to do something for myself, while I still can."

That's probably not how Cass would see it.

I thought about Ma. I would go and see her when I got back. When was the last time I'd told her that I loved her? Probably at Pop's funeral, but I couldn't remember. *That whole thing was supposed to give us something like closure, but it'd been a farce*—from the empty casket costing the same as a real burial, to all those people showing up from his school out of obligation. I was gonna give a speech, but after listening to everyone say things as unreal as his empty coffin, I just couldn't. *None of them really knew Pop the way I had*—except of course Ma.

"Shall we finish climbing this hill?" I asked, reaching for my pack.

As if I'd flipped a switch, Syd's contemplative expression vanished. He got up, and we started back up the slope.

Why hadn't Syd flown out for the funeral? He and Pop had been best friends right up until the accident. When I'd asked Syd about it up at Thousand Island Lake, he'd said, "health reasons," but that didn't make sense—he hadn't gotten his cancer until much later and they'd even met up before Ma and Pop went off on their trip. Had they had a falling out or something? Did it have something to do with Ma or me? I wanted to know the whole story, but it just didn't seem my place to ask again.

An hour or so later, the climb leveled out. The terrain became grassier and the trees less dense. We passed a junction and a small muddy-looking pond that Syd said was Scoop Lake. Eventually we came to the base of a small hill. On top was a large boulder, there was nowhere it coulda rolled down from.

"How did this huge boulder get way up here?" I asked. "Don't tell me it was pushed up by Sisyphus!"

He laughed. "It's probably a glacial erratic, deposited here by a receding glacier. The first couple of essays in the Muir book I lent you discuss the formation of the Sierra Nevada and their sculpting out by glaciers. You might find them interesting."

Crossing a wide expanse, we came to another small hill.

"Mars Lake should be just over this rise," he declared.

That was good news, 'cause I was exhausted from the climb and the heavy conversation. It would be nice to just relax by some glorious blue lake. One fit for a Roman god.

Over the top, we got our first glimpse of Mars Lake. It was not the bold blue alpine lake overlooking some majestic vista that I'd anticipated from its name. Nor was it like some opulent Roman bath. Instead, it was a wide shallow muddy-looking disappointment of a lake, surrounded by tall reedy grass. I almost expected Yoda to pop out declaring, *"Mudhole? Slimy? My home this is!"*

By the shore was a flat area with an old fire pit. It looked like an awful place to camp. Even gathering water without stepping into the mud would be a chore.

"What do you think?" asked Syd. "Maybe we should go on another two miles to Grassy Lake and see how that is?"

This spot looked miserable. But two more miles? I was beat. And Grassy Lake didn't sound that promising either.

"This is where we planned to camp, let's just stay here."

We set up our shelters and got out our cooking gear. The sun was at the treetops when, as if the God of War had orchestrated a sneak attack for dusk, we were suddenly beset upon by buzzing hordes of swarming insects. Swatting frantically, it was impossible to miss hitting eight or ten of them with each blow!

"Put on your rain gear!" commanded Syd, hurriedly pulling on his own plastic pants and jacket. Whipping out the thin yellow Chargers poncho I'd brought, I wrapped myself in it as best I could. Syd passed me some mosquito repellent, and I applied it liberally to my face and hands, but it hardly proved a barrier to Mars's onslaughting minions.

Huddled miserably with only our rain gear for protection, we hurriedly boiled water while armies of insects engulfed us. Every few seconds I had to pick out a daring soldier who'd gotten too close to my water and drowned.

When it finally boiled, I poured it into the plastic pouch of my Backwoods Buffet dinner, and after only a minute or two, wolfed down the still crunchy noodles. Syd ate swiftly too.

Swallowing the last of my noodles, I hurriedly cleaned up, then darted for the safety of my tent—clouds of hungry mozzies at my heels.

Inside, I pulled my feet in, boots still on, and like a madman zipped the door shut. At least twelve of the horrid creatures had infiltrated my defenses—buzzing around my head, looking for a chance to claim first blood.

Like Bruce Lee wielding his nunchuks in *Fist of Fury*, I struck at them with an old sock. Several leaving a streak of my own blood—a small sacrifice to Mars—against the tent wall. The floor became littered with their corpses. Outside the tent came the droning of fresh warriors. Soldiers in a war of attrition I could never hope to win.

Syd's voice came from his neighboring bivy, "Gil, there's a Chinese saying for situations like this: *Among the thirty-six ancient stratagems of war, the best choice is running away!* I think we should pack up well before dawn and escape. I'm setting my watch alarm for four-thirty."

"Sounds like a plan!" I shouted back. I could never have imagined waking up at that hour for anything. But then these weren't ordinary circumstances. Scenes from *Monty Python and the Holy Grail* with the knights fleeing while crying, *"Run away!"* filled my head.

Peering out under the tent flap, I watched the ranks of the dark army parading around my shelter. I was trapped deep behind enemy lines. It was too early to sleep, so I sat up thinking about war movies. Then slowly, I felt the need to pee.

But what could I do? The legions of Mars were massing outside my tent! A dozen scouts had snuck under the rain fly and were standing at the ready, rubbing their little hind legs together in eager anticipation, waiting to alert their comrades should I emerge from my foxhole.

I held back the urge. I resisted. But the more I struggled, the stronger the need grew, until I was practically bursting.

And then I did something I never thought possible. Pulling out my new Jetboil cookpot, I unzipped my pants and peed—careful not to miss even a drop, lest it land on the tent floor or my sleeping bag.

Making a tiny opening in the tent door, I thrust the reeking pot out as far as I could, dumping its steaming contents onto the ground. Swiftly drawing back my hand, I rinsed the pot with my bottle, quickly tossing the rinse water out after my pee and zipping up the tent. Running the searchlight of my headlamp up and down the walls, I made certain no clever enemy agent had infiltrated my defenses.

The scent of pee and moist earth wafted in from outside. At least having marked my territory, I'd be safe from marauding bears.

Relieved, I set the tainted pot as far away as possible, and using my headlamp, began studying the map, examining the route for tomorrow. Suddenly I saw our mistake—this wasn't the realm of the God of War, this was just a horrid mudhole.

"Hey Syd, look at your map!" I called to him in his bivy.

The light of his headlamp came on. There was a rustling of papers, then a voice called out, "Yeah?"

"Look at the name of the lake—right next to *Mars*."

"I don't see what you're talking about?"

"There's an *h*," I said, "obscured by a trail line."

"Oh my!" he replied. "You're right. I'm sorry. If I had known—"

"It's OK, we both missed it."

There on the map, with the faint blue letter *h* of the name obscured by a dashed trail line, it read, *Marsh Lake*.

DAY EIGHT

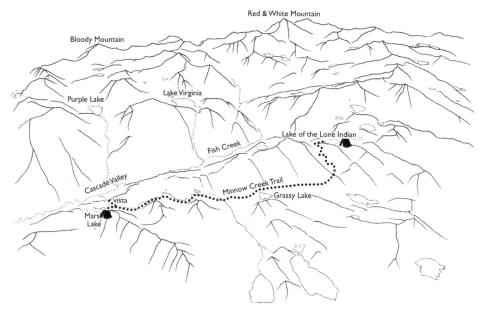

Marsh Lake (9,020′) to Lake of the Lone Indian (10,220′)
6 miles—1,420 feet elevation gain; 220 feet elevation loss

S TARS WERE TWINKLING in the predawn twilight as we made our escape from the slumbering minions of the lake.

With no sign of pursuit, we reached a junction. Syd led us down the left-hand branch, which paralleled a gentle stream, until we came to a rocky ledge at the edge of a great chasm. Here the stream picked up speed, racing through a narrow gorge before dancing over the wall in tumbling cascades.

Before us was a gaping mountain valley, maybe two thousand feet deep, and over a mile across. On the opposite wall, a broad white cataract snaked down from between a gap in the peaks. Far below, the green ribbon of a river wound its way through the trees on the valley floor. The sun had just crested the far ridge, its yellow-orange rays reflecting off the river like sparkling crystals. Beyond the far wall rose the silhouettes of distant mountains. Below us, a hawk circled in lazy spirals.

"That's Cascade Valley," proclaimed Syd, "I wanted you to see it." He pointed across, "Do you see those switchbacks winding up the far side?"

Squinting, I could just make out the pencil line of a trail zigzagging up the wall to the left of the cataract. "I hope we're not going *that* way."

"No, that trail leads up to Purple Lake. That's the way Permi and Dylan went yesterday. The JMT runs along the rim above it."

So this was the valley he'd shown me on the map.

"Years ago, your father and I hiked from Mammoth Lakes over those mountains—" he said pointing vaguely into the distance "—to the bottom of this valley, and then down to the hot springs."

"You can get to the hot springs from down there?"

"There's another trail along the valley floor. From the springs, your father and I hiked out to Reds Meadow. There's a really nice swimming hole down there," he said pointing at the river.

"It's a beautiful valley. Last night when we were trapped in our tents, I read that section of the Muir book you suggested. His image of snowflakes carving out valleys like this really struck me."

"*Tender snow-flowers noiselessly falling through unnumbered centuries, laboring harmoniously in united strength crushed and ground and wore away the rocks in their march, fashioning the landscapes into the delightful variety of hill and dale and lordly mountain that mortals call beauty.*"

"How do you remember all that?"

"I taught a course on Muir—"

"Do you think this valley was carved out by glaciers?"

"I believe so. The walls are roughly U-shaped, which is what a glacial valley looks like. A river valley is generally rough and V-shaped."

"I feel so small standing here, like an atom on the edge of a vast abyss."

"You're becoming quite literary."

"I think a bit of Muir rubbed off on me last night. He's a really beautiful writer, you know."

"Your father would have been proud to hear that." He put his hand on my shoulder, and we stood there together, breathing in the view.

Looking out over the valley gave me a sense of peace and reverence. There was something beyond myself here, something grander. Muir saw God in nature, and I could feel why. Staring at this valley was like looking up at the stars, only more direct. It was like viewing a creation fresh from God's workshop.

After what seemed like ages, Syd lifted his hand from my shoulder, breaking the spell. My pack, which seemed weightless before, suddenly pressed down on me, and everything from our talk the day before came flooding back.

"Syd," I asked, "in case—you know—I was just wondering about your religion. Are you Jewish, Christian, or what?"

"I'm a little bit of everything, I like to hedge my bets."

"What I mean is—I wouldn't know what to say, or what rites to perform, or—"

"Just say and do whatever comes from your heart. Only promise me one thing: If I do die out here, if you do have to bury me—let my kids know what happened, but first finish the trail."

Gazing across the vast abyss before us, I said nothing. *Finish the trail?* That was the last thing on my mind. *Shit—why had I even brought up religion?*

Turning back, we returned to the junction, taking the other fork south.

Was he really planning to die out here? I couldn't even imagine burying him—*was that even legal?*—let alone doing the trail without him.

We began to climb following the stream, and yet for the first time my legs didn't hurt. Maybe it'd been the hot springs, or that passage by Muir, but I was starting to feel something meditative, almost reflective in hiking. *Still, it didn't mean I wanted to finish the damn trail—that was Syd's dream, not mine.* Rather than talk about it, I walked on.

The path grew rougher, and Syd had to scout around to figure out where it went. After a few miles, we came to Grassy Lake. It was good we hadn't continued yesterday. Although a bit more attractive, this lake looked just as mosquito ridden as Marsh Lake. The bugs seemed to be sleeping, but I knew they were here somewhere, lurking like vampires in their hidden lairs, waiting to emerge at dusk.

Rounding the lake, we came upon a party of seven fishermen, each carrying a long pole and a tiny backpack. They were headed down to Cascade Valley. We greeted them in passing, neither party wanting to tarry long, lest they tempt the sleeping mosquitos.

After they went by, I said, "They're traveling light."

"They must be going 'ultralight,' catching fish and foraging, or perhaps sleeping as Muir did—on a bed of pine needles beneath a mountain bough."

Syd was just launching into an explanation of how Muir used to travel with little more than bread and tea, when a train of six horses led by a packer came clomping down the trail. The animals were heavily laden with gear, including large Coleman coolers and folding tables. We soon learned this was the supply train of the seven fishermen.

Syd let go of his lecture and after the dust settled, we continued on. At least with a string of little "trail bombs" left behind by the horses, we no longer had to hunt around to find our way.

Soon it got hilly again, and we began climbing long lazy switchbacks up a rocky ridge. Each time it seemed we'd come to the last one, it turned out there was another ridge lurking beyond. This went on for hours, although in truth it may have been less. Time seems to slow down when you're expecting something—like the way the last hour on a long airplane flight always feels the longest.

At last we reached the summit. The view soon opened up and we could see peak after snowcapped peak rolling off into the distance. Before us was a small mountain valley surrounding a pear-shaped lake, its sapphire waters sparkled invitingly. A silvery quarter-moon hung in the sky. The trail curved down in a long arc to the sandy lakeshore several hundred feet below. Another branch of the trail continued up and over the far ridge, and presumably on to Silver Pass. A short distance up from the lakeshore were a pair of tents. Close by were two tiny figures fishing at the shore.

"That's the Lake of the Lone Indian," declared Syd. "We'll camp there tonight and head over the pass in the morning."

I wasn't tired yet but stopping early sounded good.

Syd hobbled a bit. "It's my knee," he said. "It wasn't bothering me too much before, but sometimes it gives me trouble on steep descents like this." He leaned heavily into his trekking poles as we slowly descended.

When we reached the shore, I could see both fishermen. The guy on the left was over six feet tall and built like a linebacker, with a wild springy Afro that extended at least eight inches from his head.

His companion was shorter and more actively engaged in his sport, repeatedly casting out his line. He had long tightly braided dreadlocks and was trim and muscular, looking like a model for a line of athletic equipment.

Both had on high-tops and were too well-dressed to be JMT hikers. Letting his line bob in the water, the taller one waved as we approached. "Didn't think we'd see anyone else way out here," he said in a deep bass voice. "Where are you both hiking in from?"

"The Muir trail," I replied. They'd already caught two rather large trout. Having skipped breakfast, the only thing we'd had to eat all day had been cold bars, my mouth started watering as I pictured the fish roasting slowly over a fire. "Looks like you guys are having some luck, have you been out here long?"

"Not long, we arrived a little before noon. I'm Phil, and this is Mike."

Mike, who was busy reeling in his line, turned away from his fishing to say hello, but in doing so, tangled his line around his pole, then swore to himself under his breath as he tried to undo it saying, "Hi, nice to meet you both, sorry I can't shake hands right now." He began frantically twisting the pole back and forth, trying to unwrap the tangled filament.

"Do you guys mind if we camp in that spot down the lake next to yours?" I asked.

"Not at all," Phil replied.

"It'll be nice to have some company at dinner," added Mike.

"Great," I said, "and if you catch more fish than you can eat, save some for us!"

"Not likely," groaned Mike who was still struggling to untangle his line. "So far, we've only caught these two."

"*I've* caught these two," Phil corrected him.

"Hey! Whose pole is it anyway?" asked Mike, tugging more vigorously on his tangled line.

"Yours," replied Phil in his deep resonant voice, "but I'm the one who caught them."

"With *my* pole and *my* PowerBait," declared Mike, his voice rising slightly.

"True," acknowledged Phil, "but it was still my catch."

"And you said you didn't like fishing," said Mike, who had just freed his line and started to reel it in again.

"It's true. I told you. I don't like fishing," Phil said levelly.

"Well, you're gonna like *these* fish, I can tell you that," said Mike.

"That I will," Phil said nodding.

Their trout looked really good, and I caught myself licking my lips. *Shit, why hadn't I brought a pole?*

Syd and I continued to a set of campsites just up from the beach. We set up our tents and did some well-needed laundry. We were about to kick back in the sun when we saw two more hikers. As they approached, we recognized the familiar faces of Lois and Clark.

"Where are you two coming from?" Syd asked.

"Tully Hole," said Lois, looking tired.

"But we camped last night at Lake Virginia," explained Clark. "It's been a long day."

Both Tully Hole and Lake Virginia were back along the part of the JMT we'd skipped.

"How come you're camping here then?" asked Syd. "This is a bit off-trail, isn't it?"

"We're headed over Goodale Pass to VVR tomorrow," said Lois. "When we saw this lake, we decided it was too nice to pass up."

"Did you see the size of the trout those guys caught?" asked Clark.

"Yeah," I said, my mouth watering again. "I hope they catch enough for everyone."

"Well, they've gotten two big ones already!" exclaimed Clark excitedly. My heart sank. They hadn't caught any more in the two hours since we'd passed them, so they probably wouldn't have any to share. But I kept my mouth shut, not wanting to jinx it.

"Do you mind if we camp on that bluff above you guys?" asked Lois.

"Not at all," said Syd. "I hiked up there earlier. There's a large flat space and some logs set around an old fire pit."

"Maybe we can all meet up there and have a group dinner?" I suggested.

"Sounds great!" Clark smiled.

"Sure!" Lois agreed.

About an hour-and-a-half later, we all gathered on the bluff for dinner. Phil and Mike joined us, and the six of us sat in a circle preparing our respective meals.

Syd watched puzzled as I fastidiously scrubbed out my cookpot, boiling a full pot of water, only to discard it before preparing my meal.

"How are those Backwoods Buffet things?" Clark asked.

"They're not half-bad," I said, pausing for effect, "they're *all* bad."

Clark laughed.

Phil and Mike had caught just the two trout and were arguing about the best way to cook them over a backpacking stove. Phil wanted to steam them in a pot, but Mike was insisting the only proper way was to grill them.

"And where exactly are we going to find a grill out here?" Phil was asking.

"We can grill it over the stove, using a stick," explained Mike.

"You want me to run a stick from each fish's mouth to its sphincter?" asked Phil. "And aside from where we're going to get these sticks—I mean ones that aren't made of pine and all covered with sap—are you then just going to hold them over the stove with your bare hands?"

"Man, they'll be on *sticks*," said Mike, who looking around seemed to notice for the first time that the only trees up here were small pines. "OK, have it your way, steam them," he surrendered, "but when we get home, I'm taking you out to that Korean barbeque joint I've been telling you about."

"We are *not* eating Korean barbeque," declared Phil.

"And just why not?" asked Mike.

"Because it'll take a week of having you do pike jumps just to work off all that fat and sugar, that's why not."

"Hey man, who are you, my mother? You can't tell me what to eat!"

"Yeah, but I'm the one who's gonna have to push your ass through extra training if you *do* eat all that sugar-coated beef, not to mention the beer."

"Hey, who said anything about beer?"

And so it went between them. Their whole conversation about Korean barbeque making my Backwoods stroganoff taste more and more like lumpy floor wax.

Syd was cooking some pad thai noodles, and they also smelled delicious.

"How's your stroganoff?" he asked.

"Great," I mumbled under my breath as I chewed, "just like epoxy glue."

Lois was making enchiladas with rehydrated beans covered in a kinda red sauce they'd dehydrated, with real cheese Clark said was freeze-dried. They smelled amazing and only served to make my meal that much worse. Why hadn't I listened when that salesgirl at REI told me I should try my meals first?

"So, is it your mother or father who taught you how to cook that?" I asked Lois.

"My father," she answered, "he's the one from Mexico."

"That's unusual," I said, "isn't it typically the guy who's White, and the woman who's Mexican?"

"That's totally racist!" interjected Mike almost jumping to his feet. "Why can't a Mexican guy marry a White woman? Why do you guys always assume it's the White guy that marries some non-white woman? What's wrong with the other way round?"

"I don't know—" I said, caught a bit off guard. "What about your parents?" I asked Clark, trying to divert Mike's line of fire.

Clark gave me a strange look, then said, "My dad's Mexican and my mom's White."

That's odd—but that's probably why they made such a good couple. I let it go and focused on chewing on my food, avoiding Mike's critical gaze. Lois and Clark had set up two tents, which also struck me as strange. Why would a couple sleep apart, given the weight of an extra tent? Maybe Clark snored or Lois wanted her own space? She was pretty bossy. She had Clark make dinner, fetch water, open her bear canister, and even move logs for them as chairs. If she wasn't sleeping with him, why was he acting like such a dog? Maybe I should have a little man-to-man chat with Clark?

Syd turned to Mike and Phil asking, "Which way did you guys hike in?"

"We came from Vermilion," said Mike.

"We're making a loop," Phil explained. "We started where the ferry drops you off by Lake Edison. Then we hiked up here over Silver Pass. Tomorrow we're headed over Goodale Pass back to Vermilion."

"How did you guys hear about this place?" asked Clark.

"I'm a trainer at a gym near Long Beach," said Phil. "One of my clients, this older guy named Nathan, told me about it."

"Man, that dude's never gonna get rid of his belly," declared Mike. "He eats way too many carbs! And that guy never shuts up about noodles—"

"The thing is," Phil interrupted, "he's really into backpacking, and he suggested that if Mike and I wanted to do some hiking—"

"And fishing!" interjected Mike.

"*You* wanted to do the fishing," said Phil.

"Hey, who's eating them?" Mike asked.

"Who caught them?" said Phil. "Anyway, Nathan suggested we check out the area around Mono Hot Springs and Vermilion—"

"That place is awesome!" said Mike.

Vermilion, or VVR, as everyone called it, was a place where you could shower, resupply, camp, and get really great food. Supposedly they held an outdoor barbeque party every Wednesday and Saturday night that had quite the reputation. Many of the hikers we'd met, including Clark and Lois, were headed there, but Syd wanted to skip it.

"I've been to Vermilion," Syd had said, "and while they have great food, I'm really on a spiritual journey. I don't want to stop somewhere where there's a road, car-campers, and a lot of drinking." Those things all sounded to me like good reasons to go there.

"You all have to check it out," Mike declared, "they have amazing ribs, and every kind of microbrew—"

"Which you will *not* have more than one of when we get back," chided Phil.

"And there's this ferry boat that takes you across the lake. Plus, there's Mono Hot Springs, where there's also good fishing and a bunch of naturally hot pools you can soak in," Mike concluded like a salesman.

Lois turned to him, "If you guys are there, can you give Clark a ride to the hot springs? My friend is supposed to be meeting us there, but he only has a two-seater."

Clark didn't say a word. Not even a shudder. If Lois had been my girlfriend, I'd have dumped her right there! *Why was he letting her drag him like a dog across the fucking mountains, only so she could hang out with someone else? And making Clark sit in someone else's car like a spare tire?* It was too much! But Clark just sat there like a rock, ignoring her blatant infidelity.

"Sure," said Mike, "we can give Clark a ride."

Phil glared at him, "So now you're volunteering *my* car?"

"Who drove it all the way here from LA?" Mike asked.

"Still, it's *my* vehicle."

"I'm just saying—" Mike started.

"But we'd be happy to take Clark to the hot springs," interrupted Phil, giving Lois a warm smile, while eyeing Mike with his peripheral vision.

"So, you're a trainer, Phil," Syd said. "And what do you do?" he asked Mike.

"I'm a kickboxer," Mike declared proudly, "and I train people in boxing as well."

"You mean like *lucha libre?*" asked Clark excitedly, and he stood up singing, "*I am I am, I am I am!*" while dancing in place and waving his arms in the air like Rocky. He was singing the theme song, "Hombre Religioso," from Jack Black's classic *Nacho Libre*. I'd seen that movie at least a dozen times and even had the soundtrack to it. The song promptly got stuck in my head.

"No," said Mike, "that's *Mexican wrestling*. I'm a professional boxer. I fight in Vegas and places like that."

Lois gave Clark a look and he stopped singing and sat back down.

"You're a lightweight?" I asked, trying to make conversation.

At this Mike almost leapt up, complaining to Phil, "Man, why does everyone think I'm so small?"

"He's a *welterweight*," Phil intercepted Mike's anger, "but he looks smaller, so his opponents underestimate him, and then he kicks their ass."

"That's right!" proclaimed Mike and we all went back to working on our meals.

After a while, Clark spoke up. "I have a question for you guys, and I hope you don't mind me asking this, but why is it we never see any Black backpackers?"

"What are we?" snapped Mike.

"No, seriously," Clark said earnestly. "I mean, we've been on the trail for a week. And I've done lots of backpacking before. And we've met plenty of other Latinos and Asians and White people, and lots of foreigners too. But you're the first Black people I've ever met in the wilderness."

"It's because we're all hidden. We blend in with the trees," said Phil sarcastically.

"No seriously," Clark insisted, "I've been thinking about this for a long time."

"For one," answered Mike, "a lot of Black people have to support their families. We can't afford to just take off to the woods for a week or two whenever we want, and then there's the cost of all the equipment and shit."

"My client lent us the backpacks and tents," explained Phil.

"But also, it's not really in our culture," Mike went on. "I mean, I'm the first person in my family to even travel and shit."

"Just one generation ago," explained Phil, "it was illegal for a Black person to spend the night in most hotels, so our folks never experienced traveling like yours probably did."

"Yeah," said Mike, "we grew up having picnics and visiting relatives on holidays. The only real place we ever traveled to as kids was Disneyland, and that was pretty special."

"Actually," I said turning to Clark, "the ranger at Tuolumne Meadows who issued our permit was an African American woman."

"How did you know she was *African* American?" demanded Mike.

I wasn't sure how to reply, but before I could say anything, he continued, "But you see, we're starting to get places!"

"But it will take at least another generation before traveling, or hiking and camping, is part of our culture, like it is yours," concluded Phil.

"That makes sense," said Clark, who'd been listening thoughtfully.

"Time to clean the dishes," declared Lois. "Clark, can you take these down to the lake and rinse them, while I straighten up the bear canisters?"

"Sure," he nodded.

"I'll go with you," I said.

Clark and I took our cookware and headed down to the lake. As we rinsed them off, I turned to him, "Why are you hanging around with Lois?"

"What do you mean?" he asked, looking confused.

"I mean she treats you like a dog—having you make dinner, pump water, do dishes, and carry all the heavy shit."

"She's always been that way," he said, looking puzzled.

"What I'm saying is, it's OK to help out—*if* you get something back."

"Something back?" he asked, looking even more confused.

"I mean, you guys have separate tents and all, and it's cool if she's being traditional or something, but it seems like she's stringing you on," I said, beginning to get worked up. "I had this one girl I met my senior year in high school whom I totally fell for. I took her out to films, dinners, games, and shit, but somehow we never got it on. I just kept hoping. Finally, she started seeing one of my buddies—"

"That really sucks," said Clark sympathetically. But he still wasn't getting it.

"What I'm saying is, some women just like to string guys on, dangling the hope of a relationship in front of them, but always keeping the guy a safe distance, claiming, *We're just friends.* They just hold on to you for safety, waiting for their real 'Mr. Right' to show up. Keeping you as backup—*In case of emergency, break glass!*"

He stared at me mutely.

"Clark, Lois just talked about meeting *another—fucking—guy.* Can't you see that? You either have to straighten her out now, or just plain dump her on the trail with all her shit and dirty dishes!"

"You think Lois and I are dating?"

"Aren't you?"

"I mean, I love her and all—*but she's my sister.*"

"Your sister?" *Shit*—no wonder they both had Mexican fathers and Caucasian mothers. *How had I missed that?* "Oh man, I'm sorry—"

"It's fine," he said amused. "And you're right, she can be a bitch sometimes. To be honest, I feel a bit sorry for that guy she's dating."

We both laughed and finished washing our pots, but the joke was on me. When we got back, Phil and Mike were arguing about whose turn it was to do their dishes.

After cleaning up, we all sat around chatting and watching the rosy alpenglow over the mountains. We'd have made a fire, but we were above ten thousand feet and fires weren't permitted.

There seemed to be a certain special companionship between hikers that didn't exist in other places. Except for Syd, I didn't really know any of these guys well, and yet here we were hanging out and talking as if we were all old friends.

"Hey Syd," Mike asked, "do you have any idea why all the lakes up here have Indian names?"

"Yeah," added Clark, "there's Lake of the Lone Indian, Squaw Lake, Papoose Lake, Chief Lake, Warrior Lake, and Brave Lake."

"I'm not sure," said Syd, "but if I had to guess, I'd say they were named by sheepherders or early explorers after the Native Americans they met and traded with up here. Many of the east-west trails across the Sierra were originally Native American trade routes. And this is close to the old Mono Creek Trail that the Paiute Indians from Owen's Valley and Mono Lake took to trade with tribes from the Western Sierra."

"So we're at an ancient Indian meeting place?" asked Phil.

"Very possibly," said Syd. "Tribes from the east would trade salt, pine nuts, and obsidian with tribes from the west for shells, beads, berries, and acorns. You know, if you stop by a stream or river out here, sometimes you'll find small holes in the rock, about two or three inches in diameter?"

"Yeah, I've seen those before, what are they?" asked Clark.

"Those are spots where they would stop to fish and grind acorns," explained Syd.

"Wow, that's cool," said Mike.

"I used to love films about Indians," said Lois. "I don't mean the ones where they were fighting cowboys. I mean the ones that really showed how Native Americans lived."

"Hey, did you ever see that film about the bear cub that loses its mother in a rockslide?" asked Mike.

"You mean *The Bear?*" replied Phil.

"Yeah, but that wasn't the name," said Mike.

"Was there a strange dream scene with some bees?" asked Clark.

"Yeah, that's the one," said Mike. "What was that film called?"

"That was *The Bear,*" affirmed Clark.

"No it wasn't!" insisted Mike.

"Isn't the big dipper named for a bear?" asked Lois, looking up.

So it went late into the evening, until each of us grew so drowsy that we said our goodnights and retired, our small headlamps bobbing off toward our shelters in the dark.

Standing outside my tent, I gazed up at the mountains ahead. Their white snowcapped peaks seemed to glow beneath the stars. Silver Pass was up there somewhere. It was almost the same height as Donohue. I stared at Syd's tiny bivy and the cold metal shovel lying next to it. How would he hold up over another high mountain pass?

DAY NINE

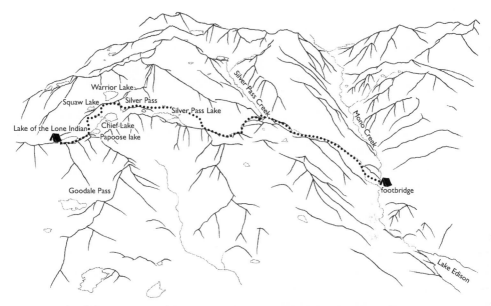

Lake of the Lone Indian (10,220´) to Mono Creek (7,970´) via Silver Pass (10,740´)

8½ miles—770 feet elevation gain; 3,020 feet elevation loss

P HIL AND MIKE WERE SNORING LOUDLY when we slipped by their tents. Clark and Lois had packed out earlier. Climbing in the crisp morning air felt good. As we reached the ridge, we turned once more to admire the lake, its waters shimmering under the newly rising sun.

We soon came to a sign declaring: *John Muir Trail*. It felt like running into a familiar friend. Following the arrow for Silver Pass, we forged on.

The two of us climbed steadily. The bare granite slope was peppered with boulders and patches of snow. Slowly we gained views of Chief Lake, Warrior Lake, and Papoose Lake sparkling below us. Looking back, I could just make out the black rocky teeth of Ritter and Banner rising up on the horizon. Ahead, we caught glimpses of another group of hikers ascending the pass, but at our halting pace they soon vanished into the distance.

It musta been at least an hour—it felt like seconds—and then suddenly we were there, gasping in the thin air at the top of the pass.

Several hikers from the group we'd seen ahead were resting here, and now began gathering up their stuff, making ready to head down the other side. We dropped our packs, taking a short spur up to the overlook.

Syd seemed to be doing better with the altitude. He'd none of the problems he'd exhibited over Donohue. I felt better too.

A woman was sitting cross-legged atop a large rock at the summit, her body half-silhouetted against the rising sun, her hair blowing in the wind. Approaching, I realized with a start that it was Kydoime. *How the hell had she gotten here?* I called out to her.

"Hey guys, fancy meeting you here," she said turning. "I thought those two snails creeping up the hill might be you."

Sunshine danced off her wild free hair. Mountains and blue lakes stretched beyond her to the horizon.

"Great to see you here," I blurted, "amazing view."

The view I was really checking out was her ample body wrapped in tight spandex against the fantastic blue sky—her two "mountain peaks" far more attractive than any of the surrounding ones.

"I thought I'd catch you guys at the hot springs," she said, "but you were gone."

"You went to the hot springs?" I asked in surprise, watching the wind play over the tiny blonde hairs running up her bare thighs.

"Yeah, I broke a bootlace. They didn't have any at the store—so I had to take a bus into town. By the time I reached the bridge it was already dark, so I camped there. At the springs a couple with a big dog said you'd already hiked out."

Shit—our night at the hot springs had been great, but it woulda been so much better if this goddess had been there too!

"We thought about camping at the bridge," I said, remembering how exhausted I'd been, "but then we decided to push on to the springs. Permi and Dylan were there too," I added, now totally regretting not having stopped at the bridge.

"That's cool," she said, "then they must be up ahead. I was wondering what happened to them."

"Where did you camp last night?" Syd asked.

"At Tully Hole—Rena and Kitty were there too."

"Really? Are they on their way here too?"

"No, they rolled into camp pretty late. I think it'll be a while before they get up and start hiking today. I gather Kitty is pretty disorganized, and Rena had to keep waiting for her to catch up."

"So, they're taking a short day?" Syd asked.

"No, Rena has a plane to catch back to Japan, so they're on a tight schedule. But they're not going over Silver Pass. They said they'll take Goodale Pass down to VVR today for the Saturday night barbeque, then skip part of the trail by hiking up to Bear Ridge from VVR tomorrow."

"Why didn't you join them?" I asked her.

"I didn't want to skip Silver Pass, or that much of the trail."

View of Cascade Valley from Silver Pass

"Wait, how did you get to Tully Hole? We didn't see you at Lake of the Lone Indian."

"Did you go up Cascade Valley?" Syd asked her.

"Yeah, I didn't want to skip the lakes, so after the hot springs, I took the trail up Cascade Valley to Purple Lake, and then to Tully Hole."

"That's about a fifteen-mile day, and almost all uphill!" exclaimed Syd.

"It wasn't that bad, except for the climb up to Purple Lake—and I found a great waterfall and swimming hole down in Cascade Valley."

I pictured Kydoime standing naked in a pool before a waterfall, the sun glowing behind her hair—even I could have walked fifteen miles uphill in sun for that!

"Could you take some photos of me at the pass?" Kydoime asked, passing me her camera. I was only too happy to oblige. Afterward she snapped several of me and Syd. She smelled like eucalyptus.

"So where are you planning to camp tonight?" I asked her.

"Well, I'm either going to camp at Mono Creek, or maybe hike a bit farther and catch the ferry to VVR, or I might head up Bear Ridge. I'm not sure yet. Depends on how I'm feeling."

"We're planning to stop at Mono Creek," said Syd.

"If you stop there, we can all hang out together," I suggested, perhaps a bit too enthusiastically.

"Maybe," she smiled, "let's see."

It was about as much of a promise as I could hope for.

We gathered our packs and started down the other side of the pass. Syd went slowly 'cause of his knee and we had to stop several times to wait.

After hanging with us for a bit, Kydoime announced, "Well guys, hope to see you at the creek," and went ahead. My heart sank as her gorgeous frame gyrated slowly off toward the horizon, while I was stuck babysitting Syd down the steep slope.

Below us was an emerald-green lake, its magnificent color momentarily distracting me from Kydoime's fading form. I asked Syd, "How come this lake is so green?"

"It's probably due to algae, but I'm not certain."

At least there was something he didn't know.

We came to an expansive plateau below a cloudless blue sky. Jumbled rocks of all sizes were strewn about. The sandy beige soil punctuated here and there by patches of dense green sedge. The soil was broken and dotted with tiny ruts and holes. From several of these poked some kind of rodent, like the prairie dogs I'd seen back in Ohio. A few stood tall on their hind legs checking us out.

"Those are Belding's ground squirrels—your father used to call them *sage rats*."

I laughed. They reminded me of the gopher in the movie *Caddyshack*.

Half-a-mile later we came to a large turquoise lake. "Let's stop for a bite," I suggested. Instead of my usual granola bars, I opened a small packet of almond butter I'd picked up at Reds. Squeeze-by-squeeze I relished the flavor—like one might savor spoonfuls of fine chocolate mousse.

"Gil, I've been looking at the map—from here to Mono Creek Bridge is only about five or six miles and mostly downhill. I'll probably take it pretty slow because of my knee. Perhaps you'd like to go ahead and pick out a nice spot for us? I can meet you at camp."

It seemed he was really saying: *Maybe you wanna run and see if you can catch Kydoime?* It wasn't even noon. Including lunch, I couldn't be more than an hour or so behind her, and even though she was fast, she'd have to stop somewhere to eat.

"Are you sure you'll be OK?" I asked. "What with your knee and the altitude and all?"

"I'll be fine," he said.

I wasn't sure it was such a good idea to leave him, but then it wasn't like we were the only ones hiking the trail. If he had a problem, someone would find him.

Packing up, I hurried down the trail. Below the plateau was a wet meadow with a gentle stream winding through a lush undulating valley. Scattered pines punctuated the landscape, each standing straight and erect above a matted bed of fragrant needles. It was a small slice of paradise, but I passed it by—my feet marching on like two soldiers, my brain focused on that statuesque Greek figure, those noble Cherokee cheekbones, and those tight American shorts.

The way leveled out crossing a small stream through a copse of trees. Several of the hikers I'd seen at the pass were picnicking nearby. They waved to me—Kydoime wasn't with them—I waved back and continued on.

Passing a second meadow, I forded another small creek, then began descending the wall of a sheer river canyon. The trail zigzagged down rugged steps of rock, forcing me to watch my footing—but I refused to slow my pace, thundering on. Passing a father and daughter hiking up, I asked them if they'd seen Kydoime, but they hadn't. The daughter said they'd stopped for lunch, so they might have missed her. Down, down, down, I trod—until at last the slope leveled out at a wide river crossing below a tumbling falls. The water was shallow, with rocks lining the side for safety, so I pushed on—barely stopping long enough to admire the magnificent cascade or think about the fact that I was actually walking through a waterfall!

Soon there was a second river crossing. I stopped, wanting to slake my thirst with the fresh cool water, but then realized Syd was carrying the filter. He would be at least an hour behind me. *Shit—never mind, I still had my warm half-filled bottle and bladder. It would be enough.* I took a long swig from my CamelBak, the warm water less satisfying in view of the tantalizingly cool river. Wading across the shin-deep flow, I splashed over the slick rocks, barely thinking about the depth until I was across. My socks and pants and the inside of my boots were soaked, but reaching the other side, I pressed on—they would dry—*I was on a mission from God!*

I burned down another mile or two of trail. Fording a small stream, I ran into four of the grungiest hikers I'd seen. Three guys and a girl, each no more than twenty, were sitting on an old log. Their packs were considerably smaller than mine, and instead of boots they had on sturdy tennis shoes.

"Have you seen a tall woman in a tight spandex top, wearing black shorts?" I asked, catching my breath.

"You mean Kydoime?" the young girl asked, she had matted pigtails and probably woulda made a cute prom date if she washed that dirt off.

"Yeah, that's her!"

"We saw her at the ferry landing. She took the one o'clock boat to VVR about an hour ago. There's another at four-thirty. You have plenty of time to catch it."

My heart sank. I dropped my pack. Kydoime had gone to VVR.

"Where are you headed?" I asked, assuming they were on a weekend excursion with such light packs.

"Canada," replied a guy in an orange ball cap with a green alligator face on it.

"We're hiking the PCT," said a tall blond kid with the nose of a bird.

"The Pacific Crest Trail," the girl explained, apparently thinking I didn't get it. "It runs from Mexico to Canada."

"You started in Mexico?" I gaped.

"Yup, at the border, in Campo," declared a stocky kid with a hairy black beard.

"But your packs are so small!"

"Never judge a man by the size of his pack," said the stocky one, grinning and pulling out his lunch.

"We travel light and fast," explained the one in the cap. "About twenty to thirty miles a day, sometimes more."

"Although we've had to slow down a bit because of all the elevation change in the Sierras," admitted the girl.

"We plan to make Canada by October," declared the blond with the beak.

"Wow! I'm lucky to make seven or eight miles a day," I confessed, "and even then, my legs feel like Jell-O."

"It's because you're carrying too much," said the girl.

"I bet you could make twenty miles easy if you lightened up," said the tall one. "For example, that big Osprey, I'll bet you got that at REI right?"

"Eh, yeah," I said, not sure how he knew which store I'd gotten my pack at.

"Thought so!" he said. "Osprey's a great brand and all—but that model weighs like five or six pounds. You should've gone with one of their ultralight packs. My ULA here is just three. That's a big difference to be lugging up and down all these peaks."

"Mine's a Gossamer Gear," said the girl, "it's a half-pound lighter than his."

"Where'd you get your packs?" I asked.

"Online," said the tall one. "All the best ultralight gear is sold through independent dealers. Sure, the big stores carry some cool shit, but they're focused mostly on weekend campers and the glamping crowd."

"What kind of tent do you have?" the guy in the ball cap asked.

"A Hubba Hubba," I replied proudly.

"That's a great tent," he admitted, "freestanding and really holds up in the wind. But it's like three, maybe four pounds, am I right?"

I nodded.

"I'm carrying a Durston X-Mid that sets up with my trekking poles and weighs only twenty-seven-and-a-half ounces."

"I don't even have a tent," proclaimed the stocky one, "just a bug net bivy."

"You gotta lighten up," said the blond guy.

"Where are you headed?" asked the one with the ball cap.

"My buddy and I are hiking the JMT to Whitney. Tonight we're camping at Mono Creek."

"That's in like another mile or two," said the guy in the cap. "We just passed there. The ferry stop where we met your friend is only a mile or so beyond that. You could camp at VVR instead, meet your friend, and take the ferry back in the morning."

"Vermilion is awesome," echoed the stout hiker.

"They have all kinds of beers and amazing ribs," said the guy in the ball cap. "There's a big hiker gathering there every night—but especially tonight—because it's Saturday. I'd definitely catch the ferry over. You can camp right there."

I'd put in one more appeal to Syd, especially if we could just catch a ferry across and be back in the morning—he might go for it.

"I'm Gil," I said, extending my hand to the guy in the cap.

"I'm Gator," he said smiling. Instead of shaking my hand, he fist-bumped me. "And this is Checkerboard," he said, indicating the girl. "And he's Taco," he pointed to the stocky one with the beard who looked up, smiled, and also fist-bumped me.

"And I'm Bret," said the guy with the nose. "I don't have a trail name yet, but if I did, it would be Smith—'Seldom Seen' Smith, like in *The Monkey Wrench Gang*."

"What's that?" asked Checkerboard.

"It's an eco-book or something about the desert. Haven't read it. But heard of it," said Taco.

"You don't get to pick your trail name," proclaimed Gator. "The rule is someone else has to give it to you. Like Taco here, who got his name 'cause he's always eating tacos."

"Best trail food there is," Taco said, grinning. And in fact, he was actually eating a taco.

"What about your names?" I asked Gator and Checkerboard.

"I go to the University of Florida—you know, *the Gators?*" he said pointing at his hat. "And also check out my shoes—" sure enough he had on alligator-patterned cloth gators over the top of his tennis shoes.

"Dirty Girl Gators," said Taco.

"That's the brand," said Checkerboard.

"And Checkerboard got her name because she's always jumping around," explained Gator.

"*Flip-flopping*," said Taco between bites.

"It means I keep jumping from one section of the trail to another," explained Checkerboard. "It's called *flip-flopping*."

"What about me?" I asked them. "What should my trail name be?"

"What are you into?" asked Bret.

"Well, hiking's alright I guess, but about the only thing I'm really into are martial arts films—so far this whole trip has been like the training scene from some kung fu flick."

The three became lost in thought, pondering the question of my name. Suddenly Taco sprang up. Stepping before me and holding a trekking pole high in the air, he commanded, "Kneel Gil!" I got on one knee and he tapped me gently on each shoulder with the pole intoning, "I dub thee, *Po*."

"*Po*," I asked surprised, getting back up, "you mean like *blind Master Po* from the old *Kung Fu* series?"

"No!" exclaimed Taco, reaching out and shaking my belly like a bowl full of Jell-O. "*Po*—like *Kung Fu Panda!*"

"*Look at my awesomeness!*" I roared, striking a silly *Kung Fu Panda* pose and doing my best movie impersonation.

Everyone laughed.

"Well, it was nice meeting you *Po*," Gator said with a grin, "but we have to hit the trail."

"Later *Brother Po*," said Taco, slinging on his pack.

"Happy trails," called Bret.

"Good luck," waved Checkerboard with a sweet smile.

And they were off—heading north for Canada.

It wasn't long before I came to the bridge over Mono Creek. On the other side was the campground. Another trail continued on to Lake Edison and the ferry.

Staring longingly for a moment down the trail Kydoime had taken, I turned and walked dejectedly over the bridge. There were no tents. Everyone was probably down at VVR having a good time. Syd would be at least an hour or two behind me 'cause of his knee, while I had just "rolled" downhill—perhaps *Po* wasn't such a bad trail name after all? My back was all sweaty from pushing so hard, and the dust and sunscreen on my face were growing crusty. What I really needed was to wash up, but I didn't relish rinsing in the icy river, and the speed of the water rushing under the bridge was concerning.

Recalling the portable solar shower I'd bought on a whim at REI, I dug the silvery bag with its long nozzle out from the bottom of my pack, filled it with water, and set it out in the sun to heat—*Po* was getting a hot shower today!

Finding a nice campsite, I pulled out some clean clothes and relaxed—not setting up my tent cause, although it was a long shot, I still wanted to try and persuade Syd to take the boat to VVR.

About forty minutes later, my shower bag was more than ready. I hiked up the trail just over a bluff. Hanging the bag from a tree branch, I stripped off my dirty clothes. The warm water felt great against my skin—it was wonderful to have a hot shower out here in the wilderness! Careful to conserve water, I shut off the flow, took out my soap and began lathering up, singing the theme song from *Nacho Libre* that Clark had sung the day before,

"I think I am, I thank I am
I'm glad I am, I'm proud I am
A real religious man . . ."

Suddenly, I heard voices and the clamor of approaching footsteps. Before I could think of what to do, a mixed group of about ten hikers—all around eighteen or twenty years old—came strutting around the bend from the other direction.

Shit—I was covered in soap!

A happy-looking blonde girl at the back of the line was bouncing along with several large colorful balloons tied to her pack. It was too late to duck down or hide, so I just waved calling out unabashedly, "Afternoon! Where are you all headed?" as if I wasn't standing under a tree wearing only my birthday suit and some bubbles.

"Hi," one of the kids called back, unfazed by my disposition, "we're off to Silver Pass Lake."

Perhaps naked men showering in the wilderness was a common sight along the trail?

"What are the balloons for?" I smiled, my willie waving in the wind.

"It's her birthday!" someone called out.

"And they make her pack lighter!" another shouted.

I watched them bob off over the bluff, the balloons bouncing in the breeze, then I rinsed off quickly and dressed—lest a party of nuns or a troop of innocent Cub Scouts should happen along next.

An hour later, Syd still hadn't shown up. *Shit—there was no way we'd make it to VVR now!* My dreams of beer and barbeque with Kydoime drained away—another lonely night of Backwoods beef stroganoff.

Frustrated, I put up my tent. Syd probably wouldn't have agreed to go there anyway.

A few other groups arrived and made camp, but none remembered seeing Syd. Growing worried, I grabbed some bars and topped off my water bottle—*there was no way I was running out of water again*—then hurried back up the trail.

It was all uphill. My quads burned from their earlier pounding—but at least I wasn't hauling a pack.

Reaching the stream where I'd met the PCT hikers, there was still no sign of Syd. *What happened to him?* I splashed across and kept going.

The temperature was dropping, and the shadows were getting longer. *Shit—why hadn't I brought my headlamp and long johns? I hadn't even eaten the damn bars!* I pressed on, every now and then stopping to call out Syd's name, but there was no answer.

I'd gotten about halfway to the big river crossing when it really started getting dark. The trail was now a faint silvery line against the surrounding trees. Moving slowly to watch my footing, I began shivering from the cold. Weird noises sounded from the forest. I heard a branch snap. *Shit—I'm either gonna freeze to death or get eaten by a bear—probably both.*

Why had I been so selfish chasing after Kydoime? This was all probably part of my karma. I was supposed to be hiking with Syd—not chasing after women and beer. After I found him we would stick together—*but where the hell was he?*

Reaching a large boulder, I sat down for a breather. The trail wound along a cliffside. I could just make out the tinkling sound of a tumbling stream somewhere in the dark. It was too cold to stay here. Standing I shouted, "Syd!"—there was no reply.

I started walking again. A faint light came on in the distance. *It was a headlamp!* Almost running, I reached the light. It was Syd!

He was resting on a large rock with his right leg outstretched and his backpack at his side.

"I wasn't sure if you'd come back, or if I'd have to set up my bivy here," he said.

"What happened?"

"I banged my ankle crossing the river. I fell in and had to change all my clothes, so I've been taking it really slow. It doesn't hurt too much, and I've taken some ibuprofen, but my knees are really shot from coming down that hill."

I was just glad to find him.

"How about if I take your pack and we go on together? It's about a mile and a half to camp. With your trekking poles and no load, do you think you can make it?"

"I think so."

Shouldering his pack and sharing the light of his headlamp, we started down the trail together. He was slow, but he wasn't limping or anything. I couldn't believe I'd been so stupid as to leave him behind like that!

"From now on I'm gonna stick with you and do my best to see that you get to Whitney."

"Thanks Gil, I'm glad you're here."

As we walked, I told him about my trail name and what the PCT hikers said about my pack.

"Well, if you like the name, *Po*, keep it. But don't listen to them about going 'ultralight.' I once tried one of those flimsy packs and it practically broke my back, and in my opinion REI's a great place for beginners to go and get fitted up. You know I remember meeting Jim Whittaker—the first American to climb Everest—when he opened their Berkeley store in 1975—"

Gladdened by his ramblings, I could tell he was gonna be alright. His pack warmed my back, and I stopped shivering.

"In a way they're right of course, you could stand to drop some pack weight, everybody could. But if you let go of too much stuff and find yourself in an emergency, what are you going to do then? The trick is to find that balance between comfort and weight. Frankly, I think you're doing fine."

"Thanks," I smiled.

Almost everyone's lights were out when we made it back to camp. I helped Syd set up his bivy.

"Do you have everything you need? Is your ankle feeling better?"

"Yes, thanks, I'll be fine. Go get some rest."

"Goodnight Syd," I said.

"Goodnight *Po*," he grinned.

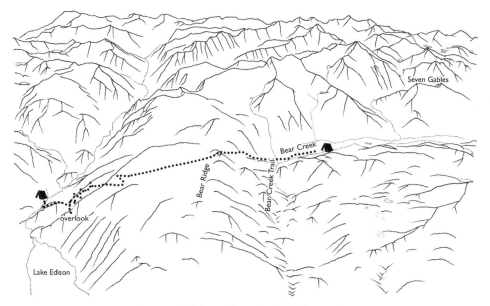

Mono Creek (7,970′) to Bear Creek (9,240′)
8½ miles—2,420 feet elevation gain; 1,150 feet elevation loss

ROLLING OVER in my sleeping bag to catch a few more Z's, I was jolted awake by a burning in my crotch. Unwrapping myself cautiously, I examined my legs—the entire region around my crotch was red and swollen. *Shit*—I musta chafed my legs while running down that hill after gettin my pants soaked. How had I been so dumb? *I'll never chase after a woman again!* Shit, shit—*ouch!* Just getting into my pants was a nightmare.

Syd was outside watching some stupid yellow birds, it looked like *he* was doing better. Wincing in pain, I hobbled over to him. "I don't know how to say this—" I began, immediately regretting my words 'cause he looked at me like I was about to announce an imminent nuclear attack. "Yesterday, the skin inside my pants got wet and now I have this horrible chafing rash. I don't think I can hike today."

"Try some vaginal cream."

"*What?* Isn't that for—you know—*women's issues?*"

"It is," he looked amused, "but it's also remarkably good for chafing rash."

"And even if I wanted some," I said, desperately trying to hold down the fire in my pants,

137

"it's not like there's a pharmacy out here, right? What am I supposed to do? Just walk up to every female hiker we meet, and say, *Pardon me ma'am, you wouldn't happen to have some vaginal cream I could borrow, would you?*"

"That would be interesting," he chuckled, "but as it happens, I have some you can use." He went over to his pack and removed a small pink tube from his first-aid kit. Legs wide, I hobbled back to my tent, applying it carefully to the affected areas. Sure enough, with the help of a little vaginal cream, I was a new man!

Returning the tube to Syd, I asked, "How did you ever come to know *that* could be used for—eh—*other issues?*"

"I read about it in Yogi's book."

"Yogi, like the bear?"

"It's her trail name. She's the author of a well-known PCT guide. Vaginal cream is one of her recommendations for chafing rash. Everyone gets it sooner or later when hiking."

"Well thank Yogi for me. Her cure feels great!" I smiled, walking around and testing my legs. The rash was no longer that painful—and I smelled fresher too!

The fire's out, we ate and packed. Syd said his foot was "a hundred percent better" so we headed up the trail for Bear Ridge.

Almost immediately, we began climbing switchback after grueling switchback. The ground here was dusted in fallen pine needles, and the air felt chilly under the shade of the large trees. A cold sweat began running down my back. Small flies and the occasional mosquito began pestering me. Swatting at the bugs and not paying attention to where I was stepping, I almost turned my foot twice on loose rocks.

"It's good the trail is covered with so many trees, or this climb would be much harder," Syd proclaimed in a cheery tone.

Was I the only one being pestered by these damn flies? Maybe it was the cream?

"See these tall straight trees?"

"Yeah," I answered with feigned enthusiasm. *They were trees, so what? We'd passed millions of 'em already—*

"These are lodgepole pines. The Native Americans used them as ridge poles in their lodges. And this one's a white pine." He pointed at another tree that looked the same as the first. "According to Wenk's guidebook, farther up we should see more of these, as well as red fir and hemlock. Each elevation has its own mini-ecosystem."

"That's great—and just how far up do these switchbacks go today?" I asked, swatting at the stupid flies.

"A little over two thousand feet, or about twice the height of the Eiffel Tower," he said with way too much enthusiasm.

That's all I needed—to climb two Eiffel Towers before lunch.

A light breeze blew through the whatever-they-were trees, chilling the mixture of sweat and sunscreen on my skin. This whole damn climb was in the trees. Why hadn't Syd told me not to bother with sunscreen today? I hated the smell of sunscreen and the sticky feeling on my skin.

Somewhere around the twentieth switchback—I lost count—we came to a grove of what Syd said were aspens. They looked like the birch trees I'd seen growing up in Ohio. Many of them had hearts with people's initials cut into their thin white bark.

"Look at these," Syd groused, "they're like those damned billboard signs they put up along the sides of highways. Why can't people just leave things pristine? Does anyone really care who P.P. and M.J. are?"

I immediately thought of Spiderman.

Just beyond the aspens Syd led us off-trail and up a bluff dotted with giant white boulders. From the top, we could see a huge shimmering lake.

We dropped our packs, eating yet another of the bland granola bars that were our unvarying snack and afternoon meal. Glancing up, I saw that we were less than halfway to the top. *Shit—this damned hill went on forever!*

"What's that giant lake?" I asked.

"That's Lake Edison. It's a reservoir really. They built it back in the fifties by damning up the river and flooding Vermilion Valley. It's used to generate hydroelectric power for Fresno."

"Is that the lake with the ferry?"

"Yes, VVR is on the far end."

Squinting, I tried to make out if there were any boats crossing the lake but couldn't see any.

"Theodore Solomons crossed this valley on his second expedition into the Sierra, in 1894, if I remember correctly."

"The guy who first dreamed up the idea for the trail, right?"

"Precisely. Solomons was continually drawn to the Sierra, despite pressure from his mother to give it up and pursue a career in law."

"Sounds like everyone's folks."

"Did your mother pressure you to study law?"

"No, that was my idea." But not wanting to get into all that, I asked, "How old was Solomons?"

He scrutinized me, saying, "He was in his twenties. He got so wrapped up in exhibiting photos from his first journey that he never really focused on his career like his mother wanted."

"So he became a local celebrity?"

"His trip into the '*terra incognito*' of the Sierra caught a certain section of the public's interest at the time. It was around then that he became friends with Leigh Bierce, the son of Ambrose Bierce, the famous journalist and author."

"Ambrose Bierce, who wrote *The Devil's Dictionary?*"

"I'm surprised you know it."

"Only parts—it was like this big book of old jokes Pop used to read from sometimes. I still remember, *Adam's Apple: a protuberance on the throat of a man, thoughtfully provided by Nature to keep the rope in place.*"

He laughed. "You have a good memory. Maybe one day you'll think about going back to school," he glanced at me inquiringly.

"What happened with Solomons?" I asked. Better to hear one of his stories than talk about my own issues.

"Solomons met with Muir to plan a route for his second expedition."

"That musta been helpful."

"Only in part. Solomons wrote that Muir was, *a truly great mountaineer . . . but a very poor sort of explorer.* Complaining that he, *could describe every place he had seen, but could seldom tell you where it was.*"

"Isn't that biting the hand that feeds you?"

"Solomons wasn't exactly known for his tact."

"He sounds like one of the partners at the firm I worked for." Syd laughed.

"Solomons took Bierce with him to Yosemite to continue his previous expedition. But they became sidetracked after hearing of the marvelous waterfalls in the Grand Canyon of the Tuolumne."

"There's a Grand Canyon in Yosemite?"

"It's part of a beautiful but somewhat treacherous river canyon that runs from Tuolumne Meadows to Hetch Hetchy. You really should see it sometime."

"Sure, if we ever finish climbing this ridge."

"Solomons and Bierce postponed their trip to photograph the canyon. Then they spent weeks lounging around the valley socializing. By the time they actually set out, it was September."

A breeze blew through the trees. Far below, the waters of Lake Edison darkened. It was nice just to hang here and listen to stories. The breeze also seemed to be helping with the bugs.

"Leading a horse and two mules, the two retraced the path that Solomons had taken out of the Sierra two years earlier. At one point they ran into a sheepherder who warned them there'd probably be early snows, but they ignored him. Not too far from where Lake Edison is now, they laid out their sleeping bags beneath an old dead pine, built a warm fire, and went to bed. During the night the tree caught fire. The two awoke to a loud cracking sound as one of the flaming branches was about to drop. Hopping away like a pair of potato-sack racers, they barely escaped being crushed and roasted."

"Aren't you always supposed to put out fires before going to bed? Isn't that what Smokey the Bear says?"

"Smokey Bear didn't exist until the 1940s. Back then, most campers kept a small fire going at night because their bags weren't much better than sewn-up blankets. But even without the fire, they should have known better than to camp under an old dead tree—you never know when one will blow over or drop a branch."

I nodded while chewing on a bar. The flavor said *peanut butter,* but "corrugated cardboard" woulda been a more apt description.

"After escaping the fire, the two winded their way through the valley below, naming it

Vermilion because of its bright red soil. From there they climbed this ridge, mapping out the section of trail we're on now."

"Did they include all these switchbacks on their map?"

"There were no switchbacks. They had to make a trail themselves and it was quite harrowing. At one point, one of their mules slipped, bouncing head-over-heels down the ridge. The two thought the mule was a goner, but even though it was carrying their glass negatives, everything was intact."

"Have you ever seen those old Shaw Brothers kung fu flicks—the ones from Hong Kong? They used to film these crazy fighting sequences where the heroes flipped through the air using wires—anyway, that's what your tumbling mule reminded me of."

"I may have seen some of those films. My son Sean used to watch that kind of thing when he was younger. As I was saying, the two really struggled up the ridge. After recovering their mule, their horse broke a leg and had to be shot. But they continued on, following Bear Creek toward a magnificent peak they dubbed, the Seven Gables. There they hunted in vain for a suitable pass. Until one morning they woke in the middle of a blizzard, trapped by snow with one of their mules missing."

"What did they do?"

"They panicked. They grabbed some food and whatever else they could carry, leaving behind their wet sleeping bags and most of their gear. Then they shot their mule to keep it from starving and set out in the storm, retracing their route as best they could."

"That's crazy."

"They figured they could get down faster without the animal, but because of the snow they were forced to navigate in whiteout conditions and didn't get very far. That night they made a crude shelter from pine branches draped across a pair of boulders. They struggled to build a fire and spent the night huddled together in their wet clothes. By midnight, Bierce was feverish. But by some miracle, the storm abated, and in the morning, they were able to trudge down to the bank of the San Joaquin River."

"So they escaped?"

"Not quite. They still had to ford the icy river and make it back with almost no supplies. Starving and frozen, on the fifth day they encountered a sheepherder who revived them with a roasting fire and gobs of steaming mutton."

"What's with all the sheepherders? Solomons' treks are starting to sound like some bad Irish joke!"

He grinned, "That's the way it was back then—the real explorers were Native Americans and sheepherders. After eight days, the two were back in Fresno, but Solomons had lost his gear, his camera, his animals, and all of his exposed negatives. Worse still, when Muir heard about their failure he declared, *Solomons was not a mountain man or he would have had sense enough to hole in, in some sheltered spot, pull in all the wood he could get hold of, and keep a fire going, instead of trying to make his way out in a storm.*"

"Well, people often do stupid things in a panic, right?"

Syd nodded.

The cool breeze picked up again causing my skin to rise in goosebumps. "It's getting kinda chilly up here talking about all this snow—maybe we should get going?"

Sometime around noon we crested the ridge. Tiny squirrels and chipmunks scampered about. The pestering flies were gone. Small gray-and-tan birds with little black masks that Syd said were mountain chickadees called to us from the trees. The path became flat. And then to my chagrin, it began heading downhill—as if to say all of our climbing had been for nothing and we could have just gone around this big hill. Which is exactly what Kydoime did, 'cause a few miles down the other side we ran into her filtering water near the top of another trail that she'd taken up from VVR. *Why did Syd always pick the hardest way?* But I stayed silent, all too happy to see the beautiful Kydoime again. Her freshly washed hair smelled vaguely of lavender. She was dressed in loose hiking pants and a simple button-down shirt. We dropped our packs and joined her beside the tiny bubbling creek.

"How was VVR?" I asked.

"Amazing. The food was terrific and the beer—well they had just about every kind of microbrew you could name. They had a big outdoor barbeque, and these ribs with this fantastic homemade sauce—"

My stomach rumbled with envy.

"Were Kitty and Rena there?" Syd inquired.

"Yeah, that's funny," she said, "they got up late at Tully Hole, and then I think they got lost once or twice, because they came in after dark—when the staff were already cleaning up."

"So they missed dinner?" I asked.

"They begged the owner to make them something, and unable to say no, he gave them each a beer and cooked them some ribs in the kitchen."

"That was nice of him," Syd said.

"Yeah, the owner and the whole staff there were really cool."

"What about Lois and Clark? Did you see them?" I asked.

"Lois was with her boyfriend. They asked about you guys."

"We slept by the bridge over Mono Creek," I grumbled, eying Syd.

"That's a nice spot. Sorry I didn't wait for you guys there, but some hikers I passed said the ferry was coming and I didn't want to miss it."

"Are Rena and Kitty on their way up?" asked Syd.

"No, they're taking a zero at VVR and Lois and Clark are heading down to Mono Hot Springs with her boyfriend—so it's just us," she said, looking at me again in a teasing flirtatious way that I wasn't sure was meant for me, or just the way she was. "Dylan was there too," she added, "but he left yesterday, when I arrived."

"What about Permi?" asked Syd.

"I don't know. I don't think Permi even stopped at VVR. He wasn't with Dylan when I got there."

We ate together, then she announced, "Well, I'm trying to make at least another ten miles today, so I'd better get going."

My heart sank. There was no way Syd and I were going make ten more miles today, even with a goddess like her lighting the way. *Shit*—I'd probably never see her again. But even if I didn't have to stay with Syd, there was no way I could keep pace with her.

She packed up, waved bye, and left us chewing on our dried bars.

After lunch, the view really opened up. In the far distance was a massive peak shaped like a gothic cathedral, with a long buttressed ridge. "What's that called?" I asked.

"That's the Seven Gables, where Solomons got trapped in the snowstorm."

"Are we going up there?"

"No, they never found a suitable pass around it. Instead the trail follows Bear Creek."

As we descended, the vegetation changed from high mountain forest to scrub and sage. Strange new insects buzzed and popped. It wasn't until we reached Bear Creek that we met with tall pines again. It was good to be back in their shade.

The creek was at least fifty feet wide. Its fast-flowing water roared and churned. An occasional tree branch swept by, caught up in the strong current. I'm not sure whether it was Paul Bunyan or some other giant who dubbed all these Sierra rivers, "creeks"—but Bear Creek was definitely not what I'd call *a creek*.

Syd was lost in his own contemplations as we followed along the bank. The woodsy smell of earth and the filtered light calmed my thoughts, and my mind drifted back to Kydoime. We'd passed many female hikers on the trail, but she was the only one who had the attributes I was looking for. My mind was just beginning to run over those attributes, when Syd interrupted my ruminations.

"Isn't that Dylan's tent?" he asked.

In the center of a clearing stood the familiar yellow tent with its propped-up awning and American flag. Sure enough, Dylan was sitting on a small green folding chair watching the river roll by. Next to his tent was a small rolled-up green tarp covering what appeared to be a bedroll. As we approached, I could smell the familiar scent of marijuana.

"Hey wow, great to see you guys again—pull up a log!" he greeted us.

We joined him by an old firepit.

"Is Permi here?" I asked, indicating the rolled-up tarp.

"Yeah, he took his collection sack up to Seven Gables. Said he wanted to check things out up there. He should be back by dinner, but you never know with Permi. And Kydoime came by about an hour ago—didn't stop—just said 'hi' and flew by like she was on a mission."

"We met up with her on Bear Ridge. She wants to make another ten miles today."

"Sounds like her," he said. "She's pretty intense. I think she's hitting MTR tomorrow."

"What's MTR?"

"Muir Trail Ranch—it's a kind of dude ranch and backpackers station."

"That's where we're getting our next resupply," said Syd.

Why did hikers always call places by their initials? VVR, PCT, JMT, MTR—even REI and HYOH—it was almost like being in the military.

"We have a reservation for a cabin at MTR the day after tomorrow," said Syd.

"We do?" This was the first he'd mentioned a reservation.

"I made it when you agreed to join me. I wanted it to be something of a surprise. A warm bed, good meal, and hot shower halfway through the trail," he smiled.

"That'll be amazing—especially a good dinner!" *Maybe they even had BLTs?* "How did you know how long it would take us to get there?"

"I didn't. I just estimated the time, adding a day as a margin of error, somehow it just worked out."

"Everything always works out on the trail," said Dylan philosophically.

"How was VVR?" I asked him.

"VVR was great. I didn't have much cash, but the owner let me work around the place in exchange for food. I also met up with Rick and Jon there for a smoke."

"The two older hikers who got the campsite at Reds Meadow?" I asked.

"Yeah, that's them. Jon has some really bad blisters. His shoes aren't fitting right. His feet were all done up with duct tape and all, so I don't know how far he's gonna make it."

"That's too bad," said Syd. "Did Permi go to VVR?"

"Nah, he skipped it. He wanted to hike up Mono Creek instead, then went cross country over Mono Divide and met me here."

"That's pretty challenging terrain," Syd looked surprised.

"Yeah, the dude really sprints it. He could do the whole trail in a week if he wanted to—but that's not his scene. He's really out here for the plants and the experience. I once saw him climb down the rocks right next to a waterfall, just to see what kinda moss grew there."

"Sounds a bit like John Muir," Syd observed.

"Kinda," said Dylan. "Only Muir was raised more of a God-fearing man."

"So you're both headed to MTR tomorrow?" Syd asked.

"Yeah, that's where we got our resupplies. I plan to hang there for a night or two, but Permi said he wants to continue up to Evolution Valley. You know, to gather more plants and have a look around. He said he'll meet me somewhere around the Muir Hut, I think."

Dylan was working on his third bowl by the time we got our tents up and gathered for dinner. His fragrant smoke blended nicely with the smell of the river. Maybe the scent would even make my Backwoods Buffet stuff taste better. But it didn't seem like anything could improve that.

"Which branch of the service were you in?" Syd asked.

"Regular army," he said as he exhaled another long puff of green sweet-smelling smoke.

"What did you do before you enlisted?"

"I was in high school. I wanted to become a civil engineer and had the grades and all, but my old man didn't have the cash to pay for college. So I signed up for the army and bought up under the Montgomery G.I. Bill—you know, so they'd pay all my tuition after four years of active duty. But then the whole Gulf shit happened, and it fucked up my head."

"I'm sorry to hear that," said Syd. "So what did you do after you got out?"

Dylan stared at the river with that half-empty look of his. "After my discharge, I couldn't hold down a job." He took another long drag, held it, then blew it out. "I tried a few things, but they never worked out. After that, well—let's just say I got into some really messed-up shit. It was pretty much the low point of my life." He sighed. "Then a friend took me to hike the trail." He turned and looked intensely at me, "Like your buddy Syd here is doing with you. And well," he turned back toward the river, "all this air and open space, it did something for me. It has a kind of spiritual power, you know? Let's just say I rediscovered God out here."

Syd nodded. "Muir wrote, *In God's wildness lies the hope of the world—the great fresh unblighted, unredeemed wilderness. The galling harness of civilization drops off, and wounds heal ere we are aware.*"

"That's beautiful. God's *wild-ness*. I like that," Dylan said, taking another long hit. "The trail got me out of a lot of bad shit. It focused my head. It was good to have a mission again. A purpose. When I got back from the trail, I made a clean break from the assholes I was hanging with. Now I work in a legal medicinal clinic, helping people out, you know, cancer patients and people in real need. Helping them get access to pot for medical reasons. They give me a lot of time off too—to hike and keep my head straight. I feel a lot better about things now. *Give, and it will be given to you.*"

Syd nodded. "This is your fourth time hiking the trail?"

"Yeah. The trail keeps me straight. You're either on the trail or off the trail. It's like the book says, *Whoever follows me will not walk in darkness, but will have the light of life.*"

It sounded like Dylan had a pretty hard life—but was all that pot really good for him? Alcohol and pot were what fucked me up after Pop died. But Dylan's issues seemed more serious than mine. Maybe he needed an even longer hike to really straighten himself up? If he could do that, maybe he could climb out of the hole he was in, get into a college program, or something? I turned to him and asked, "Have you ever tried the PCT, or that one out east someone was talking about, the Appalachian Trail?"

"I've thought about it," said Dylan. "But I heard they each pass by a lot of towns. I just want to be out here in the wilderness, away from all that. I mean, I don't mind a sedate place like VVR, that's cool and all. But I don't want to go through so many towns. Being in the mountains keeps me focused." He took another hit of his weed.

How could he keep anything clear with that much smoke?

Syd leaned back and added, "Muir said, *going to the mountains is going home.*"

From behind us a familiar voice echoed, "*This grand show is eternal. It is always sunrise somewhere; the dew is never all dried at once; a shower is forever falling; vapor ever rising. Eternal sunrise, eternal sunset, eternal dawn!*" and we turned around to see Permi striding into camp, his woven collection sack brimming with goodies.

"How was Seven Gables?" Syd asked him.

"Amazing," said Permi. "Huge peaks, hidden lakes, deep canyons—massive vertical walls! It was like circling an ancient temple."

"I'd love to see it someday," Syd said wistfully.

"I hope you'll have the chance," Permi said. "Did you try those herbs I gave you?"

"I've been mixing them into my tea each morning. They have a nice calming effect throughout the day."

Permi smiled broadly patting him gently on the back. "Glad to hear it, man!"

"What did you bring back?" I asked, eyeing his woven bag and hoping it contained something edible.

"Pinecones," he said, dumping a pile of cones each the size of small pineapple onto a large flat rock.

"What are you going to do with those," I asked, disappointed, "make Christmas ornaments?"

"No," said Permi, "we're gonna eat them man!"

"You can eat *pinecones?*"

"Not the *cones* man, the *seeds*—have you ever tasted pine nuts?"

I nodded. They used them in the pesto sauce at that Italian restaurant I sometimes frequented. But so what? And then suddenly it clicked—*pine nuts come from pinecones*. Of course! Why had I never thought of that before?

"We'll have to get them toasty to open them," Permi said.

He gathered some fallen twigs and branches and started to build a small fire in the ring. We helped him gather wood. Then I watched as he used the pine needles as fire lighter and with just a single match soon had a good blaze going. The small flames danced around the pit, the smell of wood smoke tickling my nostrils. The sun was setting, and it was amazing how mesmerizing a small campfire was.

"What kind of pinecones are those?" Syd asked him.

"Jeffrey cones. You can get pine nuts from any pine, but only Jeffreys and pinions have nuts big enough to be worth harvesting. Pinions grow on the eastern side of the Sierra. I'm hoping to try them too when we get there."

Dylan looked up, "Jeffreys are those giant trees right, the ones with the cracked orange bark that smells like vanilla?"

"Yeah, but ponderosa pines have similar bark."

"How can you tell the difference?"

"The easiest way is by the cones. Jeffrey cones are larger. And you can grab one without getting pricked. Ponderosa cones have barbs that hurt when you grab 'em."

"Like my ex," Dylan laughed.

Permi smiled, holding up one of the large cones showing us how the barbs pointed inward. "Jeffrey pines grow at higher altitudes than ponderosas, but actually they're both variations of yellow pine, and sometimes the two even hybridize, so it can get confusing."

I was still back at lodgepoles and wasn't even sure if I could recognize one of them. We'd passed some bigger trees today, maybe those were the ones he was talking about?

Permi hunted around and found a long stick with a forked end. He stuck one of the cones into the fork, holding it above the fire and rotating slowly, like he was toasting a giant marshmallow. I watched in amazement as the flaps on the cone started to bend open.

"Jeffrey pines were named for this Scottish gardener, John Jeffery, who was sent to America to collect seeds around 1850," Permi explained. "He's the one who discovered foxtail pines, which should be growing up around Whitney. Ya gotta look for 'em when you're up there. They look like whitebark pines, only with way shorter needles, like little fox tails."

I imagined a tree with bushy red tails dangling off it.

Syd spoke up, "You said Jeffrey came to America in 1850, are you sure that's right? That was before Muir came to Yosemite, the Whitney Survey, or even the American Civil War."

"Oh yeah, I'm certain," said Permi. "Everyone thinks people like Jedediah Smith, Joseph Walker, Kit Carson, and John Fremont were the Sierra's only explorers, but those guys were just looking for a way *through* the mountains. The history books always forget the people who went *into* the mountains—the botanists, man! There was another Scottish botanist named David Douglas who explored parts of California and Oregon even before Jeffrey, back in the 1820s. He's the one the Douglas squirrel and the Douglas-fir are named for."

Permi pulled the pinecone out of the fire and put it on the rock to cool. He took a second cone and started gently roasting it.

"Douglas discovered over two hundred new species. The Native Americans called him *The Grass Man* because he collected plants and wasn't interested in trading or whiskey like the other White men—so they took him for a kind of medicine man."

"That's cool," said Dylan.

"Both Douglas and Jeffrey died under strange circumstances," added Permi. "Douglas died in Hawaii. The guy who found him said he fell into a pit used for trapping animals, but that guy was a convict, so his story is suspicious. And Jeffrey disappeared mysteriously somewhere around San Francisco and was never heard from again."

"That happens to a lot of people in Frisco," Dylan said, and everyone laughed.

"Maybe he discovered a new species of carnivorous pine," I joked.

"If he did," said Permi, "no one has ever found it. But I doubt it, man. The one-legged people are our friends. Did you know that trees have feelings and can communicate with each other?"

"I believe plants and trees have feelings," said Syd. "But how do they communicate?"

"In Africa, when a giraffe grazes on an acacia tree, the tree pumps tannins into its leaves to make them bitter and drive the giraffe away. Other trees can smell the tannins, and when they do, they add them to their leaves too. It's like a tree-to-tree warning system, man."

"So trees can talk to each other through smell?" asked Dylan.

"Like we do with colognes and perfumes?" I suggested.

"Smell is a huge communicator," said Permi.

"But is that really communication?" asked Syd. "Isn't it just an evolved defense mechanism that's programmed into the trees' genes? It doesn't mean the trees are really *talking.*"

"You could say that," acknowledged Permi. "It doesn't mean the trees communicate in the way we do, but by sending signals to each other, they are interacting with their environment, and sharing those experiences with each other."

"That's true," acknowledged Syd.

Permi began roasting another cone. A blackened log glowing with warm embers dropped into the fire with a sudden crack and a burst of tiny sparks.

"The thing is, the one-legged people are so ancient and slow growing, that even if they did talk like we do, we'd never hear it. A conversation between two trees might take months on our time scale, and people—even scientists—just don't have the patience to listen at that pace."

"Can't they use time-lapse recordings, or something?" I asked.

"Maybe," said Permi, "but I think the bulk of their communication is underground. For instance, beech trees grow together in a living network connected by their roots. When a grandmother tree is cut down, the other trees can keep the stump alive by feeding it nutrients from underground. If one tree's getting more sun, it shares that energy with others, and in exchange, the other trees will pass more water to it. It's a big web of interactions, man. And that doesn't even get into how the trees relate to the different fungi and organisms in the soil."

"That's interesting," said Syd.

"They also found that isolated trees, planted in cities and gardens, live shorter lives—because they don't have any friends to connect with." Permi stuck a fourth cone in the fire.

"So trees are like people?" said Dylan. "They get sick if they're socially isolated or cut off?"

"It depends on the species. For instance, oak trees are loners. Some trees prefer company, and some prefer to live alone."

"Like people," said Syd.

Glancing from face-to-face, I pictured Syd as a stolid meditative old oak, Dylan as a cut-off beech searching for his network, and Permi as a wild pine. I was probably a fragrant spice tree, sending off pheromones in search of pollinators.

Permi took the cone from the fire and placed it on the rock. "There's a lot we can learn from our one-legged friends, if we just slow down and listen."

He handed each of us one of the toasted cones. The cone was nicely warm and the scales wide open.

"To get the pine nuts out, you have to peel open the scales, like this," Permi said as he demonstrated.

It wasn't as easy as he made it look, but after a bit of bending and twisting, I managed to get one out and eat it. I welcomed the warm piney flavor and the nut had the texture of a buttery peanut. Peeling open more scales, I began digging out and eating the delicious seeds. Syd and Dylan were doing the same, while the playful flames danced about the logs.

"Hey Syd," said Dylan, exhaling more fragrant smoke, "you told us about your cancer, and I'm sorry and all, but what really brought you out here? Why are you out hiking the trail when you're so sick and everything?"

Syd stiffened a bit, "The trail was always something I wanted to do, and when I learned I was dying, I figured this was my last chance to see it."

"Right, you said that in the springs," observed Dylan, "but I mean, you've got family, friends, people you're connected to, like those beech trees, am I right? So why come way out here and do this? The trail's beautiful and all, but if I were dying, I'd want to be with family."

It was something I'd wondered about too, and I chimed in, "What made you ask me to join you?"

Syd fidgeted with his pinecone—picking out a kernel, peeling it, turning it over in his hand, popping it in his mouth, then chewing slowly. He turned his head toward me, but I could see he was looking away, toward the fire. "We'll talk about that another time," he said quietly.

Was there something else I should know? Something about Pop? Or maybe Ma?

Syd looked halfway at Dylan and in a slow voice replied, "I do have family, yes. My wife passed away before me, but I have a great son and daughter whom I love dearly, two terrific young grandchildren, and a few close friends as well. But my cancer has progressed slowly. I've had enough time to spend with my family and friends. I've said all my goodbyes and now I don't want to become a burden. What I'm really seeking out here is a kind of spiritual peace. A kind of personal reckoning. I may have spent my life studying philosophy, but I still haven't understood the most essential question—about life's meaning." He became silent, staring into the fire.

"Are you sure you don't want a hit?" Dylan asked holding out his pipe. "This can help you find the meaning—help you to see the Word of God."

"I really appreciate it," Syd replied somewhat distantly, "but I need to seek the answer in my own way."

The fire crackled. The four of us ate our pine nuts, listening to the sounds of the forest around us.

Finally Permi spoke up. "You know Syd, I was thinking a lot about what you said in the springs while I was walking around that granite temple today—about the *Tao* and all. And also about what that guy Rob said."

"That kid building the Terminator?" asked Dylan, his face flushing.

"Yeah, but not about the Terminator," said Permi.

Dylan relaxed.

"About what he said about life arising out of chaos, or what he called *entropy*."

Syd nodded.

"I think ultimately they're the same. One *is* the other. Life *is* the void man. Like your *yang* and *yin*—both must dance together. And if we call one *life* and the other *void*, it's only because we've given them names. They're really the same thing. Like that little wave—we're all part of the water."

Syd stared pensively into the fire.

What did he mean, *life and death were the same?* I got that thing about the waves all being made of water, but it didn't mean life and death were the same—sometimes it seemed Permi really had a screw loose. And what did Syd need to tell me later? That was the real mystery.

Syd looked up from the fire. "What's your plan after this hike?" he asked Permi.

"Right now, I'm learning foraging and herbal medicine. At some point, I'm hoping to find a community of like-minded folks. Maybe get some land and live off the grid. I'm thinking either the Pacific Northwest or Colorado, but I'm open to whatever happens. I might also go and check out communities in Japan. Did you ever hear of Masanobu Fukuoka?"

"No," said Syd.

"He wrote this book called *The One-Straw Revolution*." I could sense Permi getting worked up again. "It's like a farming manifesto man! He wrote that the ultimate goal of farming is the cultivation of human beings. That farming is the art of working *with* nature, not against it. And that farmers should strive to eliminate all unnecessary labor, and let nature do the work. Fukuoka passed away at like ninety-five, but I've heard there are still places in Japan experimenting with his *do-nothing farming*. I'd love to check them out—although I don't speak Japanese, so I don't know if it would happen—but I love his way, man."

"*Do nothing and nothing will be left undone*," quoted Syd.

"Exactly," said Permi, "when you follow nature, everything just takes care of itself. That's what I'm looking for—a natural sustainable community in tune with its surroundings. When the whole collapse comes, we'll be like these pinecones, with their seeds protected and ready to grow after the fire. Seeds from which future generations can pattern their way on, from which a new humanity can bloom."

"It sounds beautiful," said Syd.

It sounded exactly like his cosmic seedpods. But how practical would his dream be? If there was a collapse, wouldn't the survivors be roaming around like in some postapocalyptic film—all fighting with each other over everything? His little utopian farm would be swallowed up, like amber waves of grain before a swarm of ravenous locusts. But staring into the flames, I didn't say anything.

"Anyone else want to smoke a bowl?" asked Dylan.

The stars twinkled in the cool night air. We sat together bathed in the warm glow of the crackling firelight. In the darkness beyond, the river murmured, insects chirped, and the occasional owl hooted. We were a tiny island, floating in the vast wild-ness around us.

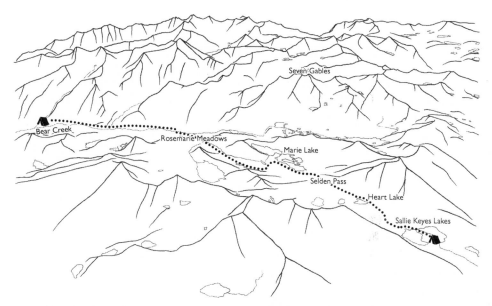

Bear Creek (9,240′) to Sallie Keyes Lakes (10,200′) via Selden Pass (10,910′)

7 miles—1,700 feet elevation gain; 740 feet elevation loss

S YD HAD BEEN MOVING pretty slowly all morning.
"You go on ahead. Wait for me where the trail crosses the creek," he urged.

From his eyes it looked like he hadn't slept much. It was just a mile or so to the crossing, so I went ahead—*maybe I could catch up to Dylan or Permi?*

Passing the trail leading up to the Seven Gables, my thoughts wandered back to Solomons and the snowstorm—*it was crazy coming out here so late in the season. How had he ever found his way outta these mountains in a total whiteout?*

Cresting the top of a small hill, I came to where the trail crossed Bear Creek and froze. *There was no bridge.* There was no log, no rock path, nothing to cross on.

The creek was over fifty feet wide. The water was raging, its surface white and churning as it roared over hidden rocks. My heart pounded and the sweat on my back began to chill. *Hadn't Syd said there'd be bridges at all the major crossings? How would we get across?*

OK, calm down—Dylan and Permi had been here, and their absence meant it *could* be crossed. The churning waves conjured up images of Pop—knocked down and dragged out to sea by some freakish rogue wave. I took a few steps back.

The large slippery-looking rocks under the surface and those poking up in the middle would make crossing here dangerous. Swimming was definitely off the table. Dropping my pack, I paced the bank, my apprehension growing.

It took Syd a really long time to show up, and even though we'd only gone a mile or so, his shirt was already soaked in sweat.

"How do we get across this thing?" I asked, rocking from leg to leg.

Syd examined the river. "I don't think it's more than knee deep," he said, wiping the sweat from his forehead. "But we should be careful, drowning is the number one cause of death in the wilderness and most of those incidents occur crossing rivers."

"Great—like this is a perfect time to mention that!"

"Sorry," he said looking tired and genuinely apologetic. "I thought you were on the swim team back in school?"

"That was a long time ago—I thought you said there'd be bridges over all the major rivers? Isn't there a better way to get over this one?"

"Let's see if we can find one," he said.

We scrambled up and down the bank in each direction, but eventually returned to where the trail crossing was. We hadn't found any stable logs or other good crossing points, and it slowly became clear that unless we wanted to go cross-country, this was the best spot to ford the rushing water.

"We'll just have to try it here," he said, with far less resolve than I was hoping for.

"Syd, I can't do this—"

"What do you mean?" he said, looking concerned.

"I mean, I don't think I can cross this. Ever since Pop died—I've never even told Ma this—but I have this thing about water. I just get all these images in my head of Pop and the beach and shit. At my last swim meet, I vomited into the pool. That's why I don't swim anymore. I can't do this."

Half expecting him to chew me out and yell, *Why the hell didn't you tell me?* I stood bracing for the storm. But he didn't shout or get upset or anything. He just stared at the ground thinking, then asked, "Do you think you could try it if we locked arms? Two people are a lot more stable when crossing that way. We could back up, or stop, whenever you need to."

He stood expectantly. I swallowed, my heart in my throat. "I can try—"

Finding a large rock, I sat down to gather my energy and remove my boots.

"Don't do that," he said.

"What?"

"Remove your boots."

"But they'll get soaked—"

"Crossing without your boots is a sure way to twist or break an ankle. You always want to keep your footwear on when crossing water."

He helped me prepare my pack, stuffing my clothes and sleeping bag into a large black garbage bag he'd brought for waterproofing and then doing the same with his gear. He collapsed his trekking poles, strapping them to his pack.

"Aren't you gonna use your poles?"

"If I was crossing alone, I would. But since we'll be locking arms, I think it's better to keep my hands free, and I wouldn't want to drop or lose one of them in the water."

The longer we took in preparation, the more anxious I became. "Is there no other way around this?"

"It doesn't look like it," he shook his head.

We pulled our packs on.

"Keep your hip belt unbuckled and loosen your shoulder straps like this," he said, demonstrating. "Many people have been washed headfirst into boulders because of their pack. By loosening it, you stand a better chance to get free should you lose your footing."

"Syd, you're not making me feel any better about this." My legs were already trembling.

We locked arms by linking our elbows and standing shoulder to shoulder. Then he inched slowly toward the water, all of my energy focused on keeping my legs from shaking as we edged toward the icy current. He went first, facing upstream and sidestepping. Soon my feet were headed into the water alongside him.

The rocks below my feet were slippery and uneven. Balancing, we moved deeper into the water. Clenching Syd, I felt like a blind tightrope walker balancing in a windstorm—only instead of wind, it was a driving wet icy current threatening to bring me down at any misstep. My legs became numb, but I was too preoccupied with balancing and pushing back images of death to notice. Step by icy step we edged deeper into the current, elbows locked. As we advanced, I could feel Syd struggling with his own footing and weak knees. We entered the center, the water pounding against my thighs and splashing up over my chest soaking my shirt. It was like a dance, leaning into the shifting flow, being pushed back, feet sliding over the rocks, sidestepping, and trying to keep my balance. All the while Syd led me slowly toward the far shore. My heart was pounding. Visions of waves and sand and ocean and Pop threatened to overtake me. I wanted to close my eyes. Holding my breath, I tightened my grip on Syd. Gradually the current eased, progress became swifter, and we reached a spot where we unlocked elbows. Springing from the water, I leapt to the solid ground of the far bank. We'd made it! Shivering and panting and just trying to stop my legs from shaking, I turned away from the water. Nausea swept over me. Dashing for the bushes, I heaved up my breakfast in wave upon wave. Eventually my breathing slowed, but my heart was still pounding.

Finding a boulder to lean on, I pulled off my boots and soaked clothes. Syd did the same. Then we wrung everything out and changed into fresh clothing, sticking the damp stuff into the netting on the back of our packs. Syd looked pretty winded from the crossing, but pulling on our packs, now laden with our damp clothes, we started up the trail, our boots squish-squish-squishing as we walked.

It felt good to be moving away from the water. Birds sang in the trees and the hot sun brought slow relief as it warmed our skin and dried our boots. Gradually my heart relaxed, and my body settled back into the rhythm of hiking.

The trail began to climb and once again Syd urged me to go ahead. Eventually I reached another stream crossing, this one shallow and safe. Hesitating momentarily, I stepped across—splashing through the ankle-deep water like a child, not worrying about wetting my already moist boots.

Coming to a trail junction, I sat to wait for Syd. There was a large meadow here with a meandering stream. The JMT continued up along the edge of the meadow. Pulling out my map, it appeared the other trail also led up to the Seven Gables region.

The sun was warm, but there was a refreshingly cool breeze. Insects buzzed about and the stream made a quiet gurgling sound. Reddish-purple flowers dotting the low green grass danced about in the breeze, their stems topped with brushlike petals.

Samantha would have probably called their bright color *fuchsia*. What did a name like that even mean? What was wrong with combining simple color names like red and purple? Did anyone actually say, *"Hey Bill, great fuchsia tie"*?

The small stream caught my eye—its clear crystal water bubbling merrily over the rocks. How was it this stream was so peaceful and calm, while Bear Creek had been so terrifying? Wasn't life the same? Is that what Permi had meant yesterday—*If we're lost in the flow, life is a joy; but facing death, it's a terror.* Was it all just a matter of perspective? What would Master Po have said? What would Syd say? Where was he anyway? He hadn't looked that well this morning. Was he OK? Getting up and pacing around, I strained my eyes to look for him. I hadn't gone that far. It wasn't like the time I'd been chasing Kydoime. Should I go back and find him?

Then I spotted him dragging himself slowly up the hill. Something was wrong. He was covered in sweat, his face looked drawn, and he was wheezing again. Staggering the final paces over to me, he dropped his pack, took a huge gasp of air, then sat hunched over.

"What's wrong?"

"I don't know," he rasped. "I'm having trouble breathing. It's never happened like this. It feels like I have a nosebleed inside my sinuses. I can taste blood when I swallow, but it's not too bad."

It didn't sound good, and although the air was cool and breezy, he was clearly perspiring.

"Maybe we'd better take a long break here?" He readily agreed.

His lips and fingernails looked almost purple—maybe it was the altitude again? We were gaining elevation and would be going over Selden Pass today, but we would be under eleven thousand feet. He'd had no trouble at Silver Pass, and that was almost the same height. My eyes jumped to his folding shovel, now sitting askew across the back of his dropped pack like the hand of some broken clock.

Perhaps he hadn't had enough to drink and was just dehydrated? That could cause nosebleeds, right? "Have some water," I offered, handing him my bottle. "What are those fuchsia-colored flowers in the meadow?" I asked, hoping to perk him up.

He took a long swig of the water. "Some sort of paintbrush, I guess."

That wasn't a good sign. Usually, he'd launch into a seminar. Maybe something in the conversation yesterday had kept him up? Or maybe he'd eaten something bad? Maybe Permi's herbs or the pine nuts hadn't agreed with him?

About thirty minutes later, he was sitting up and breathing normally.

"Are you feeling any better?"

"A little, let's get going." He got up, laboring to pull on his pack.

I followed slowly behind as he teetered along. His pace had definitely slackened. He wasn't going more than a mile an hour now, and we'd been making two or even three the day before.

"Do you want me to carry some of your gear?"

"No," he groaned dismissively, "it's not that bad."

The trail followed the small stream for awhile, then climbed up among silver-gray rocks dotted with grassy vegetation. At first, the colorful paintbrush flowers seemed to be scattered everywhere, popping up from behind tiny cracks and rocks, but gradually the terrain grew more barren with only sparse patches of grass and the occasional stunted pine. The breeze picked up, and I started to feel chilled. As we inched forward, Syd began making that strange nasal wheezing sound again.

We passed some small lakelets, then climbed a twisting trail of granite to the side of a wide shallow lake. Some ducks were huddled on the surface and a few dark birds circled overhead. The lake had several rocky islets. Dwarf pines dotted its boulder-strewn banks.

Heading to the shore, we dropped our packs for a late lunch. There was little shelter here. A gusty wind rippled the water chilling us with each blast. Even the ducks seemed to struggle when it blew.

Syd took out his rain shell and pulled it on over his damp sweat-soaked shirt. Not wanting to wear my poncho, I sat shivering in the breeze, wondering if we weren't in for a snowstorm, like the one Solomons encountered.

Lunch was more monotonous bars. Syd gnawed slowly on his, then ate some dried fruit and nuts. It wasn't much, but I was glad he ate.

"How's your breathing?" I asked.

"A little better."

Looking up, I could see some other hikers coming over the top of the pass, moving like ants down the long zigzagging switchbacks. Even though it was still a mile or so away, the climb didn't look that bad. After that we'd be descending again, and if it was all just altitude then Syd would gradually improve.

In less than twenty minutes, the hikers—a pair of couples about my age—reached the lake.

Eventually, we finished eating and like beasts of burden, took up the yoke of our packs and began struggling up the switchbacks. Syd stopped often to catch his breath. "Do you want me to take your food or something?" I offered—but he just brushed me off, grunting a short guttural, "No," with a dismissive sweep of his hand.

He was clearly in a bad mood. It was sad watching him struggle like this. We pushed on up the winding slope, the sound of the rocks grating under our boots punctuated by the sudden crack of his rain shell slapping about in the strong gusts of wind.

It took the better part of an hour to reach the pass. At the top, Syd dropped his pack and curled up behind a large rock out of the wind.

Waiting for him to recover, I pulled out my map, pressing it against the side of a boulder to keep it from flapping.

Our plan was to head down to Muir Trail Ranch and take a zero tomorrow, but that was still another seven or eight miles away. It was already getting late and at the pace we were going, it would be long past dark before we got there. It seemed more realistic to stop at Heart Lake or Sallie Keyes Lakes, which were just a few miles below the pass.

After almost half an hour, Syd pulled himself up, strapped on his pack, and we started down. To my relief, he seemed to be moving a bit faster.

Heart Lake, named for its shape, was visible down a rocky and slightly grassy incline. We soon reached its deep blue shores. The wind wasn't as bad.

"Maybe we should camp here, instead of trying to make it all the way to Muir Trail Ranch?" I suggested.

"Too rocky," was his only reply, so we trudged on.

From Heart Lake, the trail dropped down a quick jog coming to the first of the three Sallie Keyes Lakes. The lake looked perfect and there were plenty of good camping sites available, but Syd passed it by with hardly more than a glance.

At the second lake, I said, "Syd, you're clearly having trouble and it's getting late. We have at least six more miles to the ranch, and from the map it doesn't look like there are any more good camping spots between here and there. Let's just take it easy, stop here, and take a short downhill day to the ranch tomorrow. How about it?"

He paused, pulled out his map, studied it, and simply said, "OK. You're right."

We found a nice site, not too far from the lake, and made camp. By the time I'd pumped water for dinner and returned, Syd was stretched out in his sleeping bag inside his bivy.

"What about dinner?" I asked.

"Sorry, you'll have to eat alone tonight. I'm beat."

"Do you want some more mashed potatoes?"

"No, I'm not hungry."

"OK," I said, feeling somewhat nervous. *Maybe sleep would be the best medicine?*

The site was quiet. Listening to the hiss of the small gas stove, I boiled water to rehydrate another of my "gourmet" Backwoods Buffet food pouches.

There were some tents along the other shore, but they were far away, and it wouldn't be right to walk over and leave Syd all alone.

The sky over the hills took on a grayish-purple hue. Chewing on my tasteless noodles, I sat worrying about Syd.

DAY TWELVE

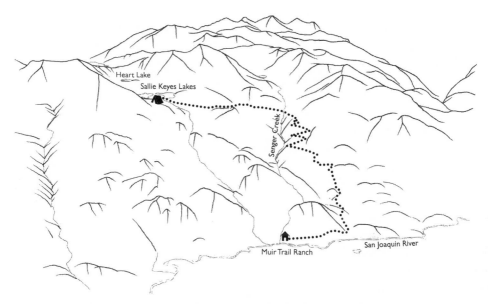

Sallie Keyes Lakes (10,200′) to Muir Trail Ranch (7,760′)
6 miles—50 feet elevation gain; 2,590 feet elevation loss

I WOKE IN THE CLAMMY PREDAWN GLOW to the sound of a low moan. Some animal down by the lake must be in pain. Burying my head in the hood of my sleeping bag, I rolled over to try and blot out the noise and sleep again, but the sound continued. It was a low soft guttural cry, like some animal wounded in the night and left to die.

Unable to get back to sleep, I pulled on my long johns and T-shirt, found my headlamp, and unzipped the tent. The sound stopped. A cold wet mist hung over everything and the headlamp did little to help me see. Stooping down, I picked up two stones, just in case this thing was dangerous. Then it started again, a long low guttural sobbing sound.

The sound wasn't animal, it was human. It was coming from Syd's bivy.

What should I do? Should I check on him, or just go back to my tent? The low sobbing continued. Dropping the rocks, I headed over to his bivy.

"Syd?" I called gently over his sobs and cries. "Are you OK?"

The sobbing grew louder. The small bivy convulsed with his shaking. Carefully, I unzipped the fine netting and peered in.

Syd was curled up, only half inside his sleeping bag, weeping and shaking like a baby. His skeletal arms clutching his bandana like a tissue.

Unsure what to do, I crawled into the small shelter, holding him from behind like a child. "It'll be all right," I said calmingly. "It'll be all right."

Syd seemed to relax into my embrace but continued sobbing into his wet bandana. "I woke three times last night," he said shaking. "Each time I couldn't breathe. I think my lungs are giving out. Or it's the thin air up here. Or some kind of internal bleeding. I feel cold. I'm dying, Gil. I'm dying. I'm not going to make it to Whitney. I'm gonna die out here in the woods."

Holding his frail bony frame to me, I repeated, "It'll be OK Syd. You'll be OK. It's just the air here. The altitude. You'll see."

"I won't be OK," he moaned softly, crying again. "My lungs must be filling with fluid. I could barely make it last night. I didn't tell you. Going over the pass, I barely made it. It took all my effort just to climb that hill. I was so happy when you said we should camp here. I should have told you then. I was wrong to drag you on this stupid quest," he wept. "I was wrong, and I'm sorry."

He blew a long steady stream of fluid into his bandana. A shudder of fear and discomfort flowed through me—was I holding another man? Instinctively, I wanted to pull back, to withdraw. Ignoring the feeling, I held tighter, gripping Syd closer to me. Embracing him in a way I hadn't let myself do with anyone since Pop's death. My tears began to flow. "You'll be OK Syd, you'll be fine," I cried—as much to him as to myself.

He sobbed, "Each time I woke up, I had to force myself to breathe. It felt like drowning. Like I was deep underwater and I had to use all my strength to come back to the surface. Each time it was harder. The next time, I'm not going to make it back. The next time, I'm gonna die."

I held him close, comforting him like a parent. Like I always wished I could have held on to Pop.

"I'm afraid of death. I'm afraid. I thought I wasn't, but I am. I'd read all my philosophy books. All my literature—all illusions. All comforts of the mind to quiet the heart's true fear. Shakespeare said it best, *To be or not to be . . . must give us pause. Must give us pause.*"

Syd stopped shaking. The ashen mist of the predawn air blew over us.

"Your father's death, Gil. The reason I skipped his funeral. It wasn't because I was sick. It was because I couldn't face your mother. The reason your father drowned, that wave that caught him—it was my fault. I told your parents to go to the Lost Coast. I told them about the camping there. But I forgot to tell them about the tides. I forgot to tell them to check the tides. It was my fault your dad drowned. I'm so sorry," he cried. "I'm so sorry." He shook again. "I loved your dad, but I forgot to tell him about the tides and he died because of me," he sobbed uncontrollably, convulsing.

I held on to his dying form, my tears flowing. "You're wrong," I cried, holding him tighter. "Pop didn't die 'cause of you. I spoke with him before they went. Pop had a map and a tide table. He had me double-check them online. He knew about the tides. He had the whole trip planned around them. The sheriff said it was a rogue wave that killed Pop. It was nothing anyone could've predicted. It wasn't even high tide. Pop's death wasn't your fault Syd," I consoled, my tears falling in streams and wetting his shirt. "If anyone's to blame, it was me. They wanted me to go with them. They asked me to go, but I refused. I was too selfish. I wanted to stay with my friends. I was a swimmer, if I'd been there, I could have saved him. But I was a thousand miles away, hanging out with my stupid friends, instead of with my parents where I belonged. I wasn't there when he needed me. It's my fault Pop died, not yours."

I cried even more, hugging him tightly. Syd squeezed my hand, "Thank you for telling me. I always thought it was me. I thought it was because I hadn't told him about the tides. But it's not your fault either. You couldn't have known what would happen. No one could."

"It was my fault. I shoulda been with him. I should've gone when they asked me."

I held on to him and could feel his body shake. In a weak voice he asked, "Is that why you dropped out? Because of your father's death?"

Swallowing hard, I began, "I never told anyone this—not even Ma—but the reason I never finished school, the reason I got that stupid paralegal certificate wasn't 'cause I dropped out. I never dropped out. I was expelled. After Pop died, the girl I was seeing dumped me, and then everything just fell apart. I moved into this stupid frat house and spent all my time lost in beer and drugs. I was failing my Law and Society class, the one class I needed to get into law school. I didn't know what to do." Holding him tighter, the words just poured out, "I cheated. I cheated in a bad way. A guy in the class showed me how to fix the professor's door so it wouldn't lock. Then we snuck in at night and photographed the exam—he'd left it right there on his desk. But we fucked up! We totally fucked up! He'd made four versions of the test and the answers we bubbled in matched one of the others. My buddy confessed, and we were both expelled. Don't tell Ma, she doesn't know. That's why I can't go back to school, 'cause I fucked up."

He was silent. I held tight to his thin frame. "What school would take me after that? That's why I never finished. Because of my own stupidity. It's what I deserve for not being there for Pop."

Syd blew a long stream of liquid into his bandana. "You can go back if you want to."

I held on. He seemed to gain strength and slowly turned over facing me. "You should have said something Gil. You should have told someone what happened." His eyes were brimming with tears. "No one will hold one bad step against you. If you apply to a different school, they'll have no way of knowing what happened. I can write a letter for you. People will understand. You're not stuck. You can always start over if you want to. Never give up on yourself."

"But I can't," I cried. "Don't you see? It's like that guy Allan said in the pool, this is my karma, my punishment for not helping Pop."

"*Fate is what we make of it*," he said through more coughs.

He shut his eyes. Holding on to him, my tears wouldn't stop flowing. "You can't die Syd, you can't!" I pleaded, shaking him. "Don't leave me here alone in the woods. We'll make it out together. We can do it! We'll go back home. We'll go back together. *Please—*"

There was no movement. Hugging him, I repeated in my head, *Please don't die! Please don't die!*

I don't know how long I lay there clinging to Syd, but slowly his chest heaved. He moved. Coughed. Then moved again. Releasing my grip, he slowly leaned up on to his elbows, then he blew his nose into his bandana in a long slow wheeze.

"Thank you for telling me about your dad," he said weakly, holding my gaze with his deep watery eyes. He steadied himself, speaking soberly like someone waking from a dream, "Listen, Muir Trail Ranch is downhill from here. It's at lower altitude. If we can get there, they'll have a phone. I'll call my kids. Explain everything to them. Tell them where we are. I think we can get a horse back to a road from there. We can leave the trail and go home. I'll go back to the hospital and you won't need to bury me out here. It's over. We can walk down to the ranch and go back. I can make it now."

Tears of hope dripped down my cheeks, "OK," I said, squeezing him tightly. "We'll walk down to the ranch together and get to a phone. You'll make it there—you'll make it!"

He fell back and lay shaking in my arms. He was so thin. So fragile.

We lay together for a long time. Dawn broke scattering the clouds and the mist. Insects began singing their rhythmic chorus. Somewhere a group of birds chirped their morning song.

Syd seemed to recover another fraction of his strength. "I'll be alright. Thank you, Gil."

When I was sure he was OK, I went back to my tent. From there, I could hear him moving around and arranging his stuff. Somehow he'd found the energy to pack.

The sun rose. We sat together quietly, eating our morning meal. It was good to see him eating, and he slowly seemed to gain more strength.

Just before heading out, I asked him, "Do you want me to help you carry some of your gear?"

"No, I can manage," he insisted, pulling on his pack as if nothing'd happened.

He started hiking, and I tagged closely behind. Was he alright now? If it wasn't for this morning, I'd hardly know anything was wrong. The best thing now was to get down to the ranch as quickly as we could.

The trail was quiet, almost ghostly. It wound by a boot-shaped lake, the last in the Sallie Keyes chain, then climbed gently over a small rise. The sun warmed the air, seeming to breathe new strength into Syd. He picked up his pace.

We went on for almost an hour, with Syd silently bearing the burden of his pack. The wheezing in his breath was gone. *Should I ask him how he was doing? Start some sort of conversation?* It was probably best not to tire him.

The trees thinned and the view opened up, revealing a steep exposed hillside covered in tall yellow sun-bleached grass. The trail wound down the slope in long sweeping curves. Far below was a forested plateau. Cutting a wide swath through the dense trees was the South

Fork of the San Joaquin River. How had Solomons ever crossed that? From the map, I knew the river led down to Florence Lake, then on by Lake Edison, but neither was visible from here. Somewhere down there was Muir Trail Ranch. We were almost there.

Through the grass we saw a woman in a tan and green uniform striding up the trail. She was still several long switchbacks below but climbing fast despite the rising heat.

I called to Syd, "It's a ranger—we're saved! She can radio for help." I squeezed past him, moving ahead to meet her.

"No," Syd said. It was the first word he'd spoken since we'd packed up.

I looked at him, puzzled.

"Don't tell her anything. I don't want her calling in the cavalry. You've got to promise me you won't say a word to her about my condition. We're almost at the ranch and I want to get there myself, on my own two legs. Just tell her we're hiking the trail, nothing more."

He looked at me with his eyes, as if to say, *Please.* It made no sense, but it wasn't much farther to the ranch. Reluctantly, I nodded, "OK." *What else could I say?*

The ranger soon reached us. Syd lingered a few paces behind. She looked almost sixty, with sun-dried skin, a kind face, and lively brown eyes. Her golden nametag read, *Ranger Abbott.* On her belt, a large radio was crackling.

"Where are you boys coming from today?" she asked in a throaty but firm granny voice.

I turned to look questioningly at Syd, but he held my eyes. Turning back, I said, "From Sallie Keyes Lakes, ma'am. We're hiking the JMT."

"Oh—" she sounded interested, "—where'd ya start?"

"Tuolumne Meadows," I replied.

"So, you crossed both Donohue and Silver Pass?"

"Yes, ma'am," I said. Syd and I had really covered a lot of ground.

To my surprise, Syd spoke up saying, "You're the first ranger we've seen out here. Somehow I thought there'd be more."

"Sometimes there are," she said, "but right now the Forest Service budget is pretty thin—and there's a lot of wilderness to cover. Can I ask your names?"

"I'm Gil," I said a bit impatiently, "and this is Syd."

"I'm Ranger Abbott, but call me Gabrielle, please. It's a real scorcher today, isn't it?"

I nodded—feeling like someone rushing his pregnant wife to the hospital and being stopped by a traffic cop.

"Do you boys have your wilderness permit handy?" she asked me, smiling.

Shit—did we have to pull that thing out? Did I have it, or did Syd?

"We do," Syd answered.

He removed his pack, setting it down carefully. Unzipping the top compartment, he drew out a neatly sealed ziplock bag. From this, he removed the pristine green wilderness permit we'd been issued at Tuolumne Meadows on our first day. He passed it to Gabrielle.

She looked over the permit, then pulled out a small red stamp from her belt pouch and stamped the bottom, signing over the stamp, and handing it back to Syd.

Good, now we can go, right?

"What happens to people who don't have permits?" Syd asked her calmly.

Was he making chitchat? We had to get down to the ranch! What was he thinking? I wanted to shoot him an angry, "let's go" glance, but couldn't with the ranger standing there.

Gabrielle looked at him, scrunched up her nose, and said in her feisty granny voice, "Generally when someone doesn't have a permit, we write 'em a ticket for five hundred dollars—for a first offense, mind you—and escort 'em out of the wilderness. The law allows us to fine someone up to five thousand dollars, or even stick 'em in jail—but it rarely comes to that."

"I see," said Syd.

"It's a real pain though. You'd be surprised how often people don't have the proper permit. I'll be patrolling a nice section of wilderness, helping injured hikers, and breaking down old fire pits—when I'll come across the illegal campfire of some half-drunken cowboys, all with no proper permits. I'll have to stop my work and confront 'em—which isn't always easy—and then escort 'em out of the forest. Sometimes it can take two, maybe three days out of my schedule. And then there's the paperwork." She looked a bit riled, as if remembering some particularly difficult encounter.

Rocking up and down on my heels waiting, I felt like someone in desperate need of the bathroom on a long car ride. *Could we please just go now?* But she just kept on jabbering.

"But that's my job. Mostly though I meet good folks like you boys, pick up trash, and get to enjoy the flowers and the sunsets," she smiled again. "Speaking of trash; what are you boys doing with your soiled toilet tissue?"

She was staring directly at me. Why did rangers always seem to ask me about my shit? "It's in our packs," I answered quickly. "I have mine in a triple ziplock bag. Do you need to see it?" *Shit—why did I say that? What if she really asked to see it and we had to waste even more time?*

"Nope, but glad to hear it," she smiled, "because there's a lot of California White Flower out there."

"*California White Flower?*" asked Syd. I nearly jumped out of my socks!

"That's what we rangers call old toilet tissue that's been scattered around by animals or just dropped there on the ground. It's the worst part of my job—cleaning up after other people's messes. It's amazing how many people will just drop their tissue on the ground thinking nature will clean it up for them. Not realizing that tissue, even the brown biodegradable kind, takes months to break down and decompose."

Oh my God, don't tell me we were going to have to stand through an environmental lecture on toilet paper decomposition? Could we just move on?

"Even when people bury their tissue, the mice and raccoons just dig it right up, scattering everything and making a mess. I carry a big bag for tissue," she said, indicating the large black trash bag strapped to her pack, "and after every patrol I make, it's full. I wish more people would just stop using tissue altogether—my friend Tess gave me a backcountry bidet and I haven't needed tissue since." Seemingly noticing my impatience, she wrapped up, "Sorry boys, we rangers seem to talk a lot about tissue, perhaps because collecting it has become such a big part of our job."

"It's understandable," said Syd. "Thanks for stamping our permit, it means a lot to me."

"Yeah, thanks," I said, hoping now we could finally move on.

"How long have you been a backcountry ranger?" Syd asked her. I had to count my breaths to keep from exploding.

"Too long—this'll be my thirtieth season. We aren't paid much either—if you're thinking of applying. Even the guys sitting at the National Park entrance stations make more than me. But they have to breathe all those exhaust fumes and answer the same fool questions all day, while I'm free to wander mostly as I like. I guess that's compensation enough. You boys have a safe hike now."

She started up the trail past us. I let my breath out slowly.

"Wow," Syd said, "that's the first ranger we've met in twelve days—I mean apart from the employees in that office at Devil's Postpile—she was the first real *wilderness ranger.*"

I stood silently, boiling in the heat—holding my tongue as Ranger Abbott slowly made her way up the hill. When I was certain she was out of earshot, I exploded, "What the hell were you doing? Asking the ranger about permits and toilet paper? I'm surprised you didn't invite her to tea! We need to get down to the ranch and get help! *Why didn't you just tell her that?!*"

Syd stood there looking down, quietly fidgeting with the stamped green permit in his hands.

I turned, waiting briefly for him to gather up his pack, then stomped down the hot slope like a soldier. Syd trailed quietly behind.

Switchback after switchback we descended in the heat. Every so often I waited for him, the gravity of my stomach pulling me down faster than his fragile legs and bad knee could handle. It was good we were heading down. I wouldn't wanna be climbing up this in the heat. I could see why the ranger had made an early start of it.

As we descended, Syd's spirits seemed to rise and his pace quickened. He began humming something classical to himself. Muir Trail Ranch couldn't be more than a mile now. We'd make it. My anger began to wane.

After several more switchbacks, we came to a steep side trail covered in loose rock, or what hikers called *scree.* A faded wooden sign next to the trail read, Florence Lake.

"This is it," Syd declared with certainty. "This is the cutoff to the ranch."

"The sign says, Florence Lake," I pointed out, not wanting to descend a steep rocky trail only to have to climb back up it if he was wrong. "Maybe there's another trail up ahead that goes to the ranch? Wouldn't the sign list the ranch if this was it?"

"No, this is the trail," he insisted. "I came here years ago with your father. We wanted to stop at the hot springs by the ranch and argued about this same sign, so we passed it and ended up missing the ranch entirely. Look at your map. The JMT leads all the way down to the river from here. This is the only turnoff. If we keep going, we'll have to backtrack about two or three miles down the river to get there."

"OK," I agreed, hoping he was right. We started down the steep side trail. It was only half as wide as the JMT and poorly groomed. Twice I slid on roots and scree almost twisting a leg. Eventually the trail crested a dusty hill, and there fifty feet below us was the gate to Muir Trail Ranch. We'd made it!

I was raring to go, but Syd stopped me. "Listen," he said, "I'm sorry about this morning." I wanted to protest, but he continued. "This is hard for me to explain, but ever since I was a kid, I was afraid of death. At thirteen, I started reading philosophy books, and by twenty-two I was in graduate school—all in an effort to understand what happens after death. The books and languages I studied, they were all ones I thought could answer the big questions, like *What is life? What is mortality?*" He paused, somewhere in the distance a horse whinnied. "But now that I'm actually the one facing it. Now that I have cancer. Well, it's all different now and the questions aren't the same. I can't explain it all. But dying isn't what's described on the pages of those books. Dying is like a door we all pass through. What actually matters is how we pass through that door. The Native Americans when facing death in battle would sing a personal death song, then bravely meet their enemy. Have you ever heard the phrase, *It's a good day to die?* That's a Native American saying."

Where he was going with this? Was he about to die?

"Yesterday, coming over Selden Pass, I was exhausted. Maybe it was my body starting to give out. Maybe it was the altitude, or something in my lungs. Or maybe it was just something in my sinuses. But I was exhausted. I didn't sleep well. All night, I felt like I was drowning. And I was scared. I was ready to give up. To call it quits and go back to that hospital and die an undignified death."

"But we made it," I said, pointing insistently down the hill. "Look, the ranch is right there! We'll walk down and phone Cass. We can get help! You're gonna be alright—"

"No," he said cutting me off. "I'm dying. We both know that. But I've chosen to die this way—*on the trail*. This is a good way to die. And if I die today, then today is a good day to die."

He seemed to draw strength from his conviction, but what the fuck was he saying?

"Something happened to me back there with the ranger," he said staring at me with a strange intensity.

"*With the ranger?*" I repeated, puzzled.

"Did you notice her name was Gabrielle?"

"Yeah, so?"

"So? Gabrielle is the female form of Gabriel, the messenger angel of God."

I stared at him in stupefied incomprehension. He wasn't really drawing meaning from that? She was probably just French-Canadian or something.

"We haven't seen a backcountry ranger since we started the trail. When Gabrielle appeared today—when she put her stamp and signature on our permit—it was like a message from above telling me, *You're on the Trail. You're on a holy mission. You can't quit now.* And I knew we must go on—to whatever end this takes us."

"You're nuts!" I exclaimed, hands on my hips. "You were at death's door just two hours ago and now you wanna go on hiking, all 'cause some ranger happened to have a name from the Bible?"

He nodded looking at me, his eyes moistening like those of a scolded child. I glared back. *What the fuck was wrong with him?* We'd made it back. He was sick. After last night we couldn't just keep going—*couldn't he see that?* When did he suddenly get so religious?

He stood there, meeting my gaze with his pleading eyes.

He looked better now. More resolute. More at peace and less troubled than before. My anger ebbed. This was his journey. His last wish. I'd promised to stick it out with him. Besides, if anything did happen, we'd be at the ranch. We'd be safe. I'd watch him, and if anything happened, we'd get help right away. We could wait and see.

"OK, enough heavy talk," I exhaled, dropping my arms.

Syd smiled saying, "Come on. We have reservations!"

So we weren't going to call Cass, head back, or find a doctor? Maybe I was the one who needed my head examined! Following him, we trod down the hill. The scent of horse mixed with dust reached my nostrils. Syd opened the gate that only moments before I thought would be our salvation, and we passed through.

Beyond the gate was a small corral with several lazily grazing horses, a log building with a shingled A-frame roof, and a cabin with a sign above it simply reading Store. A tall guy in his mid-twenties with curly reddish-brown hair and freckles appeared, clipboard in hand. He was dressed in jeans and heavy work overalls, like a cross between a rancher and a maintenance guy. "Hi, I'm Samuel," he said. "Welcome to Muir Trail Ranch. Do you guys have reservations, or are you just needing to resupply?"

"Both," said Syd. "We reserved a cabin, but we're also picking up two buckets."

"Perfect," said Samuel. Syd gave him our names and he crossed them off the list on his clipboard. "Well, let me orientate you around. You can leave your packs here for now." We happily dropped our loads by the store.

The grounds were quite extensive. Samuel showed us the kitchen, dining hall, an outdoor picnic area, and the store—which to my relief had a phone that hikers could use. At the top of a small bluff, he showed us two log structures with partially open wooden frames. "Those are our hot spring baths," he said, "you all are welcome to use them any time, but they're more popular at night. The only rule is no glass or alcohol, and that you be polite if another group is waiting to use the bath."

"Is it same-sex only or mixed?" I asked, recalling the crowd at Iva Bell.

"Is it OK to soak naked?" echoed Syd.

Samuel looked us up and down. "If *you* find some women that are willin' to soak *naykeed* with you—" he sneered, summarizing our smelly clothes, dirty faces, my belly, and Syd's skeletal frame with a roll of his eyes, "—then have at it!" he chuckled, laughing to himself.

I didn't care much for his tone, but then again we probably did look a little like the flea-bitten wandering samurai from *Yojimbo*.

Samuel led us back down to where we'd dropped our packs. "You'll be in cabin number two," he said. "You can pick up your resupply buckets over there," and with a wave of his clipboard he vanished back into the store.

A young assistant at the resupply building retrieved our buckets. "You can sort your stuff out over there," she said, indicating some picnic tables by the building. Next to the tables were a series of open buckets, all laid out in neat rows. "Those are our hiker box," she explained. "Feel free to take or leave anything you want."

Syd and I went over to the tables. "Are you sure you wanna keep going?" I asked. "We can still call Cass or your son Sean—maybe he'll know what to do."

"I'm fine now," he insisted. "I'm sorry I made you worry. It was probably the altitude and lack of sleep. I feel much better now."

Not knowing what to say, I began unsealing my bucket. Syd went back to the store to purchase more fuel and stuff.

He did look much better and maybe it was just the altitude, but it would still be best to call his kids and let them know what was going on.

In my bucket was the usual mixture of oatmeal, flavorless granola bars, and Backwoods Buffet dinners. I began rummaging around through the buckets of their "hiker box." By the time Syd returned, I'd swapped my bars and dinners for an assortment of promising goodies.

"You're really moving up in the gastronomical world," Syd praised my collection of food. "Nice choices!"

"Syd, I think we should give Cass a call—just to let her know where we are and how you're doin and stuff."

"No need," he said. "I phoned her just now from the store. She said to say hello."

"What did she say when you told her about last night?"

"I told you, that was just altitude, so I didn't mention it. I don't want to worry her."

I wasn't entirely convinced and not telling her wasn't exactly what I had in mind, but maybe he was right? Wouldn't it just cause her needless worry? She was his daughter after all, it was probably best to respect his wishes. But it didn't feel right. I guess the best thing would be to watch and wait. If he got any worse tonight, I would call her from the store myself.

After arranging our stuff, we went over to a large spring scale they'd rigged up. My pack weighed fifty-five pounds. "That's way too heavy," said Syd. His fully-loaded pack weighed just under thirty-eight pounds. "You can mail some of your gear home if you're not using it. I saw some boxes in the store. The rule is, *If you haven't used it, you can probably lose it.*"

Sorting through my gear, I began removing stuff I hadn't used—my winter gloves, extra thermals, a spare beer shirt, a harmonica that I couldn't even play, a Frisbee, the solar shower I'd used that one time, a deck of cards, a Swiss Army knife that I'd yet to need despite all its nifty tools, the pages of the map we'd already hiked over, and two of the three bottles of insect repellant I'd taken. My newly lightened pack weighed forty-nine pounds—six pounds of unwanted gear and clothing dumped! While my pack was still much heavier than Syd's, I felt pretty good about lightening up.

Taking all the stuff I'd removed to the store, I stuck them in a box and paid the postage.

"Will that be all?" asked the young attendant.

"Just one thing—that old guy who was in here a while ago buying fuel, did he make a phone call?"

"Not that I know of."

Had he lied about calling Cass? I really didn't want to confront him on it.

To our great surprise, on the way to our cabin we ran into Kydoime. She was wearing a black sleeveless T-shirt with a wide-open front held together by a laced string that accentuated her cleavage. Her hair and shirt were moist, like she'd just showered.

"Hey, you guys made it," she glowed, "did you just arrive?"

"Yeah," I said stunned, and Syd nodded. "I thought you were coming here yesterday—"

"I did, I'm running ahead of schedule. I had to stay down by the river at the backpacker's camp last night because my reservation was only for today." Her warm husky voice made my body tingle. "I kind of feel guilty moving here—most hikers won't pay the price for a room. Are you guys staying here too, or in tents?"

"We're in cabin number two," said Syd.

"We're neighbors then! I'm in cabin one," she said smiling.

"That's great!" I blurted. "We were just about to check out our cabin and do some laundry, wanna join us?"

"I just finished all that, but I'll catch up with you guys at dinner, OK?" She gave me another of her winks, then continued on toward the store.

Her hips swayed as she strode away, her legs perfectly formed.

"Come on," said Syd, calling me back to the planet, "let's go do our laundry."

The cabins were log-frame buildings with green canvas roofs. The door to ours was open and had no lock. Inside were three small tightly-made beds. There were real pillows and sheets and a folded towel on each bed.

The bathroom and showers were in separate wooden stalls behind the cabins. The dirty face with the weeks-old mangy beard staring back from the mirror was hardly my own. My hair was all matted down and twisted. My skin covered in black grime.

"Hey Syd," I shouted from my stall, "I look like some kinda mountain man!"

"Must be all those Backwoods meals you're eating!" he called back.

It was the longest, steamiest, most refreshing shower I could remember.

After doing some much-needed laundry, Syd suggested we take a walk over to the backpacker's campsite. He seemed to be doing much better.

Wandering through the sea of tents, we heard Led Zeppelin's "Stairway to Heaven" emanating from up on a rocky ledge. Following the sound, we found Dylan seated under the awning of his yellow flag-draped tent kicking back and enjoying the afternoon sun— with what else? A bowl.

"Hey guys, great to see ya! Wanna smoke?"

"Thanks, but not right now," Syd replied. "I was looking for Rena. I heard she might be coming here tonight."

"Haven't seen her yet, but Kydoime is down at the ranch."

"Yeah, we saw her a while ago," I said, thinking of her lacy black outfit.

"Oh, that's right, you guys are staying at the ranch, aren't you?" he asked, apparently just absorbing the fact that we were clean and didn't have our packs on. "Mighty pricey."

"Yes, it is a bit expensive," agreed Syd. "Listen, if you see Rena—"

But he didn't need to finish his sentence 'cause scrambling over the rocks with her ginormous blue backpack came a familiar voice in broken English, "Syd! Gil! Dylan! You all here? Happy to see you! Trail was soooo hot and I missed turnoff! Had to come back up trail from river to get here!"

"You had to walk back almost three miles?" asked Syd.

"Trail here marked Florence Lake, not Muir Trail Ranch," she said, making an exaggerated, almost cute, unhappy face.

"Yes, it's very confusing," he agreed. "Where's Kitty?"

"Kitty slept in at VVR. Big hangover. I couldn't wait because of plane ticket. But Kitty said she'd catch up in couple days. I think so. She move so fast. So happy to see you guys! Is this backpacker's camp?"

"Yes," said Syd, "but we have a room with an extra bed. You can use it if you'd like. There's a shower and a home-cooked dinner too. I think we could sneak you in."

"Really!?" she squealed.

"If you leave most of your stuff here, they'll think you're just another guest of the ranch."

"I can watch your stuff," volunteered Dylan.

"Really?!" said Rena, "A bed? A shower? And dinner!"

"And you can stay for free," added Syd, closing the deal.

Within minutes Rena had grabbed a few essentials and was ready to go.

I turned to Dylan, "Why don't you join us too? No one would see you shower and the dinner has to be better than trail food. Whaddya say?"

"Nah," said Dylan, "I tried earlier and that tall kid who checks people in, the one with the attitude, kicked me out."

"You mean Samuel?" I asked. He'd kinda rubbed me the wrong way too.

"Yeah, Samuel," Dylan continued, "Kydoime was hassled by him too. She said he was a real asshole. That's why I pitched my tent up here. So I could smoke my shit and not be bothered. There's a warm pool in the meadow, and it'll be sunset soon. I'm just fine hanging out here. But thanks for the offer."

"Where's Permi?" asked Syd.

"He hung with me last night but left in the morning. Wanted to hike up to Evolution Creek lookin' for mushrooms—I hope he found the *right kind*, if ya know what I mean," he cocked his head, half grinning. "I'll catch up ta him tomorrow at the Muir Hut."

We all said bye to Dylan, sneaking Rena into the ranch and showing her where the showers were.

About thirty minutes later, a clean and smiling Rena came bounding into the room, her hair dripping from inside a wrapped towel. "Wow, showers soooo good! Thank you!" she glowed. She'd changed her clothes too. "You sure it alright, I stay here? Not get noticed?"

"It'll be fine," said Syd. "There are so many people here, they won't even know. Maybe later we can all go soak in their hot spring baths."

"They have hot springs too?" Rena asked wide-eyed. Syd nodded. "*Sugoi!*" she exclaimed in Japanese, clapping her hands and jumping. Syd smiled.

Maybe it was Rena, but Syd had certainly recovered his strength. Probably it'd just been the altitude—like up on Donohue. Now I could just relax and enjoy this place!

We all headed back up the hill, one merry group, to the predinner "happy hour" Samuel had told us about.

On the outdoor benches by the corral was a huge spread. A crowd of ranch guests—obviously not hikers from their neat "cotton kills" button-downs and jeans—were socializing and enjoying the aperitifs.

Syd and Rena got some wine and cheese. I grabbed a cold Sierra Nevada and a heap of grapes and crackers. Then we spotted Kydoime sipping wine off by herself at the end of one of the benches. "Gil! Rena! Syd!" she called out happily when she saw us. "Come join me!" We ambled over. "I'm not really into the ranching and horseback crowd," she confessed. "Is Rena staying here too?"

"We sneaked her in," I confided in a low tone. Samuel was prowling the party, and I didn't want him to get wind of our little act of subterfuge.

"Oh, that's so cool!" she grinned looking a little bubbly, as if this wasn't her first glass of wine. "If anyone asks, you can tell them she's in my cabin. I was supposed to be assigned a roommate, but she never showed up, so now I've got a single."

"Will do," I said, and passed the word to Rena who was deep in a conversation with Syd about the medical benefits of some kinda Japanese herb.

Kydoime and I both went back to the benches to get more drinks, then found a quiet spot away from the crowd.

Leaning on the fence she asked, "So is that your father you're hiking with?"

"What, Syd? No. My Pop passed away years ago. Syd was his best friend. I'm hiking the trail with him 'cause he has cancer and needs someone to help him get along."

"That's really sweet. I'm sorry about your dad. I guess I just assumed you were out doing the father-son thing."

"It does kinda looks like that—although I'm not sure how anyone could mistake Syd for Pop."

She glanced at my stomach smiling something to herself. "How bad is he?"

"Not good. But he's a tough old geezer. I think he'll make it."

"Not everyone would be out here doing what you're doing. That's really admirable."

"Thanks. So have you always been into backpacking and stuff?"

"Do I look like an outdoors girl?" she said, grinning. Before I could think of some witty line, she winked and added, "I read that book, *Wild*, you know, about the woman who hikes the PCT alone, and I thought, *If she can do it so can I!* So I quit my job and came out here. Before this I was selling medical equipment to hospitals, like scanners for diagnosing your friend. How about you? What do you do?"

"I'm in law," I answered—my usual line. I mean, she didn't need to know all the details, right?

"You're a lawyer?" she asked, looking skeptical.

"I was originally a journalism major at Northwestern, but I switched to law after Pop died. I figured I had to find something a little better for paying the bills. But I kinda got disillusioned with all that, so now I'm taking some time off, helping out Pop's old buddy, while I sort out what I really wanna do—"

Syd and Rena wandered over with a new load of grapes, and we all hung out chatting. Trying to impress her further, I told a couple of bear jokes, making everyone laugh—even Syd. He was just starting to rave about some old film called *My Dinner with Andre*, when Samuel wandered over.

It looked like he had sniffed Rena out, and now like a detective at the end of a mystery, was about to announce his discovery and evict her from the party. But instead he swaggered over to Kydoime. "Sorry about yesterday," he said in a slurred voice that was more drunk than apologetic. "I just found out the ranch is letting me go—tonight's my last night—so I was wondering if maybe you and I could go check out the hot springs together?"

"Sorry Sam," she snapped, "but tonight I'm soaking with these guys." She wrapped her arms around me and Syd, "And since we don't have any swimsuits, we'd like to soak in private please."

Samuel looked at us, his expression twisted up in a snarl that was a cross between jealousy and stunned amazement, his eyes questioning, *How exactly was it these two were about to soak 'nay-keed' with the best-looking woman at the party?* But he said nothing. He just slunk away, tail between his legs, heading almost mechanically toward the bench of wine and beer.

"Sorry," Kydoime said to us when he'd gone. "I didn't mean to speak for you, but he's been bothering me my whole time here, and I really do hope you guys will join me soaking later."

I certainly wasn't going to object. Both Syd and Rena readily consented.

After cocktail hour, the dinner bell rang. Smuggling Rena in, we all enjoyed a fabulous home-cooked meal—snarfing down huge portions of everything. The only one who ate more than me was Rena, taking pictures of each item first. For a tiny girl, she certainly packed an appetite!

After gathering our towels, we all headed up the hill to the bath houses. A silvery half-moon hung in the sky. The building had an open roof, and its interior was adorned in moonlight that gave everything a magical pearly glow. The large bathing pool was constructed of carefully placed stones, laid out lovingly in swirls and curves like a Japanese spa. The walls were made of polished fine-grained beams. There was a bench and a smaller pool with a wooden bucket for rinsing off. The whole place could easily hold a group of ten and was indulgently spacious for our intimate tribe.

There was an awkward pause as we entered. Syd went first, removing his shoes by the door, then slipping out of his clothing, and using the large wooden bucket to rinse his naked body.

Following Syd, I removed my clothes. Then taking the wooden bucket, I poured it gently over my head, trying my best to suck my gut in. Stepping slowly into the warmth of the pool, I was relieved to discover it was only a few feet deep. Finding an underwater bench, I sat back embraced by the gentle ripples of the soothing springs.

Rena, unabashed, and probably used to bathing at hot springs in Japan, slipped out of her clothes folding them with expert precision, and stepped into the small washing pool, rinsing off with the bucket.

I watched as Syd's eyes ran over her tiny body, following her as she moved slowly over to the seat next to his. "Welcome," he said in a soft voice.

"So happy be here!" she whispered, touching his shoulder gently.

Kydoime was last. She fiddled with her boot laces. Stuck her socks into her boots. Then asked cautiously, "How's the water?"

"Great," said Rena.

"Come on in," said Syd.

I just watched, a silent voyeur in the moonlight.

Kydoime slid off her pants, revealing skin-tight panties that perfectly hugged her voluptuous thighs. Then she removed her top, dropping it into a crumpled heap. Finally, she slipped out of the panties and bending down, began rinsing.

Riveted, my eyes ran over the strong high cheekbones of her perfect face, catching a flash of her moonlit eyes. Then down to her exquisite Amazon body outlined in the shimmering light. Finally, my gaze paused on her full upturned breasts.

Approaching the steps, she looked like a marble statuette come to life, her body lit by dancing reflections of the silvery light on the rippling water. Like a living centerfold, she stepped naked into the pool, coming toward me, seating herself just inches away in the warm water. "This is great," she whispered, her warm breath tickling my ear. All I could do was nod dumbly.

The four of us sat together for some time, watching the moon set over the trees. Listening to the lapping of the water. And me catching secret glimpses of Kydoime's amazing body swelling up toward me from beneath the ripples.

We spoke of nothing—the trail, the dinner, the people we'd met, the beauty of the trees. The real conversation lay unspoken beneath the water.

Slowly Syd and Rena began a more personal exchange about Rena's past, Syd's children, her travels, and his current condition. Rena gave him a long hug and the two sat holding each other in silent human intimacy, like two bare trees entwined for support against the inevitable buffeting of ravenous winter winds.

Kydoime, maybe becoming conscious of our eavesdropping, turned toward me and ran her hand along my shoulder, eliciting gentle electric thrills. Then she whispered softly in my ear, "Would you like a back rub?"

Could I say no? Looking into her penetrating eyes and nodding, I let myself float gently into her lap, cradled between her firm legs. Her hands were amazing. I closed my eyes, relaxing into the strength and expertise of her skilled fingers, which moved silently over the knots and soreness of my two weeks on the trail.

When she finished, I lay there in her arms as she gently stroked my hair, floating like a child in the womb, her touch growing more intimate, her thigh rubbing mine.

Syd and Rena were no longer embraced and were now sitting close together whispering to each other. I think they were talking about some Japanese Buddhist story, but honestly, the way Kydoime was rubbing my thigh and my head was floating against her soft breasts, they could have been discussing a raging forest fire about to sweep down over the ranch and I'd still have been blissfully smiling.

Kydoime started to tease my ears. This was the sign to change places, so I floated up onto my side and whispered to her, "Would you like me to massage you?" Hoping that she wouldn't be disappointed by my lesser but still well-regarded skill as a casual masseuse—something I'd learned really opens doors—and legs—back in my frat days.

"No," she whispered in her husky voice, running a finger more intimately down the inside of my thigh. "How about instead, you and I go back to my cabin for the night?"

Was this for real? I thought shit like this only happened in bad romance novels. "Eh, alright—" I sputtered. She gave me a strong squeeze, and I followed her swaying hips back up the steps and out of the pool, whispering to Syd as I passed not to wait up. He smiled, giving me a wise knowing look. Soon I was drying off and pulling on my clothes, ready to follow Kydoime to the ends of the Earth if that's where she led me.

Kydoime headed out. I turned to see Syd and Rena wave at me. It was good Syd had found someone he could connect with. Rena seemed very sweet.

But my thoughts of Syd and Rena faded like the reflection of the moonlight in the pool as I followed Kydoime back to her cabin. Our clothes seemed to melt away as we got inside. I went to hug her, my typical prelude to a kiss, but instead she just pushed me back onto the bed. Running her expert hands over my chest, she climbed on top whispering, "Now I hope you don't mind, but I kind of like to take control—"

DAY THIRTEEN

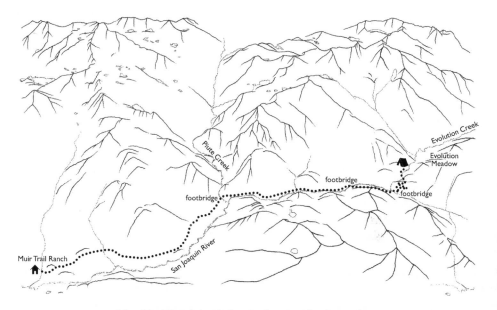

Muir Trail Ranch (7,760′) to Evolution Valley (9,240′)
7½ miles—1,730 feet elevation gain; 250 feet elevation loss

KYDOIME WAS STANDING by the mirror, wearing only a loose black shirt cut just above the navel and her tight pink panties. She was combing out her hair, while carefully pouring oil from a tiny bottle into her hands and rubbing it in—her sheets scented like eucalyptus, my head swimming from lack of sleep.

"Do you like the smell?" she smiled, seeing I was up. "It's essential oil. I use it to keep my hair manageable and fresh. It also keeps the bugs away."

"It smells great, just like you," I winked, recalling the animal-like scent of her body.

She walked over and rubbed a dab of the oil on my forehead, "You're cute. Better get dressed now. Time for breakfast."

Reaching out my hand to caress the tight curve of her thigh, she pulled away. "Uh-uh-uh," she teased. "That was for last night. Today we have miles to go before we sleep." She went back over to the other bed and pulled on a pair of skintight shorts, then went back to teasing out her hair.

"Last night was amazing," I said, sitting up.

"I enjoyed it too—although you were a bit slow the last time," she teased, giggling to herself.

173

"Yeah, so—" I started a bit awkwardly, "—what does this whole thing mean for us?"

"What do you mean?" she gave me a wry smile—a teasing gleam in her eyes.

"I mean, you and I—after last night?"

"You mean, are we *lovers? Married? Joined at the hip? No!*" she laughed. "Last night was just trail sex. You know, you're working out all day, walking the trail in the hot heat, and sometimes you just need a release. *Trail sex.* That's all."

"That's all last night meant to you?"

She stopped combing her hair and looked at me quizzically. "To tell you the truth—that guy Samuel, you know? The one who checks people in?"

I nodded.

"Well, he was really creeping me out. The night before you guys came I was staying down at the backpackers' camp, and he came by all drunk and staggering. Telling me how hot I was. And asking if I wanted to go soak with him. I turned him down of course, but he was a real ass about it. It took two other guys to make him leave."

So that's what Dylan meant.

"Last night I'd had a couple a glasses of wine, and then I saw him there at the party, and well, I really wanted to push his buttons. And you were standing there, so I made certain he knew we were going soaking together."

"Was that all it was then?"

"No," she crooned gently, comforting me with her eyes. "After that, well, you were kinda cute, then one thing led to another in the pool and I got kinda hot—" she suddenly looked at me seriously, as if weighing something. "Don't worry. I don't expect anything from you. You're as free as a bird." She smiled, walked over, and kissed me affectionately on the forehead where she'd rubbed the oil in. "You know," she whispered, "you're really kinda cute. Someday I might even fall for a guy like you—" she jiggled my naked beer belly, "—*if you weren't already pregnant!*" and giggling, she went back to combing her hair.

Only trail sex? How could last night have meant so little to her? As she preened herself, my eyes feasted on the sublime curves of her body. Last night had been perfect. A gorgeous woman, no long courtship, and no strings attached. With most of my dates there'd been that awkward moment in the morning—the lies, the gathering up of clothes, and the escape—all before they could remember to ask for a number. Here was the real deal. Total noncommittal freedom. The perfect night with the perfect woman. Kydoime had just said to me what I only dreamed I could say to someone in the morning—and yet somehow I was the one feeling disappointed.

Gathering up my strewn clothes, I pulled 'em back on. "I'll see you at breakfast then," I said awkwardly, heading for the door.

Interposing, she stopped me, planted another gentle kiss on my forehead, then pinched my ass. "It was great. I really enjoyed it. I know you're hiking with that old man, but if you can catch up on the trail, then maybe we can do this again?" She giggled. I slipped out the door—the scent of eucalyptus and the touch of her kiss lingering on my forehead.

Syd looked chipper as I came in. Rena was still sleeping, and he was quietly organizing his gear. He looked fresh and awake, better than I'd seen him all trip. Quite a change from the morning before.

The sound of my boots on the wooden floor woke Rena. Stirring in her bed, she opened her eyes, "*Ohayou!* Good morning!" She sat up, smiling energetically. "I slept soooo well," she said, stretching her arms. Getting up, she folded her sheets neatly, then quickly assembled her stuff. "Thank you so much for letting me stay in real bed." She was still in her hiking clothes from yesterday. There was no evidence that she and Syd had done anything but share the room.

Syd turned to Rena apologetically, "Sorry we can't take you to breakfast this morning. I think this time they may notice you. But I'll see if I can pack you a little something for lunch."

"I understand," she nodded. "Don't want to get you in trouble. See you at hiker's box. Bye." She gave him a warm squeeze, then slipped out the door waving like a schoolgirl—it amazed me that she was thirty-eight.

Syd looked melancholy. "She's a sweet kid, if I were twenty years younger—" He stood watching the empty doorway, then turned to me, "So how was your night, *Casanova?*"

"Good. Really good. But *Casanova* needs a shower before breakfast."

Casanova would be a cool trail name—better than Po. But a guy couldn't get any action with a name like that. What woman in her right mind would sleep with a guy named Casanova? Why had Taco named me Po? Why not *The Dragon Warrior*, or something really awesome?

Showering slowly, each scene from the night before played back inside my head. It'd really been the perfect night.

At the mess hall there was no sign of Kydoime. Hadn't she said she'd join us for breakfast? It was just like with Samantha, there was no point in getting all wrapped up in a woman. Still, the food was amazing. Hot coffee, real orange juice, a variety of breads, bacon, eggs, jam, and even real hash browns. Syd and I ate heartily. The only thing I didn't sample was their oatmeal.

The ranch staff had laid out various meats and condiments and stuff for making trail lunches. Remembering the BLT from Reds, I piled bacon, lettuce, tomato, and mayonnaise between two thick slices of wheat toast, grabbing an apple for good measure. Syd prepared two large sandwiches, packing each one carefully into a separate bag and adding an assortment of fruit to each.

We found Rena at the hiker boxes. She'd just finished collecting an interesting variety of food items. Syd stealthily passed her the bag with the fruit and sandwich he'd prepared. When she looked inside, her eyes grew wide, "*Sugoi desu ne!* You don't know how much I love food!" She gave him a warm hug, making me wonder again if all they'd done was sleep last night.

"See you on the trail," Syd smiled. "If you want, you can camp with us in Evolution Valley tonight."

"Yes, I like that," Rena said. "I still have to pack, but I try and catch up."

The hike from Muir Trail Ranch to Piute Creek was a rolling three-mile jog through a shady forest. The birds were singing and an occasional squirrel chittered up a tree to herald our approach.

The map showed that Piute Creek was a tributary of the San Joaquin River. Judging from the fast-flowing water, it was probably a pretty major one. Much to my relief, there was a large gray metal footbridge at the crossing.

We soon began ascending a spectacular rocky gorge that followed along one branch of the river. The water here was almost an iridescent green, alternating between wide lazy flows tumbling gently over polished rocks and turbulent white water roaring down through narrow channels. Low succulents lined the sunny exposed bank, but a cool mist from the churning water kept the going pleasant.

An hour or so later we came to a second footbridge. "If I'm not mistaken," observed Syd, "this bridge and the other were built back in 1916 or '17, from the original funding allocated for the trail."

Crossing, we stopped for lunch under the bridge. Pulling out my BLT, I breathed in its fresh wheat toast aroma, slowly savoring each bite of bacon, lettuce, and juicy tomato in gastronomic ecstasy—like an astronaut returning to Earth after subsisting for months on tubes of protein gel. Even my simple apple was exquisite. Several groups of hikers passed by waving to us from the bridge. We waved back but were in no rush as we enjoyed our shade and the music of the water. The whole thing reminded me of one of my childhood picnics with Pop. Only after a long break did we reluctantly don our packs again and start moving.

This side of the river was less rocky and more forested. After crossing a third bridge, we reached a steep cliff face that had to be a thousand feet tall. The trail wound up it in long sweeping switchbacks. Syd appeared in high spirits as we zigged and zagged upward. *Was this the man who was at death's door just a day ago?* It was hard to believe. Maybe all my concern had been misfounded?

Near the top, the trail met Evolution Creek at a spectacular cascade—the white water falling in braids into an emerald-green pool, then tumbling down in a succession of granite steps. We paused to take in the view.

"I've been thinking about the reason you were expelled," he said.

I swallowed, waiting for the boom to hit. This was exactly how Pop had always begun his long chiding lectures.

"If you write a letter to your university, explaining why you cheated, what happened with your father, and how it affected you—being very apologetic of course—I think there's a good chance they'll readmit you. If not, you can always apply to another school. If you don't list your previous university on your application, they'll have no way of knowing that you were enrolled someplace else."

"You're not disappointed in me?"

"I am. Academic dishonesty is a very serious thing. Real victories and satisfaction come from pride in our achievements. When we cheat, we're really cheating ourselves. Even though your reasons are understandable, you still made a series of bad choices."

I nodded.

"But I believe you've suffered enough. Now it's time to move forward."

"So you really think I could get back into Northwestern, or another college?"

"I do. I might even be able to help you get into Cal—I still have a certain amount of pull there—but it would mean another four years of study."

The bubbling falls churned the pool below. Ma would certainly be proud if I got into Berkeley—even if it did take another four years. I'd some equity built up in my condo and could always find a part-time job as a legal assistant or something. I just might be able to make that work. But would I still wanna go into law? Working as a paralegal had shown me the tainted underbelly of that industry, and I couldn't imagine spending the rest of my life writing legal contracts. But what else could I do? Literature was cool, but it didn't pay—even Pop had quit that—and I was no philosopher. Maybe I could go back to journalism? That'd been way better than law. Journalism would let me make a difference by writing about political corruption or social inequity. And researching an article was like being the detective in a mystery novel—uncovering the facts, then presenting them step by step to the reader. Pop always said I had a talent for writing. Maybe I should go back to that?

"We'd better get going," Syd said, interrupting my thoughts.

A little beyond the falls the trail began to level off. We entered a wide forested valley that soon gave way to a yellow-green meadow surrounded by distant peaks. The grass waved invitingly abuzz with birds and bees. This was the gateway to Evolution Valley, the name evoking some special primitive spot in the Sierra. The valley was fenced in on both sides by rocky forested slopes covered in the now familiar lodgepole pines. Evolution Creek cut broadly through the center. The path ahead forded the creek, with a split in the trail and a sign suggesting an easier ford upstream. But it didn't look that bad here—the creek was wide and slow with a shallow pebbly bottom. It couldn't be more than ankle deep. Nothing like the raging white water and slick rocks of Bear Creek.

"Are you OK crossing here?" Syd asked.

"I think so. But how will Rena know which way we went?"

Using a trekking pole, he scratched the word *Rena* into the sand, with a large arrow pointing across the river. "I think she'll see that."

It woulda been nice if we could catch up to Kydoime, but she was probably miles ahead by now. I'd even forgotten to get her phone number. Why was it the things you really wanted were always out of reach, while those that you didn't dropped abundantly into your lap?

The creek was deeper than it looked, rising above my knees in the middle. Pausing nervously, I took a deep breath, then pushed across, making it to the far bank.

The trail wound through the trees skirting the meadow. We soon passed a lovely campsite nestled in the rocks. Unfortunately, there was already a group here. Saying hello, we gave them a description of Rena so they could let her know we'd been here.

Winding up and down over small hills, we came to a pair of empty sites. The first bordered the meadow, the second was larger and more forested. Selecting the former, we dropped our packs and made camp.

It was still a bit early for dinner, so we sat cross-legged on some fallen trees by the meadow. We rested admiring the waving grasses and colorful wildflowers, while listening to the birds sing in the warm afternoon sun. Dragonflies hovered about. Permi had told me they eat mosquitos, so it was good to see them here.

Syd looked pretty relaxed, maybe I could have a little fun with him like I'd done with Pop when I was a kid. "So, this is Evolution Valley?" I asked with feigned indifference.

"The entranceway to it," he said looking out over the grassy plain toward the mountains in the distance. "This part is called Evolution Meadow."

"It's kinda disappointing, don't you think? I mean, given its name and everything?" It was all I could do to keep from snickering.

"What do you mean?" he said, his eyes widening in surprise. "Don't you think all this is beautiful?"

"Sure, I guess, but when I first heard the name Evolution Valley, I kinda expected it to be full of strange creatures—ancient dinosaurs or something—you know, with tall prehistoric jungle plants, right? Not just another grassy meadow with a river."

"Like something out of an Edgar Rice Burroughs novel?" he raised an eyebrow.

"Like, *Jurassic Park*, you know?"

"You imagined we'd hike all the way up here, only to get eaten by a velociraptor?" he said, narrowing his gaze.

"Not exactly," I replied, trying hard not to smile, "but I was expecting something a bit more impressive than *this*," I said, dismissing the whole idyllic scene with a wave of my hand.

He rolled his eyes. "I happen to think *this*," he mimicked my hand gesture, "is amazing. It's one of the few mountain meadows to have escaped grazing by the *hooved locusts* of the sheepherders—as Muir called them. This meadow is just as it would have been thousands of years ago, and I happen to think it's grand." His face reddened a bit, like I'd upset him.

"I was just pulling your chain. I think it's a beautiful meadow too. You take everything way too seriously—you should lighten up."

We sat looking out over the meadow. Syd began to do some meditative breathing, while I let my mind wander, thinking about Kydoime. What did she mean by *only trail sex?* Could I have been just anyone? Just another penis? Was that really my karma—to be dumped by everyone I cared about, just like I'd dumped Pop? Or was it like Syd had said— was I somehow able to change my fate?

A yellow-brown bird fluttered by, alighting briefly on the curved stem of a tall wild-flower. The plant had speckled globelike flowers, dangling like little yellow Christmas bells, their orange-tipped clappers waving in the light breeze.

"What kinda flower is that?"

Syd sat breathing rhythmically, as if he hadn't heard me. Then slowly turned his head to examine the flower. "I'm not certain. I think it's a kind of lily, but let's find out."

He led me back over to camp. From his pack, he pulled out a book that I hadn't seen before, *Wildflowers of the High Sierra and John Muir Trail*, by Elizabeth Wenk.

"Isn't that same person who wrote your guidebook?"

"It is. Wenk's really a plant biologist. She did her doctoral thesis at Cal on the effects of rock types on alpine plants."

"She went to Berkeley?"

"I never had her in any of my classes, but I knew her thesis advisor pretty well. Apparently, she still comes up to the Sierra every summer. It's possible we'll run into her."

Syd took the book and walked back over to where we'd been sitting. "Let's see what she has to say about this one." He thumbed expertly back and forth through the photographs until arriving at one matching the plant, "I thought so—it's a Kelley's lily or *Lilum kelleyanum.*"

"Wow, that's cool," I said, comparing the picture to the lily. "But doesn't having all these books in your pack get heavy? I mean, I know your pack is lighter than mine and everything, but wouldn't it be even lighter without the books?"

"It might, but I wouldn't want to be without them. As Barbara Tuchman said, *Books are companions, teachers, magicians, bankers of the treasures of the mind. Books are humanity in print.*"

"How many are you carrying?"

"Just three, now that you have my copy of Muir."

What was his other book? Looking across the field, I noticed small dancing butterflies with orange and white bands running along their delicate black wings. "What kinda butterflies are those?" I asked.

"Aren't you forgetting your Kelley's lily?"

"I already know what that is—you just told me." *Was he having some sort of short-term memory failure?*

He looked at me for a while, "You know, it's very comforting to name things, but there's also a blindness that comes from naming."

"Whaddya mean?"

"Take the Kelley's lily. After you knew its name, you stopped seeing it."

"I still see it. It's right over there," I pointed.

"What I mean is, after you learned its name, it lost its fascination. The Chinese writer Lu Xun once wrote, *Beyond my garden wall, you can see two trees. The first is a jujube tree. The second is also a jujube tree.*"

"Now why do you think he wrote it that way? Why not just say, *Beyond the wall there are two jujube trees?*"

"Maybe he was being paid by the word?"

He laughed, "Seriously Gil, think."

"Perhaps he wanted the reader to pay attention to each one?"

"Exactly," he smiled. "Just like people, each tree is an individual. It has its own twists and turns, its own bark and pattern of branches, its own character. His jujubes may be the same kind of tree, but they're not the same tree."

"So what you're saying is, I should pay more attention to each Kelley's lily, not just move on to the butterflies?"

"Try it. Lie in the field. Get to know the lilies. Their similarities. Their differences. In the same way you would get to know people. Muir used to spend entire days observing just a single plant or animal. Many artists do the same. It's what you have to do if you want to really see nature."

What he said made sense, but I was no Muir, and I barely took the time to get to know people, let alone plants. But it wasn't like I had a full schedule or something. Walking slowly over to the lilies, I plopped down in the grass and looked again.

They all looked pretty much the same. A few had a couple more flowers. A few had less. Some were yellower, some more orangey. So what? What was the point of just sitting here? Syd seemed to think it was worth it. Maybe this was like in *Tai Chi Master*, when Jet Li's character sits and meditates about the nature of water, learning the secret of tai chi boxing in the process. Maybe there was something hidden in the flowers that Syd wanted me to discover?

Staring more, I noticed the unopened flowers looked like long green seedpods. Permi woulda liked that. A couple of the plants had flowers that were wider, more open, less globelike—more like little stars. A couple had perfect globes. Some were deep orange, some almost golden. Some were tall, some short. The orange-and-black butterflies landed more often on the orange flowers. Each plant had its own character, like women. I began thinking up names for each of 'em: The short one with the sunlike flowers, Rey. The large orange one with all the butterflies was Romeo. The flashy golden one in the middle, Elektra. The orange one with all the black specks, Tigress. The one none of the birds visited, Lady Snowbird. The plant with all the pointy stems, Barb. And the one with all the unopened flowers, Budd.

My legs began to ache. It was getting harder to come up with names. Who was I fooling? I was no biologist. How did people like Muir sit all day long doing this?

Stretching my stiff legs, I got up, walking back. Syd was sitting cross-legged, like someone doing yoga.

"Did you learn something?" he asked.

"I see what you mean, each flower is different. Although I don't think I'm really a naturalist like Muir."

"It's a good start. Slowly you'll notice more."

We walked back over to camp and began preparing for dinner. As we gathered our stuff, our ears were assaulted by the loud prattling of teenage boys approaching from the other direction.

The sound grew louder. Pretty soon, a troop of Boy Scouts dressed in olive and brown uniforms came into view. They were led by two middle-aged and slightly rotund Scoutmasters. The Scouts stopped at the forested campsite, scattered their gear, and began pitching their tents. One of the two adults waved at us and smiled, as if to say, *I'm sure it's alright with you that a group of noisy teenage boys keep you up all night with their incessant jabbering.* It was something like the pleasant smile a mother with a crying infant gives you after squeezing into the middle seat on a thirteen-hour international flight.

The Scouts soon had their tents up and a raging fire going. The smell of smoke and the sounds of boyish revelry wafted over our peaceful camp.

"Do you think we'll see Rena tonight?" I asked Syd.

"Doubt it," he said, heating his dinner. "It's going to be dark soon."

But less than a minute later, a happy female voice shouted from the trail, "Syd! Gil! Wow! Glad to catch up you guys at last!"

"Rena!" came Syd's surprised exclamation. "Great to see you! I wasn't sure you were going to make it."

"People at other camp told me you here, or I already stop. I see your arrow at river too. What you making for dinner?" she inquired with great interest, dropping her blue monster.

"I'm cooking curried chicken with raisins and currants," replied Syd.

"*Aa, sou-ka,*" she said eyes wide. "Looks delicious."

"Try some," he offered, holding out a spoonful for her to taste.

"Oh, so good!" her face lit up. "Best backpacking meal! Did you make yourself?"

"The recipe is from a backpacking cookbook called, *A Fork in the Trail.*"

Rena pulled out a small address book and wrote something down, which I guessed was the name of the cookbook.

"What you cooking?" she asked me.

"I'm making ramen noodles."

"Ah—instant ramen like Japanese," she smiled—but she didn't seem as impressed as she'd been with Syd's chicken.

"You're really coming up in the world," Syd said with a wink.

"Yeah, I found all kinds of stuff in those hiker buckets. Sure beats Backwoods Buffet."

Rena got out her cooking gear and began mixing the contents of three small bags into a stainless steel pot of water.

"What are you making?" Syd asked her.

"Couscous curry, I found in MTR hiker box too," she practically glowed. "Has couscous, dried fruit, veggies, garlic, plus I add in bit of oil," she said.

After cooking, we all traded tastes of our meals. Food was by far the number one conversation topic on trail. Backpackers talked incessantly about what they ate, what they wished they ate, and what they wanted to eat when they got home.

The number two topic had to be gear. *What sort of pack is that? Where'd you get those trekking poles? How do you like that tent?* were all common greetings among backpackers—in the same way someone at the office would ask, *How's it going?*

Weight had to be number three. Even though no one in polite society would ever ask your weight, on the trail people would think nothing of asking the weight of my pack, my tent, or any other item I happened to have out. Backpackers were more obsessed with weight than a swimsuit model at a smorgasbord—which was funny, 'cause backpackers on the whole—Syd excepted—were not a thin lot. Most could stand to lose a pound or two. In my case, thirty. Yet it seemed most backpackers would gladly fork over hundreds of dollars to reduce the weight of their spork by several ounces—never dreaming that for the price of a few less slices of pizza, they could drop their body mass by far more. But then maybe that wasn't the point—'cause pizza was the number one food backpackers seemed to crave on trail. Not me. For me, it was BLTs. After Reds Meadow, I just couldn't get the taste of BLTs outta my head. It was strange. I'd never really liked BLTs before, but now every break I found myself thinking about them.

We finished eating and Rena went over to set up her little orange tent.

Afterward, Syd asked, "Do you guys want to take a walk in the meadow and watch the stars?"

"Yes," Rena nodded.

"I think I'm just gonna relax here," I said, not wanting to be a third wheel.

They headed off—it didn't look like there was anything romantic between them—it was more like a grandfather taking his granddaughter on a stroll. And yet there was a certain spark of mutual understanding between them, something I wished I could find in my own relationships.

Looking at the large inviting fire at the Boy Scout camp, I wandered over to say hi. Maybe we could discuss food or pack weight?

One of the two large Scoutmasters met me a bit away from their fire. He looked to be in his midforties, with a short stubbly beard that'd probably grown out on trail.

"I'm Rodge. That's my coleader Seymour by the fire, pleased to meet you."

"Where did you all hike in from?" I asked—actually, *this* was the most common conversation topic on trail, followed closely by food, gear, and weight. Mentally, I renumbered my topics.

"We're from San Jose, but we just came back down from Muir Pass. We were supposed to hike over it and head out in Bishop, but one of our boys got sick."

"Is he OK?"

"Don't know," he said somberly. "He has bad altitude sickness. Worst I've seen. Just became unresponsive and started babbling to himself as we approached the pass. Complained of a real bad headache and then became dizzy and disorientated. At first, we weren't really sure what it was, but then we ran into a ranger and she said we'd better get him down, so we turned around. We're headed back to Florence Lake tomorrow."

"Did he get any better?"

"A bit. He's sleeping in his tent now. We gave him some ibuprofen, like the ranger suggested. She said she'd come by tomorrow morning to check on him."

"I hope he's alright. Be sure to give him plenty of fluids," repeating what Syd had told me was the best treatment for altitude sickness.

"Hope you don't mind us camping next to you. We'll be quiet. It's been a long day for us. This was about as far as I think any of the boys could have made it."

"It's fine." They had a sick kid—we could live with a little noise. "Let us know if there's anything we can do."

"I think we have the situation under control. We'll be back down below seven thousand feet tomorrow. It should be alright." It sounded more like he was trying to convince himself than me.

Wishing them well, I headed back to our camp. When Syd and Rena returned, I told them about the boy.

Syd was thoughtful. "That's a tough situation. It would be better if they could get him down to a lower altitude tonight. We're still over nine thousand feet up here. But I guess they have a whole troop to consider. Let's stop by and see if there's anything we can do for them in the morning."

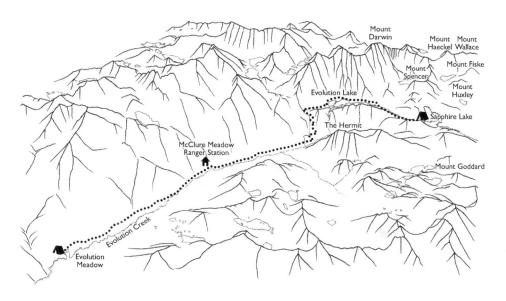

Evolution Valley (9,240′) to Sapphire Lake Outflow (10,900′)
7½ miles—1,840 feet elevation gain; 180 feet elevation loss

"Gil, are you awake?" Syd was rustling my tent.

"What?" I asked groggily, extracting my head from the hood of my bag.

"I heard some talking at the other camp, so I went over to see how that kid was doing."

"Yeah?"

"I spoke with one of the Scoutmasters and it's not good. The kid's still dizzy and disorientated and he can't walk. It may be cerebral edema. It's rare at these altitudes, but it's not unheard of."

"That sounds bad."

"I'm going to get my gear together and hike up to the ranger station. You and Rena can meet me up there later."

"How far is it?"

"About two miles."

"I'll go with you."

Syd woke Rena and she wanted to go too. The three of us had our gear packed in less than twenty minutes—it's amazing how fast you can get ready when you have to. Rodge and Seymour thanked us profusely.

It took just under an hour hiking in the chill with our headlamps to reach the log cabin of the McClure Meadow Ranger Station. We knocked urgently on the heavy wooden door. The ranger, a middle-aged woman, stood blinking in the doorway in her heavy gray bathrobe as we explained the situation. She was quite polite for someone who'd been woken up before dawn, but perhaps she was used to people calling at all hours. She thanked us, shut the door, and within minutes reemerged in her ranger's hat and uniform, hurrying down the trail toward the Scout camp.

"That was a good thing," I said after she'd left.

"They're fortunate the ranger was here," observed Syd.

"What do you mean?"

"Rangers spend the bulk of their time in the field. They're not often at their station."

"I just hope the boy is OK."

"Me too," echoed Rena.

"I think he will be," affirmed Syd. "Shall we make breakfast?"

It was pretty early, but my stomach was already rumbling. Syd and I dropped our packs—only now becoming aware that we'd been carrying them nervously the whole time the ranger was changing.

"You eat. I take nap," Rena said yawning. Dragging her gear over to the far side of the station, she spread out her tent like a ground cloth, laid her sleeping bag on top, and soon was fast asleep. It never ceased to amaze me how women could fall asleep almost anywhere.

Syd and I cooked our oatmeal as dawn slowly broke over the meadow. After, he woke Rena gently, "We're gonna keep going. Do you want to camp with us tonight around Sapphire Lake?"

"Uh-huh," she nodded sleepily.

A bit past the station we spied a lone gray dome rising majestically above the meadow, its cap bathed in the predawn glow. With its hairless head and broad shoulders, it struck me as *The Guardian of the Valley*. If it didn't have a name, I'd call it Drax. "What's that thing called?" I asked, pointing.

"That's The Hermit. It's one of the peaks Solomons named."

"Solomons was here too? I thought he was chased out of the mountains by a blizzard?"

"He was. But it wasn't long before the young explorer was organizing his next expedition—much to the chagrin of his poor mother, who wanted him to find a respectable job."

"Sounds like Ma. She was really freaked out when I lost my job."

"Everyone's mother spends a lot of time worrying—it's part of the occupation. You never did tell me why you lost your job."

"Let's just say the managing partner and I disagreed over the number of hours in a fortyhour work week."

"I see," he chuckled.

"It's no big deal. I can easily get another job—there's no shortage of lawyers in LA. Although I'm seriously considering what you said about trying to get back into

Northwestern or maybe applying to Berkeley. But tell me more about Solomons. It's still kinda early and I don't wanna think about the whole future-career-thing right now."

"The year after his disaster in the snowstorm, Solomons mounted his third expedition. This time with Ernest Bonner."

"Why did he keep changing partners? Why didn't he ask one of his previous companions to go again?"

"It may be because of his personality—he was pretty brash and tended to alienate people—or it might just have been difficult to find anyone with that much time off. Imagine asking your old boss for a two-month-long vacation."

"He woulda just given me the year off."

"The two started out by taking a packhorse up to the camp Solomons had abandoned the year before, hoping to scavenge some of his old equipment. But most of it was ruined. There was a moment of excitement when Solomons found his old eight-by-ten wooden box camera, but when he went to pick it up, it fell apart—all of the glue had dissolved."

"So could they take photos then?"

"Oh sure, Solomons didn't take chances. He'd brought along a newer more portable four-by-five camera."

We wound along the edge of the meadow. It was wide enough here that we could stroll side by side. Yellow and brown birds chattered in the trees. The morning air was crisp and the sky a tranquil blue.

"Believing they could cover more ground without an animal, the two returned to Florence Lake, leaving their packhorse in the care of a sheepherder. Then they set out on foot, each carrying about a sixty-pound pack."

"Wait—what about all those glass plate negatives? You know, all the undeveloped photos he took the year before? Did he ever find those?"

"Ah yes," recalled Syd, "he did. But he left them in the care of the sheepherder, who despite young Solomons' orders, let curiosity get the best of him and opened the box. When Solomons finally developed them, all of the plates were black."

"That sucks."

"Yes, it was really a loss." We greeted and passed a couple of hikers heading north, then Syd went on with his story. "Proceeding on foot, Solomons and Bonner followed an old sheep trail, arriving at the confluence of the South Fork of the San Joaquin River and Evolution Creek."

"At that third bridge?"

"That's right. Solomons was searching for a path to the Kings River Basin that would be navigable for pack animals—and no such pass had yet been found. Exploring Evolution Creek first, the two of them cached most of their food, scrambling up that high rock face we climbed yesterday, and crossing the meadow you were so disappointed with."

"So that's when he named The Hermit?"

"Yes, they took almost the same route we're following today."

The trail ended abruptly at a crossing. There was no bridge, and the surrounding area was pretty rough and overgrown. Scouting through the brush, we located a brace of fallen logs and cautiously crossed over, mindful of not slipping.

"You know," I said, "just scouting around through the woods here for a good crossing point was pretty tough. How did Solomons go all this way without a trail?"

"Cross-country is never easy. I'm pretty sure he stuck to the meadow and the flat areas when he could. But you're right, many parts must've been quite harrowing—like scrambling up the rock face. People don't often think about it, but we're really lucky to have a trail to follow. We have a lot to thank the early explorers for."

Pulling out the map, I saw this was the last water crossing before a long stretch of uphill. The sun was rising, and it was getting warm. There was no way I was going to run out of water again. "Let's stop here for a snack and pump more water," I suggested.

While we were eating, Kitty came jogging up to the far bank. Her clothes had clearly seen some trail miles. Syd pointed to the logs and she strutted across, her wispy sun-bleached hair waving in the breeze.

"Hey guys!" she huffed. Without waiting to catch her breath, she pulled out a small squeeze filter and headed over to the stream. I'd seen a few other people using those. They looked much easier than Syd's old pump.

"Did you find Rena?" Syd asked.

"Behind the ranger station? Yup, I found her. That girl can really sleep! Said she doesn't want to hike till noon, can you believe that?"

"To each their own," Syd defended. "I hear you guys had quite the time at VVR."

Kitty flushed, "I guess she told you huh? I'm paying for it now—gotta get up to Wanda Lake or maybe even Helen tonight." Kitty finished filtering and slung her pack back on over her sweaty shirt. "Gotta run, great seeing you guys again!" she waved, heading off at a fast jog.

"She certainly seems to be in a rush," I said.

"She's making up miles. From what Rena says, she'll hike like that for a day or two, crash, then do it again."

"Why not just go slower, like us?"

"Everyone has their own style and Kitty's young. She reminds me of some of the freshmen I taught at Cal—the ones who were always procrastinating then pulling all-nighters to catch up with their assignments."

"I went through that phase my freshman year."

"We all do—she's just that way about trail miles."

After filtering we hit the switchbacks—long lazy zigzags snaking up a chiseled rock face in the heat. Syd dropped behind me. Passing the base of The Hermit, I reached a granite shelf extending at least a hundred yards to a broad azure lake. It was framed by a towering sawtooth range of six or seven massive granite peaks dotted in snow. The waxing moon was just rising over the ridge. It was like one of the grand scenes out of Muir. Each element perfectly placed to form a masterful composition—as if God himself had painted the landscape from water and stone.

"*A fraternity of titans!*" Syd exclaimed, placing a hand on my shoulder, and surprising me from behind.

"It is," I marveled, catching my breath.

"That's what Solomons called it. He was so impressed that he named this Evolution Lake and the six peaks surrounding it after the great evolutionists, Darwin, Haeckel, Wallace, Fiske, Huxley, and Spencer."

Syd dropped his pack and I followed, resting on the warm stone. Looking at his map, he identified each of the peaks in turn. There were several tents down by the lakeshore, and the still quiet of the mountain air was punctuated by the occasional shout of campers testing the frigid water.

For once I had an interesting lunch. Using my cooking pot, I added water to some yellow powdered garbanzo beans, mixed in some dried fruit and nuts, and soon had a tasty hummus paste that I contentedly dipped crackers into.

"You're really trading up on your meals," Syd praised.

"I'm just happy to be eating anything but bars."

As we ate, Syd continued his story. "Solomons and Bonner made their base camp up where we're heading today, around Sapphire Lake. The next morning, they set out to summit both Mount Wallace and Mount Darwin," he indicated two of the imposing peaks.

Evolution Lake

"Wow, that's just nuts, climbing just one of those would be exhausting."

He nodded. "They got up early and reached the top of Mount Wallace, measuring its height with an expensive new barometer they'd brought along. Then they attempted Mount Darwin but were stymied a few hundred feet below the summit. Solomons proclaimed the peak, *barred to all human beings*, but of course it was eventually climbed. Then they slid back down on the glacier."

"Can you really do that?"

He sat up taller, "It's called *glissading*. Sitting on your butt, or sometimes kneeling like a skier, you can slide down a snow-covered mountainside in a matter of minutes."

"Isn't it dangerous?"

"A little, but it's worth it. I've glissaded down the slopes Mount Shasta several times, and I can tell you it's better than any amusement park ride."

"Doesn't it hurt your butt, sliding down on all that ice?"

"Not if you do it right. You slide down in the late afternoon when the snow and ice are soft. The snow sprays up between your legs, slowing your descent, but it's still a wild ride. You use an ice axe to steer with and to arrest your slide, should things get out of control."

"Wow, I can't picture you doing that."

"I wasn't always this age," he chided. "There was one time your father and I, along with a buddy of ours, got caught in a whiteout attempting Mount Shasta and had to get back down quick. The snow and ice hadn't melted yet—and let me tell you, it was one hard ride. When the three of us reached the bottom, the seats of our jeans were torn open and our butts were badly cut and scrapped. But none of us had felt a thing because of the cold."

"Ouch!"

"The funny thing is, we all went camping up at Ashland Oregon afterward—you know, to see their famous Shakespeare Festival—and when we went swimming at the campground—well, let's just say the other guys in the locker room looked mighty strangely at the three of us with our matching black-and-blue butts."

We both laughed. Pop had never told me *that* story.

"Getting back to Solomons—the next day he and Bonner headed back down to where they'd cached their food. Still searching for a pass, they headed up the San Joaquin River, struggling up the icy slopes of Mount Goddard without the aid of climbing tools. Can you imagine Solomons' vexation when after nearly reaching the summit, he realized he'd forgotten his barometer back at their previous camp?"

"Oh no—seriously?"

"He had no way to measure the altitude. But from the top he did manage to spy out what would eventually become Muir Pass—the navigable stock route he'd sought to the Kings River Basin. But the forgotten barometer was just the beginning of his troubles. A freak snowstorm forced the two to shelter on the summit, passing the night huddled beneath some small tamarack pines."

"Sounds miserable."

"It was. In the morning the two tried to reach the pass but were driven back by freezing rain. To escape the weather, they crossed into a canyon below Mount Goddard. What Solomons called the Enchanted Gorge, passing through the neck of two peaks he dubbed, Scylla and Charybdis."

"From the *Odyssey!*" I blurted.

"I'm glad to see you know your Homer, your father would have been proud. If I were in better shape, I'd like to see that gorge. It's part of a very remote region called the Ionian Basin. Solomons wrote that it was one of the strangest and most fantastic places he'd encountered. He believed the gorge would become a world-famous tourist attraction. But he was wrong. From what I've read, its remote location, steep talus, and choking vegetation, make it one of the least accessible spots in the Sierra. Even Steve Roper's *Sierra High Route*—which is a more challenging cross-country alternative to the Muir Trail—avoids it in favor of the surer route over Muir Pass."

"There's a *more challenging* alternative to the Muir Trail?"

"Anything is a trail if you follow it. There's no reason you have to tread in someone else's footprints."

I could think of many reasons. "So what happened to Solomons?"

"At the foot of the Enchanted Gorge they came to Simpson Meadow. From there the two explored neighboring Tehipite Valley, which Solomons wrote was second only to Yosemite in splendor. The two then followed the well-trodden sheep-route over Granite Pass, arriving tattered and hungry but in good spirits at the horse trail into Kings Canyon—at what is now Roads End."

"So did he go back to explore the pass he saw?"

"Sort of. Solomons returned the following summer with two young Sierra Club members, Walter Starr and Allen Chickering. But falling ill, he left the mountains about a week into their journey. Starr and Chickering went on, becoming the first to cross from Yosemite to Kings Canyon with pack animals—but not by the high route Solomons was seeking. Years later, Walter Starr's eldest son, Walter Starr Jr.—or "Peter" as he preferred to be called—explored the regions along the Muir Trail, taking copious notes that he hoped to organize into a guidebook. But tragically, he died in a solo climbing accident up in the Minarets. His father later organized his notes and published them posthumously as *Starr's Guide to the John Muir Trail and the High Sierra Region*, which for many years was the best guide to the trail."

"I think Pop had a copy of that book—it had a big folded map in it, right?"

"Yes, it was one of the books we liked to flip through when planning trips back in our Berkeley days."

"So did Solomons ever reach the pass?"

"No, he left that to others, instead venturing up to Alaska, where he made a small fortune in coal mining. He later used the money to build a ranch up near Yosemite. But it wasn't until he was in his sixties, when a friend invited him to join their trek, that he returned to see the then nearly completed trail."

"So it took him from fourteen to sixty to realize his dream?"

"As you might imagine he had grown pretty stout and had to get back in shape for the trip. Actually, he looked a little like you did back when you showed up at my place."

"Gee, thanks."

"Honestly, you've lost quite a bit of that beer belly since we began."

I did feel a bit thinner. Probably a combination of all the miles and those awful bars and Backwoods meals I'd been eating.

"Why have I never heard of Solomons before? I mean I'm not exactly an expert on the history of the Sierra or anything, but you'd think a guy like that would be more famous."

"As I said, he could be pretty brash. He also had a falling out with the Sierra Club. All of which probably resulted in him being less well recognized than he should be. It wasn't until much later that he was formally honored by the naming of Mount Solomons. We'll see it when we reach Muir Pass. It's not far from there."

"So in the end, he joined his *fraternity of titans*."

"That he did," Syd smiled, "that he did."

We both stared for a while across the waters at the majestic congregation of peaks Solomons had discovered. This was a beautiful area and a fitting spot for a mountain commemorating the young explorer.

Skirting the lake's left bank, we heard the whir-whir-whir of a red-and-white Park Service helicopter. It came rising swiftly over the ridge, flew low above the lake, then headed down toward the valley below.

"Do you think that's for the boy from the Scouting troop?" I asked.

"Could be," he said thoughtfully.

"I hope the boy's alright." It had been years since I'd gone to church or anything, but silently I said a prayer for him.

At the far end of the lake, we reached the creek again. A series of boulders spanned the water like stepping-stones, and we leapt from rock to rock. Passing a series of cascades, we came to a flat area where the stream widened out into a beautiful lakelet at the foot of Mount Spencer. We'd planned to camp up at Sapphire, but this spot was so beautiful neither of us could pass it by. We made camp about a hundred feet off the trail.

Other hikers passed us on their way to Sapphire, but we never saw Rena. When night came, we cooked our dinners on a granite ledge above the stream.

It seemed ironic that Solomons had named such a divine spot for the six great evolutionists. "Syd," I asked, "do you believe in fate? Do you think stuff happens for a reason? That it's all part of God's plan—like Dylan said? Or that everything is just random?"

"I'm not sure I believe in divine providence—if there is a God it's beyond us to know its purpose. But there's a well-known Chinese idiom I'm fond of called, *Old Man Sai Loses a Horse*. The story goes something like this," he began,

> One day old man Sai loses a horse when it jumps his corral.
> Everyone in the village tries to console him, but the old man asks, "How do we know this is really unfortunate?"

After some time, the horse returns leading a fine stray. Everyone in the village comes to congratulate him, but the old man asks, "How do we know this is really fortunate?"

Sometime later his son is thrown while trying to ride the new horse, breaking a leg. Everyone comes 'round to console him again, but again he asks, "How do we know this is really unfortunate?"

Soon after, the country goes to war and soldiers come to his village looking for conscripts. This time his son is spared because of his leg.

"The point is," Syd concluded, "we never really know what fate is. Sometimes a tragedy may really be a new opportunity."

"Like what you meant by *fate is what we make of it?*"

He smiled.

It seemed that Syd was doing better. I certainly was. The spot we were in was magnificent with its high peaks, rocky walls, and gentle cascades. I found myself looking forward to the hike tomorrow and seeing the pass Solomons had spotted. Maybe this was what Pop had felt out here, the expansiveness and sense of adventure?

When I tucked in, I pulled out the Muir book Syd had lent me, eager to read another chapter.

DAY FIFTEEN

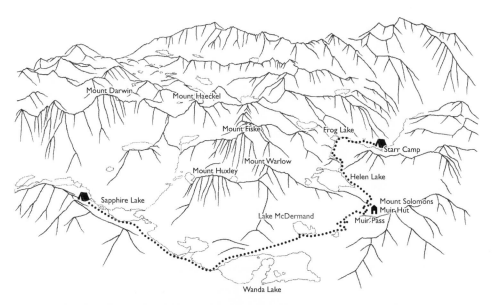

Sapphire Lake Outflow (10,900′) to Starr Camp (10,320′) via Muir Pass (11,980′)

7½ miles—1,090 feet elevation gain; 1,670 feet elevation loss

T HE AIR WAS THIN, and Syd and I had to halt occasionally to catch our breath. Muir Pass was somewhere up the gray talus-covered slope we were climbing. At almost twelve thousand feet, it would be the highest we'd been so far. Even though Syd was making slow progress, he was in high spirits.

We'd gotten up late, passing Sapphire Lake and catching up to Rena who musta passed us in the morning. Rena was up on a rocky slope that was dotted with white flowers by a small rivulet trickling into Wanda Lake. She was wrapped in a red flapping windbreaker and cooking cranberry pancakes on a large frying pan she had balanced over her tiny stove.

She practically beamed when we came over, displaying a small glass jar of honest-to-God Vermont maple syrup.

"You're carrying that?" Syd gaped.

"Yes," she nodded vigorously. "I found at MTR. Is heavy. That's why I make now. Please to try pancakes."

She poured the syrup over the tiny pancakes and using her spatula—I couldn't believe she was carrying a frying pan and spatula—gave us each one. They were amazing. The sugary maple syrup sublime against the bittersweet warm cranberries. Chewing slowly, I relished each tiny bite. Pop woulda loved to be here now, tasting pancakes with real syrup up in the mountains. The small white flowers danced in the breeze. It was heaven.

"These are outstanding," Syd praised.

Rena sparkled like a new parent, cooking another round for each of us.

She really was Iron Woman. Her pack musta weighed over sixty pounds, but here she was on her first hike outpacing even experienced hikers—with time enough to stop and cook pancakes. Like Gogo Yubari, the kick-ass schoolgirl in *Kill Bill*, you never judge a person's ability by their size!

"Did you ever catch up to Kitty?" Syd asked.

"No, I oversleep at ranger station," she said, making a sad face. "Yesterday I only make it to Evolution Lake, so now I need catch up Kitty again, but first make pancakes and enjoy sunshine!" she smiled broadly.

Eventually Syd got up and quoting Muir declared, "*The mountains are calling and I must go!*"

Now we were somewhere on the ridge below the pass, Syd's energy fueled by Rena and her pancakes. I'd learned from our previous climbs that most initial peaks were false ones. The real pass was always far above what at first appeared to be the summit. So as we moved slowly toward the ridge, I held some strength in reserve, mentally prepared to ascend yet another slope, and then perhaps one or two more.

Some hikers were coming down from above. "You're almost there!" declared a thin woman with a green pack and blonde pigtails.

You're almost there—that could mean almost anything—out here it was more of a greeting than a true measure of progress. The other phrase I'd learned to be wary of was, *Mile, mile and a half,* which always seemed to be some arbitrary distance between four and six miles.

"We're almost at the ridge, or the actual pass?" I pressed.

"Almost at the pass!" she exclaimed. "The Muir Hut's right there, see?" She pointed at what appeared to be a large pile of rocks.

Encouraged, but circumspect, I held my pace up the rocky switchback, Syd close behind me. The trail rounded a large boulder. Ahead I saw the hut. She was right, we were there! It was almost as nice as the pancakes.

The hut had been hard to see from below 'cause its brown, gray, and orange bricks all looked cut from the granite littering the slopes around us. The building was octagonal, with a circular brick roof stepped inward to a point, like a giant stone beehive, or one of the LEGO buildings I'd fashioned as a kid. There was a single entrance with a heavy wooden door facing north, a squared-off stone chimney on the eastern side, and a small glass window with a long brick lintel like an eyebrow peering west. A metal plaque by the door read, *To John Muir, Lover of "The Range of Light." This shelter was erected through the generosity of Frederick Schwarz, 1931, Sierra Club, U.S. Forest Service.*

"Who was Frederick Schwarz?" I asked.

Muir Hut

"He was a professional forester who wanted to make a personal contribution toward the Muir Trail," Syd explained. "William Colby of the Sierra Club suggested that he build a shelter up here for travelers, like the ones in Italy he'd seen in *National Geographic*. They had the plans drawn up by Henry Gutterson, a well-known San Francisco architect."

"How do you remember so many details?"

"Hal Roth wrote about the hut in *Pathway in the Sky*. It's one of the books I read before our trip. And Wenk also talks about it in her guide. I read it again last night. Shall we go in?"

The inside was dimly lit. There was a musty smell like an old cave. The door was split, so we cracked open the top half to let in a bit more light and air. The roof was gorgeous, its concentric brick design like the inside of a Navajo basket. A stone bench ran around the interior. Against one wall was a small fireplace that'd been bricked up. Someone had left a pair of weathered deer antlers on the mantle, and beside it was a plaque with a picture of John Muir, a Sierra Club emblem, and a short dedication. Over the fireplace was hung a string of Tibetan prayer flags. But most impressive, to me at least, was that high up on the interior wall hung a large cloth American flag. I smiled knowingly, like one in on a secret, recognizing the flag that Dylan had carried all the way up here in tribute of John Muir, America, the trail, and whatever other personal significance it held to the hearty vet.

It was cool inside, so after looking around, we headed back outside. Latching the door, we sat in the sun eating our lunches, the occasional gust of wind echoing off the mountains and rock.

"Muir Pass was one of the biggest challenges the early explorers faced in finding a route for the trail," said Syd. "Although Solomons spied the pass from the summit of Mount Goddard, he never actually investigated the feasibility of guiding stock over it."

"So, who was the first person to use the pass?" I mumbled, chewing a mouthful of almond butter.

"Technically it was George Davis and his geological survey party who made the first crossing with stock. But it was J.N. LeConte who really established its feasibility as a pass, linking up all the separately explored sections of the JMT into one contiguous trail."

"You told me about him, his father was a University of California President, right?"

"That was his uncle John who taught physics. His father was the geology professor famous for championing Muir's theory of glacial erosion. J.N. was very much like him—over his lifetime making forty-four extended trips through the Sierra. Unlike Solomons and Brown, LeConte viewed wilderness expeditions as social outings, almost always travelling with a group. On some trips he would mule-in food and supplies, establishing a large basecamp where he and his companions held rowdy dinners around oversized bonfires—often celebrating their victories with drink and cigar."

That sounded more like my idea of camping—way better than choking down packets of Backwoods Buffet huddled over a tiny stove. Then again, it probably wasn't very ecological to burn all that wood—especially if everybody started doing it. And it probably wasn't that safe either—what with all the wildfires California was experiencing lately.

Syd went on, "Perhaps because he was an engineer, LeConte was the first to recognize the need for a reliable map unifying the scattered observations from earlier expeditions. In the winters, he poured over the archives and in the summers, he did fieldwork to fill in the gaps. On each of his trips he carried both a mountain theodolite and an aneroid barometer."

"What are those?" I asked. "You said yesterday that Solomons had a barometer for measuring altitude, and I forgot to ask you how it worked."

"A theodolite is an instrument similar to the tool surveyors use. LeConte used it to determine the location of mountains by triangulation. A barometer measures air pressure, from which you can determine altitude."

"Is that why it's so hard to breathe up here? 'Cause the pressure's lower?"

"Precisely. At lower pressures, there's less oxygen. LeConte used the data he gathered to make the first accurate map of Yosemite and Kings Canyon, which he published in the *Bulletin of the Sierra Club.*"

"Who paid for all that?"

"Mostly himself. You could call it his summer hobby."

"Did Solomons know him?"

"I told you how Solomons accompanied LeConte on his ascent of Mount Ritter. Both were the same age and both members of the Sierra Club, although of very different backgrounds. Solomons grew up in a cramped San Francisco apartment, while LeConte was raised among the Berkeley elite, accompanying his father on outings since an early age."

I nodded, still working on my almond butter. Syd's stories reminded me of the picnics Pop used to take me on—only Pop tended to tell me about Greek legends and stuff, rather than exploration and history.

"Eventually LeConte decided to pick up Solomons' work, mapping out a High Mountain Route along the crest of the Sierra. He began by searching for a pass across this divide. On one trip, he actually climbed right up to where we're sitting now, but looking down the other side, he described the terrain as *savage black gorges that would be impossible to get an animal down*, and so on the brink of discovering Muir Pass, he abandoned it."

"Wow, he was so close."

"Discretion is the better part of valor, and from what I've read, the other side of this pass is pretty rough going."

"Wait—you mean it's going to be harder *going down?*"

"Remember, we have a trail to follow, the early explorers didn't, so it shouldn't be too bad for us. But finding a navigable pass through this region turned out to be quite a challenge."

"So how did they actually find it?"

"Several years later, LeConte tried again. This time starting from the other side in the Kings River Basin. From there, he made several attempts to locate a pass, but none of the routes he found were suitable for stock."

"So what happened?"

"The following year George Davis and his survey team reported making it over this pass with their pack train in the snow. After hearing about it, LeConte and his friends Duncan McDuffie and James Hutchinson set out to hike the entire length of the proposed trail. The group started at Tuolumne Meadows in the summer of 1908 and followed essentially the same route we took to get here. When they reached where we're at now, the same point LeConte had turned back from earlier, they pushed on, leading their animals down the other side. It was a harrowing descent, and the poor animals' legs were badly cut by the loose rock and talus. But they made it to the Middle Fork of the Kings River, arriving at what is now called Le Conte[†] Canyon."

"Wow, I'm glad we have a trail."

He nodded. "From there, his team continued south, exploring the territory originally sketched by Bolton Brown, and arriving twenty-eight days later in Kings Canyon—having made what was effectively the first trip along the JMT."

"Wait, I thought the trail ended at Whitney, not Kings Canyon?"

"The section to Whitney wasn't added until later on. In those days there was no good stock path down to Whitney and it was much more practical to begin and end on the western side of the Sierra. Even today, with modern transportation, we'll still have to take a number of long bus rides to get from Whitney Portal back to your car in Yosemite."

[†]Although J.N. LeConte generally shortened his family name from "Le Conte" to "LeConte" in publications, the U.S. Geological Survey (USGS) employs the legal two-word variant of his name in features named for J.N. LeConte.

"I see. So is LeConte considered *the father of the JMT?*"

"I wouldn't say that. LeConte did become the second president of the Sierra Club, and he certainly helped carry along the project, but many people were responsible for the creation of the trail. Solomons had the vision and explored much of its northern part. The artist Bolton Brown scouted and described many of its southern regions. LeConte checked the feasibility of the route and made detailed maps. Many early explorers including Muir and Whitney also had a hand, not to mention the Sierra Club, which got a bill passed for the construction of the trail. And the Forest Service employees, who did the actual construction work. It was the combined effort of a great many people that resulted in what's often called, America's Most Famous Trail."

Breathing in the rarified air and looking out over the landscape, I marveled at just how many people it'd taken to allow me to be sitting here now.

"You know, I mentioned it earlier, but that peak there—" Syd motioned toward the large peak towering over the south end of the pass "—is Mount Solomons, and the two lakes surrounding the pass, Wanda and Helen, were named for Muir's two daughters."

It really was incredible we'd made it here. Thinking about Dylan's flag made me proud that America had a true wilderness trail over these mountains, preserved for all people by our National Park and Forest Services. Organizations that John Muir, through his explorations, writings, and efforts, helped to create. Just one man—an American immigrant from Scotland wielding a pen and carrying a knapsack—had changed the world for the better. There might be no real "father" of the JMT, but it seemed fitting that this trail and this hut were both named for John Muir.

Looking out over the pass and up at Mount Solomons, I admired how well the small stone hut blended in with its surroundings. Then it occurred to me, "Hey, where's Rena? Shouldn't she be here by now?"

"Not really, she likes to take long naps in the afternoon sun, then hike later during the cooler part of the day."

"That doesn't sound half bad."

"For her, it's fine. But at our pace, it would mean making less than three miles a day."

I laughed. He was right of course.

"Shall we start down that 'savage gorge' to Le Conte Canyon?" he asked.

I didn't like the sound of that, but agreed, and soon we were heading over the crest.

Syd was really growing on me. He reminded me of Pop—his stories, his love of nature, and his deep guiding wisdom. I was glad he'd made it here to see the places he'd read about. Maybe he was right. Maybe I could change my fate? Muir had changed a whole world with just his pen—maybe I could change mine too?

Crossing the top, I saw why LeConte had turned away from this. The trail wound over jumbled black stone down a steep descent to Helen Lake. In many places Syd and I struggled with our footing, each of us narrowly avoiding twisting an ankle on several occasions. At the bottom, the trail crossed the lake's outflow, then ran up and down steep ledges where it was not well marked. At several spots we had to scout around to be sure we were on the actual trail.

Eventually we reached an unnamed lake, the banks of which were teeming with large black tadpoles. Some of 'em were already in the process of changing into frogs, sporting long yellow-spotted legs.

"Do you know what these are?" Syd asked enthusiastically.

"Yeah, they're baby frogs."

"They're rare Sierra Nevada Yellow-Legged Frogs. They're an endangered species."

"They don't look very endangered to me." They were so numerous that you could practically walk across 'em.

"They're a species indigenous to the Sierra Nevada that have been pushed almost to extinction by the introduction of nonnative trout. They used to be everywhere up here, but now they're only in a handful of lakes. John Muir once described these 'happy frogs' in *The Mountains of California*, where he mused about how they got here suggesting that, *either their sticky spawn was carried in on the feet of ducks or other birds, else their progenitors must have made some exciting excursions through the woods and up the sides of the canyons.*"

I laughed, imagining a troop of tiny frogs in blue Cub Scout uniforms with yellow ties and tiny brown hiking sticks, all climbing up the canyon wall in search of lakes.

"Do you see that tree?" he asked.

He was pointing up at a majestic golden-brown tree that'd been stripped of all its bark and leaves.

"You mean the old dead one?"

"That's a whitebark pine. Notice the needles at the tip of that one branch? It's not dead, but it looks like it's struggling. Whitebark pines are some of the oldest trees on the planet. Sadly, many of them are dying now because of fungus, beetles, and wildfire—all aggravated by climate change."

"Isn't there anything people can do to save 'em?" I asked, remembering what Permi had said about trees having feelings.

"Not likely," he shook his head. "Although, I read that a small fraction of these is naturally pest resistant—just like some people have a natural resistance to certain diseases. So it could be that in time the more resilient ones will make a comeback, but it'll be a long while before anyone knows for certain."

I took a photo of the tree, standing on the ridge overlooking the surrounding mountains like a wizened old sage.

"I want to stop here for a while, watch the frogs, and meditate," Syd said. "Why don't you go on to Starr Camp and find us a site. I'll meet you there later, it shouldn't be far."

"Are you sure? Last time I went ahead, you twisted your ankle crossing that stream, remember? Maybe we'd better stick together."

"It's less than a mile and pretty flat," he assured me, showing me how to find Starr Camp on the map.

"Why is it called Starr Camp?"

"I'm not sure, but I suspect it has something to do with Peter Starr, whom I told you about yesterday."

I guess no one could know everything. Leaving him there in quiet cross-legged meditation, I headed on. Syd really had a patience for sitting and observing things that I couldn't share. I really enjoyed the scenery here and all, but there was no way I could just sit all day staring at a tree or a flower. The real beauty of the hike came at the end of the day, when you could just stretch out your legs and chill. That and the people we met. My night with Kydoime began replaying in my head. The gentle hills and tumbling creeks merging with images of her curving body. Suddenly I jerked to attention—having almost walked right by the turn off to Starr Camp. The camp was below the trail on a wide shelf overlooking a meadow with a stream and small lake.

A tall light-haired hiker was camped there. He had a small tarp propped up on trekking poles for a tent. His muscular chest practically jumped out of his tight black BodyPump T-shirt. He was sitting on a large rock watching me while chewing on a long stick of hard salami.

"Hi," I greeted him. "I'm Gil."

"Jack," he replied, taking my hand firmly, "Pleased ta meet ya!" He'd a vaguely Australian-sounding accent, with sharp blue eyes, and a grinning sun-creased face.

"Is this Starr Camp?"

"Ay," he answered, gnawing on his salami.

"Do you mind if my buddy and I set up our tents over there?" I asked, indicating a spot at the other end of the ridge.

"Have at it!"

"Are you from Australia?"

"Nah—New Zealand."

"Which way are you hiking?"

"North, for Evolution Valley," he pointed back up the way I'd just come from.

"Are you doing the JMT?"

"Just a section mate, then baggin' a few peaks—I'm more of a mountaineer than a tramper."

"You came all the way out here from New Zealand just for that?"

"Nah, I'm working as a postdoc out at Stanford, this was all the time I had off."

"So you're doing some sort of research work? In what?"

"That's refreshing."

"What do you mean?"

"It's like whenever I tell someone I'm Kiwi, they always wanna know something about *Lord of the Rings*. You're the first person to ask about my research."

"*Lord of the Rings?* Oh, 'cause it was filmed there, right?"

"Yeah, musta had the same conversation fifty times already. You know, how to find the spots it was filmed, when's the best time to go, and all that. Straight up—Tourism NZ should just start promoting Ring Tours—they'd earn a bloody fortune! But my research is in biomedical engineering."

"That's cool. I know what you mean—almost every conversation I have out here seems to be about food, gear, or pack weight."

Jack laughed. Before long I was listening rapt as he told me about getting trapped by a storm somewhere in the New Zealand bush.

"So there we were mate, the river was massive and the creeks we'd crossed the day before were too swollen for us to backtrack. It was getting pretty desperate, and our only option was to try and sidle the gully right over an active slip then bush-bash out to—"

He was interrupted by Rena calling down to us, "Gil! Quick! Syd in trouble!"

Without pausing to grab any of my gear, I hurried up the slope, Jack following.

Rena led us back up to the lake where Syd had been watching the frogs. He was lying there on the ground by a pool of vomit. The smell was pretty bad.

"Syd!" I called out to him. "Are you OK?"

He leaned up on one arm opening his eyes. His face and hands were covered in a mix of dirt and dried puke, but at least he was conscious.

"I'm having a bad bout of vertigo," he said weakly. "It happens sometimes with my condition. When I open my eyes the whole world seems to be spinning around."

"Here, let me help you clean up," I said, kicking some dirt over the puke, then using his water bottle to wash his face and hands while getting him into a sitting position against a rock. I felt his forehead, at least he didn't have a fever or anything—*why did he always get in trouble when I was away?*

"I have medicine for this," he said, "but I left it back home. I'm sorry."

"Wait. Cass gave me some pills! Maybe it's one of those?"

"Perhaps," he groaned.

"Can you walk?"

"I don't think so. I tried, but I keep falling down."

"The camp's not far," I said, after checking his breathing and stuff as best as I could remember from first-aid class. "This is Jack. I think the two of us can support you back— would that work?"

"We can try."

I strapped his pack onto my back, then Jack and I each took one of his arms over our shoulders, taking his weight between us. It was surprising how light and boney he was.

Syd could barely stand and kept his eyes closed as we walked. Along the way he threw up twice, both in dry heaves. Each time we set him down and I cleaned him up after, giving him something to drink.

It was hard carrying his pack and walking him down the trail at the same time, but Jack was strong, and after about twenty minutes we'd made it to camp.

Rena went down to the river and pumped some water for us while Jack and I got his bivy up and helped get him inside with his sleeping clothes.

Going through my pack, I found the pill bottles Cass had given me.

"This is it," he said, opening one of them and swallowing a pill with some water.

"Cass told me those were sedatives—"

"They're antihistamines, but they have a sedative effect. I'll probably sleep till noon. Tomorrow's a short day anyway. I'll be fine now—I just need some rest."

Rena knelt down giving him a long hug and listening to his chest, "Are you sure you be OK now?"

"I've had this before, don't worry," he gave her a slight squeeze.

"Should I stay tonight?" she asked. "Kitty up ahead. I said I join her, but if you need, I stay with you."

"I'll be alright. Please join Kitty—she'll worry about you. You gave me your email address. I'll write you when I'm back."

"OK, take good care," she hugged him again. Then with tears welling up in her eyes she said bye to us. We thanked her. She seemed to struggle for a moment under the weight of her pack before continuing down the trail.

After zipping up Syd's bivy, we headed over to Jack's camp to let him rest.

"He seems pretty ill. I'll stick around to see if he needs help in the mornin'," Jack said. "Thanks, that'll be great," I said, glad for all the help I could get.

"No worries, mate. Is he a relation of yours or something?"

"He was my Pop's best friend. I'm helping him hike the trail."

"He's lucky to have ya."

"It's sorta like having Pop back—except I can't imagine having to go through everything I did when Pop died all over again."

"I know how ya feel. I lost this girl I was seein' to cancer. It's what got me into the medical field. It's a tough one—but better to have loved and lost, than not to have loved at all."

"*Old man Sai loses a horse,*" I murmured.

"What's that?"

"Nothing—just something he said once—I think it's his way of telling me: *nothing ventured, nothing gained.*"

"That's it mate. That's spot-on."

"Whaddya think the easiest way outta here is? I mean, if I have to get him back to a hospital or something?"

"Your closest exit is out by South Lake, over Bishop Pass. It's not far, but you'd never make it, he's knackered and it's a pretty rough climb. If he's not right by mornin' you'd best call rescue."

Maybe we'd need to find a ranger again. At least Jack would be here to help.

DAY SIXTEEN

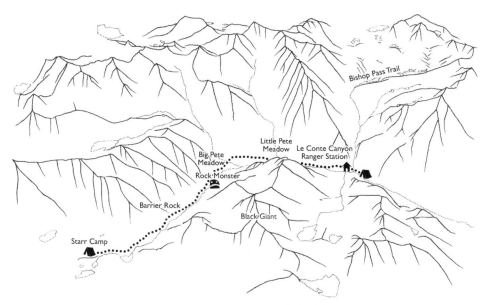

Starr Camp (10,320′) to Le Conte Canyon Ranger Station (8,720′)
4 miles—60 feet elevation gain; 1,660 feet elevation loss

S YD GOT UP at around ten saying he was feeling much better. The vertigo had passed,
and he could walk again.

"You sure you're alright?" I asked. "You had me pretty scared yesterday."

"I've had a few episodes like this. They always pass. It's good you had that medicine.
I'll be fine."

"Just let me know if you need anything—we'll stick close together today, OK?"

He nodded.

"This is Jack from New Zealand," I said, "he's the one who helped me get you back here."

"From New Zealand? Where they shot *Lord of the Rings?*"

"Ya see what I mean?" Jack shot me a glance. "Well, if you guys are all good here, then
I'd better get myself going. I'm tryna make Evolution Valley today."

"What's the plan?" I asked as Syd ate. I'd already breakfasted with Jack.

"A short four miles to Le Conte Canyon Ranger Station."

"There's a ranger station?"

"Yup."

That was good news—if he did need help, at least there'd be a place to find it.

"Why are we stopping there?"

"That's where we're getting our next resupply. I've arranged to have it horsed-in over Bishop Pass, instead of hiking out to Onion Valley like most people do. It'll save us two days, and we won't have to visit a town."

That was more good news. If there was another emergency, they could probably carry him out on horseback. It also explained the name, "Rainbow Pack Outfitters" where we'd mailed our third buckets.

"How much did that cost?"

"They bring in people on camping and fishing trips all the time, so asking them to carry a couple of extra buckets wasn't very expensive. The only downside is we'll have to carry twelve days of food to Whitney, but I figure you've got your hiking legs now."

So he *was* still planning to go on.

He packed up and shouldered his pack as if nothing'd happened. He looked OK, the pills and extra sleep musta worked, but I couldn't help feeling in my gut this was the start of something worse.

Just beyond camp we gained amazing views of Black Giant, a serrated black ridge rising up like some dark guardian over the surrounding peaks, its arms spread wide as if to envelope them in its grasp. Below it were boulder-strewn slopes dotted with splotches of white snow, still clinging tenaciously to the shadows despite the heat.

Syd's pace was normal and he wasn't outta breath or anything, but I continued to watch him.

The trail descended, passing a series of cascades and crossing a large gray granite slope.

Syd paused to comment, "Notice anything special here?"

I scanned the way we'd just come. There were two small waterfalls in the stream we'd been following. The trail just behind us cut steeply through the middle of a slick granite slope that looked like it'd been polished smooth by the erosion of water. There were a couple of dark stains on the rock, but that was nothing new. The trees along the slope were all the tall familiar lodgepole pines. No one else was coming down the trail, and there were no strange birds flitting about. The sky was clear. There really didn't seem to be anything special, other than the normal beauty of being up in the Sierra, which it was all too easy to get used to. Perhaps that's what he wanted me to notice?

"I don't see anything unusual—unless you're talking about the two small waterfalls along the river?"

"No, although they're lovely. Look again at the section of trail we just came over."

It was steep, but there was nothing remarkable.

"Sorry, I just don't see it."

"This is Barrier Rock. The trail here had to be blasted out of solid rock—and it was quite a job too. Bits of it kept cracking off because of the way it layers. This may not look like much but making a trail here was one of the trickier bits of work they had to do when making the JMT."

My eyes ran over the granite slope again. Sure enough, there were chip marks in the rock and areas that musta been blasted out. How'd I missed seein that? There were also spots where someone had carefully cemented small rocks into place to level the trail, and even steps cut into the sheer wall. The work blended in so well it looked like the trail naturally crossed the rock.

Syd pointed up the slope, "Had they not blasted out a path here, the trail would have crisscrossed the river, requiring a pair of bridges. The builders wanted to do everything they could to keep the route as pristine as possible."

The two of us stood staring at the trail in quiet admiration. Syd sure seemed to be back to his chipper self.

"You know there's a funny thing about bridges," he added. "If you hike a lot in the woods, or even drive up a scenic highway like the one through Big Sur, you'll notice most tourists stop for photographs in front of bridges. There's something about the contrast between man-made objects and a natural landscape that attracts people."

"Maybe it's an urge to conquer nature? To make our mark on the landscape?"

"Perhaps, but here is something even more fantastic—the surveyors and trail workers created a route that blends in—without bridges. This is the kind of work I admire."

I'd heard somewhere that a perfect Japanese garden was one where the rocks and plants were indistinguishable from those found in nature. That ultimate perfection was invisible to the eye. The people who'd cut the trail into this rock were definitely master landscapers—it'd certainly fooled me.

We continued on. My mind drifted. How had they made this trail? It musta been a ridiculous undertaking. Not to mention all the environmentalists. Just getting a group of them to agree on anything was daunting. Soon we came to a clearing at the side of a tiny meadow. There was an enormous boulder here, at least twice my height. A wide crack ran horizontally across the front, like an enormous gaping mouth. Someone had placed stones inside it, arranging them to look like giant teeth. The whole thing resembled a great dinosaur skull or an enormous rock monster. It even had two large sunken dents on either side, resembling eye sockets. Dropping my pack, I climbed inside its mouth and had Syd take photos of me being "eaten" by the monster.

Reviewing the pictures, it dawned on me that this was exactly what Syd had described earlier. I was taking photos with a man-made creation in nature. But so what? If the trail and all of nature were art, then so was this giant rock monster. Maybe Syd had a bias against man-made art, or the intrusion of man-made objects, but I didn't. So long as they blended in or enhanced their surroundings, what was wrong with a few bridges or rustic stone buildings? I loved the way the Muir Hut grew out of its surroundings. Sure, roads and cars could be made less obtrusive, and billboards could be done away with, but not every landscape needed to be pristine. I liked this toothy rock monster!

"Syd, who actually made the JMT? I mean—you told me before about the explorers and all. But who actually did the work? You know, before helicopters and jackhammers and all—how did they do this? It musta cost a fortune."

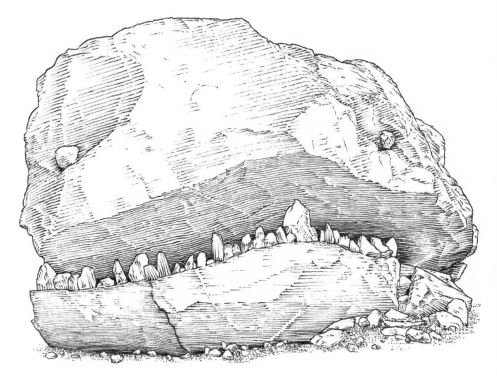

Rock Monster

He stroked the growing beard on his chin, "Let's see now, I believe it was William Colby who first began to garner public interest in constructing a physical trail."

"You mentioned him once, who was he?"

"He was a lawyer from San Francisco who helped Muir in his fight over Hetch Hetchy, and who eventually became the Sierra Club's third president. Colby organized the Club's first Summer Outing, leading about a hundred people into the Yosemite High Country."

"A hundred? Isn't that a bit too many?"

"They didn't have restrictions or permits in those days, but it was a large group for a fragile wilderness area, that's true. The attendees were very impressed, and the following summer Colby took almost twice that number into Kings Canyon. Slowly the number of outings grew, but they were limited by the lack of regular trails."

"How'd they get all those city folks to rough it?"

"These were *outings*, not backpacking trips. They had lecturers, entertainers, and packers. It was something of a grand social event. I think it was around 1914 that the political manager for the Governor of California attended one of Colby's trips. After seeing the need for well-maintained trails, he offered his support. Wasting no time, Colby drafted a bill for the creation of what would become the Muir Trail."

"Did it pass?"

"Yes, and it had tremendous public approval. It was signed into law the year after Muir died, issuing an initial ten thousand dollars for the construction of the trail."

"Ten thousand? I couldn't even get a decent car for that!"

"True, but in those days workers were paid only a few dollars a day. Back then, ten thousand dollars was about the price of a nice home—which isn't much, but it was the first of five such appropriations, and some of the costs were borne by the Forest Service and other sources as well."

Working at a law firm had taught me how to quickly calculate prices. "Actually, that's pretty reasonable costwise," I concluded after doing some mental math. "One of our clients had a construction company, and if we estimate the trail to be two hundred miles long, and the cost five times that of a house, it works out to a bit less per mile than it does to make a paved road today—and this is just a trail. How long did it take them to finish it?"

"Quite a while. They couldn't just start work after the bill passed. First Wilbur McClure, the state engineer, had to approve the plans. He took two trips on horseback up and down the proposed route, making changes and adjustments until he could certify it was workable."

"Is that the same McClure for whom McClure Meadow back in Evolution Valley was named?"

"The same. Of course, there were many challenges. They had to cut through rock, move boulders, plan switchbacks, and figure out the best places to ford rivers—or where absolutely necessary, build bridges."

"Like the ones we crossed on the San Joaquin?"

"Yes, and all of the work was done by hand—with shovels and pickaxes, star drills, and dynamite. Probably the two hardest parts were Forester Pass and the Golden Staircase, which both required extensive blasting. But in 1933, when Solomons returned to hike the trail in his sixties, it was more or less as you see it now. The last parts were finished in 1938."

"Twenty-three years after the bill passed," I mused.

"Or fifty-four years after Solomons first had his vision."

"That's only about ten trail miles a year. If we made public roads at that pace, we'd still be working on the highways linking New York to California."

"Remember there's heavy snow covering the Sierra all winter. The best they could do was work about three to four months a year. And all their food and construction supplies had to be packed in on mules. It was a massive undertaking."

"I'll bet. I hadn't really thought about it before, but it's pretty impressive. I'm glad you brought me here. I don't think I'd ever have seen it on my own. You're like my own personal John Muir." Syd flushed. He was pretty modest sometimes. "You know, it took a while, but I'm starting to really see what people love about the wilderness. There's something down-to-earth and primal about being self-sufficient out here."

"When Thoreau left society to build his cabin in the woods, he wrote, *I wanted to live deep and suck out all the marrow of life, to live so sturdily and Spartan-like as to put to rout all that was not life.*"

"Maybe that's what Pop saw in Thoreau—being out here really reveals what's important. You know, I've felt more alive on this trip than my whole life since college."

He smiled.

How'd life become so harried that people had forgotten the importance of wilderness? Places like this grounded us to our very humanity. Our politicians spent so much energy squabbling over tax breaks, when small investments like the trail could do so much more for the greater good. Maybe more people needed to come out here and reflect on what really mattered? I looked up. The rock monster stared at me with its toothy grin.

"Shall we get going?" Syd asked.

I nodded. As we walked, my eyes followed the long line of dirt beneath my feet. It was amazing how many people had come together to make this possible.

Less than thirty minutes later we were at the junction to Bishop Pass. The ranger station was a short jog away. Its front door was locked. A dated message said the ranger would be back in two or three days.

"This is where we'll get our resupply," said Syd. "There was no note for us, so I can only assume they haven't gotten here yet."

"So we're camping here?"

"It'll be what hikers call a *nero*-day."

"Let me guess, a *near-zero* day, right?"

"Precisely. We can relax, do laundry, and just take it easy."

"Fine by me." It would be good just to chill and see how Syd was doing. Besides, the last time I'd done laundry was way back at MTR and I was starting to smell like Yojimbo again.

We made camp just south of the ranger station. The site was surrounded by fragrant pines above a bubbling stream. We did laundry and "showered"—dumping water over our heads with our bear canisters. Syd looked skeletal. After yesterday, it was a wonder he was still doing this—although his skin did look a bit less yellow, probably from all the sun. My own skin was tanned and my belly and legs seemed tighter. Both of us were starting to grow beards. Mine was wild and scraggly, making me look like Jack Nicolson in *The Shining*. Syd's was gray and wispy. We'd probably look like a pair of tramps by the time we reached Whitney. Just as we were drying off, we heard a familiar voice.

"Syd, Gil, I find your camp. Wow, you really look like big bear!" Rena giggled, pointing at my naked belly. *Why was it every time I washed off in the wilderness, someone always came along?*

"How everything? Still dizzy?" she asked Syd.

"I'm fine," he said, and she smiled.

Rena pretended to look the other way as we dried off and dressed—at least she didn't pull out her Nikon—then followed us back up to camp.

"I thought you'd be far ahead of us by now," Syd said.

"Yes," she said glancing down, "but last night growing dark and I get lost again. Only hour ago find the trail."

"I'm glad you're alright. If you can stay, I have some special stuff packed for dinner that we can all share," he offered.

"No, can't," Rena said with obvious reluctance. "Have to make Whitney and catch plane. Sorry, if I know before I meet you, would change schedule. I hope make Mather Pass today."

"That's quite far," observed Syd.

"I know, but I can do!"

"I believe you can."

Rena gave him a long hug, then pulled on her big blue pack and headed off. Syd looked noticeably saddened.

"Do you think you'll go to Japan and see her after we get back?"

"I'd love to visit Japan again— " he trailed off. "I've made it farther on the trail than I ever expected to. But even if I could, I wouldn't want to burden her with a dying old man."

"Wait—just how far had you expected to make it?"

He looked like a deer caught in the headlights. Turning away he said, "Yesterday or tomorrow, does anyone really know how long they have?"

"Yeah, I get that," I said straightening up. "What I mean is, if you knew you might die out here, why bring me along—you know, given everything that happened with Pop and all?"

"Because *you* need this as much as I do, maybe more," he said meeting my gaze.

"Whaddya mean?"

"Look into yourself and ask the same question."

Shit—was he really gonna pull the Master Po thing now? There was no way I was letting this go!

"Syd, what I need from you is some honesty. Yesterday was really scary. We're at a ranger station now. If we need to hike out, we can, or maybe we can get a horse or something. What I need to know is, *can you make it or not?"*

He took a deep breath and glanced down, "I don't know. Yesterday wasn't a good sign. My doctor said the vertigo might return if the cancer progresses. I'm frightened too. I want to try, but there are no guarantees. If that's too much for you, we can hike out here. I'll accept that. We've already made it halfway."

I stared at him. *"You know the Odyssey, right?* I mean—I know you do—you quoted Tennyson's poem about it on the second day—*striving, seeking, and not yielding—"*

"Of course."

"You see, I never really liked that story. Pop read it to me when I was a kid, and I know it's a great book and all—but the things is, Odysseus never really cared for his men. Like that whole thing with the cyclops. Instead of simply sailing away, he taunts the monster— out of pure vanity. And when it begins tossing boulders at their ships and all his men beg him to stop—*does he listen? No!* He reveals their identity, dooming them to wander for years. And even with his wife—she stays loyal the whole time, bravely fending off her suitors. But not Odysseus, he sleeps with Circe, staying with her for almost a year, and then Calypso, for what, seven more? Even his old dog was more loyal than he was! What I mean is, don't be like Odysseus."

He nodded.

"The one I really admired was Aeneas, you know from Virgil?"

"It's been a while—"

"Pop was fond of that too. Aeneas survived Troy, which actually fell 'cause of the giant horse Odysseus thought up. So Aeneas assembles all the survivors—even carrying his own father outta the burning city on his back—and helps them to escape, eventually founding Rome. But unlike Odysseus, Aeneas really cares for his men, trying his best not to lose any—and even when he does, he really mourns 'em."

"I see."

"What I mean is, I need you to let me know what's happening. Like at MTR—you didn't really call Cass, did you?"

"No," he said, bowing his head.

"I don't know why you need to make it to Whitney so bad—but if it's that important, I'm gonna do my best to help you. I just need to know if we really stand a chance. I need you to be honest with me. That's all."

"I can't promise anything, and some of my symptoms have been troubling lately, but somehow I believe the two of us will make it to see that sunrise—"

"That's good enough for me. I'll do my best to get you there. I just need to know you really believe it."

Relaxing, I patted him on the back. We finished our camp chores, then I lay out in the sun reading Muir.

At around four, we heard the clomping of horses and headed up to the junction. Riding the lead was a deeply tanned woman with long brown hair and a wide leather cowboy hat. She looked like the beautiful rancher's daughter from some Clint Eastwood flick—all that was missing was a shotgun. Strung behind her were three pack horses with leather saddlebags and a ton of gear.

"Is one of y' fella's Syd?"

He nodded.

"I'm Esperanza," she said while dismounting. "I've got two buckets for y'all."

My eyes feasted on this lithe young cowgirl. "Would you like a hand with that?" I offered.

"I can manage," she said—her flowing hair and perfect features stirring more than a passing interest in me. *Shit—why hadn't I ever learned to ride a horse? What could I say to a girl like this?*

She removed our buckets, placing them down away from the horses.

"Would you like to stay and join us for dinner?" I ventured.

"Nah, can't, although I'd like ta—and thanks for the offer," she grinned broadly. "I have ta get th' rest a these things up to the pass, so th' trail crew can use 'em."

She climbed back onto her mount, saying, "Y'all just leave your trash and anything else ya wants to have packed out in these here buckets. Stick 'em under th' veranda in front a th' station and I'll pack 'em out in the mornin'. Be certain not ta include anything that might attract critters. Have a lovely evening," she waved, gently nudging her mount.

A grassy equine aroma lingered in the air as she rode off. This was the first woman since Kydoime we'd met out here whom I'd found attractive. There really wasn't much hope for me getting together with some cowgirl from Bishop, but standing by the dusty trail, I pictured myself in a western bar clinging to the mechanical bull for just a chance at getting to know her.

"Come on," Syd called me back as the dust was settling. "Let's get these buckets down to camp and pack up our canisters."

Lugging the heavy containers wasn't easy 'cause the metal handles had been cut off—probably to protect the sides of the horses—so we had to cradle the buckets in our arms, waddling back to camp like a pair of penguins. But it wasn't far, and we began unpacking them like two happy children opening their presents on Christmas Day.

"Hey look," I said, pulling out several metallic orange packages, "twelve packs of Chicken Parmesan—*Mmmm, Backwoods Buffet again!*"

"You certainly know how to embrace variety," he said. Then holding something up added, "Perfect, new toothpaste."

After packing, I stuffed my trash into the empty bucket, using it as a chair.

"I have a surprise tonight," he announced.

"What's that?"

He pulled out two white foil-lined bags, holding 'em up for me to see, "Fresh country fried chicken, coleslaw, biscuits, and gravy!"

My jaw almost dropped. It took all of my control just to keep from drooling. "How—?" I asked.

"Ruby and Greg who run Rainbow Pack Outfitters are old friends of your father and mine from way back. When they heard we'd be hiking the trail together, Ruby insisted on including some of her home-fried chicken for us. And for another surprise—" he added theatrically, and like a magician produced a large bottle of dark wine from within his bucket, displaying it like an auctioneer, "—a bottle of Royal Escort Port from Prager Port Works in Napa Valley. I've been saving it for a special occasion and thought it would be a fitting one if we made it to the last stretch."

"Wow," I was stunned. Truly overwhelmed. *No Backwoods Bob tonight—we were having fried chicken and Port wine!*

"Shall we open it?" I asked.

"By all means," he said, ceremoniously handing me the bottle.

Peeling the foil off the top, I stared at the embedded cork.

"Syd," I started, "I don't have a bottle opener. I mailed my Swiss Army Knife back at MTR."

"I thought you had one. I didn't pack a corkscrew either."

We sat and stared at the unopened bottle.

"Perhaps we can just break the neck open on some rocks?"

"This is a twenty-year-old vintage Port. A rock might crack the bottle. Besides, we wouldn't want to leave broken glass in the wilderness."

"How do we get it open then?"

He scratched his head. We were like two monkeys on an island trying to figure out how to open up a coconut.

"I know, let me get a pointed stick!"

Searching around, I found a dry stick and broke it off into as sharp a point as I could manage without a knife, then tried wedging it in with a twisting motion—but the end wouldn't penetrate the firm cork. As I pushed harder, it snapped, almost causing me to drop the bottle in surprise.

"*Shit!*" I exclaimed. "That didn't work. What about a sharp rock?"

Placing the bottle down, I began searching around for a long sharp stone, but none were the right size. "How did ancient man do this?" I cried in frustration.

"I don't think ancient man had to open wine bottles," said Syd, looking somewhat amused by my efforts.

"We must have something that can open up this damn bottle!"

I began rummaging through the top of our packs. None of our cookware had a detachable metal handle. My spork was too wide. Syd's cutlery and most of our other gear was plastic. Even my trowel was too big—although I think Syd would have freaked if I tried opening his fancy bottle with my poop-scoop. We just had nothing in our packs capable of removing a cork. What kinda outdoor survivalists were we?

Dejected, I returned to my seat on the orange bucket. Syd looked as disappointed as me. "Well, we do have the chicken," he consoled.

We each opened a bag of chicken—which wasn't warm, but wasn't cold either—and started digging into our meals. It was delicious. We sat ravenously devouring the meal, licking our hands and lips. All the while that dark bottle stood there mocking us, like a single raised digit holding up the proverbial finger.

"We can wait for Esperanza to come back," I suggested. "She must have a corkscrew or something we can use." The idea of sharing a bottle of wine with her was also appealing.

"That won't be until sometime tomorrow—and if we miss her, we'll have to lug the bottle all the way to Whitney."

"I've got it," I snapped my fingers, "the ranger station! There must be something there we can use!"

Jumping up, I headed up the trail. But going all the way around the station, there was nothing. No discarded nail or screwdriver or anything—the meticulous ranger had stowed everything away and locked up.

The sun slowly sinking, I wandered back to camp.

"Any luck?" Syd asked hopefully.

"Nah—nothing."

Chewing on another leg of chicken, I eyed the bottle.

"Isn't there anything in Wenk's guidebook about how to open wine bottles in the wilderness?"

"I don't think so."

"There must be something—" I grumbled. "If only they hadn't clipped the handles off our buckets, then we could bend the wire into—hey wait a second, I've got it!" Jumping up, I ran to my tent, bent to the ground, and returned wiping off the prized object on my pants. "We can open it with this!" I proclaimed, holding up one of my red metal tent stakes in triumph.

Syd smiled.

Sticking the pointy stake into the neck and twisting, the cork gradually yielded. Scraping away the tiny bits of wood like a surgeon, I slowly worked my way down to the dark treasure within. Some bits of cork had fallen into the wine, but I don't think Syd or I cared. Passing the bottle ceremoniously to Syd, he took a sip, swished it around in his mouth, swallowed, and pronounced his approval. Then he took a longer draught, returning the bottle to me.

Swallowing like a thirsty sailor, I let the warm sweet beverage roll down my throat, bits of floating cork adding a sort of woodsy flavor. After the first draught, I took another long swig, this time letting some of the wine slosh around in my mouth and appreciating its subtle flavors and soft sweetness. It was heaven.

Sitting there like two happy old drunks, we passed the bottle back and forth, finishing our chicken, and laughing about all the hardships of the trail.

DAY SEVENTEEN

Le Conte Canyon Ranger Station (8,720′) to Palisade Creek (8,690′)
6½ miles—710 feet elevation gain; 740 feet elevation loss

I AWOKE TO THE SUN glaring on my tent and a raging headache. Syd was still snoring away. Somehow, he'd managed to position his shelter in the shade.

"Syd," I shook his bivy.

"What time is it?" he groaned.

"Late, we overslept."

He rummaged around inside. "It's almost eleven-thirty!" he declared.

"It was the Port, but it was worth it."

"Alcohol and altitude don't mix."

We struck camp in slow motion, leaving our buckets under the porch for Esperanza. It was almost one when we headed out. My head was throbbing and my shoulders were straining under the burden of our resupply. Was it just me, or was the sun brighter?

Crossing a small metal footbridge, we wound our way down into Le Conte Canyon. Here the stream we'd camped at merged with other tributaries, forming the imposing

Le Conte Canyon

Middle Fork of the Kings River—its roaring waters churning down a series of cascades to our right.

The scenery in the canyon just kept growing more magnificent, lifting my spirits and making my shifting pack more bearable. Flashy birds with black heads and bright orange and yellow breasts caught my eye. Syd called them grosbeaks. Twisty red-barked manzanita lined the trail. Lodgepole pines dotted the left slope like Christmas trees, while spires of granite rose up beyond the river on the right. Dominating these was The Citadel, jutting up above the others like an ancient watchtower—its ramparts guarding the entrance to a wide ravine. Beside it tumbled a tall white falls that split into three jagged branches, like forks of lightning, before reuniting again and plunging into the river.

At the end of the canyon was a bend in the trail, with a large campsite framed by lodge-pole pines and a massive granite boulder. Beyond it spread a lush yellow-green meadow of waving grass. Winding through the center was the Kings River, now broad and gentle forming lazy oxbows—the scent of clean water and damp hay reminiscent of my childhood.

"Let's stop here and take a break."

"Sure," he concurred.

Dropping our heavy packs, we drifted out into the meadow, enjoying the magnificent views and the feel of squishy grass beneath our feet. Had I been a pioneer, I woulda built my cabin here.

Syd pointed at two peaks near the south end of the canyon. "That's Observation Peak," he said indicating the farther one, "and that one is Mount *Shakspere*."

"Wait, you mean *Shakespeare*, right?"

"No, *Shakspere*. It was named by Francis Farquhar, who was the editor of the *Sierra Club Bulletin* and later became a club president. He and a small party of club members were the first to climb it, but somehow the mapmaker made a spelling error."

"That's crazy, why not just fix it?"

"Some things just happen that way." He pointed to a tall peak at the end of the ridge. "I may be wrong, but I believe that's Mount Woodworth, which was first climbed by Bolton Brown."

"The art professor from Stanford who made your drawing?"

"Precisely. We're past the region where Solomons' explorations ended and are beginning to enter *Bolton Brown territory*."

As he said it, we were both startled by the sound of a large bird flapping overhead, which had somehow been frightened out of its hiding place in the brush. Near to where the bird had emerged, a man in high boots and an explorer's cap appeared from among the tall grasses and came striding over. In his hand was what looked like an old-fashioned rooftop TV-aerial, shaped in a series of progressively smaller arrow heads. What did he hope to receive with that old thing?

We met him by the bend in the river. A neatly trimmed salt-and-pepper beard covered his deeply creased skin.

"Well hello there," he said, "hiking the JMT?" I couldn't quite place his accent, part British maybe, but with a blend of Californian. Syd introduced us.

"I'm Jim," the man said cordially.

"What are you doing out here with that antenna?" I asked. "Searching for aliens?"

"No," he grinned, "tracking birds. I'm out doing a field project on the habitat of Sierra Sooty Grouse. The antenna helps me locate the ones we've tagged."

"Are there other people out here doing research work too?"

"Oh sure, but most of them are off in remote locations—the Sierra's a great place for observing nature apart from most influences of man."

"How long are you out here for?"

"Another week, then I move on to my next location."

"You picked a great spot. This meadow's gorgeous."

"And it's appropriately called *Grouse Meadow*," noted Syd.

"That it is," said Jim. "You guys should see it in winter!"

"Winter?" I started. "Do you have a cabin out here?"

"Nope, just a tent and a good old sleeping bag."

"How do you keep from freezing your balls off?"

"Sometimes you don't, but we have to track the birds in each season," he grinned toothily. "Barely see anyone out here in winter, but summer's a different story."

"How do you get way out here in winter? Isn't everything snowed in?"

"Generally, I snowshoe in. But I'm getting a bit old for snow camping now, so these days my younger assistants do most of the winter counts. Recently I've been using a Forest Service cabin up near Mount Pinos as a winter base—it's good to have heat and a shower," he said smiling.

Summer camping was fine, but winter camping? That was just nuts.

"Did you notice the sundew plants?" he asked.

"Sundew?"

"You're standing right next to some." He was looking at my feet.

Following his gaze, I spied a small leafy plant with long fronds like a fern. The tips had small hairs on them with pink dew clinging to the ends.

"That's a Sierra Sundew, it's a rare carnivorous plant."

It was good we hadn't stepped on it.

"There aren't many places you find them," he continued. "Let me see if I can find one that's eating something." He bent down. "Here, this one's caught a large fly."

Sure enough, the sticky projections were slowly curling around a struggling black fly trapped in the pink goo. Grossed out, I turned away.

While we were standing there Esperanza rode by leading her team back up the canyon. The three of us called out and waved, but she didn't see us.

Jim said she brought supplies out for him once a week, and we had a long chat about the excellent quality of their chicken dinners.

Past Grouse Meadow the trail descended steadily, coming to a junction just above the confluence of the Kings River with Palisade Creek. A metal sign pointed left for Mather Pass and ahead for Simpson Meadow.

"Isn't Simpson Meadow one of the places you said Solomons went?" I asked.

"All the major explorers traveled through there, it's the most direct route to Kings Canyon." Syd pulled out his map. "Before the Golden Staircase was finished, hikers either had to go out over Granite Pass to Roads End," he said tracing the route, "and then back up to Woods Creek this way—or take this much more rugged route up over Cartridge Pass to the South Fork of the Kings."

"But there's no trail there—"

"There used to be, but it hasn't been maintained, so they don't show it on the maps anymore. Bolton Brown once struggled up that creek with a very disagreeable mule. I'll tell you about it sometime, but it's getting late and we probably should get going."

The trail began to ascend. It wasn't steep, but the twelve days of food in my pack combined with the stiffness from my hangover all made it exhausting. Syd seemed to be dragging too. Passing a broad campsite between the trail and the creek, we both glanced at each other knowingly, then dropped our packs.

The camp had a nice smell to it. After setting up my tent I asked him about it.

"There's a large Sierra Juniper there," he pointed. "They're beautiful trees and often highly fragrant."

To me it looked like an aged pine with a thick orangey-brown twisted trunk, or one of those fake trees they made cell phone towers look like. Walking over I sniffed its rough bark.

"Isn't this the same kinda wood Ma puts in all her sweater drawers?"

"I believe that comes from cedar."

The creek was down a steep incline, and I struggled down and back to fetch water. Then sitting on a log by Syd, I pulled off my boots to stretch out my feet and relax.

"You know," I said, "I've been thinking a lot about things, and well, everything on this trip so far has been a lot like a martial arts film."

His face lifted into the hint of an amused smile.

"But you know," I went on a bit hesitantly, "usually by this point, the Master begins teaching his student something of his art." I looked at him expectantly. His eyes sparkled in the sun, but I couldn't tell if he was following me or not. "What I mean is—aren't you going to teach me something about woodland survival, like how to make a fire from two sticks, or trap wild animals, or something?"

He became contemplative, then said, "I think you'd better ask Permi to show you those things—he's the *survivalist*. You know, your father once took a class in *primitive skills*. I remember huddling miserably in the rain, while he tried for over an hour to start a fire with a bow drill. Finally, he gave up and we just used some matches. The wilderness can be pretty humbling. It takes a lot of skills that most of us have lost to survive out here. I admire Permi for trying to learn them. But even he's a student, and he's been at it for many years. Primitive man would have grown up in the wild, learning skills from older tribe members—much like we spend our childhood learning reading and mathematics in school."

He seemed to notice my disappointment.

"But there are a few things I *can* teach you," he offered.

I looked up, ready to begin.

"Try keeping still and just listening with me to the sounds of nature for a while. See what you observe."

This was exactly like when Master Po in *Kung Fu* had asked young Caine to stop and listen to everything around him. Caine was shocked when the blind Master could distinguish the sound of a grasshopper moving at his feet. In fact, that's how Caine came to be called Grasshopper. Eager to be like Caine, I closed my eyes and listened.

I heard the creek—a distant tumbling sound of water churning over rock. The music of birdsong reached my ear. Listening deeper, I became aware of Syd's breathing next to me, the sound of rustling needles when the breeze blew, my own heartbeat, the scent of pine, the smell of earth, and the fading warmth of the afternoon sun.

Syd asked, "Do you hear that? Someone's coming up the trail. They should be here soon."

I listened intently but heard only the creek and the birds. Was this a trick? Did he have his eyes open? Was he hearing something I'd missed?

I opened my eyes, blinking. His eyes were still shut. I glanced up and down the trail. No one was coming.

"What are you talking about?" I asked.

He opened his eyes. "You'll see." An amused smile played across his face.

I waited impatiently. Several minutes later a pair of backpackers passed our camp, waving as they hiked by. Was it just a coincidence?

"Listen again," he said.

Obediently, I shut my eyes. What'd he heard? What was the secret?

Sometime later he announced, "Someone else is coming, this time from the other direction."

Sitting quietly, eyes shut tight, I listened carefully for what he was hearing. But the only sounds were the birds and the creek and the pines. As much as I strained, I could hear no voices or footsteps—*what was I missing?*

I opened my eyes again, staring both ways. There was no raised dust, no sign of anyone. I waited. Several minutes later a trio of hikers came tramping down the trail, just as he'd said.

This was too weird. Had the trail given him super wilderness powers? He wasn't really Master Po, was he?

"How'd you do that??"

"Listen and I'll tell you."

We sat silently—eyes shut. After about ten minutes he said, "Someone else is coming now, can you hear that?"

"No." All I heard were the same natural sounds as before.

"Don't you hear the bird?"

I could almost feel the amusement in his voice. "The bird?" There was a bird in a tree somewhere chirping, *Peep! Peep! Peep!*

"Yeah, so?"

"That bird is *alarming*. It flew up to that branch and is shouting out in bird language, *Look out! Danger! Somebody's coming!* Whenever you hear a bird alarming it means someone or something is coming—usually in a rush. The squirrels do it too. It's a kind of wilderness alarm system."

The bird did sound agitated—why hadn't I noticed it before?

"If you walk quietly, the birds don't alarm. But that's not how most people walk. Most people walk with a purpose, and when they do it alarms the birds."

I opened my eyes again. Sure enough, several minutes later a group of four women came jogging down the trail, their trekking poles flashing like they had a train to catch.

I smiled. It was a great natural warning system—how'd I never noticed it before? Maybe with time I could even hear a grasshopper? From now on, I would walk more slowly and try to observe more.

We took out our dinners. *Shit*—Backwoods Buffet again. Boiling water, I cautiously poured it into my orange package and waited. Maybe their Chicken Parmesan would taste better than the others? I hesitatingly inserted my spork. Out came a familiar looking orange-yellow lump of goo. I tasted it. It was exactly the same as their Backwoods lasagna— *there was no difference!* The exact same synthetic shit with a different label. Bob stared at me from the side of the package, mocking me with his stupid grin. *Shit—why hadn't I listened to that salesgirl?*

"We need to sleep early tonight in order to beat the heat up the Golden Staircase tomorrow," he said.

"Fine by me." I mumbled choking down the last of my meal. An early sleep was just what I needed.

That night I dreamt of Kydoime. Lying back, she began kissing me, working her way down from my neck to my chest. Slowly I became aware of her warm wet saliva clinging to my stomach. Gasping in horror, I opened my eyes to see her naked body transforming into a giant sundew plant, her sticky tendrils wrapping around me, the goo the same orangey-yellow as my Backwoods Buffet! Struggling to break free, I woke up twisted and sweaty inside my Bonfire bag.

The air was unusually warm and heavy. The steady trill of insects broken only by the sound of Syd's snoring. Quietly unzipping my tent, I tiptoed across the bare ground to the ledge above the creek, sitting on one of the cold rocks. Silvery moonlight reflected off the water. Pop had once brought me out to a place like this. Sitting together by the stream he'd said, *One day, years from now, you'll remember this place*—how had he known?

I watched the water churning over the rocks.

What exactly had Syd meant yesterday when he said *I needed to come here more than he had?* Was he trying to tell me I needed this trip to help me let Pop go?

Part of it was never actually seeing a body—some tiny part of me clung to the hope that he might still be out there, might someday be coming back. But in my heart I knew it wasn't true. One of Pop's favorite quotes jumped to mind, *Time is but the stream I go a-fishing in . . . Its thin current slides away, but eternity remains.*

Was that it? Was Syd saying, *Even though Pop was gone, his spirit remained?* It felt that way sometimes—especially near water—like he was watching over me.

Syd was just like Pop with his deep love of wilderness, stories, and history—but they also shared something deeper and more spiritual. It was hard to place my finger on it, but the two were kindred spirits. After spending so much time with Syd, I could feel what'd bound the two of them together.

I wanted to love Syd too, like Pop had—wanted to share my grief and bare my soul— but he was dying, and wouldn't I just have to go through all this pain again when he died? Wasn't emptiness the only thing that really remained—*like the last ten years of my life?*

DAY EIGHTEEN

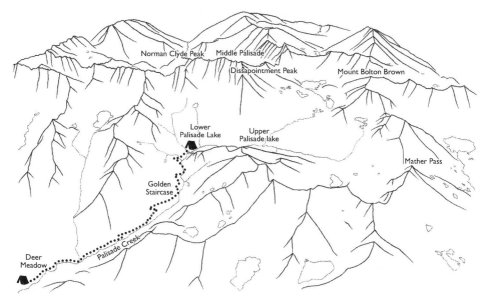

Palisade Creek (8,690′) to Lower Palisade Lake (10,610′) via Golden Staircase

4¼ miles—2,020 feet elevation gain; 100 feet elevation loss

T HE LANDSCAPE here was almost bipolar. The cliffs on our left were a rocky desert of loose talus and sagebrush, while on our right a lush pine forest lined the course of the raging creek. The trail wound in and out of the trees, teasing us with cool shade, then pounding us with dry heat.

Although we'd woken at sunrise, all those little morning chores added up, and it wasn't until nine that we'd actually got going. I tugged on my straps to balance the load better. The air was heating up and we'd need to carry a shitload of water up the Staircase. Nothing about today's climb appealed to me. Judging from how pensive Syd was, I don't think he was looking forward to it either.

The words to Led Zeppelin's "Stairway to Heaven," which Dylan had been playing back at MTR, began rolling around in my head. "Why do they call it the Golden Staircase?" I asked.

"I believe it's because around sunset the rocks take on a golden hue. It certainly is a staircase—the whole thing had to be cut and blasted out of the rockface by Palisade Falls. What worries me is it's an almost two-thousand-foot climb with no water. Judging from the sun today, we probably should have started out much earlier. As it stands, we'll be climbing it right in the midday heat."

That wasn't very reassuring. Passing Deer Meadow, we continued until we came to what the map showed was our last chance for water. Dropping our packs, we began pumping.

"Drink as much as you can and take at least three liters up the Staircase."

Chugging a full bottle of water, I filled up my CamelBak to the two-and-a-half-liter mark—just shy of the full three liters. At over two pounds a liter, I was adding more than five pounds of extra weight. Even with the heat, it should be more than enough to make it to the top.

Syd, being overly cautious, filled his bladder to the top and stuck an extra bottle of water in his pack for good measure. Then he had us both apply extra sunscreen.

"Woah," I groaned pulling on my pack. "This thing must be over sixty pounds!"

The hip belt dug into my sides, and I had to readjust it twice before it was sitting comfortably. Whatever the weight, it was definitely more than I'd carried all trail. Syd didn't look any happier under his burden. Hunched over and staggering forward, we advanced toward the looming yellow cliffs.

The sun was climbing steadily and as we cleared the last bits of forest, the heat struck us full on and the temperature jumped to at least a hundred. Syd pulled out his hiking hat, while all I could do was tie my bandana around my forehead like a jogger. We were only at the base, but already sweat was dripping down my neck. This couldn't be good.

The monster before us rose almost straight up into the sun. Squinting, I could make out two broad ledges below the ridgetop, each roughly a third of the way up. The rocks radiated yellow in the baking heat. It looked more like a golden oven. Taking a deep breath, I started up the first switchback. A few solitary trees dotted the trail, but none offered any real shade. The air felt like a dry sauna. It wasn't long before Syd fell a couple of turns behind. I worried about him having another episode of vertigo in the heat but my pack was too heavy and it was too hot to stop without any shade, so I just pressed on. There had to be a tree or something up ahead I could wait under. Besides, looking down I could see most of the trail below, so I'd know if something happened and could always go back.

The first section passed teasingly close to Palisade Falls. It was an impressive sight, and I paused briefly to admire it but there was no place to stop and drink unless somehow you sprouted wings.

The sun pounded down. Drawing tiny, measured sips from my CamelBak, I let the water swish around in my mouth before swallowing. There was no way I was repeating my experience at the bridge after Reds Meadow.

The trail below wound back and forth, the trees below shrinking to resemble those from a model trainset. Syd was about two hundred feet below me but making steady progress. There wasn't a sliver of shade anywhere. Nothing to cool the air, I took slow breaths between my teeth, but it was little help and I slogged on.

Sweat trickled down my face, forcing me to stop, wring out my bandana, and wipe off my sunglasses. Salt burned my eyes. Several people passed me on their way down, all eager to be getting off the hot rocks and only exchanging a perfunctory greeting in passing—they'd obviously started out much earlier than we had.

Twenty or thirty minutes later, I heard a metallic *clank, clank, clank*, echoing down the trail. What the hell was that? It grew louder as I climbed. Rounding a switchback, I came across a team of three heavily muscled men laboring shirtless under the hot sun in orange hardhats. A beefy guy dripping with sweat was breaking up rocks with an enormous sledgehammer. Below him, a thick-mustached Latino guy and a well-tanned younger man with glistening olive skin, were both struggling with crowbars to level one of the massive stepping-stones along the trail, shimming it with the broken rock fragments. Except for the lack of orange jumpsuits, they looked exactly like a chain gang from the movies.

"Hey," I hailed the younger guy.

"Ow ya goin'—pretty hot day to be climbin' the trail," he responded in an accent that sounded vaguely Australian—kinda like Jack's, but deeper.

"Worse to be working on it in this heat, isn't it?"

"You said it mate," he grinned, wiping his forehead.

"How'd you guys get here?"

"We hiked in from Deer Meadow. Our basecamp's down there."

"What are you doing way up here?"

"Working on the trail—" which I guess was kinda obvious "—we're trail crew."

"What's trail crew?"

"We work for the Park Service—clearing brush, repairing trail, whatever they need."

"And you camp out here?"

"Yeah, we hike in each morning."

The other guys took a break from their work as we talked.

"How do you get your food and supplies?"

"It comes in by horse, sometimes by choppa."

"And you're paid?"

"Not very good," the Latino guy chimed in, "but it's enough. Most workers are volunteers. But if you like it enough and want to stay out here for the summer, there's paying jobs like ours."

"Looks pretty tough," I said.

"Beats loafin' around the city drinkin' beer," replied the younger guy. "Ya get paid to live outdoors, can't waste the money ya earn, and get in better shape than at any fitness center—ya can't beat it!"

"Thanks for doing this," I offered. What else could I say to three guys laboring in hundred-degree heat to make a few steps along the trail a bit more level for people like me?

"Keep outta the heat!" said the younger one. I smiled and continued on. What would Syd and these guys talk about? Probably the history of trail crew, I laughed to myself.

After two more baking turns up the long switchbacks, I saw a ranger coming down the steps. She was moving with the gait of a mountain goat.

"It's a scorcher," she said when we met, her sharp hazel eyes taking me in the way a sergeant sizes up a new recruit.

"Yeah," I huffed, wiping another load of sweat from below my bandana.

"It's still a long way up, are you carrying enough water?"

"I've got a couple of liters in my CamelBak."

"That's good. Do you have your wilderness permit handy?"

"Eh, no," I stammered, "my buddy Syd down there has it. He's about ten, maybe fifteen minutes behind me."

"In that case, may I have your name?"

"It's Gil," I said. She scribbled it down on a small notepad. "May I ask you something?" I inquired.

"Sure," she smiled.

"About four days ago, we were camped next to a troop of Boy Scouts. One of the kids had really bad altitude sickness or something, so my buddy Syd and I let the ranger down in McClure Meadow know. Anyway, we saw a helicopter, and I was wondering if the boy was OK?"

"He's fine. They choppered him down to the hospital in Bishop. He was discharged yesterday."

"What was wrong with him?"

"Altitude sickness. A mild cerebral edema or swelling of the brain. It happens sometimes. It was good you helped them out."

"Is that common?" I asked, thinking about how Syd had been at some of the passes.

"We get a fair number of calls involving altitude sickness, especially up on Whitney where city folk think they can just stride up to fourteen thousand feet without any conditioning. But edemas are rare—the majority of cases are simply dehydration. When we have to send a chopper, it usually involves broken bones. You'd be amazed how many people slip off logs crossing streams."

"Wow, that's exactly what my buddy said. If you do need to evacuate someone, who pays for the helicopter?"

"Inside the park, we do. Outside—don't ask. Just hope that if you ever need one, you have some really good insurance paid up, the deed to a small gold mine, or you're too poor for the whole industrial complex to bother chasing you. And don't get me started on the issue of health insurance for backcountry rangers—as a *seasonal employee* we have to foot the bill for our own insurance." She seemed to be getting worked up but caught herself. "Anyway," she said more evenly, "if you don't have any other questions, I need to be getting down to the trail crew below."

She strode down the mountain, while I slowly dragged my feet up the sunbaked rocks. *Shit*—she was right about health insurance. Why did every other country but America have some form of nationalized insurance? What would I do if I needed to be flown out like that kid? I didn't wanna think about it. That's what'd originally drawn me to journalism—reporting on social justice—and what I'd thought I'd be doing when I went into law. Who knew I'd spend my days working on business contracts? Mulling over my past, I ascended slowly. The trail ahead was empty. I guess no one else was crazy enough to be out here in this heat.

Eventually I reached the first ledge. The final ridge still hovered a thousand or more feet above me, but I was more than a third of the way up now. The air tasted like a dry sauna. Looking down, Syd was nowhere to be seen. Parts of the trail were obscured by rock. He must be down there somewhere. I pulled out a granola bar and standing with my pack on in the full sun, choked down half of it with two small gulps of water. Even my bladder was starting to heat up and now tasted warm and flavorless.

Unable to stand the baking sun, I started back up the steps hoping Syd would be OK in this heat. At least there was a ranger down there. My thighs strained under the load of my pack—the Golden Staircase was becoming the Scorching Stairmaster.

The song "Stairway to Heaven" began rolling through my head again. I couldn't remember all of the lyrics, so I just kept repeating the parts I remembered—climbing my Golden Staircase toward Heaven. Time and steps became a blur, but eventually I made it to the second ledge.

Stopping made me feel hotter, so I moved on, taking swallow after swallow from my bladder. And then my blue plastic tube drew up the sound of sucking air. *Fuuuck.*

The ridge was still far above me, the trees tiny dots below. I had to be two-thirds of the way up. Better to go on than go back. Should I wait for Syd? He had that extra bottle of water. But he was far behind and there wasn't a drop of shade anywhere. Besides, what if he was also running out of water? I pressed on, ascending step after step in the pounding heat.

My mouth began to dry out. *Fuck*—why hadn't listened to him? I should have taken three liters of water and an extra bottle like he had. The lyrics from "Stairway to Heaven" morphed and merged in the heat of my climb, until I began repeating the phrase *And I'm climbing a staircase to Heaven* over and over in my brain like a mantra.

Breathing through my nose, I tried to retain as much moisture as I could, but it was no use. My saliva dried up. My tongue started to swell. Lines of heat seemed to emanate from the rocks. I became dizzy.

The ridge was a few hundred feet above me, rippling in the hot air like a mirage. Pressing on, sweat crusting on my burning neck, boots dragging over the ground, I looked up to see a couple in matching brown shorts descending rapidly toward me. My eyes focused on the tall brimming water bottles strapped to the sides of their packs. When they reached me, I skipped all the usual introductions. "Do you have any spare water?" I gasped like a desert toad.

"Sure," the woman sung in an angelic voice, pulling off a bottle with a concerned look and handing it to me. "You can drink from this."

Unable to speak more, I nodded my thanks and gulped down nearly a quarter of the bottle, coughed several times, then took another swallow—the cool refreshing water lubricating my system like the Tin Man's oil can in the *Wizard of Oz.*

"Thanks," I uttered, wiping my brow. "That's a lifesaver!"

"It's really hot out," she sympathized.

Her partner, who was about thirty with dark hair, nodded in sweltering agreement. "Don't worry, it's not that far to the top. There's a small stream up there you can fill up at."

"That's great," I sputtered, my throat still parched. "That's the best news I've had all day."

"Do you want a bit more water?" offered the woman. "You can pour it into a bottle if you need to. We have more, and we're headed down."

I took another swig. "Thanks, this should be enough. My buddy's coming up behind me. He's an old guy, thin, with a raggedy green Kelty pack. Please give him what's left if he needs it," I said, passing her back the half-empty bottle.

"Of course," she smiled.

"Thanks again, I really appreciate it."

"Have a good hike," waved the man, and they continued down the trail.

Refreshed, and hopeful about the presence of a stream above, I started back up the hot rocks. The sun baked down on me, and my mouth began to dry out again. Why hadn't I taken that woman up on her offer and dumped some of the water into my bladder? But then there was Syd to think about. How was he holding up? Wouldn't he be happy when the woman offered him half a bottle?

I could feel myself losing energy. My stomach began to cramp. All I'd eaten up this awful rock was half a bar. The rest was still in my pocket, but I had nothing to wash it down with. Staving off my stomach with the promise of food at the stream above, I began to recite my mantra—*And I'm climbing a staircase to Heaven*—the words looping over and over again in my mind.

My tongue began to dry out. Like Sisyphus pushing up the rock, the ridge hung forever above me. But then, like in every film I'd ever seen about people lost in the desert, I rounded an outcropping and heard the faint tinkling of salvation.

I pushed myself on—up, up, up—the magnetic music of the water drawing me forward. Finally, I crested the ridge. As always, it was a false summit. But it didn't matter. I could clearly hear the flowing water now. Rounding a large boulder, I saw the creek. It was fifty or sixty feet below, down a steep questionable-looking incline. I decided to risk it. Dropping my pack and laying it beside the boulder, I crawled into the tiny bit of shade the rock afforded. I rested in the cooler air, regaining my breath. Then fiddling with the flaps of my pack, I pulled out my blue CamelBak bladder. A tiny pocket of water remained at the bottom. Opening it, I thirstily sucked up the remaining drops.

I was about to carry it down the incline when it hit me—*Syd has the pump*. Would it be safe to drink unfiltered water? All the commercials I'd seen promoting *pure mountain water* suggested it was fine. But then Syd and Steve had warned me about *Giardia* on the first day; that amoebalike parasite that causes terrible diarrhea and dehydration. That was the last thing I needed up here, away from any doctor or medical assistance and without insurance. *Shit*. I scrunched up in the shade of the boulder waiting for Syd, my mouth as dry as sanded wood.

No one came. A fat bucktoothed marmot climbed around on the rocks above, watching me as if to ask, "*Does that pack contain any food?*" I eyed him curious to see if he would approach, but he kept his distance.

At least thirty minutes passed. Where was Syd? *Shit.* He wasn't that far behind me. I'd sent that couple down with water for him, and the ranger was there too. If he didn't show soon, I'd have to get water from the stream and go looking for him. Why was it every time we got separated something seemed to happen? I lay curled up under the boulder waiting.

More time passed. Unable to stand it, I crawled out from under the rock, almost dizzy in the sweltering heat. Staggering back to where I could see down the last few switchbacks, I squinted, shading my eyes and searching for Syd. Nothing. Remembering my pack and the marmot, I scrambled back to the rock. The marmot hadn't moved. I crawled back into the shade of the boulder. *Where was he?*

More time passed. Then the marmot looked up the trail, froze, and scrambled away. There was a *click, click, click* noise. Was it trekking poles? I strained my ears. The sound grew louder. A short tense eternity later, I spotted Syd ambling up the trail. My heart leaped with joy. Calling to him hoarsely, he lumbered over, dropped his pack, and joined me.

"That was a hell of a climb," he said.

"Are you alright? Did that couple give you water?"

"They offered. They told me they'd met you—but I really didn't need any. I still have half a bottle left."

He was OK and still had half a bottle left? I was almost pissed at him for *not* running out of water! My head swam. My thirst was killing me. "Do you have your filter?" I sputtered.

"Sure," he said pulling it out and passing me his bottle with a concerned look. "Why don't you finish this off first?"

The water was warm from all the sun. I swallowed anyway, the thirst-quenching liquid almost burning as it went down. Taking his bottle, the pump, and my bladder, I headed down the incline. It wasn't easygoing but using one hand and sliding down on my butt, I reached the stream, plunging my head into the cold water in celebration. Pumping his bottle full, I greedily gulped it down, reveling in its cool sweet contents. Pumping it full again and filling my bladder, I drank more of the cool water until my thirst was thoroughly slaked.

Climbing back up with the awkward bladder and bottle looked daunting at first but proved easier than getting down. Soon I was back in the boulder's shade happily eating, drinking, and chatting with Syd—as if this whole afternoon had been just a lazy stroll in the park.

He pulled his map out and studied it. "It looks like only three-quarters of a mile to the lake. We should cross a stream or two and then be there. From here, the trail should be a lot more gentle too."

"That's good. Did that ranger check your permit?"

"Yes, she did."

"I asked her about the Boy Scout. She said the kid's alright."

"I asked her the same question. Sorry I took so long, I met up with her where that trail crew was working. The five of us started talking about the history of trail workers in the Sierra. I guess I just lost track of time."

Shit—I should have known. "It's fine," I said. "I'm just glad you made it."

We packed up and crawled out from under our rock. The sun wasn't as intense as it'd been earlier.

Syd was right—from here the trail was a lot less steep. We soon came to the banks of the same stream I'd climbed down to earlier. There were plenty of shady spots. *Shit. If I'd gone a bit farther, I could have just waited here and wouldn't have had to climb that wall. I could even have washed off!*

Summiting a low rise, we came to a point overlooking a long ridge-lined valley with a steel-gray lake stretched across it, its surface rippling in the light breeze. A rocky wall reached down to the right bank. Beyond the lake rose four sharp granite peaks whose profiles looked like pyramids, the rightmost one dotted with patches of snow at its base.

"That's Lower Palisade Lake. We'll camp there today," Syd said. He'd get no opposition from me. We hadn't covered more than four-and-a-half miles but it was late afternoon and we were both spent.

There were a fair number of tents scattered about the lake, most close to the outflow. We found a nice spot on a small ridge and made camp.

After resting a bit, we headed down to the water. At the shore, tall clumps of sedge gave way to a sheltered sandy beach. No one was around, so Syd and I stripped down. The air was considerably cooler than it had been when I was climbing the Staircase. Syd jumped in, dog-paddled a short way out, and returned shivering but looking clean and pleased with himself. Just watching him in the water made my heart race. It woulda been great to join him, but there was just no way. Rinsing off by the shore, I scrubbed off as much salty sunscreen as I could, the chill air against my skin surprisingly refreshing.

Back on the rocks at our camp, we watched the fading light dance over the distant summits, breathing in the clean scent of water wafting on the light breeze. The sunsets up here were incredible, with their pastel tones and lingering alpenglow. Sure, there were fantastic sunsets over the beaches in LA—but I was always too busy working or stuck in traffic to see them. Up here watching the progression of colors over the peaks was our evening entertainment. How had we grown so apart from this simple pleasure in our modern lives? How much more would people cherish this God-given orb if every day we paused to watch displays like these? The swelling moon rose up over the lake from between the peaks, completing the picture. Muir had called the Sierra "The Range of Light," and I could see why. We'd earned this view climbing the Staircase, and now it seemed to me it really was a staircase to Heaven.

As we ate, Syd pointed out some of the surrounding peaks. "That one over there," he indicated a rough peak at the end of a ragged ridge left of the lake, "is Middle Palisade. It's one of the ten peaks over fourteen thousand feet in the lower Sierra and was first climbed by Francis Farquhar."

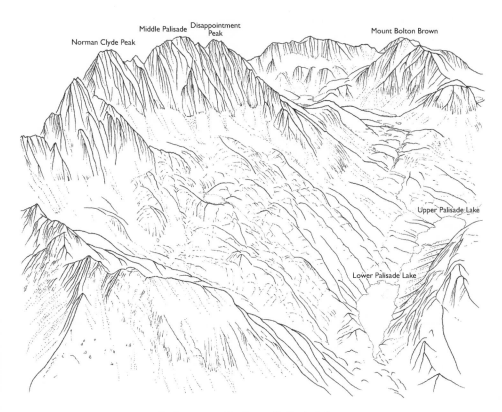

Peaks surrounding Lower Palisade Lake

"The one who named Mount Shakspere?"

He nodded. "That one to its right is called Disappointment Peak. It was named by a climber who thought he'd gone up Middle Palisade, but discovered he was on a different summit with no way over to the taller one."

"That sucks." I pointed to a tall rocky-looking summit to the left of Middle Palisade, "Is that also a fourteen thousand footer?"

"That's Norman Clyde Peak, which is just under fourteen. It was named for one of the most famous mountaineers in the history of the Sierra. Clyde was something of a recluse, who spent the greater part of his life up here making over a hundred and thirty first ascents, most of them solo. He was the one who located Peter Starr's missing body up in the Minarets, long after everyone else had given up."

"Wait, did you say *Clyde?* When I complained about lugging my backpack to school,

Pop used to tell me about this old-time mountaineer named Clyde who carried this gigantic ninety-pound pack stuffed full of books up and down the Sierra, was that him?"

Syd laughed. "That sounds like something your father would say. Although most of the stuff in his famously overweight pack was probably climbing equipment, he was known for taking works of literature with him, often in the original Greek or Latin."

It was funny hearing this now. As a kid, I'd always doubted that story.

"Do you see that large triangular peak just beyond the lake on the left?" he asked.

There was a gap where the moon was rising, a lone solitary peak to its right and a cluster of three pyramidlike peaks to its left. The tallest of these was bathed in a bright golden light.

"That's Mount Bolton Brown."

"Did he climb that?"

"No, but it was named in his honor. Brown never reached this point, but he drew many sketches of it, describing the terrain in the *Sierra Club Bulletin*."

"If he never came here, how did he sketch it?"

"After coming to Stanford, Brown visited Yosemite and Lake Tahoe, but he was bothered by all the tourists and roadside attractions. He longed for something wilder—a truly undiscovered country to explore."

This sounded like the beginning of one of Syd's long stories. Settling back, I chewed my Backwoods meal, while marveling at the surrounding scenery.

"In 1895, the same year that Solomons discovered Evolution Valley, young Professor Brown made his first trek into Kings Canyon—which in those days was a three-day hike from the nearest road in Fresno. He aimed to climb Mount Clarence King, but the summit proved too steep, and he returned to Fresno. Inspired by the vast unexplored territory of the Southern Sierra, he returned a few weeks later equipped for a longer expedition. This time he led a very disagreeable black mule named Jack. Practically dragging poor Jack over the fords and hills, he headed north over Granite Pass to Simpson Meadow."

"The spot we passed the turnoff for yesterday?"

"Precisely. In fact, both Brown and Solomons were there on almost the same date. Solomons was exiting The Enchanted Gorge, while Brown was tugging Jack up the trail."

"Did they meet?"

"I don't think so, it's a pretty big area. If they had, it would probably have been recorded somewhere. It's interesting, because that was Solomons' last major exploration into the Sierra, and essentially Brown's first."

"So, Solomons was handing off the torch to Brown?"

"Figuratively speaking, although neither man knew it at the time. I think I told you, but Brown not only was an artist but also an avid climber. From Simpson Meadow, he scrambled up the highest peak in the vicinity, Mount Woodworth, becoming the first to climb it. From the top, Brown could see the entire Palisade Range, which is where we are now. He remained until late afternoon, making numerous sketches of the peaks and canyons—including the one that was eventually to bear his name."

The last glow of sunlight was now touching the crests.

"Later he described this region as, *the wildest and roughest part of the whole Sierra*, adding that, *From all accounts, it has never been explored. Even the sheepmen do not go there, because there is no grass.*"

"He got that wrong."

"What do you mean?"

"It wasn't that there was no grass—there's plenty of grass here," I said pointing at the tufts all around us. "The reason the sheepmen didn't come here was 'cause they didn't wanna climb the Golden Staircase, or however you got up here before they blasted that thing into the rock."

"You have a point," he chuckled. "Anyway, after seeing all these peaks, Brown was smitten. They called to him. So he headed up the Middle Fork of the Kings, dragging poor Jack."

"Up to that junction we were at?"

"No. In those days there was no trail and Brown found the going quite rough. So he turned east at Cartridge Creek—along the route of the old JMT that I showed you yesterday—hoping to find an easier passage there. But he had no such luck. He spent three aggravating days just trying to get his mule up that canyon, but Jack kept slipping and somersaulting down the rocky slopes. After each fall, Brown had to unpack him, knock down boulders to smooth the way, then drag the reluctant mule back up the slope and repack him."

"That's nuts."

"Because of the slow progress, his provisions began to run low. He was debating whether to turn back when he ran into a shepherd who told him of a pass next to Mount Ruskin through which he could reach the South Fork of the Kings. Elated at not having to backtrack, Brown dragged poor Jack up the slope. Leaving him at the pass, he made a harrowing ascent of Mount Ruskin, making more sketches from the summit. He recorded some twenty-six sparkling lakes and named Split Mountain. Then he descended with Jack to the South Fork of the Kings."

"That sounds like some pretty rough terrain."

"It was. People say the trail there has all but been reclaimed by the wilderness."

"Did you and Pop ever take any cross-country trips?"

"We did take a few off-trail expeditions, yes. Mostly scrambling up and down talus slopes to summit some interesting peak. Although there was one season we tried to reach Tehipite Valley by heading up the Middle Fork of the Kings River from Yucca Point, in Kings Canyon. That was a huge mistake. As we got up the canyon, the river became too treacherous to wade across and the banks steep and thick with thorny gooseberry. At one point your father nearly stepped off a fallen trunk onto a rattler. It's the only trip we ever turned back on. By the time we'd scrambled out of that gorge, we'd both torn up our legs and our hiking pants, and each of us had a case of poison oak that lasted a week."

I chuckled. "Pop never told me about that one."

"Your father always wanted you to join him hiking. I don't think his telling you about that trip would have encouraged you."

"That's true. I'm glad I finally got out here, but I don't think I'd have made it without a trail to follow."

"The mountains are a very different experience cross-country, although it's a lot easier above the treeline."

"I guess its best some regions don't have trails—that way people who wanna can still experience them in the way the early explorers did."

We ate in silence for a while, admiring the pinkish-purple glow basking the peaks. Today's climb was tough enough—I couldn't imagine bushwhacking up canyons and talus slopes without a map or trail.

"So where did Bolton Brown go after he reached the river?"

Syd finished the last of his dinner, took a long sip of tea, then resumed, "At the South Fork, Brown saw a sharp pointed peak that he named Arrow Peak. The peak called to him, but he was low on food, his shoes were all torn up, and he needed to get back to Fresno. Brown spent a restless night debating what to do. By morning the lure of the peak won out, and he found himself racing toward it—prudence to the wind."

"He sounds a lot like Muir."

"Very much so. The mountains called strongly to both of them. On top of Arrow Peak, he did more sketching, making the first rough maps of the territory. Returning triumphantly, he packed Jack and headed down the South Fork. But poor Jack had suffered enough of Brown, and Brown had suffered enough of Jack. After four more arduous days of struggling and somersaults, Brown finally gave up. Shouldering as much gear as he could carry, he abandoned Jack, making a forced march back to his camp in Paradise Valley. From there he made his way back to Fresno, recording enthusiastically, *I was shockingly ragged and sunburned and dusty, but I had had a glorious vacation.*"

"So did Brown ever make it to the Palisades?"

"No, after that he headed farther south."

"If mules were as difficult as Jack, why not just go on foot—like we're doing?"

"Because there were no places to resupply. They were making their way across unexplored territory and needed to take enough food and equipment for up to a month or two. Just think about how heavy our packs are with only twelve days of food. There was no lightweight equipment back then. Plastic had yet to be invented. Everything was canvas and bedrolls. They didn't even have Backwoods Buffet," he grinned. "It just wasn't possible to mount an extended exploration without stock."

"So they'd make a basecamp somewhere, like you said LeConte did with his friends, and then explore outward on foot?"

"That was generally the itinerary. Solomons' trip with Bonner was the exception. But that trip lasted for only sixteen days, and the two exited the mountains hungry and exhausted after starting out with over sixty pounds each."

He sipped his tea, "After reading Brown's description of the Palisades, J.N. LeConte headed up Cartridge Creek, naming Marion Lake for his wife who accompanied him. Using the lake as their basecamp, the couple explored the Palisades region, including climbing Split Mountain—making it the only fourteen-thousand-foot peak in the Sierra to have had a first ascent by a woman."[†]

I didn't wanna think about climbing anymore. Lugging my Osprey up the Stairmaster had been enough for me. Stretching out my legs, I watched the last of the alpenglow fade from the summit of Mount Bolton Brown. The moon rose higher, and the first of the evening stars began to emerge. It was a beautiful night—but we still had Mather Pass to get over tomorrow and from the map and the guidebook, it looked worse than our climb today.

I got what people saw in places like this—the wide-open country, alpine lakes, and sunsets were all amazing—but climbing the peaks was another story. Maybe I'd gotten too used to just driving down to Redondo Beach to enjoy the sun or hang out playing volleyball? Maybe there was something to be gained from summiting a mountain—but for me, just getting over these passes with Syd had been enough. Why would anyone want to work any harder? What was it about mountain tops that called to people anyway?

[†]New evidence suggests Split Mountain may have been ascended by Frank Saulque and party in 1887, prior to the LeContes' climb.

DAY NINETEEN

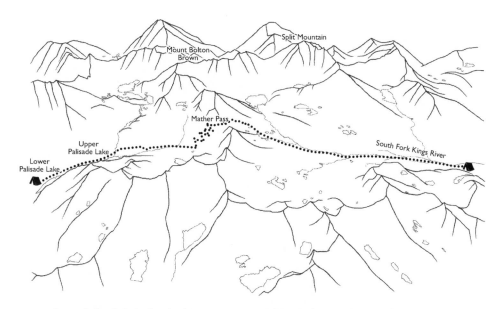

Lower Palisade Lake (10,610′) to Kings River SF (10,040′) via Mather Pass (12,100′)
9 miles—1,500 feet elevation gain; 2,070 feet elevation loss

S YD SEEMED NERVOUS—each time he'd had trouble was at altitude. Maybe he had some sort of brain swelling like that boy? Looking up, I scanned the snow-dotted cliffs high above. Where exactly was the pass? A chilly breeze was blowing. It didn't feel as hot as yesterday, probably 'cause we were a lot higher now.

There were two Palisade Lakes, and we were now above the second. The trail had zigzagged up from the first then back down toward the second, before starting its real ascent. This meant we'd be climbing up everything we'd just lost all over again. If the trail would just keep going up, instead of coming back down all the time, we'd be well over the height of Whitney by now. Who knows, we might even be at the moon! But if they didn't go up and down, they wouldn't be mountains, right?

"Mather Pass was named for Stephen Tyng Mather, another Cal alumnus," Syd said as we climbed, distracting me from the cliffs above.

"Who?"

"The first director of the National Park Service," he gazed at me in surprise, as if everyone knew who the first National Park Service Director was.

He looked at me expectantly. "How did he get the job?" I asked, playing along.

He launched right into his usual lecture, "Legend goes that after visiting the parks in Europe, he wrote a letter to the Secretary of the Interior complaining about how poorly our own national parks were being run."

The old saying was right, *Old professors never die, they just lose their class.* I smiled as he prattled on.

"The Secretary was none other than Franklin Lane, who was also a Cal alumnus. Supposedly Lane replied, *Dear Steve, if you don't like the way the parks are being run, come down to Washington and run them yourself!* So he did. Of course, that's probably a fabrication. Mather was a self-made millionaire through his Borax mining businesses, which is probably what really got him the job."

"What's Borax mining?" I feigned interest—seriously, who does history lectures while climbing a mountain at seven in the morning?

"Did you ever hear of Twenty-Mule Team Borax?"

"The washing powder?"

"That was his."

"So he cleaned up in the washing business?"

He grimaced. "Regardless of how he got the job, he used the position to strengthen the Park Service and promote our national parks. But he also added the concessions—the tourist hotels and shops where you can buy souvenirs, T-shirts, and that sort of thing," he sneered, "which today has become something of an issue with conservationists."

"Didn't I hear that Yosemite was going to have to rename the Ahwahnee Hotel and several other landmarks, 'cause the previous contract holder claimed the rights to the names?"

"Let's hope not. Frankly, there are a lot of people who'd prefer the parks were run a lot less like a business. Although to be fair, in Mather's day the parks were struggling to accommodate everyone who wanted to see them, so he saw the addition of concessions as much needed infrastructure. Mather also put a lot of his own money into the parks and was a good friend of Muir's. All in all, we owe him a lot."

The trail was little more than a line winding its way through a field of jumbled rocks and strewn boulders. The air was growing noticeably thinner, forcing Syd to stop talking and focus on his breathing. I trailed slowly behind. There was no way I was separating from him again.

Placing one foot in front of the other, I took short breaths, sipping slowly from my CamelBak. This time I was carrying the full three liters plus an extra bottle—the additional weight offset by the food I'd eaten. Following him, each small step we took brought us a little closer to the barren peaks above.

Slowly my breathing became more rhythmic and my mind numbed—I began thinking about Samantha. *Why could I never get her out of my head?* She'd been amazing—brains and a bod. Why'd she dumped me just when I needed her the most?

Breathing grew harder. Syd had to pause every few hundred feet to catch his breath, and I welcomed the breaks.

The slope was gray and desolate—barren fields of scree and talus. A spirelike ridge of sawtooth rocks rose menacingly overhead. Nothing grew here. The trail was little more than a two-foot clearing through the midst of an enormous boulder field, wending its way slowly toward some unseen goal above. It was getting colder, and the wind began to snap in gusts as we climbed.

After moving to LA, I'd had a string of short relationships. Women practically buzz around guys with legal degrees. But inevitably each one fell apart. Was it my fate never to have a lasting relationship? Wasn't that my punishment for abandoning Pop?

The trail grew steeper, with high rock steps. My thighs ached, but I followed Syd—stair after stair—lost in the memories of my past. Maybe that was the thing about climbing a mountain—without distractions all you could do was focus and reflect.

I thought about Kydoime, about the morning after. That black cutoff top and those sexy pink panties. Her words, *it's just trail sex*, still burned.

Was this how the women I'd slept with felt in all those short relationships? Had I ever really gone out with someone I cared about—or had all I'd really wanted just been sex?

I could see the top, maybe five hundred feet above now. Switchbacks twisted back and forth through the fallen rock. It was incredible anyone had built a trail here—that the whole damn thing didn't just come sliding down.

Syd climbed on. That night we were drinking he'd told me about his wife. They'd had a deep relation—like Ma and Pop—sharing everything. Why couldn't I find someone like that?

People passed me coming down. I nodded, but didn't really see them, lost in my reflections. Mechanically I circled a protruding rock, rounded a switchback, and there we were. The top of the pass. Finished.

The pass was a kinda dirt strip running across the gap between the peaks. A stiff wind was blowing over the crest. At least eight or ten people were up here. Several were milling about, but most were resting and catching their breath among the rocks. Three older women with matching teal bandanas were busy taking each other's photos. The wind muffling out the sounds of conversation with its constant gusts.

Syd took shelter from the gusts behind a large rock, and I followed. When he had rested a bit he said, "Wasn't certain a few times back there, but we made it. Over twelve thousand feet—the highest we've been!"

"Wasn't Muir Pass also about twelve?"

"Just under."

"How are you feeling?"

"About as good as can be expected up here." He sat for a while, his chest rising and falling. Then he closed his eyes, lying back on his pack against the rocks to rest.

Sitting on the cold hard stone, I realized I hadn't had a single real relationship since Samantha. Not one.

Syd sat up and we ate, then we found another hiker to take photos of us. We stood side by side, arms over each other's shoulders, both with thumbs up. Dirty sweaty brows and dark sunglasses at the top of the first director of the National Park Service's pass. Glad to be up here, but just as glad to be heading down.

The back side of Mather Pass proved almost as challenging as the front. It was a long winding descent down a sandy reddish-brown slope of slippery pebbles. At the bottom was a high scrub desert, dotted with dank pools of standing water that not even a thirsty cow would touch. The afternoon sun beat down on us as we wandered through this vast wasteland.

I recalled that guy Jose at the hot springs joking about how his father had wished he'd slept with more than one woman, and his wife Gizella saying life was really about *a good home, good food, and healthy children.* That's what I needed. That's what my family was before the accident.

"Syd," I asked, "how did you meet your wife?"

"We met in college," he replied, getting a spark in his eye. "She was beautiful as a picture then, and still was on the day she died."

"Ma said she was in an accident."

He looked down. "Actually, she passed away in the hospital afterward."

"How did it happen?"

"It was almost three years ago," he said stiffly. "She was coming home on the highway following some errands, when some kid in a fancy car passed her on the right. He swiped the car in front of her, who braked suddenly, and she slammed into him. Then she was hit again from behind. The funny thing is, she seemed OK when I got to the hospital. We even laughed about it. But then she died the next night from brain hemorrhaging."

"I'm sorry to hear that."

"I got to see her before she died, but I never had the chance to say goodbye."

We hiked on in silence over the barren hills.

It'd been the same with Pop. I'd never stopped to tell him how much I'd loved him, and then he was gone. Maybe Syd's cancer was like my own pain? Had it been triggered by his wife's death, by his regret and loss?

We began to see patches of grass and small sparse pines again. The air grew more fragrant and earthy. Crossing a trickling stream, we stopped to rest.

"I forgot to point out Split Mountain," he lamented, "but there it is." He pointed up at a tall peak at the end of a rough serrated ridge. "I guess from the east it looks more dramatic—the top is supposed to be divided like a sharp V."

Taking our bottles and bladders, I went down to the stream and began pumping water. How did couples like Syd and his wife manage to keep the flame alive? I guess the first step would be finding a partner I truly connected with. That would be hard. It was lonely being single, and it was so easy to meet other lonely people. Damn it! I'd just have to try. Ma used to say, *The first step to solving any problem is the awareness that there is a problem.* I'd just have to stay focused. No more hooking up with women I didn't plan to be with. No more acting like a dog. That would be my new pact. *Shit*—why did Ma's wisdom always ring true after the fact? Maybe there was a self-help book I could buy? Something like *Dating for Dogs*. Nah, even if it did exist, it would probably just be a romantic guide for pet owners.

I carried the water up to where Syd was resting on the bank. "Syd, how were you able to maintain such a long and happy marriage?"

He looked at me strangely, tilting his head slightly, then became thoughtful. "It's not easy, and I'm not sure I can explain exactly how to do it. It takes patience. It takes the right person. And it takes work. You have to listen to each other, and you have to want to put the other person ahead of your own desires, because you love them."

"I thought relationships were about compromise?"

"Not in my experience. If you always have to compromise, you're either with the wrong person, or you're not putting her needs ahead of your own. When you really love someone, you naturally think of them before yourself. There's no need to compromise. I'm not saying it always works like that. Sometimes you have to stop and ask yourself why you want something, what is it your partner desires, and find a balance between conflicting needs that makes you both happy. It takes a lot of inner listening. But the first step is patience."

Why was patience the first step? Patience for what? I got that you had to love the other person. That sorta went without saying. But after you found the right woman, wouldn't everything just sorta work out? Or was that all just some Disney-inspired fantasy? I couldn't really recall Ma and Pop ever fighting, but maybe I'd just been too young?

"Thanks Syd."

He looked at me expectantly, but when I didn't say more he asked, "What made you ask about my marriage?"

"Nothing, I was just thinking about some of my old relationships."

"I see," he smiled, reminding me of Master Po from *Kung Fu* again. I could almost hear him calling me, Grasshopper.

"How much farther to camp?" I asked.

"Perhaps another five miles. I was planning to camp at Bench Lake today, but now I think we should stop when we reach the South Fork of the Kings."

"How much farther is the lake?"

"Another mile, mile and a half past the river, but it's all uphill on the other side."

That was hiking code for, *I don't know*, and probably meant several miles of steep climbing.

"Let's just stop at the river," I agreed.

The trail made a long steady descent, entering a forest of lodgepole pines. We soon began to catch glimpses of a large river tumbling off to our left, its sound carrying through the trees. The fresh scent of pine was everywhere. Chipmunks and squirrels darted about, and birds leapt up heralding, *Peep! Peep! Peep!* as we passed. I'd yet to master the *wilderness kung fu* of silent walking.

The five miles rolled by quickly, and in less than two hours we emerged at a large flat area dotted with tents and campsites at the South Fork of the Kings River. This was the river Solomons and LeConte had tried so hard to find a passage to, and the one Brown had climbed down to with Jack after sketching the Palisades.

The river was quite wide and the water rushed by, but there was a shallow ford where the trail crossed it and it didn't look too bad, nothing like Bear Creek.

On the far bank, a large party had brought in mules. Two packers were busy gathering them up and tethering them to the trees. The mules were making their characteristic braying sounds and you could hear them clearly over the roar of the river. Syd and I went up the bank a bit, so we wouldn't be across from them. Settling on a nice flat spot a few hundred yards above the river, we dropped our packs and made camp. This time Syd went down to the water to pump while I relaxed, looking at the map and rereading Muir's adventure in the windstorm.

After a while it dawned on me that Syd had been gone an awfully long time. Concerned, I followed the narrow path he had taken down to where he should have been pumping water. Instead, he was sitting cross-legged by the river balancing stones.

He'd already made two pillars—or what might better be described as "balancing statues" of medium-sized rocks. They weren't simple piles like the cairns we passed along the trail, rather Syd had balanced his stones *endwise*. His first stack consisted of four rounded stones that looked like vertical gravity-defying oval beads. His second was composed of three upside-down triangles, each balanced on its vertex with the wider end magically suspended above, the stones getting progressively larger up the stack. The topmost one was twisted at a right angle, making it look like one of those giant Easter Island heads.

Syd was starting a third stack, trying to balance a large, inverted triangle on top of a smooth oval base. The water bag lay empty beside him.

"Oh, hi Gil," he said, looking up from his work, inadvertently letting the larger of the two stones fall. "Sorry, got lost in rock art."

"How do those things stay up?" I asked. "Chewing gum?"

I lightly touched the pillar of oval stones to see how he'd fastened them together, jumping back in surprise as the tower crashed down in an avalanche of stones.

"Well," he smiled, "that demonstrates two things—the impermanence of existence and that you have a child's mind."

I grated. "Sorry about your statue, but what exactly do you mean by *child's mind?*" I never could stand anyone implying I was immature.

"It isn't derogatory. It's an expression from Eastern philosophy."

"Ah," I said, not understanding.

"There's a story from ancient Japan about a man who pays a call on a famous Zen Master, it goes like this," he began,

The man humbly enters the chamber where the Master is taking his morning tea.

"How can I help you?" the Master inquires.

The man bows deeply and in a supplicating voice petitions, "Master, please help me find the truth and calm my mind. Teach me how to reach Nirvana and become one with the Universe."

To which the Master simply replies, "First have a cup of tea," passing him a small ceramic cup.

"Thank you," the man bows politely.

The Master lifts the teapot and begins pouring into the man's cup. He continues, even after the cup flows over and the tea begins spilling over the table.

"Master, the cup is full!" exclaims the man, trying not to be rude while backing up so as not to get scalded.

"Ah," observes the Master, "and so is yours! You cannot learn what I have to teach until you come to me with an empty cup."

Syd finished and smiled with anticipation. It was just like one of Pop's stories—without a real ending.

"And what is that supposed to mean?" I asked, never having had the patience for riddles.

"It means," he sighed, apparently disappointed that I hadn't grasped the significance, "that the petitioner had preconceived notions of what Buddhism is, and so long as he retained his expectations, his metaphorical cup of tea was full. He would be unable to receive the true teachings of the Master because his preconceived notions would get in the way of any real learning."

"Yeah, that makes sense, but what does it have to do with being childish?"

"Your gentle touching of the stones to see how they were held together was like a child testing a hypothesis. Now that your hypothesis is shattered, you're open to the real answer. A child's mind is like an empty cup—ready to receive what is poured in."

"*OK Master*," I said, bowing low and putting on my best Asian accent. "*Kindly teach this humble grasshopper how stones are balanced.*"

We both laughed.

"It's quite simple. It just requires patience." He picked up one of the oval stones, turning it in his hands. "Most stones are not perfectly smooth. They're rough and have tiny bumps—even these round-looking river rocks." He held it out for me to feel.

Running my fingers over the smooth-looking stone, I felt what might have been tiny flat areas and bumps but wasn't really sure. I nodded, and he continued.

"When you put one stone on top of another, you must first feel where the stone's center of gravity is—where it wants to stand up in order to balance. You can't balance a stone at an angle, all of its mass must be centered."

He placed the stone endwise on the one he was using as a base, then delicately moved it from side to side, feeling it out, until it was almost balancing.

"Once the mass is centered, the stone will balance if you can align two of the smooth surfaces. You do this by feeling the way it moves. When the two line up perfectly, you can let go." He turned the stone gently. Suddenly it seemed to "fit" and he pulled both hands away like a magician, leaving the stone still and perfectly balanced.

"Wow!" I exclaimed, almost clapping.

"That's really all there is to it. Of course, adding another stone on top of the first requires more patience, but the idea is the same. It's really a great exercise for calming the mind."

He selected another oval stone and started to balance it endwise on top of the one he'd just stood up, motioning to me to give it a try.

Sitting down, I selected what looked like an easier rock to balance—a beginner's rock—then choosing a fairly flat base, attempted to stand it up. At first the stone wobbled and fell each time I let go, but slowly I got the hang of it. Finding the center of gravity, and then the sweet spot where the two stones came together, I slowly adjusted the stone. After about ten minutes, I had a single stone standing on end. Marveling at my achievement, I motioned for Syd to see my masterpiece.

"Excellent," he praised, "now try adding another stone to the stack."

He'd already balanced a second stone on his pile and was selecting a third.

Picking out a smaller, but promising-looking rock, I turned it carefully in my hands, finding its center of gravity. Placing it delicately atop my first stone, the first one promptly collapsed, destroying ten minutes of labor.

"I can't do it," I declared.

"You can," he assured me, "but it takes patience."

I tried again, but this time I couldn't even get the first stone to stand endwise. Pissed off and frustrated, I threw the stupid rock into the river, making a huge splash.

"Now you really do have a child's mind," he chided, laughing.

"There must be some trick!"

"No trick. Just patience. My friend Tony who taught mathematics once told me if his students couldn't solve a problem in under five minutes, they declared it *impossible* and gave up. Or worse, they looked up the answer and learned nothing. Often, they would leave everything for the night before, doing poorly because they didn't have enough time to relax and absorb the material. The pressure of *having to learn* making it impossible *to learn*."

Now he really sounded like Pop.

"You're saying that I'm trying too hard?"

"Just relax and *be the stones*. No goals. No pressure. That's the only way to master anything." His eyes twinkled, "That's why stacking stones is so calming. It's a kind of meditation. If one stone doesn't fit, don't force it. Try it at another angle or try a different stone. The rocks have a lot to teach you, if you listen to them."

Taking a deep breath, I calmed myself and tried again. Getting the first stone to stand on end wasn't too hard this time. Selecting a second oval-shaped stone, I found its center of gravity, then placed it on top the first one. Again, the first stone tumbled over. I put down the second stone and stood the first one up again. This time supporting the first stone with my hand, I placed the second on top and felt around for that sweet spot between the two. It took some time. Rotating, feeling, and experimenting. I'm not sure how long it was, but eventually I felt the two stones merge into one. Then supporting both gently, I moved them around until the bottom stone lined up again with the base. This time both stones felt right. Gently, I removed my hands. The two stones were standing end to end!

"I did it!" I called to Syd, showing off my first two-rock pillar.

"Nice," praised Syd, who'd just placed a fourth stone atop his own pillar. "I think we'd better finish gathering that water now."

The two of us worked together, carrying the water up to camp.

He was right of course—I couldn't stack the stones until I relaxed my mind, and once I did, it was calming. I don't think I could have done three. Well, maybe. Maybe with practice. And then it clicked: *A good relationship is like stacking stones; it takes patience, listening, and finding the right balance. And even when things fell down, if you had the right frame of mind, you could stack them back up, or find a new balancing point. The key was patience and an open mind.*

My Backwoods dinner wasn't exactly the crowning glory of our evening, but as I chewed it down I thought about the stones.

Had balancing them been Syd's way of teaching me the secret of a good relationship, or was that just my own serendipitous interpretation? It didn't matter. Going forward, I would try to find balance in my own relationships. Now I could see why he'd been so successful at his. It wasn't 'cause he'd found the one-in-a-million person who matched him perfectly—although there was something of that too—it was 'cause he'd figured out how to balance things, so it stood up over time.

DAY TWENTY

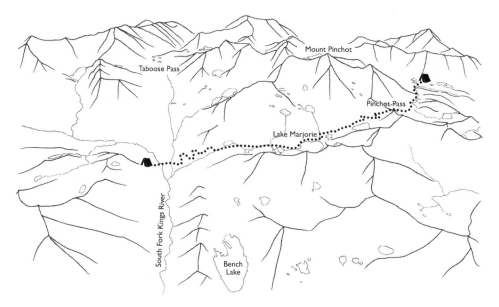

Kings River SF (10,040′) to Unnamed Lake (11,090′) via Pinchot Pass (12,130′)

6½ miles—2,210 feet elevation gain; 1,160 feet elevation loss

T HERE HAD BEEN A STORM somewhere up in the mountains last night, and while it had only drizzled down here, the bright flashes and booming of thunder had kept me up for hours.

Heading down to the river to wash up, I found the water deep and raging. *There was no way I was crossing that!*

"The water's really high," I declared upon returning to camp, my stomach in knots.

"It must have been all the rain—let's see how it is at the ford," he said.

We lined our packs with his black plastic garbage bags, packing everything inside like we'd done at Bear Creek. By the time we were ready to go, the mules and everyone else were gone. Somehow, we were always the last ones outta camp.

The spot where the trail forded the river was especially wide, but the current looked pretty intense. At the pass yesterday, I'd overheard a group talking about how some PCT hikers had died crossing here during a high snow-melt year. I'd tried not to listen but couldn't help it. Turning to Syd I said, "This thing's almost waist deep now. Look at that flow. We shoulda crossed it yesterday—isn't there some other way around this? Can't we go upstream a bit? Or wait till it subsides or something?"

"No. This is supposedly the best ford, and it may be a day or two before it goes back down. It's wider and shallower here. The other campers all made it across. We'll lock arms and face against the current, like we did before. We'll be fine."

Fuck—the river was really raging. But Syd had been right at Bear Creek, and we'd made it across that. And everyone else had made it across here too. *Fuck.* "OK," I agreed—immediately regretting it.

We unbuckled our hip belts and loosened our pack straps like before. Then we linked arms. My heart was pounding. I didn't wanna do this. I hated water. Nausea welled up inside me. Pop's face, all puffed and distorted and wrapped in seaweed, flashed before my eyes. I froze.

"I can't do this," I said.

"You can," Syd urged. "Just keep hold of my arm, face upstream, and follow me. Don't think about the water, just edge forward and focus on my arm."

He led me gently, pulling me toward the water. Nervously, I followed. My mind racing. My eyes were half-closed as I tried to block out the knowledge of what I was doing. The icy water gripped my ankles, then ran into my boots. Suddenly it became much deeper. The current was strong. Too strong. My grip on Syd's arm tightened. Despite the flat rocks, I had to lean into it, fighting the current to keep from being pushed over. Bending my knees, I leaned forward, found footing, then forced my leg on, dragging it against the flow. Teeth clenched, heart pumping, we edged on. The water splashing up over my shirt. The current shifting about me like a wrestler looking for an opening. The cold water numbed my legs. My pack with its open belt shifted about. But I went on, drawn by Syd's guiding arm.

Suddenly, I slipped. In that moment, I lost my grip on Syd. Turning, I saw him carried off on one leg and into the raging current.

"Syd!" I cried. Ripping off my pack, I hurled it toward the far shore, not looking to see whether it made it or not, my eyes fixed on Syd. His body was limp. He'd hit his head against a rock and was being dragged sideways by the mass of his pack, his head underwater. I dove in after him, struggling with the current and the drag of my boots. Kicking and stroking like on the last lap of a swim meet, I propelled myself forward with a burst of energy. Reaching him, I lifted his head out of the water. There was an ugly gash on his forehead and blood was streaming everywhere, but he was breathing and his eyes were open. He looked stunned. Supporting his weight, I made boldly for the shore, Syd clinging to me, the river merely an afterthought.

Climbing the far bank, I laid him down on the soft ground, pulling his pack off, while he spat out water.

"You were right," he coughed, "the river was deeper than I thought."

My head was spinning, "Don't move. Just try to relax. Are you OK? How's your head?"

He reached up and felt his forehead, only now seeming to notice all the blood.

My limbs began shaking. Tears streamed down my face. Wiping them away, I searched the bank frantically for my pack. It was lying upside down, half in and half outta the water. Dragging it over, I dug through the sealed bag for my first-aid kit.

He was bleeding badly. Cleaning up the gash with several antibiotic wipes and some cream, I applied a large butterfly bandage to staunch the flow. Back home he mighta gotten a stitch or two—but out here it was the best I could do. Then I went through the whole drill from swim team about checking for a concussion. His eyes could still focus. He'd have a nasty bump, but best I could tell, he'd make it.

Still soaked and shivering, my stomach reeled. Staggering up the bank to some bushes, I hunched over and vomited in two successive heaves.

Straightening, I wiped my eyes. Someone on the far bank was watching me, shimmering in the sunlight like an apparition. It looked like Pop. He seemed to be saying something. And then it hit me. I had just slipped on a rock. Pop had died when a freak wave caught him. *It was all the same.* You couldn't prepare for life's accidents. Pop coulda died at any time—it wasn't my fault for not being there. There was no way I coulda been with him every moment of his life. There was no way I coulda protected him from every possible accident.

My stomach cramped and I fell to my knees, heaving in wave after wave until I had expelled all the anxiety and pain inside me and there was nothing left to come out. My tears streamed into the ground. *Pop's death wasn't my fault.*

The apparition on the far shore seemed to flicker and vanish.

Struggling up, I wiped my hands on my pants, then brushed away the tears making a mess of my face. The sun shone down. Everything felt lighter. A huge burden lifted from my soul.

Kicking some dirt over the mess, I staggered back to Syd.

Had that really been Pop? Or just some trick of the light?

"What happened to your face and clothes?" Syd asked when he saw me.

"Nothing," I said, "I just became a little more grounded." And then the words gushed out, "Pop's death, that slip in the river, it all just happened—there was nothing I could've done! I wish I'd been there for Pop, like I was for you, but none of it could've been predicted—*none of it was my fault.*"

"Of course it wasn't—"

"The crazy thing is—my friends all tried to tell me that before—that shit just happens. That it wasn't my fault. And it made good logical sense and all—but it wasn't until just now that I got it."

He gave me a warm hug, holding me tight like Pop woulda done.

"I'm glad you found that peace," he said.

Had there been a higher purpose in his taking me on this trip? Or was that all just random too?

We sat together for a long while. The river still frightened me, but something inside had shifted. Eventually Syd leaned forward, dusted the dirt off his pack, pulled out his trekking poles, and stepped about cautiously testing his legs. "I'm fine," he declared, and began changing outta his soaked clothes and dumping the water from his boots.

I changed too, washing my face and wringing my clothes out as best I could and sticking them in the mesh netting at the back of my pack to dry.

"Do you wanna camp here tonight and just rest?" I suggested.

"Let's sit here a while longer, then keep going."

We stayed about thirty minutes more, drying in the sun. After checking his eyes and reflexes again, I followed Syd up the canyon wall, letting him take the lead. Despite the accident, he was moving at a pretty good clip.

My realization about Pop's death seemed to lighten my load. Birds were chirping. The air smelled like pine. Filtered sun warmed my skin. I was glad to be here.

The shovel on Syd's pack swung back and forth. It wasn't a clock ticking away the time he had left, it was a metronome keeping beat with the music of life—telling us to dance and sing and revel in the time we were here!

We climbed together—a thousand feet up the steep bank to a granite shelf. At the top, I wasn't even winded. I felt elated. Joyous at being in the wilderness. In the place Pop loved most.

Syd pulled out his map and looked around. "There should be a ranger station up here. Maybe we can have them take a look at my cut?"

We searched around for the station, but never found it, coming instead to a signed junction for Taboose Pass. Shortly after, we reached the turn off for Bench Lake. It was a mile-and-a-half detour from the JMT.

Flustered at not finding the station, he consulted his guidebook. "According to this, the station is only a large tent that gets taken down when the ranger is away, so I guess the ranger is out—and it looks like we should probably skip Bench Lake too. We still have Pinchot Pass to cross."

"We could camp at the lake and do the pass tomorrow," I suggested, looking at his bandage.

"Better not, we only have one reserve meal. It's too bad. The lake's supposed to overlook the river with a beautiful framed view of Arrow Peak."

"The mountain Bolton Brown climbed? The one that called to him after breakfast?"

"That's why I wanted to camp there yesterday, but given everything, I'm glad we didn't push it."

We headed on, passing gorgeous rock-framed pools and tiny streams. We were entering a semicircular amphitheater of high peaks, or what mountaineers called a *cirque*. Somewhere up there was Pinchot Pass. We advanced reverently, like two supplicants approaching the throne of the gods.

We soon spotted Lake Marjorie, with spellbinding cobalt blue water and a soft grassy bank nestled between boulders and slopes of talus. Neither of us had to ask the other—we both headed for the shore.

At the lake were four other hikers. A couple dressed like a pair of modern hippies were seated on some large rocks taking lunch in the sun. At the bank, two guys in typical backpacking garb were fishing.

We stopped on some rocks. Pulling out my first-aid kit, I checked Syd's bump. His forehead was badly bruised, but the wound looked clean and the bleeding staunched. Applying fresh ointment, I rebandaged it. Leaving Syd to relax, I headed over to the fishermen. The first guy was portly and deeply tanned with curly black hair, looking like he was from India or something. His companion was gangly with a burnt freckled face and wispy blond hair.

"Where did you guys hike in from?" I asked. *Trail conversation topic number one.*

"Yosemite Valley," the blond replied in a vaguely British accent. "We're hiking the JMT."

"So are we," I said. "We started down at Tuolumne."

"I'm Ken, and this is Azder," he smiled, "and they're Jay and Christie." He pointed toward the hippie-looking couple, who smiled and waved.

Syd ambled over, and I introduced him.

The two cast their lines out, reeling them in slowly—their sparkling golden lures dancing across the water. Each of them brought in a medium-sized trout—they promptly knocked the fish out on the rocks then stuck them in a large plastic bag brimming with other fish.

My mouth began watering. "How many did you guys catch?"

"Those two make ten," Ken replied.

"Isn't there a limit of three apiece?" asked Syd.

"I believe it's five up here," said Ken, "but we all have licenses, so we're alright."

Christie motioned for us to join them.

She was a slim, graceful-looking Asian woman with a wide flat face and dark hair tied up neatly in a pinned bun. Jay looked like a cross between a surfer and a yoga teacher. The two were sharing a lunch of hummus and pita bread. They were almost too clean for a couple of backpackers.

"That's a nasty looking bump!" Christie gasped when she saw Syd's forehead.

"I fell in the river. Gil here saved me."

"I have some chamomile teabags," she offered. "You soak them in warm water and lay them over the wound to help heal it." She began digging through her pack.

"I thought that was just for drinking," I said.

"Oh no," she said. "Chamomile's a powerful herbal remedy that helps reduce inflammation, boost the immune response, and is better at treating wounds than most ointments."

"Christie studied herbal medicine in Hong Kong," Jay explained. He had an accent too, almost British like Ken's, but with a slightly different flavor. They were quite the international group, but then many of the people we'd met out here were from overseas.

Christie smiled broadly, presenting Syd with two carefully-wrapped tea bags.

Ken and Azder wandered over and pretty soon we were all seated together on the rocks enjoying lunch.

"Are those the famous Sierra Nevada Golden Trout?" I asked Ken, pointing at the bag of fish.

"Nope, they're Brown Trout."

"Golden Trout is practically an endangered species," said Azder. "Years ago people stocked the lakes and rivers out here with Brown Trout, but stopped when they found them displacing the native fish."

"But the Brown Trout remain," continued Ken. "In a way, we're helping the ecosystem recover by fishing them out."

"Did you want to take a few?" Azder offered.

"Really? Can you spare some?" I looked at him, my mouth watering like Pavlov's dog.

"Sure, I've got a couple more in my pack. Here, take these two," he said, handing me a plastic bag with two good-sized fish.

"We'd better get going if we're gonna make Woods Creek," announced Jay. "It was nice meeting you both, maybe we'll see you on trail?"

"Thanks for the trout!" I smiled.

They packed up, heading on toward the pass at a pretty good pace.

"Wow, we'll have fish tonight," I said when they'd gone.

"You'd better double bag that and keep it away from your clothes. You don't want to meet another bear."

"Are you sure you're OK to do the pass today?"

"I'm fine."

A *Peep! Peep! Peep!* sound caught our ears. We both turned to see a group of seven older women donning a rainbow assortment of brightly colored packs and matching boots go chattering by on their way up to the pass.

Packing up, we trailed them at some distance, slowly losing ground.

Syd and I climbed at a steady pace, each of us alternatingly taking the lead, resting here and there for the other to catch up.

I began to think about Ma and how much she worried about me. I'd really screwed things up after Pop died. After we got back, I would call her up and tell her about everything—even what'd happened at school.

I pictured the balancing rocks again and thought about Kydoime. She was certainly attractive, but did we really have anything in common? Is that what my sundew dream was about? Was my subconscious mind trying to warn me about meaningless relationships?

The next time I saw her, we would just talk, nothing more. That would be hard—like a dieter with chocolate cake. But fat chance of me seeing her again—she was probably days ahead by now. I'd need to find someone new.

My thoughts were interrupted by an elderly woman leading a gear-laden llama down the trail. I guess mules and horses weren't the only form of stock.

The remaining climb was comparatively easy, and soon I was sitting among the rocks admiring the view from the top of Pinchot Pass. Syd was still a couple of switchbacks below. It was early afternoon, and a cool steady breeze was blowing. Far in the distance white puffy clouds were drifting toward the pass.

At the top were the older women with the colorful packs and boots. They were all wearing matching teal bandanas around their necks like the women I'd seen on Mather—was this a thing? The women were chattering away, swapping bits of sandwich packed with tuna, salami, cheese, and other mouth-watering items. I envied them.

Hungrily, I pulled out my bag of less-than-appetizing bars, selecting one that promised to taste like coconut, but didn't.

"Where did you all hike in from?" I asked the woman sitting closest to me, a stout brunette in a pink cap.

"We started down at Reds about a week ago," she replied with a thick German accent.

"Are you from Europe?"

"I'm Swiss, but I've been working in Sacramento for a number of years. We're all part of a local hiking group of Sierra Club Singles."

"Are you going all the way to Whitney?"

"We were," a thin blonde piped up.

"But it just isn't that much fun anymore," finished the one I was talking to in her strong accent.

"And I need to get back to work," interjected another.

"How about you?" the one with the accent asked me.

"I'm going all the way to Whitney," I said—maybe too proudly, 'cause my answer seemed to disappoint the band.

The woman replied simply, "Well good for you," and returned to chatting with her group. I returned to chewing on my bar.

A lot of people we'd met were heading back. From my own informal survey, it seemed less than half would be finishing the trail. Of course that didn't include the PCT hikers, who were a completely different breed.

Syd appeared, greeting the women on his way over. He looked pretty winded, the bandage on his forehead still firmly attached above the swelling.

"Made it," he declared catching his breath, "that was quite a climb."

"Not as bad as Mather."

"Or Donohue."

He pulled out some salmon jerky and a less-than-appetizing-looking bar. The group of women started packing up, then strutted down the trail together, still chattering away.

Syd and I sat, watching the fluffy clouds gather.

"What percent of people who start the JMT actually finish it?" I asked him.

"I'm not sure, I believe about seventy percent or more finish."

"What do you think the main reason people give up is?"

"It's funny you ask. A few weeks before we left, Cass handed me a copy of an online survey she'd found listing the top reasons hikers quit the trail. I don't remember the exact statistics, but the number one reason by far was, *Couldn't make the planned daily miles.*"

"So they underestimated how kick-ass the trail really is?"

"That's not exactly how I would put it, but yes. Most people setting out to do the trail have only the standard two-week vacation, so they plan to hike about fifteen miles a day in order to complete it within that time."

"Wow—we're only making six to eight a day, and it's already killing me."

"We're pretty slow. Most people average about twelve miles a day—although some in excellent physical condition do achieve fifteen or more."

"The PCT hikers I met said they were doing twenty-mile days, and Kydoime's doing more than twelve, but she takes a day off every now and then."

"That's the other thing people don't figure in. We haven't taken any zero-days, although we've had a couple of short ones. Many people who can do twenty- or thirty-mile days on weekends, think they can do the same thing day after day out here, which just isn't realistic given the body's need for rest, the daily elevation change, and overall altitude of the JMT. So they end up frustrated and behind schedule, which means running out of time and food. Many just don't plan realistically for how difficult this trip really is."

"That makes sense. What were the other reasons?"

"About what you'd expect—poor preparation, weather-related issues, river crossings, snow, and physical problems like blisters, twisted legs, and altitude sickness. A few also listed loneliness, getting lost, and gear failure—but those were pretty rare."

"No one got mauled by bears?" I asked, remembering our night of *cowboy camping*.

"Animal attacks are pretty rare. Although I'm sure some people are forced back after losing food because of improper storage."

"How does anyone doing fifteen miles a day find time to relax and do camp chores, like laundry?"

"There's a term called *hiker trash* that some people proudly apply to themselves."

I laughed, feeling a lot like *hiker trash* myself, with my sweaty shirt, blackened finger-nails, and matted hair.

Syd laughed too. It was good to see him happy and relaxed. His clothes might be becoming raggedy, and his appearance unkempt, but physically he seemed better than when we'd started. The trail had been good for him.

We packed up, descending a series of quick switchbacks down the other side, which soon flattened out to a dusty undulating plateau dotted with enormous glacially-strewn boulders.

"Did I ever tell you who Pinchot was?" Syd asked, pronouncing the name *Pin*-cho.

"No, but I was pretty sure you'd be getting around to it."

"I'm not a big fan of Gifford Pinchot, although he did die of leukemia—so at least we share that in common."

Why did he have to say shit like that? It wasn't funny or ironic.

"Pinchot grew up in a family that made their fortune from lumber speculation. He attended Yale and then, through a number of connections, became the first chief of the U.S. Forest Service—using his post to promote commercial logging interests."

"Sort of like the fox guarding the henhouse?"

"Yes, although he did advocate for conservation and worked hard to prevent clear-cutting and other destructive processes common at the time. But unlike Muir who championed wilderness for wilderness' sake, Pinchot advocated *the conservation and renewal of natural resources for the service of man*."

"Sounds like many of our elected officials."

"*What really gets them elected—the people or the money?* Anyway, Pinchot and Muir clashed repeatedly over the damning of Hetch Hetchy. A battle that Pinchot won through the clever omission of facts."

"So why name a pass along the Muir Trail for him?"

"I believe the pass took its name from Mount Pinchot, the tallest of the mountain peaks surrounding it. J.N. LeConte named the peak on one of his surveys, probably because at the time Pinchot had founded the Society of American Foresters—an organization dedicated to the preservation of forested lands. It wasn't until later that he and Muir clashed. Back when LeConte was first exploring these parts, Pinchot was regarded as a staunch environmentalist."

"Everything's relative."

"Working in the legal industry, you would know," he thrusted.

"Now you're spinning the facts," I parried.

"Touché!" he said, acknowledging the point.

We both laughed, continuing down the boulder-strewn path toward the greener and more forested area below. Overhead black clouds began to appear. It looked like we might get some rain.

We walked for the better part of an hour until Syd complained his knee was bothering him.

"Let's stop down there," he suggested, indicating a small lake a short way off the trail.

The lake was muddy and full of small black insects and tadpoles. It was good we had a water filter. We made camp well above the shore. The sky was too threatening for laundry or other chores, so we sat down to rest below a grove of trees. No sooner had we settled back on our air mattresses, then a small gray-black rodent about the size of a chipmunk came bounding down chirping a shrill and angry *chirr*. I clapped my hands. It squealed a sharp *pillillooeet* sound and scampered off.

"Gil, meet the famous Sierra Douglas squirrel," he smiled.

"I thought it was some kinda dark chipmunk."

"It looks like one," he agreed, "but without the stripe. They eat pine nuts and are quite territorial. Muir devoted an entire chapter to them in *The Mountains of California*—I think it's in the book I gave you. The squirrel's named for the botanist Permi was telling us about. Did you hear his call before he ran away?"

"Yeah, *pillillooeet*," I said, imitating the sound. A similar cry echoed down from the branches above.

"You seem to have his calling card," he said grinning.

"Just call me Doctor Doolittle," I said, putting on my best English accent while tipping an imaginary top hat. Syd laughed.

"Muir wrote that the sound was also the Native American name for the squirrel."

The trees grew silent. Syd boiled one of the chamomile bags Christie had given him, carefully covering his wound and lying back to let it soak in.

"*Why do Communists drink only herbal tea?*" I joked.

"You know, I've been meaning to say something to you about your jokes. You often use them as a substitute for real conversation."

"What do you mean?"

"Take that cocktail party at MTR. Most of the time you were with Kydoime, you were telling jokes. There's nothing wrong with using one to break the ice, but don't fall back on them as a way to escape real conversation. You asked me about relationships yesterday. One of the most important ways to build a strong relationship is to open yourself up to someone. Let them see who you are. Otherwise, what are you going to talk about when the jokes run out?"

He had a point. Who would guess this old guy—with the dripping teabag on his forehead—was really a kinda Zen Master. Ma was right, he had a lot to teach me.

I wanted to open up and share everything, like I'd done with Pop, but catching sight of that cancerous purple blotch around his shoulder, an unsettling feeling held me back.

There was a rustling noise in the branches above. Suddenly the squirrel leapt from the tree to a neighboring one—effortlessly gliding through the space in between. Then it scampered down the other trunk in crazy halting circles turning this way and that, like a nervous child crossing a busy street.

"Did you see the way he jumped?" I asked Syd. He nodded, balancing the bag on his forehead.

I looked back to where the squirrel had just been, but now he was gone. "That's strange, he was just there, and now he's—" I spied him darting into my backpack. "Hey!" I yelled, jumping up and racing over clapping my hands.

The nimble minx shot out like a bullet, scampering back up his tree.

Sealing up my pack, I went back over to sit with Syd, keeping a watchful eye so there'd be no second assault.

All the while, unbeknownst to me, the little soldier was circling round our camp, using my tent as cover, and now came creeping up on my pack from the far side. This I didn't discover until I heard a soft chewing sound from my pack and walked over to investigate.

Upon reaching it, the little thief darted out again, turning to hiss *pillillooeet* at me before scampering back to his treetop fortress.

"That little *pillillooeet* just chewed a hole in my pack!" I yelled to Syd.

"Did you take the fish out?" he asked.

Shit—the fish! Of course! I slid the bag out of the pouch that the little bugger had nearly chewed through—fortunately it hadn't gotten to the fish. With the help of some duct tape, I patched it up, "*If you can't fix it with duct tape—you haven't used enough!*" I recited. *Shit—* did I really have a joke for everything?

I brought the fish back to where we were sitting.

"You're lucky that pack wasn't in your tent," he admonished. He sat back up and after rinsing well, I helped him apply a fresh bandage. His forehead was still pretty bruised and swollen.

Suddenly, something hard dropped onto my head. "Ouch!" I yelled, reaching down to discover a spiky green pinecone.

"*Pillillooeet*," the rodent's familiar battle cry issued down from the ramparts of the tree. I chucked the pinecone up at my assailant, missing by a wide margin.

"It seems you've made a friend," Syd laughed.

Picking up the pinecone, I turned it over in my hands. Recalling the delicious pine nuts Permi had roasted for us, I tried peeling it open. My fingers were soon black with sap. I hadn't even managed to open a single flap. I guess you needed a fire. Giving up, I tossed the stupid thing aside, then began rubbing the sap from my fingers.

No sooner had I sat down, then my little assailant scampered down from his tree, made a dash for the discarded cone, and immediately began peeling it open like some classroom know-it-all showing off their solution at the board.

Surrendering, I picked up the bag of trout. "How do you think we should cook these?"

"Let's try steaming them."

He found two flat stones. Rinsing them, he placed them in the bottom of his pot, adding a small bit of water. Then he carefully set the fish on top of the rocks, steaming them. Despite the lack of salt or seasoning, they were the finest thing we'd tasted all trip.

My first course was followed by a second of Backwoods Buffet muck—all the worse in comparison to the fresh trout, Bob's grinning face reminding me of the damn squirrel.

Rinsing everything carefully to remove the scent of fish, we kicked back to watch the gathering clouds.

"You know, there's something I've been meaning to ask you all trip," I said.

"What's that?"

"Was I the only one you asked to go, or did you call up a bunch of people?"

"I only called you."

"Really?"

"Really. Do you remember what I told you about the tides that morning at Sallie Keyes Lakes, when I couldn't breathe?"

"You thought Pop's death was your fault, 'cause you'd forgotten to tell him about the tides, but actually it was a rogue wave that got Pop."

"Right, I'd never known that. I'd been afraid to talk to your mother about it. Afraid to go to the funeral, because I'd thought it was my fault."

"It was nobody's fault, just like with me and Pop," I insisted, my emotions welling up.

"But that's why I asked you to go, because I believed it was my fault."

I stared at him, blinking.

"You didn't know it, but I'd been keeping an eye on you. I'd heard from your mother that you'd been having trouble since your father passed. I thought bringing you on this trip would be my own penance. That you needed a jolt to set you straight, and this was my last chance to do it."

"So you asked me to go 'cause you thought Pop's death was your own fault?"

"Yes. Honestly, I wasn't certain it was such a good idea. Especially at first when I met you, it seemed like a mistake bringing you here. That's why after the bear incident when you wanted to go back, I didn't argue."

"I'd no idea. I never knew why you asked me. I thought maybe Ma put you up to it, or you just needed a partner and thought I'd be like Pop. But now I'm really glad you brought me. And glad we didn't go back after the bear. This trip has really changed me. It's shown me things I never knew about myself. Especially today. I always thought Pop's death had been my fault, but now I know it wasn't. You saved me today as much as I saved you."

We both blinked back tears watching the clouds.

After some time he asked, "Why? What made you think I'd asked anyone else?"

"Just before I picked you up, Cass told me you'd asked a bunch of folks, but all of them had said no."

He rose up a bit from his seat, his face flushed, "How would she know who I asked? I called a number of people, sure, but it was only to ask them about the trail and get their advice on how best to prepare for it. *You* were the only one I asked to join me. Everyone my age has either passed away or gave up on the whole outdoors thing years ago."

"You were right, I needed this."

"We both did," he exhaled, leaning back against his improvised chair.

The sunset imparted a rosy glow to the dark clouds, but it wasn't long before thunder rumbled and lightning flashed. We began gathering up our stuff. The air had a fresh scent. I could almost smell the coming storm.

Somewhere nearby there was a shrill, "*Pillillooeet!*" as the rain started.

"Good night *Pillillooeet!*" we both called together, laughing as we dashed for our shelters.

I stayed up reading Muir's chapter on the Douglas Squirrel, while listening to the rolling thunder and pelting rain, the tent lit up by the occasional lighting flash. It was both frightening and exhilarating.

Just before shutting off my headlamp Syd called out, "*So why do Communists only drink herbal tea?*"

"*Because proper tea is theft*," I shouted back. I heard him groaning in his bivy.

DAY TWENTY-ONE

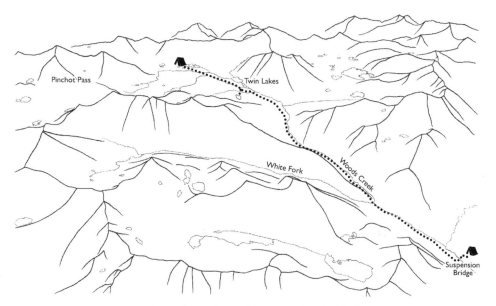

Unnamed Lake (11,090′) to Woods Creek Bridge (8,530′)
5¼ miles—80 feet elevation gain; 2,640 feet elevation loss

IT'D RAINED THE BETTER PART OF THE NIGHT, leaving the ground soaked and a slight chill in the air. My tent was still damp when I packed it away. The small drops of water didn't look like much but added noticeably to the weight of my pack. The feisty little squirrel was nowhere to be seen. I'd stayed up reading Muir's essay on the Douglas squirrel, as well as another chapter about his favorite bird, the water ouzel. Muir had a beautiful way of describing things, and it woulda been nice to have had another look at the squirrel before we hiked on.

At around Twin Lakes, Syd led us a short jog off-trail to a small pond. The reflection of a tall blue-gray peak to the southwest was perfectly framed in the still water. The peak had two long sweeping buttresses leading up to a razorlike ridge that was steeply gabled, making it look like the roof of a Gothic cathedral.

"What's that mountain called?" I asked.

"That's Mount Clarence King. A friend of mine told me this was the best view of it from

Mount Clarence King and Mount Cotter

the trail. That smaller peak to the left is Mount Cotter. We'll pass under both of them on our way up to Rae Lakes."

The view was extraordinary.

"The peak was first climbed by Bolton Brown," explained Syd. "He was on a two-month long honeymoon out here with his bride Lucy. If you recall, he'd tried to climb the peak on his first trip but stopped shy of the summit because of the steep vertical cliffs on the ridge."

"It looks really dangerous," I agreed—its peak had a triangular spire.

"But Brown was an expert mountaineer, and this time he'd brought a special lasso with him. Catching one end over the peak, and hoping it would hold, he pulled himself up—dangling in a sling over a sheer two-thousand-foot drop until he managed to squirm over the top."

"That's just crazy. What did his bride say?"

"I don't know, she stayed in camp. But she joined him on many of his other less technical climbs. The two of them were like a pair of mountain goats."

"So why wasn't the peak named for him? I mean, I know that other peak at Palisade Lakes was named for Brown—but who was this Clarence King guy? Is he the one for whom Kings Canyon was named?"

"Kings Canyon takes its name from the Kings River, which Spanish explorers of the early eighteen hundreds called *El Rio de los Santos Reyes*, or *The River of Holy Kings*. Do you remember I told you about Josiah Whitney, the chief of the California Geological Survey at around the time of the Civil War?"

"The one who called Muir an ignoramus over his theory of glaciers?"

"That's right," he chuckled. "After exploring Yosemite—this was before Muir came there—Whitney sent his botanist William Brewer and his topographer Charles Hoffman up the South Fork of the Kings River, to search for the sources of the three major rivers in this area—the Kings, Kaweah, and Kern. The two were accompanied by James Gardiner, an assistant surveyor; a packer named Richard Cotter; and a young twenty-two-year-old assistant geologist named Clarence King."

"How do you remember all those names?"

"It was a very famous expedition."

"Didn't Whitney go too?"

"No, he'd had difficulty up on Mount Dana in Yosemite—probably due to altitude sickness. After that, he directed his expeditions from his desk, using Brewer as his commander in the field."

"It's funny they named the tallest peak in America for someone who got altitude sickness."

"Yes, it is a bit ironic." He continued, "Brewer's team headed up the South Fork of the Kings. Climbing out of the canyon, the group was overwhelmed with the scale and ruggedness of the Sierra. The jagged snowcapped mountains were much taller and grander than any of them had imagined."

"I know the feeling. Sometimes from the top of a pass I feel I'm looking out the window of an invisible airplane—staring down at all the valleys and ridges with their lakes and forests spread out to the horizon. When I'm climbing up, I keep asking myself what I'm doing here, but each time I get to the top and see that view, I feel it was worth it."

He smiled, a knowing look in his eye. "Brewer and Hoffman climbed a high peak that they later named Mount Brewer—we should be able to see it when we're up on Glen Pass. From its summit, they were awed to discover an even taller range of peaks to the east, still draped in early season snow. His team wanted to investigate the new range, but Brewer wisely judged the passage across the snow to be too dangerous. Nevertheless, young Clarence King begged Brewer to let him and his friend Cotter have a shot. After much pestering, Brewer assented. According to King's account, which many consider overdrama-tized, the two struggled up and down over ice-covered cliffs—risking death at nearly every step, with little more than a length of rope between them to stop a fall. Finally crossing the snows, they reached the foot of the high range they'd spotted from Mount Brewer. Climb-ing what King took to be the tallest of the peaks, the two assailed its heavily-crevassed slopes, reaching the top only within inches of their lives. Upon summiting, King rang his climbing hammer against the tallest rock, declaring the peak to be "Mount Tyndall."

"Wait, I thought the highest peak was called Whitney?"

"I'm coming to that."

"So who was this Tyndall guy?"

"He was an Irish physicist who became enamored of mountaineering. His book, *The Glaciers of the Alps*, was probably what inspired King. Anyway, after surveying the sur-rounding peaks, King and Cotter were shocked to discover two others taller than Tyndall. They named the highest of these Whitney, in honor of their chief. But the two were run-ning out of food, so they were forced to return without attempting Whitney. Afterward, King begged Brewer to let him try again. And once more Brewer assented. This time King took a more southerly approach but was unable to find a course up to Whitney."

"How is it he couldn't find the tallest peak in the Sierra?"

"It's not just a matter of finding a peak, you also have to find a route up it. That's the real challenge of mountaineering. It wasn't until the early nineteen hundreds that climb-ers began to use pitons and belays. In King's day, all climbing contained some element of what we'd now call *free soloing*. Your father and I tried our hand at mountaineering back in our day, and I can tell you, even on a so-called easy route, it's still quite challenging."

I couldn't picture Pop as a mountaineer, although he did have a couple of old photos of himself posing on rocky slopes with his old mountain axe in hand. "So did King ever climb Whitney?"

"Some years later, he made his way to Lone Pine—the small town below Whitney at the end of the JMT—hoping to summit from the eastern side. There he climbed a cloud-shrouded summit and from a break in the clouds spotted Mount Tyndall standing to the northwest. Triumphant, he returned to Lone Pine, declaring that Whitney had at last been conquered."

"So he was the first to climb it."

"No, King got lost in the clouds. The peak he climbed turned out to be Mount Lang-ley, which is just southeast of Whitney. Ironically, the peak he'd spied through the clouds wasn't Mount Tyndall at all, but actually Whitney."

"So first he climbs the peak northwest of Whitney, and then he climbs the one south-east of it?"

"Exactly, he kept missing the mountain!"

"So when did he find out he was on the wrong peak?"

"Several years later, another climber summited Mount Langley and found King's sum-mit register, proving King had been on the wrong mountain. Well, that didn't stop King.

Jumping on the first train back to California, he set out once again. This time approaching Whitney from the southwest and finally summiting the true peak. But upon reaching the top, he discovered a small monument and a record of the parties who had beaten him to it. He returned home deflated."

"I know the feeling. I once broke a school record at a swim meet, only to have the kid after me beat my time. So who made it up first?"

"A trio of fishermen from Owens Valley named Begole, Johnson, and Lucas, followed by two other parties. King's was probably the fourth assent. The fishermen wanted to call the mountain Fishermen's Peak, and the case went to court. But in the end, the name Whitney stuck. Interestingly, Muir was probably the next person to climb Whitney. At first, he made the same error as King, summiting Langley by mistake. Realizing his error, he ran down, attempting to summit the actual peak the same day. But Muir underestimated the distance. At around midnight, well shy of the summit, he was forced to dance around just to keep warm up on the barren rocks. Finally, with no food or shelter, he turned back. Then he tried again. This time starting from the eastern face, successfully reaching the summit by what is now called *The Mountaineer's Route*."

We sat admiring the view of Mount Clarence King. Syd's stories about the early explorers always impressed me. Looking out at its cathedral-like summit, I couldn't picture anyone hanging from the top by just a lasso, or King and Cotter sliding down steep icy walls with only a rope between them. There weren't any maps or trails back then, and most of their equipment musta been unimaginably primitive. It was just a different era and maybe even King's inflated accounts were an understatement of what those early explorers actually faced.

Somehow, I'd really grown to enjoy Syd's stories. There was something primal, almost sentimental, and deeply human in this oral tradition. I wouldn't have believed it before—immersed in the rapid consumption of instant media—but now it seemed to me this intimate human sharing of information was yet another slice of our being that'd been given up in exchange for our modern lives. It was only out here in the wilderness, where a person had time to step outta things, that one recognized how much we'd traded away without ever really knowing the value of what we were giving up. Maybe that was the pull we felt from nature? A tug at our own roots, a reminder of who we were, and what was really at the ground of our existence.

Syd looked at me, and I nodded. Getting up, we returned to the trail. From here, we descended into a rocky river valley. At the bottom was Woods Creek. The trail paralleled the gorge, remaining tantalizingly far above it in the afternoon heat.

Eventually, we reached a signed junction. An arrow pointed ahead toward Road's End and Paradise Valley, while another labeled John Muir Trail pointed left. To my surprise, there was music drifting up from the direction of the river. Following its sound, we came to a large suspension bridge dangling over the heavy rapids. The music was coming from a campground on the far side.

"Sounds like a party!" I exclaimed.

Syd tipped his head back, shut his eyes, and recited,

> When through life unblest we rove,
> Losing all that made life dear,
> Should some notes we used to love,
> In days of boyhood, meet our ear,
> Oh! how welcome breathes the strain!
> Wakening thoughts that long have slept;
> Kindling former smiles again,
> In faded eyes that long have wept!

He opened his eyes, then added, "Thomas Moore."

"That's beautiful." And with Syd's benediction, we approached the platform leading up to the bridge.

The thing was an old wood-and-wire affair, long steel cables curved down from tall wooden A-frames supporting a series of shifting planks. The dangling assembly swaying seemingly in time with the music. A sign cautioned, *One person at a time on bridge.* Somewhere across the gap, a steel guitar was crying out a bluesy tune.

"After you," insisted Syd with jovial politeness that clearly masked his nervousness.

"Why thank you, sir," I replied, mounting the scaffold. The planks shifted and swayed beneath me. Clutching the safety lines I advanced cautiously, slowly finding my balance. It was kinda fun actually, the way the bridge danced in the breeze to the rhythm of my steps, the music luring me on like a Siren. Syd followed, his old bones rattling in the wind.

Beyond the bridge a party was underway. About a dozen musicians were gathered in a circle, each playing various instruments that they musta packed in. I counted two guitars, a banjo, a saxophone, at least two flutes, several harmonicas, a fiddle, and all kinds of drums. Someone had even brought a long ornate didgeridoo that was painted with orange, black, and yellow bands like a coral snake. Beside the circle was a large pile of logs in a dug-out pit. The scent of marijuana hung everywhere.

Most of the musicians looked about twenty- or thirty-something, although several were older. They were dressed in a wide variety of outfits. One vaguely Indian-looking woman wore a decorative sari of green, crimson, and gold. Two other women wore tie-dyed sarongs in wild swirling psychedelic patterns. One of the drummers had on a colorful African-looking outfit, awash in browns, yellows, and reds. One guy even wore a top hat and tux. When one of the musicians finished, another started in, the songs and styles shifting at the whim of whoever took the lead, the others jamming along behind.

Surrounding the scene was a large hillside campground dotted with colorful tents of every shape and size. It was a bit like Reds Meadow, only more spread out. A number of campers were strolling about, others just relaxing and enjoying the music. Many looked like they'd just gotten here and were as surprised as we were to discover the gathering.

A Black guitarist was playing an old Lightnin' Hopkins blues song. The seated campers swaying left and right to its rolling storylike melody.

Syd stood listening to the music, slowly taking in the scene. "It looks like quite an event."

"Yeah," I agreed. "Where are we going to set up camp?"

"Maybe over there by those trees?" he suggested, indicating a spot at the far edge of the campground. "It should be an interesting evening."

"What do you think's going on? Is it some sorta festival?"

"Beats me. I've never seen anything like it out here. It's probably illegal—but it looks pretty fun. They probably timed it to coincide with tonight's full moon."

"I thought you weren't into stuff like this, isn't that why we skipped VVR?"

"I never said I wasn't into music—I just don't like the whole car-camping scene."

His attitude seemed a bit contradictory, but maybe he was just loosening up? We wove in and out of the various tents, our packs swaying to the rolling rhythm of the music.

We settled on a spot beneath some trees by a patch of red manzanita bushes, just up from a stream that flowed into the main creek. It was close enough that we could hear the music, but far enough that we could still get some rest.

Making camp, we filtered water and rinsed off. Then propping up our air mattresses against a log, we settled in to enjoy the music. Every genre from rock to blues, country to new age, indigenous to jazz, and even rap and hip-hop was represented at one point or another in an endlessly-shifting kaleidoscope of sound and celebration.

A guy with long dirty-blond curls dressed like one of the musicians in a flowing outfit staggered by. Stopping him, I asked, "Hey, who put this whole thing together?"

"Together?" he answered in a disconnected manner, looking pretty stoned. "I don't really know. My sister hooked me up."

"How did they plan it?" I asked him. "I thought every trailhead had a quota?"

"I'm not really sure," he stammered, "there's only about fifteen or twenty of us that I know of—the rest just kinda showed up—hiking the various trails, I guess. They do this every year, gathering somewhere in the mountains each time. My sister turned me on to it. She's dating one of the guitarists."

I thanked the guy who then wandered off. We made an early dinner, enjoying the music while watching the flow of people around us. The sun was still well above the horizon, dancing in and out of fluffy white clouds that drifted lazily over the surrounding peaks. Despite the early hour, someone was already lighting the bonfire, and there was a growing number of people dancing around the circle.

"Do you want to smoke the stuff Dylan gave me?" Syd asked.

"Sure," I agreed, somewhat surprised. "Did you bring a pipe?"

"I was just about to ask you."

"Give me a minute," I said, disappearing to search among the tents. What I was after didn't take long to find, and I soon returned clutching an empty beer can, holding it aloft like a trophy. With the help of a tent stake, I soon had it converted into a pipe—a trick I'd learned at the frat house.

We laid back smoking Dylan's medicinal herb. The music took on a slow mystic spin enveloping my body with its warm vibrating pulse. The clouds glowed in brilliant pink and purple hues, their shapes shifting into dragons, faces, animals, and castles—my feet grounded to the earth, my spirit soaring up into the mountains, the whole range of light illuminated.

The sun rolled away, and the stars emerged. Soon the voluptuous round queen of the night rose up over the mountains, drowning out the jealous stars and draping the trees with her pearl white damask.

"Do you want some magic Lethe water?" an older man in loose-fitting pants and a tie-dyed magician's robe asked a second time before I became fully aware of him standing there. He was proffering a pewter cup of a vaguely gin-and-strawberry-smelling concoction. His question called me back to awareness, and I shook my head no. To my surprise, Syd took the cup, swallowing much more that I would've deemed wise from a stranger offering "magic water" in the woods.

"Thanks," said Syd, wiping his mouth. "That's great, what's in it?"

"Oh, you know, strawberries, oranges, a bit of gin, and well—my own special brew," the man trailed off with a mischievous smile.

Syd grinned, offering his hand to the man who looked to be about his own age. "I'm Syd, what's your name?"

"My friends call me Kyron," he answered, taking Syd's hand. "Enjoy the music," he sung, wandering off.

Woken from our long trance, Syd and I arose, and as if under an enchantment, found ourselves drawn toward the center of the music and the raging bonfire. The style had shifted from its earlier mellow assortment into the steady dance beat of *boots 'n cats 'n, boots 'n cats 'n, boots 'n cats 'n* by the drummers who were seated in a circle by the fire. Surrounding them, a pulsating throng of dancers—mostly campers—cast up huge shadows, licking like flames over the surrounding forest. The dancers swayed and gyrated to the rhythm, an undulating mass of bodies. Women in shorts danced with T-shirts tied above their navel, a few almost topless. Guys wore baggy pants, some with open button-downs displaying well-muscled chests.

"It's like lekking birds!" exclaimed Syd, raising his voice above the pounding of the drums.

"What's *lekking?*" I asked, cupping my hands over his ear so he could hear me.

"It's when groups of birds display their plumage in order to find a mate," he shouted back.

I laughed. It really did resemble a mating dance—and there would certainly be a lot of paired-up sleeping bags tonight. Maybe I could find someone to warm my synthetically-feathered nest from among the writhing dancers.

"I'm gonna join in!" I yelled to Syd, leaving him to watch as I merged with the oscillating crowd.

Flames leapt up, the old moves coming back, twisting and swaying to the primal rhythm of the wild jungle dance. Spotting several young doves, I moved in—but all rejected me. I moved on, a hunter circling the flames.

And then I saw her. Kydoime—her shirt tied up like a Persian belly dancer—expertly gyrating among a pack of chiseled hikers, all vying for her favor.

Our eyes locked. "Gil!" she called out to me, motioning for me to join her.

Finding myself at the center of this menagerie, I danced for all I was worth, my hips bending to the rhythm of Kydoime's Dionysian thighs. Her flock of Satyrs looking astounded at being displaced from the full attentions of their goddess by the sudden appearance of some returned Odysseus—disguised as an unkempt pot-bellied guy in dirty hiking garb.

As the song shifted, she planted a passionate kiss of reunion on my sweaty brow, shouting into my ear, "Let's get out of here!" Grabbing my arm, she dragged me off in the direction of the surrounding forest, to the gaping astonishment of her herd.

"Where did you come from?" I asked when we no longer had to shout. "I thought you were at least two days ahead of me by now."

"I probably would be," she grinned, "but then I got my period. I took a couple of zero-days up around Bench Lake. I get 'em really bad sometimes, with heavy bleeding and cramping."

I cringed, "*Whoa—too much information!* You know that kinda talk really turns men off, right?"

"Seriously? Like everything I do and say needs to be for the benefit of attracting men?"

"That's not what I meant—"

Why were women always twisting my words around? But better not to argue, adding, "I hear Bench Lake is gorgeous."

"It was," she smiled. "I took a couple of short day-hikes. That's where Randy Morgenson disappeared."

"Who?"

"You know, from that book, *The Last Season*, about the ranger who vanished out here? It was right along the Muir trail. Don't tell me you never heard of him?"

I shrugged, and she dropped it. Syd would probably know what she was talking about. Right now, with her hand in mine and the eucalyptus scent of her body, my attention was focused elsewhere.

"So how did you come to be here?" I asked, still amazed at finding her, and even more amazed that she had dragged me off from among that circle of fetching suitors.

"I camped here last night. I was packing up kind of late, when a couple of people wandered in asking me if this was the Woods Creek Bridge. We started talking, and when I heard there was a group of musicians coming, I moved my tent a bit out of the way and just hung out. It's been great so far, and now it's even better because you're here," she squeezed my hand tightly.

We wandered hand-in-hand through the moonlit forest, my heart thumping to the distant beat of the drums. The lingering high from the pot giving everything a surrealistic quality, like that moonlit image of Syd's.

We brushed through branches of pines as she led me up a narrow footpath. Suddenly the trees opened up to reveal a small clearing with her green tent in the center—a tiny island of paradise in an ocean of trees.

We sat on some downy needles before her tent. She pulled out some chocolates and we slowly fed each other the tiny morsels. Gradually we went from chocolates to kissing, and from kissing to more kissing. Before I knew it, we were making love on the soft needles.

Sometime later, we crawled inside her tent—her sleeping bag opening like a silken mattress below our entwined bodies.

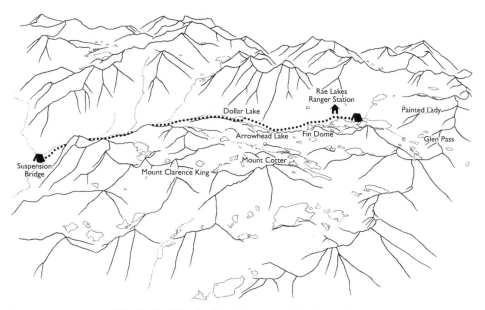

Woods Creek Bridge (8,530′) to Rae Lakes (10,570′)
6½ miles—2,180 feet elevation gain; 140 feet elevation loss

I WOKE COLD AND NAKED in a green tent. The flap was open, and a cool breeze was blowing in. *Where were my clothes?*

Emerging naked, I stepped out into the clearing.

Kydoime was sitting dressed and cross-legged on a large fallen tree nibbling on something. She smiled when she saw me, teasing, "Is *Adam* awake and ready to enter the garden?" Giggling to herself like a playful child she said, "You do know God created *Eve* first, but then she made Eve promise to tell Adam that *he* had been first."

I laughed, walking barefoot and naked to her across the fallen pine needles. We embraced, exchanging passionate kisses in the warm golden dawn. "I could get used to this," I whispered.

"C'mon Gil," she protested, pushing me away gently. "I told you last time, it's only *trail sex.*"

"Then why," I prodded, cocking my head slightly, "among all those cut-up guys you were dancing with last night, did you choose me?"

269

"Oh, come on," she taunted, "don't you know? I love a man with a tummy!" She giggled again, patting my stomach, then looked at me sideways for a moment. "You really don't know, do you? It's because you're different. Like that old man you're hiking with—not many people would do that." Then in a mocking tone she added, "Besides, the whole 'dad bod' thing is in now, and everyone knows, *it's better to sleep with someone you know, than someone you don't.*" She pushed me away again.

We both laughed, but it was really hard to know what she was thinking.

"Would you like some dried pomegranate seeds?" she offered.

They were sweet and tart, like her.

"Your stuff's over there," she indicated a neatly-folded pile of clothes. "I aired them last night while you were sleeping, so they wouldn't stink up the tent—they really could stand a wash."

"Are you sure there's nothing *Adam* can't do for *Eve*?" I asked, smiling broadly, hoping she'd be tempted again by the serpent.

"No, I'd love to. I really would. There's something—I have to move on today. I'm way behind schedule, and I need to make up my miles."

"Will I see you up at Rae Lakes?"

"I really wanted to camp there," she said longingly. "It's supposed to be gorgeous. But I have a friend meeting me with my resupply up at Onion Valley, and I'm already a day late. So I need to hoof it over both Glen and Kearsarge Passes today. Are you going to Onion Valley?"

"We got our last resupply horsed-in over Bishop Pass and are headed straight to Whitney."

"Then maybe I'll catch up to you around Forester?" she smiled, patting my stomach again, and giving me another long kiss. "But now I need to hit the trail." Pushing me gently aside, she headed over to her tent to finish packing. Everything but her sleeping bag was already neatly stacked against the log.

She was a real mystery. Beautiful and soft when she wanted to be, yet strong and independent too. Different from all the women I'd known. Her shirt hugged her body as she packed up the tent. Why did she have to be on such a tight schedule? It would be incredible to spend another night with this goddess. But she wasn't the sort to change her mind. *Shit*—I hardly knew anything about her. Why hadn't I woken earlier, so we could have talked? Or spent a little more time last night before jumping into bed? I guess it'd been the drums and the pot. If we did meet up at Forester, maybe we could spend a whole day together then? Syd's phrase "child's mind" popped into my head—best to be open and ready and just accept what comes.

Syd—shit! I'd forgotten all about him. I'd left him at the bonfire after he'd drunk that "magic water." I had to get back and find him. Hurrying over to my clothes, I pulled them on, gave Kydoime another kiss, and said a quick goodbye. My shirt smelled like eucalyptus—she musta sprayed it with something.

Back at the tent, Syd was packed up and waiting. It was a relief to find him there.

"Well, if it isn't Briar Rose, back from the enchanted forest," he mocked.

"Who?" I asked. Syd's references could be pretty obscure sometimes.

"Nevermind, it looks like someone had a good time."

"Yeah, Kydoime was at the dance."

"I know, I saw you two together. You dance pretty well."

"I took a course at the frat house. It was a graduation requirement." He laughed.

"How was your night?" I asked.

"It was interesting. I'm not sure I can put it all into words."

His eyes took on a dreamy quality and I sat down and listened.

"I don't know if it was the marijuana, or something in that drink I had—but after leaving you, I wandered up the trail a bit, away from everything. Finding my way down to the stream in the moonlight, everything lit up under its soft glow, like in a Bolton Brown drawing. I sat there, just watching the water flow by. It was like looking at life. Then I saw a small trout hidden among the rocks, almost motionless, its body waving gently back and forth, keeping it steady against the current.

"As I watched, the moonlight took on an almost iridescent rainbowlike glow. It's hard to describe, but I could almost taste the different colors. The trees of the forest seemed to grow faces and I could almost touch the silvery network of roots and fungi running off from my hands beneath the soil, my entire body rooted to the spot."

There musta been something in that drink he had, like the 'shrooms I'd taken in my frat days.

"The flowing water became the eternal stream of time. The trout would eventually die and be carried off to the ocean, but new things would be born and live on from its remains. I realized I was the fish, and the fish was me. That everything's connected. That we all swim for a while against the current, until one day we're carried off by the flow."

"How do you interpret all that?"

"Like that Zen story I told you—we're all just waves bobbing in the ocean, our form appears temporary, but in fact we're all eternal. All part of the water. Only this time, it wasn't just a metaphor. This time, I could feel it with all my being. I began weeping. Weeping for the fish that would die. Weeping for myself. Weeping for the stream, for all life, for everyone lost in this delusion. Weeping for the joy and beauty of the endless current.

"And then I felt my mind beginning to dissolve. At first it was frightening, but then I embraced it. No longer me, nor the fish, nor the water—but everything at once. I could feel the earth and moon, the breeze over the mountains, the flow of the stream. Past and present. All connected in an endless dance."

"It sounds like you had a vision of God."

"No—it wasn't that. Not in the Western sense at least. Not in the sense of one all-powerful, all-knowing being. It was the opposite. It was like being completely absorbed into everything, part of all nature. It was a spiritual sense that all was one, all was connected, and yet all was separate too. As if everything were God, and yet everything had its own perspective onto itself. Like the jewels in Indra's net. Like a giant spiderweb covered in dew drops, in which every drop holds the image of every other drop. I can't really describe it, but for what seemed both an instant and an eternity, I no longer existed, but was a part of everything."

I nodded.

"And then I came back. I felt cold. Felt the chill of the earth under me, and I came back to the trout, still swimming in the stream. Only now the moon had jumped across the sky and was behind me. That's when I saw the deer. A doe, standing pale and white in the moonlight across the stream. It sniffed the air, then looked right at me—looked straight through me as if I were transparent. It called out, and a small fawn came bounding out of the trees to drink with her."

He sat, eyes closed, and I didn't interrupt.

"Eventually the pair wandered back into the forest. I could no longer see my trout. I looked up at the sky. The moonlight drowned out the Milky Way, but I could see millions of stars beyond the mountains glowing in a supernatural light, and I thought, *This is the wilderness as Muir saw it—this is the face of God.*"

"So you do believe in God?" I asked gently.

"Not in the sense of any scripture, but I do feel an awe and reverence—that there's something more, something spiritual that lies beyond our senses and imagination."

"I told you, we're all just playing a great cosmic video game."

He opened his eyes, holding my gaze thoughtfully for a long moment.

"That's the problem Gil, we have no way of knowing for sure. Is what I experienced last night real, or was it just what I wanted to believe? Was I really connected to everything, or was it all just a drug-induced fantasy born from my own mind? That's what I've been sitting here pondering."

"I guess it's like you said about the wave and the water. It just depends on how you look at it."

He sat quietly for a time, then got up, "You'd better pack and eat. It's starting to get hot out, and it's a long climb up to Rae Lakes."

It was good he was alright, that kinda experience could've taken him in any direction— but probably for him being grounded in nature was the safest place to experience such visions. Maybe this would help him become more at ease with his own mortality?

The trail wound mostly uphill, but it wasn't nearly as steep as the passes we'd been over. Climbing a low rise, we passed two hikers heading north. They had large open chrome umbrellas hooked to their shoulder straps. One had a solar panel attached to the top, his earbuds emitting the tinny vibrations of whatever it was he was listening to.

"Where are you coming from?" I asked them.

"Mexico," the first one responded, "we're doing the PCT." The other seemed lost in his musical haze.

"What are the umbrellas for?"

"Sun. We used them when crossing the desert. They're better than hats or sunscreen, or a sweaty raincoat when it pours."

It made sense, better than the sticky sunscreen I was using. "Aren't you worried about Mary Poppinsing off some cliff in the wind?"

"We don't open 'em when it's blowing."

So what did they do if it was both windy *and* rainy? But we just said goodbye and hiked on—*NOBO meets SOBO.*

The guy with the earbuds had the right idea. It woulda been great to have brought along some tunes. All trip, the same two stupid songs had been repeating over and over in my head, like a pair of never-ending earworms: Led Zeppelin's "Stairway to Heaven" and the theme song from *Nacho Libre.* That guy with the umbrella could choose from thousands of songs, while my own internal radio had only two selections. Then again, if I'd brought music, Syd would probably have lectured me about "shutting down my ability to be reflective"—which would probably be true too. Back in LA, whenever there'd been nothing to do, I'd pull out my phone, do some gaming, watch a video, or something. But here there was nothing like that. At first it was disconcerting, almost frightening. But gradually the random thoughts streaming through my head had become a source of contemplation and reflection. Back in the world of perpetual entertainment, it was way too easy to get lost in the noise. But out here was all the time in the world to think and reflect. Maybe that's what people meant by *getting away from it all.* Although it seemed like it was really *getting* back *to it all.* Would I still be able to find this feeling back in LA?

Syd was up ahead, no doubt lost in his own reflections. We continued on in this way, until he suddenly halted, pointing up at the two prominent peaks above us. "Those are Mount Clarence King and Mount Cotter."

They were the two peaks we'd seen from the small lake the day before. The view wasn't as good up close. It was like my life in LA, the farther I got from it, the more clearly I saw it.

About thirty minutes later we came to Dollar Lake, a small roundish lake sparkling in the noonday sun. The trail wound up around the side. Some young hikers had stopped here—their packs abandoned by the lakeshore. They were taking turns climbing a large jutting rock and diving off in their underwear. Two of the women were topless but somehow I felt little interest in boobs. They were beautiful to be sure, like in nice paintings or sculptures. But my real interest now was in getting to know someone for who they were, not what they were. One of the girls leapt in a perfect dive, ripples echoing out from where she pierced the water. The image of Kydoime sitting on the tree trunk came back to me. Where was she from? What was her full name? After saying bye, I'd given her my number, but had never gotten hers. Who was she? Was it really just *trail sex?* A shout and a big splash from one of the guys caught my attention. It was obvious he wasn't a swimmer, his arms thrashing awkwardly and his legs breaking the water as he struggled for the shore. When he reached the bank safely, I went on, following Syd.

We soon came to Arrowhead Lake. There was an old brown metal bear box here, the first I'd seen out in the wilderness.

"There used to be a lot more of them," explained Syd, "but they're being phased out now that everyone's required to carry individual canisters."

The box made a nice chair. While he went down to the lake to pump water, I stroked my unfamiliar beard, my eyes drifting over my hands. Despite washing them every night, it still looked like I'd been working in a coal mine. What did the rest of me look like? The last time I'd really seen myself, or even had a real shower, was at Muir Trail Ranch.

When Syd returned, we ate the usual bars. He was looking pretty grungy too. Fitter, but filthy. Which would Cass notice first when she saw him?

Less than an hour later, we were overlooking the second of the three Rae Lakes. It was one of the most beautiful chain of lakes we'd seen all trail—azure water with sandy shores and perfect beaches—the sky above a cloudless cobalt blue. The water was jumping with fish, making me wish again that I'd brought a rod. The lakes were nestled in a small valley, surrounded by gigantic peaks. Most prominent was Painted Lady—a rival to the great pyramid, its slopes glowing rosy pink in the warm sun. Also amazing was Fin Dome, a tall triangle jutting up above the lakes like a giant shark's fin. We were high up again, well over ten thousand feet, and the air was crisp and pleasant with a flavor like seagrass.

From our vantage, we could see tents dotting the most attractive beaches and sites. There were swimmers, fishermen, and lazy sunbathers hanging out. It would be hard to find a nice site. Rounding the crest of a small rise, we passed a turnoff for the Rae Lakes Ranger Station, and sure enough moments later a scraggly-bearded guy in a green and gray Park Service uniform came strolling up the trail in our direction, whistling.

"Hall-oo," he called in greeting when we were several yards apart.

We stopped and said hi. He smiled a broad smile. Then seemed to notice Syd's bandage, the still black-and-blue area around it, and the shovel dangling from his pack—the twin of his own.

"What happened to your head, and what's that shovel for?" he queried.

"Long story," Syd answered.

The ranger cocked his head slightly, "You both have your permits?"

"We do," Syd replied, "would you like to check them? We're hiking the JMT."

Syd really seemed to relish having his permit checked.

"No need," the ranger smiled, straightening his head. "I'm in a bit of a rush. Apparently there's been a big group making a ruckus down at Woods Creek, and I need to check it out. We got a number of complaints about loud music, late-night partying, and an illegal bonfire. You guys didn't see anything, did you?"

Syd looked as if he was about to detail the whole thing. I guess it was wrong for people to party in the wilderness like that. Their bonfire coulda started a fire or something. And there were certainly people seeking peace and solitude, who didn't wanna hike into a loud musical gathering. But we shouldn't be the ones to rat them out.

"No," I interjected, cutting Syd off. "We didn't see anything, but then we were camped up near Pinchot Pass last night," I lied. "Beautiful view of Mount Clarence King from up there."

Syd shot me a sideways glance but stayed silent.

"So there weren't a large number of tents down by Woods Creek when you went by?" the ranger eyed me a bit suspiciously.

"Come to think of it, it was a bit crowded there," I said.

"Where are you guys camping tonight?" he asked.

"Somewhere up here, but it looks like most of the good spots are taken."

"Ah," said the ranger, "not if you know where to look. If you keep on the way you're going, then take a right at the small spur and follow it down—you'll find some nice empty sites, right there by the lakeshore. Great fishing too."

"I thought we had to camp at least a hundred feet from water?" Syd said.

"Technically, yes," said the ranger, "but there are some well-established sites down there that are acceptable exceptions to that rule. You two have a great time. I've got to get going." He headed on the way we'd come.

Following the ranger's directions, we found a series of three empty campsites—each better than the one before. The last was situated on a small ledge overlooking the second lake, with a tiny slope leading down to a private beach and an amazing view of Fin Dome. Dropping our stuff, we made camp. Then we headed down to the beach to relax.

It was sunny and the water called.

"Syd," I said turning toward him. "Will you try something with me? I wanna try swimming again." Surprising even myself with my request.

"Sure, what do you need me to do?"

"Nothing," I said looking at his bandage. "Just stand by the shore and make sure I'm OK."

Checking that no one was around, I stripped off my clothes, piling them carefully on a log, then edged naked toward the water with growing trepidation.

"Ever since Pop died, I haven't been able to do this. I've tried a thousand times, but every time I've chickened out."

"I know," he said reassuringly.

"But that day at the river when you fell in, it was all instinct and I swam. I wanna see if I can do it again."

The icy water lapped at my feet. I began trembling—certain that when I stepped in, I would see Pop's bloated face again. I couldn't do it.

Taking two steps back, I squeezed my eyes shut, trying to imagine I was in my childhood room at home, far away from the water. That I was safe at home. Safe with both my parents.

"What are you doing?" Syd asked gently.

"I'm imagining myself at home, back when I was a kid. A therapist I once saw taught me how to do this, to help me clear my mind and keep the images I see of Pop away. He said if I could imagine someplace safe, that I could enter the water."

"That reminds me of the story of the man who went to see a great shaman about his incurable disease. The shaman prepared a special remedy for him, but just before administering it, said, *This medicine will only work, if when you swallow it, you're not thinking of a monkey.*"

It took me a second, but then I got it. "So you're saying, trying not to think of Pop will only make me think of him?"

"Precisely," he looked at me earnestly. "Your trying to push him away only makes his image stronger. Why not try the opposite instead? Embrace your father's image. Focus on him as you enter the water. Ask him why he's appearing to you, what he has to teach you. The worst that can happen is you turn back."

Shit—that didn't make any sense. My legs were trembling again. But what could I lose? It felt like something Master Po would say. *Shit*—why had I wanted to do this anyway? Inching forward on the cold sand, I stepped into the icy water, its level quickly rising to my knees, goosebumps covering my skin.

I closed my eyes. Pop's face, all bloated and drowned and covered in seaweed hung before me. My heart raced. A wave of nausea swelled up. I had to get out of here. Outta the water. Holding my ground, I focused on Pop's image, asking, *What do you have to teach me?* He hung there. I moved forward, my thighs entering the chill. His ghostly visage stared at me. I took another step. Pop's face seemed to shift, his head cut and bruised, like Syd's. Another step. The water wrapped around my chest. I dove—Pop's image vanishing like a fleeting ghost, washed away by the cool pure water. Swimming out strongly, I stroked hard for a small islet about a hundred yards offshore—my body warming to the effort. Twice my left leg threatened to cramp up in the cold, but I eased through it and soon reached the rocky outcropping. Climbing onto a large promontory, I stood dripping in the warm sun. "I did it!" I whooped, the icy water streaming off my head.

Surveying the sparkling waters around me, I dove back in, swimming back to our small beach, triumphant.

Syd smiled proudly, like Pop woulda done. Stepping onto the sand, I hugged him tightly, squeezing him to me. He hugged me back, my dripping naked body soaking his flannels.

When I let go, he gave me a warm fatherly look, broken only by the butterfly bandage on his bruised forehead and his stubbly three-week-old beard. He grinned, waving a wet hand over my head, and like a priest at a baptism intoned, "Now you are reborn."

Tears began streaming down my face. I hugged him again. The image of Syd's face and Pop's blending in my mind.

Suddenly a *Peep! Peep! Peep!* sound caught my ear and I let go. What would it look like, a crying naked man hugging a wounded old coot? *Why was it every time I got undressed, someone always came along?* Stepping quickly to the log, I pulled my pants on.

Sure enough, a couple was checking out the campsite next to ours. Fortunately, they were quite a ways off.

I turned back to Syd saying, "I thought you weren't religious?"

"I never said that. I said I'm a little bit of everything, I like to hedge my bets."

Nodding in slow recollection, my scalp tingled as the sun dried the water from my matted hair. He was right—I was reborn.

Syd began stripping off his own clothes, apparently unfazed by the couple.

"What about your head?" I asked, eying his bandage.

"The bleeding's stopped. I think the chamomile really helped. After washing off, I'll put the other tea bag on it, change the bandage, and add some more ointment. It should be OK."

Syd took only a quick dip before coming back to shore. He was clean and smiling—drying himself off with his bandana. Standing shirtless in the sun beside him, the mountain breeze washed over me. "That was great!" I exclaimed.

"Any better and we'd be illegal," he grinned.

I laughed. It was the first time he'd made a joke that was actually funny. But he was right, he was looking noticeably better. He needed a shave to be sure, but his body was fuller, his skinny limbs almost toned, he still had the big blotches, but even the bump on his forehead didn't look too bad.

I wasn't looking that shabby myself. My stomach was almost flat, my legs and thighs muscular, my arms trim again. Hiking was the best fitness plan and therapy I'd ever had.

We dressed, combed out our matted hair as best we could, and lay back in the sun enjoying our little slice of paradise. Despite the fading eucalyptus smell, my clothes were getting pretty stanky, but it was just too nice here to think of chores.

Syd went over to the shore, sat down, and selecting some large oval stones, began balancing them end to end like he'd done before. When he was done, he knelt down as if to say a prayer, then came back to sit with me.

"Is that a monument to your wife?"

"No, not specifically. It's just my way to celebrate being here. A way of putting my joy into physical form. Although my wife is certainly a part of that feeling because I carry her spirit with me."

"You must really miss her. The loss musta been very painful for you."

"It was sad that she had to die in that way. But in the end, we all learn to let everyone and everything we love go."

"Whaddya mean?"

"When you get to be my age, or sick like I am, you really come to understand the saying, *you can't take it with you*. At one point in my life, I spent a lot of time gathering things. Nowadays, I spend a lot of time dispersing them, seeing that they make others happy—like that Bolton Brown drawing I'm giving you."

"That'll always mean a lot to me—especially now that you've told who he was. But while what you said is true about possessions, people are different, right? We don't collect people or give 'em away—they're taken from us."

"No—people are not taken from us, because they were never ours to begin with. The only real thing we ever own is ourselves. Everything else is just borrowed from the universe and, at some point, we must return it all."

"But people aren't things—they're people. And when they're gone, they're gone. They're different from stuff like books and paintings."

"The only difference is that with a person both of you have a choice whether to stay together or not. Otherwise, it's the same—when it's their time, all we can do is say goodbye. Everyone leaves this life eventually. Everyone goes back to the ocean."

"OK, philosophically, sure—but don't you miss your wife?"

"Yes, I miss her dearly. She was my partner and my best friend. We loved each other. But I'm glad for the time we had, and I'm glad she left before me."

"Whaddya mean? Wouldn't you rather she was here now? To be with you through your cancer and all?"

"No, not at all. It's a blessing that she went first. Seeing me sick would just have made her suffer. And I would have spent too much of my own energy worried about her. I miss her of course, but it was her time to go. When someone dies, the only thing we're left with is the choice of whether to focus on the gap in our lives or to celebrate the joy they've left behind. For me, I choose the joy. All the small gifts her company afforded me. All the lessons I learned from her. All the memories of the times we spent together. A part of her spirit lives on inside me and inside our children. I think if she's watching us now, she'd be happy to know how much we cherish her memory, rather than being consumed with grief over her loss, over something we can't hold on to."

"But wait, can't you experience both the joy of what she meant to you and the sadness over her loss?"

"No, not in my experience. The two emotions are opposites, and if you try to hold on to both, you'll only have melancholy. I'm not saying I never feel sad about Katrine's death. Sometimes the pain of her passing washes over me and I cry, or I sit silently for a time thinking of her. In the end, it's the remembrance of the joy she brought into my life that consoles me. Prolonged grieving over a loved one is just attempting to cling to something that's gone, but the joy that they've brought us is something that can fill our hearts forever."

Was I still grieving for Pop, or was it really for myself? The reflection of Fin Dome stood tall in the water. Why hadn't I been able to let Pop go? To say my goodbyes and make my peace like Syd had done? Even at Pop's funeral, standing by his empty coffin, everything had just seemed so surreal. Was I just focused on my own grief? Sore inside for the loss of someone I missed, instead of glad for the things he had given me?

Heading down to the shore, I found several jumbled rocks and began balancing them slowly as Syd had taught me. Soon I had a small monument to Pop standing next to Syd's. Kneeling, I prayed, *Pop, I hope you can hear me now. Thank you for everything you've given me. For everything you taught me, and for everything you inspired me to become. Thank you for leading me to Syd, he's a good friend and teacher. Please forgive my mistakes—especially about my schooling. I promise I'll make it right when I get back. Did you see me swimming again? I wish you were here. I really miss you. I'll always love you, Pop. I'll always miss you.*

My tears began flowing—rushing like a flood after years of being held back. Then slowly my heart rose, his presence shining on me. Syd was right. Pop was gone, but his spirit lived on inside me. It was up to me now to carry his light forward.

Standing up slowly, I walked back to where Syd was waiting. He put his arm over my shoulder and we sat together, looking at our two pillars reflected in the tranquil blue water, like two beacons at the edge of the ocean.

After a long time he spoke, "Bolton Brown's the one who first discovered this valley, naming it, Another Paradise."

"*Another Paradise*," I repeated, "the place I'd finally let Pop come to rest in."

We sat together. I didn't want to go anywhere, just wanted to stay here in the sun by this lakeshore forever.

"Did Brown come here on his honeymoon?" I asked, his stories making me feel like I was sitting with Pop.

"It was several years after that—he came here with his wife and their new two-year-old, naming the largest of the lakes Lucy and the island in the center Eleanor's Island for his daughter."

"That wasn't on the map?"

"His names didn't stick. Several years later, William Colby of the Sierra Club renamed the lakes for his own wife, Rachel 'Rae' Colby, and that was the name that got printed on the map."

"Why? If Brown came here first, shouldn't his names have had priority?"

"Naming can be a pretty political thing. Brown gave names to almost all the lakes and peaks in this region, but only a few remain. For instance, he envisioned this whole ridge above us as a giant dragon, naming the peaks, The Head, The Fin, and The Tail. And Glen Pass he originally called Blue Flower Pass. But only Fin Dome and a handful of his other names were ever officially adopted."

The ridge did look like a dragon. Pop had loved reading me stories about dragons. It was fitting that one now guarded his secret paradise.

"Brown musta named The Painted Lady," I ventured.

"No, he called that peak, The Pyramid. Later it was given the unfortunate name, The Colored Lady. Then in the 1950s, it was discreetly changed to The Painted Lady."

"It's good to have at least a few mountain peaks named for women. It seems like most of the mountains we've seen are named for men, and most of the lakes for women."

"That's the old tradition."

"Originally, I thought Whitney was named for a woman, before you told me about Josiah Whitney." He laughed.

We sat by the lake, watching Fin Dome's reflection grow longer in the water. Eventually hunger called.

Syd turned to me, "Do you think we should knock the stones down, or leave them standing?"

"Won't they eventually fall down on their own?"

"They will, but some people are pretty opposed to leaving any sort of man-made objects in the wilderness. They see even rock art as a kind of pollution."

"Fuck 'em! They'll fall down anyway—and there are millions of rocks here. Some people just have to complain about everything."

"I agree with you but was just asking. I didn't worry about it last time by the river, because they'd be washed down anyway and wouldn't disrupt the landscape, but here by the lake, I don't know."

"I guess that makes sense. If people started building 'em everywhere, they'd become like some sorta rock graffiti, marring the landscape, and ruining it for those who came here to get away from man-made things for a while."

"It's good you can see that. It's always best to try to see both sides of things."

"OK, if they're still standing in the morning, we'll take 'em down, leaving things as pristine as we found 'em."

He nodded, and we walked back up to camp.

The couple at the next site had just finished getting their tents up and while Syd went back down to pump water, I strode over to say hi. Suddenly, I recognized the tents. It was Lois and Clark! Among all this wilderness, they'd somehow managed to find the one spot next to ours.

"Hey there!" I shouted, waving to them.

"Gil!" Lois exclaimed, and Clark stood up. "Is that you guys camped over there by the lake?" she asked, looking as amazed as I was.

"Sure is, great to see you both again. Last I heard, you were headed to Mono Hot Springs with your boyfriend."

"It was nice to soak and relax, but I prefer being back on trail. Wow, imagine running into you guys way out here."

Clark gave me a big bear hug, "Great to see you again."

"Let's all have dinner together," I invited.

"Are you still eating those Backwoods Buffet things?" Lois asked.

"Yeah," I confessed, "still choking 'em down."

"Well, I have some homemade chili you can try tonight."

"That would be amazing," I said, smiling.

Soon we were all seated together on the small beach. Lois cooked a big batch of vegetarian chili, to which she added freeze-dried cheese and ground-up tortillas, giving each of us a huge helping.

"It's our last meal before our resupply," she explained, "so we can afford to splurge a bit and share."

"Hey, this is *amazing*," I praised, tasting the chili, "and being from the Midwest, I know chili."

"Thanks," she beamed. "I play with the ingredients and flavorings a lot, but the basics are an old family recipe."

"Sis cooks the best food," Clark declared, "and then she spends hours dehydrating it all. We've had a different meal almost every night. She's the best cook on the trail—although we never seem to lose weight," he patted his stomach.

"Wow, we should hike with you guys," I exclaimed.

"You can," offered Lois. "We're heading out over Kearsarge Pass to Onion Valley tomorrow. You're both welcome to tag along."

"What's in Onion Valley?" I asked.

"Nothing much," she said.

"Pretty much just a campground and a parking lot," answered Clark.

"But the Mount Williamson Motel in Independence runs a guest shuttle up and back, and accepts resupply packages," explained Lois. "The hostess is a former JMT hiker. We have two rooms reserved for tomorrow and their breakfast is legendary. Plus, they have laundry, real beds, and showers. There's probably even a store in Independence where you could replace those Backwoods meals of yours."

"Wow, do you think I could find a BLT there?"

"You're obsessed with BLTs aren't you?" Clark jumped in.

"Whaddya mean?"

"You couldn't stop talking about them back at The Lake of the Lone Indian, and you're still obsessing about them now."

"Was I? I don't remember— "

"All night at dinner, while you were choking down that Backwards Bob glop of yours and staring wide-eyed at those two guys with the fish like you were going to die from hunger."

"Phil and Mike?"

"Yeah, those guys, and all you kept saying was how when you got back, the first thing you were going to do was have a BLT."

"It's the bacon," I said, "and the bread—that wheat bread aroma. And the mayonnaise, and sweet tomatoes."

"Not the crispy lettuce?" Lois teased.

"That too," I said, my mouth watering, despite her fantastic chili.

"Well come to Onion Valley," enticed Clark. "We can always squeeze you guys into my room—if one of you doesn't mind taking the floor. There's got to be a couple of restaurants in town. I'm sure you can find your BLT somewhere."

"I'm just looking forward to fresh fruit and juice," Lois said.

"I want a big fat hamburger with tons of ketchup, and fries," said Clark. "And definitely a beer! And after that a pizza!"

I was sold. I was long past sold. I was salivating.

"What do you think, Syd? Can we stop at Onion Valley?" He'd been quiet the whole time.

Syd gave me one of his looks, "We're already carrying enough food to get to Whitney. A trip to Onion Valley and back would cost us three days at least. It just doesn't make sense. You can get a BLT in Lone Pine when we finish the trail."

The air hissed out of my dream like a fallen soufflé. He was right of course. He hadn't said it, but he had no desire to leave the trail or visit a town. He'd paid to have us resupplied by horse so we wouldn't have to exit at Onion Valley. We were only a few days away from Whitney, and he was looking more and more like he'd make it. We couldn't get off the trail now. I owed him that.

"Sorry guys," I said, the words painfully leaving my lips, "but Syd's right."

"That's OK," said Clark. "We understand. It's kind of nice not to have to leave the woods."

"Hey, at your pace, you'll probably catch back up to us before Whitney. Do you think you guys could bring me back a BLT from Onion Valley?"

"We could, but it would be pretty gross," said Lois. "The lettuce and tomatoes would get brown and soggy, and the bacon and mayo would probably go bad in the heat. You can't keep a BLT fresh for long, even with a refrigerator."

She was right. I'd just have to endure a few more nights of my Backwoods Buffet. I looked down at our two monuments and suddenly missed Ma's cooking.

DAY TWENTY-THREE

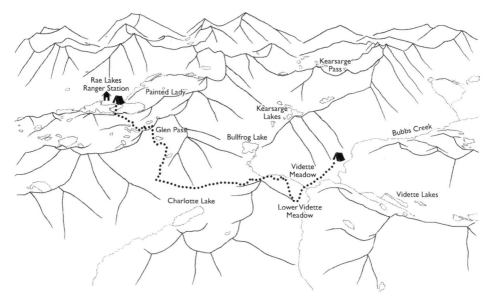

Rae Lakes (10,570') to Vidette Meadow (9,570') via Glen Pass (11,970')
6¼ miles—1,550 feet elevation gain; 2,550 feet elevation loss

I WAS CROSSING A LONG MOUNTAIN VALLEY through a squishy green meadow, when up from the grass popped a trio of sexy full-figured onions. They had big eyes, large lipstick-red mouths, and long spindly limbs extending from their round yellow bodies. Their skin was peeled back just enough to see their juicy wet flesh bursting out from beneath their skimpy bikini tops. They danced and sung and made me cry with their strong sweet juices—calling me to go with them to Onion Valley.

Bounding after them, three tall dark orange carrot men with yellow birdlike legs popped up from the meadow. The one in the center began singing a bluesy song about the joys and wonders of Onion Valley, while the other two accompanied him, blowing long brassy-yellow saxophones. Soon luscious green pepper people swinging their hips in brown dried-grass miniskirts appeared, followed by squishy red tomato ladies in stringy black-thong bathing suits—all forming a crowd of dancing singing vegetables like some over-the-top musical production. The whole ensemble calling me to Onion Valley.

They led me toward a wide gap between two triangular snowcapped peaks, complete with singing bighorn sheep on top. The gap gave off a golden glow, with a trail winding across it to the magical kingdom beyond. Dancing tubs of mayonnaise, two-legged female hamburgers in soft tender buns, spinning cans of beer, and even a BLT sandwich, all sung and danced—calling me up over the pass to Onion Valley.

Struggling after them, a thunderous godlike voice shook the peaks bellowing out the single command, "*No!*" Rising up like some giant apparition before the pass was the disembodied face of Robin Williams, God rest his soul, with wild unkempt hair and a stringy brown beard. His immense head looked down, and in a booming voice uttered the words from the film *Jumanji*, "In the jungle, you must wait, 'til the dice read five or eight!" Only now it was Syd's voice calling me and everything vanished, my body sweaty and twisted inside my Bonfire bag.

"Gil, are you alright?" he was shaking the tent. "I thought I heard you shouting—"

"Yeah, I'm fine," I answered, unwinding my bag and poking my head out through the top. *Great, just great—now I was dreaming about food.*

Getting outta the bag, I began arranging my stuff, then joined him outside for breakfast. There was no wind. Our two monuments and Fin Dome stood perfectly reflected in the still mirror of the lake below us. My eyes lingered over them, then hearing something, I turned to see Lois and Clark over at their campsite cooking breakfast. Probably cranberry pancakes or some other gourmet meal. But I didn't walk over—it would just make me think more about food.

Lois and Clark were still getting ready when we passed their camp. They said they'd catch up to us at the pass—no doubt they would.

The trail ran along a narrow isthmus dividing the second and third lakes. The northern lake was rockier and less inviting, but there were still a few scattered tents. Some early risers were up fishing by the lake.

"Why are there so many hikers on this part of the trail?" I asked Syd.

"It's part of a popular circuit out of Kings Canyon called the Rae Lakes Loop. A few miles after Glen Pass they'll head down Bubbs Creek, and we'll be back in Terra Incognito again."

We wound up the side of a large foothill, gaining a spectacular view of the lakes. Gazing back down at the clear shining waters of my rebirth, I felt airy and free.

In the soft breeze, I caught a whiff of a sweet musky smell, like someone had peed after eating too much asparagus. Hopefully it wasn't a patch of California Whiteflower—used toilet tissue scattered by inconsiderate hikers. Turning to find the source, my eyes caught the head of a cluster of violet-blue flowers poking out of a crack in the surrounding rock. Each looked like a tiny blue lollipop with a ball of delicate flowers radiating out from the tip of its stem. They were small and easily overlooked, maybe three or four inches high, with delicate fernlike leaves.

"Hey Syd, check out these little blue lollipop flowers—are these why Bolton Brown called this place Blue Flower Pass?"

"Do you know what you've found?!"

"Eh—blue flowers?"

"*Those are Sky Pilots!* They're one of the rarest plants in the Sierra. They only grow in talus fields at altitudes above ten or eleven thousand feet and only flower for a couple of days. I've looked for these each time I've come to the Sierra, but so far I've never seen them in bloom. You must have some special providence to have found them here on your first trip."

I didn't mention the smell, but they were beautiful, and it felt good to have found them. Pulling out my camera, I photographed the tiny balls—capturing the brave pioneers in their rocky home. It was tempting to pick one—to press it in the Muir book and show Ma. But knowing how rare these were, I took only photos.

With some regret, we moved on. The trail wound around some small pools nestled among empty talus fields, then began ascending the pass in long sweeping switchbacks.

Climbing was almost routine now, and I soon dropped into a steady rhythm. My mantra—*And I'm climbing my staircase to Heaven*—repeating in my head as I pressed on mechanically, like one of those old-fashioned windup toys. Syd followed a few switchbacks behind.

The summit was crowded with backpackers. Most of whom were too clean to be hiking the JMT. One couple had even brought their six-year-old daughter.

Scouting around for a place to drop my pack, I spotted Jay, Christie, Ken, and Azder relaxing among the boulders.

"I never thought I'd catch up to you guys again," I said in surprise.

"Wow, hey Gil! How are you and Syd doing?" asked Azder for the group.

"Pull up a rock," said Jay.

"Where are you guys headed today?" Azder asked.

"Not sure," I confessed dropping my pack. "Somewhere close to Forester Pass I'd imagine."

"That's where we're going," said Azder, "after we meet up with Ken's mum."

"His mother?"

"Yeah," he nodded. "She's done the JMT twice and loves getting out here when she can. She's bringing us our resupply so we don't have to hike out over Kearsarge Pass."

"But there's four of you—that must weigh like eighty pounds?" I said, picturing Ken's "mum" built something like the Incredible Hulk.

"Nah," Azder laughed. "From here it's only three days to Whitney, so it's more like twenty pounds of food."

"Which she can carry easy," Ken added.

I couldn't picture Ma, tough as she was, hiking in twenty pounds of food over a high mountain pass. But then Syd was carrying far more, and he was older and more frail than she was. Maybe the whole age thing was just my own prejudice? Come to think of it, a lot of people in their sixties and even some in their seventies or more had passed us on the trail. Actually, it woulda been pretty cool meeting Ma up here.

"I just hope she finds us," said Christie.

"We took an extra day fishing at Rae Lakes," Ken explained.

"Yeah, so we'd better get going," Jay urged, hastily finishing up his lunch.

The four of 'em got up, strapped on their packs, and headed off.

A short while later Syd came trudging up. "Whew," he said wiping his brow, "wasn't sure I'd make that last stretch—the rocks looked pretty dangerous."

"Yeah," I agreed. "You just missed Jay, Christie, Ken, and Azder."

"They were up here? I would have liked to see them again. I imagined they'd have been a lot faster than we were."

"I think it's because we haven't really taken any breaks. It seems like everyone else does, so it just kinda evens out."

He dropped his pack and we both ate lunch—bars of course. As I chewed on mine I tried to imagine it was a BLT, but somehow thought of a monkey.

"Do you see that tall pyramid-shaped peak?" he asked between bites, pointing at a crest rising above a long sharp ridge to the southwest.

"Yeah."

"That's Mount Brewer, the peak from which they first spotted Mount Whitney."

"So that's where King and Cotter started out from?"

"You'll see what a difficult journey it must have been when we cross Forester."

"Have you been over Forester before?"

"No. I haven't been up Whitney either. Except for Rae Lakes, which I visited once with my wife, and a trip up Kern Canyon I took with my son Sean, I haven't really hiked this part of the Sierra. But we've got the guidebook and maps, we'll be fine."

As we chewed our insipid bars, the familiar forms of Lois and Clark came striding up. They were joined by a pair of older hikers. As they drew closer, I recognized the lanky forms of Rick and Jon, the two sixty-something Midwesterners from Reds Meadow. The pair were still hiking in jeans and button-downs, although they looked considerably more trail worn. Rick was still clean-shaven and had on his sun-faded cowboy hat, while Jon now sported a scraggly gray beard and had a bad sunburn beneath the dirty blue bandana wrapped over his head.

Expelling a streak of spittle into the rocks, Rick declared, "Well shoot, that was a fun climb." Then noticing Syd and me, he exclaimed, "Well, fancy meeting you two up here— had a nice trip up from Reds Meadow?"

We exchanged the usual greetings and stories from the trail.

"You remember those obnoxious kids who kept complaining about snoring?" Jon asked me.

"Yeah, I remember."

"Well, apparently they ran into an old granny ranger somewheres around Silver Pass. Turns out they were hiking without any permits. They were camped in a large meadow and had built up a big bonfire in an illegal ring."

"And they'd been harassing female hikers," added Rick.

"What happened?"

"Well, from what I heard, they each got a thousand-dollar citation and were escorted out from the wilderness," said Jon.

"Serves 'em right," I said, wondering if the ranger was Gabrielle.

"How's your feet?" Rick asked Jon.

"No better," said Jon, who'd been working on his laces and now gingerly pulled off his boots and socks. Both of his feet were a mass of silver duct tape.

"What happened?" Syd asked.

"Blisters," said Jon.

"His boots are a size too big," Rick spat.

"Borrowed 'em from my cousin," Jon explained.

His feet looked awful. Yellow puss was oozing out from between cracks in the silver tape.

"Ohhh—that looks bad," said Lois. Clark nodded sympathetically.

"Gonna do the whole hike anyways," declared Jon. "It doesn't hurt too bad."

"You should get medical attention," said Clark. "That could be septic."

"That's the plan," said Rick. "We're hikin' out ta Independence today, gonna visit a clinic and get 'em patched up, then take a few days rest."

"When you're retired, it doesn't matter how long ya take to finish the trail," said Jon.

"Well, you're welcome to get a ride with us," offered Lois.

"Maybe you can find some better fitting boots," Syd suggested.

"Nah," said Jon. "These are fine. I just need ta wear thicker socks."

While Rick tended Jon's feet, Lois and Clark pulled out their lunch. The two had brought tabouli mix, which after blending with water and olive oil, they stuffed into pita bread along with ground cashews and dried shredded apricot. Staring like a ravenous racoon, I bit and chewed the rest of my awful bar.

Syd finished his own lunch, and packing up, we said goodbye to the four. Clark promised he'd bring us both some snacks from Onion Valley. We waved, then headed down the far side.

The descent was steeper than the way up. The trail hovered high above a few lonely pothole lakes. The ground was dotted with alpine scrub grass. There were a couple of strange perfectly circular patches where absolutely nothing grew. Were these made by lightning strikes or some sorta underground mineral toxic to plants? Syd woulda known—but he was lagging behind again 'cause of his knee.

After a long dry stretch, the trail rounded a rock wall opening up to a clear view of Charlotte Lake nestled among the trees far below. Waiting for Syd, I sat in the sun enjoying the view.

When he caught up, we descended a long sparsely-forested ridge down to a dusty trail junction for Kearsarge Pass. Soon we came to a second, then a third junction—all marked for Kearsarge Pass.

"It seems this pass is really popular," I remarked, "this is the third trail that goes there."

"They form a kind of triangle, depending on which way you're going."

"So who was this Kearsarge guy? Did he discover the pass?"

"No, it's a funny story actually. During the Civil War, the pro-Confederate prospectors named the region around Lone Pine, The Alabama Hills, for the *CSS Alabama*, the

Confederate States' most successful warship. Not to be outdone, the pro-Union prospectors named the pass above the hills, Kearsarge Pass, for the *USS Kearsarge*, the ship that sunk the *Alabama*."

I laughed.

"This branch of the triangle heads up by Bullfrog Lake. I wanted to stop there and see the lake, because that's where Bolton Brown's family made their basecamp, but my knee's starting to swell up again—so I think we'd better skip it and just keep going down to Vidette Meadow."

"Sure," I said, nodding.

The trail to Vidette Meadow went steeply downhill. On the way we passed a couple of nice-looking campsites by a small stream, but they were occupied. Attracted by a distinctive smell, I discovered a patch of wild onions growing down by the bank and picked a bunch for dinner. Permi woulda been proud!

At the bottom of the hill, the trail came to a T. When Syd caught up, we turned left. "The other fork follows Bubbs Creek down to Kings Canyon, completing the Rae Lakes Loop," he said.

We soon came to a wide grassy meadow surrounded by mountains. "This is Vidette Meadow," declared Syd, who was limping slightly. "This morning, I thought we might make it all the way to the base of Forester, but now with my knee acting up, I think maybe we should stop here and take an easy day tomorrow." It sounded fine to me.

We hadn't gone far when we came to a spacious campsite by the river. There were already a couple of tents here, but there was enough space for two more without crowding. Approaching the stream, we ran into Christie and Jay filtering water. Christie gave us each a wide smile of welcome.

"Nice to see you guys again," I said. "Did you meet up with Ken's mum?"

"We did," Jay replied, "there was a bit of a mix-up over where she'd be, but we found her."

"Are those wild onions?" Christie asked, eyeing the bunch I was carrying.

"Yeah," I said, holding up my harvest.

"Wow," she bubbled, "so those *were* onions! See, I told you," she needled Jay. "I thought so, but Jay wasn't sure."

Handing her a couple, she broke off a leaf. "Mmmmm," she sniffed. "Are you cooking us dinner?"

Syd came to my rescue, "We'd be happy to share what we've got, but you might not like Gil's cooking. He's been feasting exclusively on Backwoods Buffet."

"Those freeze-dried chemical things that you cook in the plastic pouch?" Christie sneered, wrinkling up her nose and making me wish for the thousandth time I'd listened to that salesgirl.

"Is it OK if we share your campsite?" Syd asked.

"Sure, there's plenty of space," said Jay.

"Azder and Ken took Ken's mum up the creek fishing," Christie said. "Maybe if they catch something, we can cook them with your onions?"

"Wow, that would be amazing!" The thought of fresh fish and onions sounded like something out of a dream.

Picking a site far enough away from their tents to afford them some privacy, we dropped our packs and made camp. It wasn't long before Azder, Ken, and his mother returned carrying eight large trout.

Ken's "mum" was a fairly fit-looking woman, a bit younger than Ma. She had short silvery hair and a graceful smile accentuated in an earthy manner by a pair of slightly crooked front teeth. We made the typical round of introductions.

"The boys and Christie all call me *mum*, but my proper name is Jennifer," she said.

"How was the hike in?" Syd asked her.

"A lot tougher than I remember. And it doesn't help any that I have a gimpy knee. But it's probably the weather—I almost got turned around at the pass. Looks as if we're in for a spell of rain."

"That would explain it," said Syd. "My knees always seem to act up when the weather turns."

The two began chatting about their health problems, like older people always seemed to do when they got together. Leaving them, I went down to the stream to wash up.

Christie was there, naked and scrubbing her back with a small towel as best she could while standing ankle deep in the cold water. I was about to slip away discreetly when she turned and saw me.

"Sorry," I said embarrassed. "I'll just find a spot downstream."

"Why not join me if you're gonna wash up," she smiled, almost beaming.

Why not? Because you're naked and your partner is nowhere to be seen, a voice in my head warned. But disarmed by her warm smile, I stripped down, wading shyly into the pool. Standing beside her, I rinsed off, my eyes half averted.

"Do you think you could help me get my back?" she asked, holding out her small towel. What would Jay say if he found me scrubbing her back? But I accepted the proffered towel.

Christie's body was trim and fit, like Michelle Yeoh in *Crouching Tiger,* and her open carefree personality practically contagious. Soon we were scrubbing the dirt from each other's backs, Christie acting as if it was the most natural thing in the world. It felt quite pleasant, but in the back of my head alarm bells were sounding.

"Are you and Jay a couple?" I asked, hoping she wouldn't mistake my question for some sorta opening line.

"We are," she replied cheerfully. "We met at Phayao in Thailand working as WWOOFers. We've been together since."

"What's a WWOOFer?"

"You never heard of WWOOFers?" she asked surprised. "I thought everybody knew what they were."

She had a way of talking that made me feel at ease. "No, I've never heard of WWOOFers, except for the speakers I mean, what are they?"

"A WWOOFer is a kind of organic farm worker, like an exchange student," she smiled unabashedly while balancing adroitly on one foot to scrub her toes. "It stands for *Willing Workers on Organic Farms*, or *World Wide Opportunities on Organic Farms*—I forget which. Basically, you volunteer and they sponsor your visa, provide food, and a place to stay in exchange for farm work. Phayao is a famous farm in Thailand—I'm surprised you never heard of it."

"Wait, did you run into a guy named Permi? About my height, thin, goatee? Really into plants—"

"Yes!" she brightened, her smile so wide it looked like her face might split. "We camped with him up at Evolution Lake. He and another guy named Dylan who smoked a lot of herb and had a big yellow tent. Those guys are great."

Jay suddenly appeared at the bank, startling me. I was about to explain that we were only washing off, when Christie said, "Gil here knows Permi."

"Really?" Jay looked surprised. "That guy's rad—he may join us in Colorado this fall."

Jay came down the bank to where I was standing naked with his partner, stripped off his cotton shirt and loose pants, and soon the three of us were naked in the stream, washing off and chatting like a trio of innocent school children.

Afterward, we dried off in the sun, dressed, and headed back—talking as easily as if we'd known each other our whole lives. There was something beautiful and open about the comradery that hikers seemed to share, but which was so rare in the outside world—or maybe it was just Christie's contagious innocence that put everyone at ease?

By the time we sat down to eat, I knew all about the worldwide organic farming movement, how to join, and even which farms were considered the best places for a neophyte like me. If every farm was populated with people like Christie and Jay, then maybe I needed to try my hand tilling the soil. *Nah*—farming always sounded romantic, but when you got down to it, it was really hard work. All manual labor and hauling wheelbarrows. Not for me. Still, the warmth of their open kindness made me wonder whether there was a dimension to life I was missing.

Ken and Azder had gathered wood and built a small fire. The smoke and the crackle of the logs gave the whole camp a warm homelike feeling. We gathered around it for a communal dinner with fish, fresh onions, and some wine that Ken's "mum" packed in. Syd shared some Spanish rice he'd brought, and I contributed some mashed potatoes—glad not to have to choke down another packet of Backed-up Buffet.

"So Gil here's told me he's an unfulfilled paralegal whose thinking about going back to school and this is his first backpacking trip," Christie announced a bit too openly. "What do you do Syd?"

"I'm retired," he replied. I was pretty sure he wasn't gonna get into the whole cancer thing.

"This is your first backpack?" Azder asked me in surprise.

"Yeah, it's pretty tough."

"I'll say," said Ken. "The JMT's a pretty rough place to start."

"If it wasn't for Syd here, I'd probably have quit a bunch a times, but I'm helping him finish the trail."

"If you like, you can go back with me mum," Ken offered. "She's been looking for someone to hike out with—and the four of us can take Syd."

"No way," I jumped. "Syd and I are a team." They nodded. "Actually, I'm really starting to enjoy being out here—the simplicity of everything and the people."

"We've been trying to get him into farming," said Jay.

"Backpacking really strips things down to their essence," agreed Azder.

"I also love the space it gives you for thinking," I said. "It's really helped me to work things out."

"What did you do before you retired?" Christie asked Syd.

"I was a college professor at Berkeley," he answered matter-of-factly—in the same way someone might say, *I flipped burgers at Denny's.*

"Seriously?" said Azder. "In what subject? What department?"

"Philosophy, with a specialty in East Asian thought."

"Wow, that's so cool," exclaimed Christie. "So you know all about the *Tao* and the *I Ching?*"

"I know a lot about Taosim," Syd replied, "but far less about the *I Ching.*"

"I'd love to hear more about that," she smiled. "You know I'm studying to be a teacher too."

"What do you want to teach?" asked Ken's mum.

"Not college or anything," she said looking down and uncharacteristically shy. "Probably elementary or middle school—I love working with kids."

"Christie and I are hoping to start a school like the one I attended growing up in Johannesburg," Jay interjected.

"We want to introduce a more holistic curriculum than the schools we've seen here," Christie finished.

"What would the main difference be?" I asked, especially curious 'cause as a principal, Pop had often talked about different teaching methods around the dinner table.

"It's the approach," Jay explained. "Take botany—in our middle school, the first thing we did was go outside and pick different flowers. Then we dissected them, making pencil sketches of the various parts."

"That sounds great," said Azder, "nicely combining inquiry and observation, like a scientist would, and very hands-on."

"All of our lessons were like that," Jay continued. "After, we went around the room looking at everybody's drawings, noting the similarities and differences. It was only then that the teacher introduced the names of the common parts and their anatomy. In our math lesson, we learned how to describe the swirls the leaves and branches made around the stem. Even the songs we sung that week in music and the poems we read for English all related to flowers."

"That's very different from how my science classes were taught," I reflected. "When we learned about plants, we just had to memorize the names of all the different parts—it was really boring. I think that's why I never got into science. It was always just a bunch of disconnected facts."

"That's what a lot of people think," said Azder. "Science is actually quite fun, like being a detective."

"If I were to change one thing about our school system," said Syd, "it would be to extend the day to six in the evening, when most parents get home from work. From three to six, students would do supervised homework under the guidance of teaching interns. That way in the evening, parents could spend quality time with their children, instead of pushing them to do homework. And children whose parents weren't experts in a particular subject, would still be able to get the support they needed—leveling the playing field for all children."

"What about fun?" I asked. "What about soccer, swimming, music, and after-school activities? Not every kid wants to spend their day cooped up in a classroom doing homework. Besides, how would you get the money for that?" That was the question Pop had always asked about such proposals.

"Students who are doing well could certainly participate in such activities. And I believe I know someone who'll be writing articles promoting social justice that can help garnish support for such programs," he winked at me. "Meanwhile you keep studying to become a teacher, Christie. I think you'll make a wonderful instructor."

"Thanks," she said with a deep almost motherly smile.

Writing to promote social justice? I hadn't said anything about that. But he was right, that is what I'd been mulling over going back to school for. Once again, he reminded me of Master Po—seeing the world clearly despite his blindness. Pop used to say, *If you have built castles in the air, your work need not be lost; that is where they should be. Now put the foundations under them.* I guess it was time to lay my own foundations.

When I tuned back in, Azder and Ken were busy debating the merits of genetically modified plants.

That's how it went the rest of the evening. Sitting around the campfire like old friends, chatting about everything and enjoying each other's company as the warm flames danced over the logs. Occasional claps of thunder boomed in the distance, momentarily silencing the chirping insects, and clouds rolled in obscuring the stars. But somehow it just made everything more intimate.

DAY TWENTY-FOUR

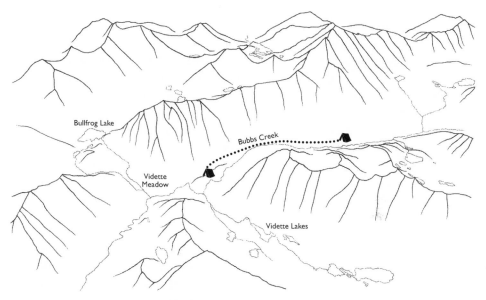

Vidette Meadow (9,570′) to Bubbs Creek (10,480′)
3 miles—910 feet elevation gain; 0 feet elevation loss

O UR HIKE TODAY was almost too easy. The weather was foggy and Syd's knee was acting up, so we'd decided to take a "nero" or near-zero day, heading just up to the treeline at the base of Forester. Jay and his group had packed up early, hoping to make the pass if they weren't blocked by thunderstorms. Meanwhile, Ken's "mum" was planning to take a zero day. *And do Sweet Fanny Adams*, as she put it, heading out the day after.

Less than two hours after we'd started, Syd stopped at a large wooded campsite, announcing that this was it. It wasn't even noon yet.

The weather had cleared as we'd hiked. The sky was deep blue punctuated occasionally by gray cumulous clouds, which like stray sheep seemed to rush off in search of their lost flock. The air had that special clarity that comes after a rain, making the nearby mountains look closer and more spectacular.

Next to our camp was a large shelf of smooth granite extending out to a beautiful swimming hole in the river. We hung a clothesline and set about washing all our stanky clothes. It'd been a while since we'd done laundry, so we washed everything except for what we wore—even our long underwear and sleeping caps got a good scrubbing. It took us the better part of an hour, but finally the long taut line hung low above the bare granite, look-ing like the cable of a suspension bridge.

Kicking back, we pulled out our bars and relaxed in the warm sun. We were halfway through eating when the thunder started up again, the clouds began congregating, and it started to pour.

"It's a Sierra shower," declared Syd. "They start fast and end fast."

Gathering up our stuff, we left our clothes hanging, heading for the shelter of my two-man tent. Syd and I huddled inside. There was just enough room for the two of us to sit up. Through the flap, we watched as the rain soaked our clothes, the bottom ones now touch-ing the rock. Syd had clipped them to the line using small plastic bread clips he'd saved as wilderness clothespins, so at least they wouldn't blow away, but they wouldn't dry either.

"What do we do about our clothes?" I asked.

"Nothing. When the rain stops we'll wring them out again—they'll be dry by dinner, you'll see."

We sat, listening to the pitter-patter on the taught fabric. It woulda been nice to play cards, but I'd mailed my deck home at MTR.

"Do you know any camping jokes?" I asked.

"No, but let me share a poem with you that I've been thinking about lately. It's by Du Fu, one of China's greatest poets from the Tang dynasty." He closed his eyes and recited,

> Alone, the wild goose refuses food and drink,
> his calls searching for the flock.
> Who feels compassion for that single shadow
> vanishing in a thousand distant clouds?
> You watch, even as it flies from sight,
> its plaintive calls cutting through you.
> The noisy crows ignore it:
> the bickering, squabbling multitudes.

We sat listening to the rain. The poem really seemed to sum him up—the lonely old philosopher calling out for his lost flock, ignored by the multitudes. It might almost be a kinda epitaph. Pop woulda understood this well. Was that who he was calling out for now?

"That's quite sad," I said finally—not giving voice to my thoughts.

"Most of Du Fu's poems have a melancholy tone," he said, opening his eyes. "The trans-lation isn't perfect, for instance in the original it's wild ducks, not crows—but I think this rendering captures the spirit better in English."

"It's strange—I never really thought the Chinese wrote poems. I mean, I guess they did. Everyone wrote poems, right? One of my friends was really into that Persian poet Rumi and all. But when you think of China, you think of kung fu, Chinese food, the Great Wall, and stuff like that—not poetry."

"That's a Western view. China has a rich poetic history and perhaps some of the greatest poems the world has ever known. Classical Chinese is an ideal language for poetry because each word is monosyllabic with a corresponding tone, resulting in a composition that is naturally musical. And each character is a picture, so a calligraphic drawing of a poem appeals visually, intellectually, and emotionally—"

"Eh, Syd?" I interrupted. "You're lecturing."

"Oh, sorry," he flushed. "I just love Asian literature so much that I get carried away whenever I have the opportunity to talk about it. Katrine used to complain too."

"At least you found a job you love. How many people get to say that?"

The rain beat harder for a few moments, then slowed.

"How much longer do you think this rain will last?" I asked.

"It's hard to say. Hopefully not that long."

We sat, watching rivulets of water run down the fly.

"I can tell you an ancient story from Zhuangzi," he offered.

"OK, if you promise not to turn it into a lecture."

"I'll try. Zhuangzi lived in the fourth century BC, during China's Warring States Period. According to legend, he spent his life wandering across China, sharing his Taoist parables. Perhaps his best-known story is *The Butterfly Dream*. In it, he dreams he's a butterfly—but upon waking, he puzzles as to whether he's a man who dreamed he was a butterfly, or a butterfly now dreaming he's a man—"

"You're lecturing again—"

"Sorry, Zhuangzi's story of *The Caged Pheasant* goes like this," he began,

> A marsh pheasant has to take ten steps to find a scrap of food.
> It must walk a hundred paces for a paltry peck of water.
> Yet despite this, it doesn't wish to be locked up in a cage.
> Even were it dining like a king, it would not be happy.

"That's us today—two caged pheasants trapped in the rain!"

"True, but with your Backwoods dinners, I'd hardly call you *dining like a king*."

We both laughed.

"You know, that story's a lot like my life in LA. I have a nice condo and all, but I feel kinda trapped. I'm not really that happy in the legal industry, but then I don't wanna be poor either. Yesterday you talked about writing, do you really think I should go back to school? Won't that cost me a lot a time and money for a job that probably pays less anyway?"

"If you're only chasing money, you'll never be happy."

"Maybe, but without money life can be pretty miserable."

"Laozi said, *When there is no desire, all things are at peace*."

"That's deep—did you ever see that old TV Series *Kung Fu?*"

"I saw a few episodes back when it aired in the seventies, why?"

"Do you remember Caine's teacher, blind Master Po, the one who called him Grasshopper?"

"Vaguely, I do recall the grasshopper thing."

"It's just that sometimes the things you say remind me of Master Po."

"Perhaps because he quoted a lot from the *Tao Te Jing?*"

"Maybe, but you really remind me of him."

He sat looking kindly, the hint of a smile on his face, exactly like Master Po.

"I have a story similar to the one about your pheasant. I don't remember where I heard it, maybe from Pop or the *Reader's Digest.* But what you said about loving your work made me think of it." I began,

> There's this businessman who goes down to Mexico. He comes across a fisherman resting in a boat by the beach. In the bottom of the boat are three large tuna. The businessman asks him, "How long did it take you to catch those fish?"
>
> The fisherman opens his eyes and replies, "Not long, maybe a few hours, why?"
>
> "Well, if you spent a little longer," the businessman suggests, "you could catch more."
>
> "True, but why would I want to do that?" asks the fisherman. "These three are plenty for me and my family."
>
> The businessman explains, "If you caught more fish, then you could sell them at the market and make a profit. Eventually you could buy a bigger boat."
>
> The fisherman asks, "What would I want a bigger boat for?"
>
> "With a bigger boat, you could catch even more fish. Eventually you could afford several boats."
>
> "Why would I want all those boats?" asks the fisherman.
>
> The businessman smiles, "Because you'd hire them out of course, you'd start a fleet. Then you'd make even more money. Eventually, you could move to the big city, and run the whole enterprise from there."
>
> "But why would I want to do that?" the fisherman asks.
>
> "That's the best part," says the businessman. "After ten or fifteen years, you could sell the whole thing. You'd have made a small fortune."
>
> "What could I do with that?" asks the fisherman.
>
> "With all that money, you could find some sleepy village to retire in, go fishing every morning, and sleep under the trees in the afternoon!" proclaims the businessman.
>
> The fisherman looks puzzled saying, "But that's what I'm doing already."

Syd smiled. "Yes, that's a famous story by Heinrich Böll. I think in the original version, it was an American tourist who encounters the fisherman."

"If you already knew the story, why'd you let me finish it?"

"Because it's a good story and because I liked the way you told it. Besides, it really gets at the heart of what Zhuangzi was saying. Chasing wealth is often like being trapped in a cage. I used to tell my kids, *Do what you love and it'll never feel like work.*"

"That's what Christie and Jay were saying yesterday. This whole trip has really made me think a lot about things I never paid much attention to."

"Sometimes we need to rediscover ourselves. Recreation is needed for *re-creation*."

The wind picked up. The tent shook, then sprung back.

"You and Ma are right. I should go back to school. I've been spending too much time chasing money and women. I need to focus more on myself, on my own feelings and needs."

"You mean you think chasing money and women has been focusing on somebody else's needs?"

The tent shuddered again.

"OK, maybe you have a point there. But what I mean is, everyone says that having a lot of money and a beautiful girl is what a guy should want, right? But isn't that just like those stories? Isn't that just a kinda material trap we get lost in? I mean, shouldn't we really be working on finding out what it is we really want, not just chasing what someone else tells us is good?"

"I think what you're saying is you need to discover what's really in your heart."

"Yeah—isn't that like what the Buddhists say, *happiness comes from within?*"

"No, it isn't," he replied curtly, sitting up a bit straighter.

"Whaddya mean? I thought the central idea of Buddhism was to be natural, to follow the *Tao*, to get in touch with yourself in order to find inner peace."

Syd remained silent for a long time, keeping his eyes closed.

Finally he said, "Those are all Western interpretations of Eastern thought. All perhaps except finding inner peace." He sat thinking for a while, then asked, "How would you define happiness, Gil?"

"Happiness is— " I struggled with the question. "Happiness is— Wait, is this a trick question?"

"No, no trick. Take your time. How would you define happiness?"

I turned the question over. Answers like, *wealth, a good companion, long life*, or *lots of time* would just be falling into his *Caged Pheasant* trap. Finally it hit me, "It's pretty simple—happiness is when you feel good."

"Certainly," he nodded, "but that's a very Western definition. That's the definition that every advertising agency in the world wants you to have, because what happens when those good feelings stop?"

"You want more?"

"Exactly. You want more. And so you go back to the marketplace looking for another product to satisfy your desire, but it never lasts, am I right?"

I nodded.

"When you finish that special meal, when you purchase that new car you've had your eye on, when you buy that certain something you've been saving up for, you feel good. But almost immediately after, the feeling fades, and you're right back on the treadmill, looking for the next thing that will satisfy you."

"You make it sound like a drug."

"It's exactly like a drug. The advertising agencies want you drugged, so you don't wake up and realize you're just chasing your own tail. You think you want all those items they're selling, but you don't. I'll bet you have a closet full of things you thought you needed but didn't."

He was right, I had half a closet filled with boxes of stuff that I'd never really used but couldn't bring myself to toss out either.

He continued, "I believe the reason people are so attached to their mobile devices is the same phenomenon. There's a moment of excitement when you get a new message or bit of interesting news, then when the feeling fades, you check it again, hoping to get another one, like those treats they train animals with."

I nodded. "You know," I gazed at the tent wall, "I hate to admit it, but that day we climbed Mather Pass—I realized that's what I've been doing with women and sex. I mean, I meet some girl, and take her out and all, but what I'm really thinking is, *How can I get her into bed?* But once I do, I'm no longer interested. So I dump her and move on."

"It's good you've been able to see that about yourself, although you don't seem to realize calling women *girls* also shows a lack of respect and objectification."

"I never noticed that—I guess I should pay more attention to my language."

"Your language reflects your thoughts. You told me before that you want to find someone to share your life with. Up until now it sounds like women and sex have just been a game for you."

"So now that I've mastered the game, I should level up? Find someone I respect and try having a relationship that lasts, instead of just trying to have sex? Is that it?"

"Mutual respect should always be the prelude to a relationship. But if you just view it all as a new game, then eventually you'll grow tired of that too. Whenever we chase feelings, we run the risk of being trapped by them. The thing that gives us pleasure becomes an addiction."

The rain fell in a sudden torrent, streaking down the fly. The air inside the tent was cool and humid and it felt cramped—scrunched up with Syd, my sleeping bag, and stuff—but I was glad for the company and shelter.

After a bit, he continued, "The sign of an addiction is that we continually crave more and more. We crave more because we're chasing good feelings, and feelings, as you've admitted, are fleeting. No, you can't just substitute one game for another. You have to do something entirely different. You have to get out of the game."

"I don't follow," I said, hoping he wasn't going to tell me to become a monk or something.

He looked at me and asked, "You try to hold on to good feelings, right?"

"Yeah."

"But you can't, because feelings are fleeting. So you chase after that same feeling again and again, hoping that the next time, it'll last."

"Yeah, OK, that sounds like what I've been doing."

"And you probably also try to avoid bad feelings, like pain and suffering, am I right?"

"Of course, no one wants to feel bad."

"Some people do. For some, pain is a kind of addiction too."

"OK, but what's your point? I mean, most people, at least most *normal people*, seek pleasure and avoid pain—that's kinda obvious, right?"

"Yes, it is. But what most people don't think about is how ephemeral those feelings are. They try to hold on to them, forgetting that they never last. An analogy that some people use to describe this is waves at the beach."

"Waves?"

"Imagine that you're standing at the beach, way down by the ocean, and waves are coming in."

"OK." I pictured a tropical island somewhere with white sand beaches and blue waves washing in.

"Now imagine that some of those waves bring pleasurable feelings. Most people would try to cling to those, to make them last, even as the water is flowing away around them and washing back out to the sea. And after the wave fades, they would seek more, trying their best to be hit by a wave of pleasure, and maybe this time hold on to it."

What he was describing sounded a lot like my life.

"Now imagine that other waves bring in painful feelings."

I pictured a dark wave heading for the shore.

"Most people would try to dodge such waves, push them away, or shake the water off them, even though some unpleasant feelings are simply unavoidable."

"Yeah," I agreed—that was kinda like how I'd dealt with losing Pop.

"The person on the beach would spend all their energy chasing and trying to hold on to the fleeting pleasurable waves, while trying to dodge and push away the painful ones."

It sounded like some sorta video game.

"That's what most people spend their lives doing. Chasing and dodging ephemeral waves of transient feelings. Trying to hold on to the good, while pushing away the bad. Even though you can't really do either, because all feelings fade, like waves on the beach."

The rain grew softer.

"OK, I get that, but what else can you do?"

"Don't play the game. Don't spend your energy on the waves. Buddhism and Eastern thought don't teach us to seek our own inner happiness. That's what Western culture and individualism teaches. Buddhism teaches *the transcendence of desire*. It teaches that because all feeling are fleeting, we must accept our feelings without trying to hold on to them or push them away. The most famous tenant of Buddhism is *desiring is suffering*. Once you understand that, you can step entirely out of the game."

"How?"

"By just letting the waves of feelings roll over you. Acknowledge them. Enjoy the good, suffer the bad, but realize that they are all just feelings, like waves of water. Don't try to cling to them or chase after them. Just accept them as they naturally ebb and flow."

"And you do that?"

"I try to. I don't always succeed. Sometimes I get caught up in trying to hold on to good feelings or avoid something that's painful. But knowing this, I generally become aware of what I'm doing and let it go. The mind likes to play tricks on us. It tries to lead us astray. Some people use the analogy of a rider guiding an unruly elephant. Our body, our feelings, our desires, even part of our subconscious mind is like a great elephant that tries to lead us away from pain, chasing whatever gives us the most pleasure—regardless of whether it's good for us or not. Our conscious mind is like the rider on the elephant's back, who must constantly strive to keep the elephant under control. It's not always easy. The elephant tries to lull its rider to sleep. Tries to bribe its rider by promising more good feelings. Or tries to anger its rider and shake him off. So the rider must stay alert and conscious of the elephant's tricks. Only then will the journey be peaceful."

"Like when someone hands you a slice of ice cream covered chocolate cake, but you know you're supposed to be on a diet?"

"That," said Syd, "is the one time I always let the elephant win."

We both laughed, listening to the music of the rain.

Maybe he was right. Maybe the secret of relationships was just observation. Just enjoying being with someone you loved, while not trying to achieve anything. Like balancing stones. Was that the secret to all happiness? Staying centered and not being swept away by the waves?

Wasn't it the same with Pop? Wasn't the best thing to celebrate those we loved while they were here, letting them return to the universe—like the waves and the water—when they passed on?

Somewhere in the distance thunder rumbled. Cautiously opening the flap, I peered out at our wet clothes. The line was hanging lower, many of the items were now touching the rock, but nothing had been blown off. Hopefully Syd was right and the storm would pass. The conversation was interesting, but it felt stifling just to sit here all day.

"What do you do when you're stuck somewhere and you just wanna pass the time?" I asked him.

"Generally, I meditate."

"That's what you were doing when I was looking at those flowers in Evolution Valley."

"Yes, it helps one to find inner balance. Some brain studies even suggest that we reach our happiest state during meditation. It's very good for relationships too. It can help you to stay calm and not be led astray by emotions. It's one way to experience the waves I talked about without clinging to them."

"Sorta like the clarity you get from walking in the wilderness?"

"It's exactly like that. The calm and clarity that come from meditation and long walks is very similar."

"Can you teach me how?"

"Sure, but don't expect too much at first, it takes practice. Begin by stretching out your legs, get comfortable, and sit like this," he got into a cross-legged position, resting his hands gently atop his knees.

It felt like I was about to do yoga or something.

"Now simply focus your attention on your breathing."

"Should I close my eyes?"

"It's up to you. Some people do, others prefer to focus on a single point."

Closing my eyes, I listened to my breath flow in and out.

"Don't count breaths or try to control them. Don't try to do much of anything. Just observe your breathing and let your mind clear."

My mind kept jumping to different things—the feel of my hands on my knees, the wet laundry, the cool moist air, the sound of rain striking the tent. I opened my eyes. "I can't do this. I keep thinking of one thing and then another."

"That's normal in the beginning. Simply accept the distractions, then focus back on your breathing. Watch your breath rise and fall. Observe it come in and go out. If you have thoughts, acknowledge them, then let them wash away like the waves on a beach."

Closing my eyes, I tried again. Each time something distracted me, I accepted it, then let it go, focusing back on my breath, watching it flow in and out. Slowly my mind began to settle. The sound of rain rose and fell gently, like my breathing. Time passed.

How was Jay's group doing? Had they made it over the pass? Where was Kydoime now? And Permi and Dylan, Lois and Clark? Was the rain just over this valley? What would the whole Sierra look like on one of those satellite weather maps?

Shit—my thoughts had wandered off. Pushing them aside, I concentrated on the rise and fall of my diaphragm. The gentle flow of air going softly in and out. Trying to do nothing. Listening to my breath.

Was I really just going to sit here all afternoon, doing nothing?

Hey! Be quiet! Stay open to the experience. Syd has a lot to teach. Relax and try something new.

What can I learn from this that isn't already in some self-help book? Did I really plan to do this every day? How would I find the time? Was I gonna join some sorta hippie commune or something?

"Syd," I said, opening my eyes, "I started following my breath, and for a few minutes I was doing OK. My mind was blank, and I felt calm. I was really getting it. But then, well, it's hard to describe, but I had all these other thoughts and I got distracted."

"Thoughts like how foolish it is to sit and meditate all day long?" he smiled, looking like Master Po again.

"Yeah, how did you know?"

"Because that's what almost everyone experiences the first time. The mind tries to trick us and distract us from what's important. They call it, *the monkey mind*, and the more you fight it, the stronger it becomes."

"Like the elephant struggling with its rider?"

"Exactly. Don't try to fight it, just acknowledge the thoughts that come to you and they'll go away."

"Whaddya mean? If I don't fight against it, won't all those annoying thoughts just keep popping up in my head distracting me?"

"That's one of the main tricks of the monkey mind. Like a pestering teenager, it wants you to argue with it. That's how it gains strength. When you argue with it, you just end up feeding it energy."

"But if I don't argue, how do I get it to shut up so I can practice my breathing?"

"It's like the waves I was telling you about. Don't try to push your thoughts away or hang on to them. Just let your thoughts wash over you. Observe them and acknowledge them. If you find yourself thinking, *I feel like a fool*, then just acknowledge the thought that *you feel like a fool*, and let the thought wash away, then focus back on your breathing. If you find yourself daydreaming, recognize it, accept that you've been distracted, then focus back on your breathing."

"OK, I'll give it another shot."

"Good. I'll meditate with you."

We both sat cross-legged, eyes closed, breathing slowly.

My chest rose and fell, irregularly at first, but then calmly and rhythmically in sync with Syd's breathing.

The rain began pounding the tent again. It didn't sound like it would let up. *Shit*—I was focused on the rain, not my breathing. OK, not a problem. I listened to the rain, that's fine, it's natural, now back to my breathing. I felt my diaphragm rise and fall again, but my mind kept drifting—paying attention to the wind, to Syd's breathing, to a rock under my butt—each time I let it go and came back to my breath.

Gradually my thoughts calmed, the distractions faded, and my breathing became rhythmic. Almost like napping.

How is this meditation different from napping?

You're that "monkey mind." I see what you're doing. I won't argue with you. Letting the thought go, I focused back on my breathing. Time passed.

I was doing it! I was really meditating. I was guiding the elephant!

Shit—I wasn't doing anything. It was that tricky "monkey mind" again, distracting me by telling me I was in control. I see what you're doing there, but it won't work. Picturing its words flowing away like waves on the beach, I focused back on my breathing.

Thoughts aren't waves, you can't sit here forever.

True, *thoughts aren't waves and I can't sit here forever*, I acknowledged, picturing the words flowing away. Listening to my breath. In, then out. In, then out.

My breathing slowed. The rain faded from my consciousness. Only my breath existed.

How long was it? Five minutes? Twenty minutes? An hour? But after a time, my legs felt cramped and my stomach empty. This wasn't the monkey mind, this was my body talking. Opening my eyes, I came slowly back to the inside of the tent, like waking from a trance.

"Syd, I have to stretch."

"That's understandable," he said lifting his gaze. "How do you feel?"

"I feel peaceful. Relaxed. Like I've just had a good nap, only I wasn't sleeping or really awake either. It's hard to describe, but once I figured out the tricks of that monkey mind, I was able to focus—although I did get distracted a lot."

"You've done very well for your first session. Meditation is like anything else, it takes practice. Try sitting for a while each day. Then see in a week or two how it affects you."

"I'll try," I said. So far no answers or insight had come to me, but it was calming, and this was only the first step. Maybe Syd was right. Maybe the answer to life's problems wasn't to be found in a self-help book, maybe the answer was really just sitting and accepting one's feelings. Calm, without desire. Like walking in the woods.

The rain had stopped, and I peeked outside. There was still a fine mist, but it looked like the sun was trying to break through. I slipped my boots on and went out. The air had a cool cloudlike quality, like I'd stepped into a new world. The pine needles were hung in tiny silver droplets reflecting the diffuse light in all directions, like a thousand tiny universes.

Walking to a distant tree, I unzipped my pants and peed. Then walked back to the clothesline. The clothes were soaked and damp. Wringing them out one by one, I left them hanging.

"It's not too bad out here," I called to Syd, "maybe we should eat?"

"Good idea."

We got our cooking stuff out. Syd pulled on his rain pants and jacket, while I sat on a garbage bag in just my T-shirt.

I looked at him sitting next to me in the mist, the lonely old goose. Had I been pushing him away 'cause of the pain I feared at his loss, rather than enjoying the time we had together? Was that what I'd done in all my relationships since college? Pushed everyone away because of my fear of loss? Maybe that was the secret—*loving also meant accepting loss.*

Thunder echoed over the distant peaks.

He said, "You know, before you study meditation they say, *Mountains are just mountains, and rivers are just rivers.* But after you begin your practice, *Mountains are no longer mountains, and rivers are no longer rivers.*"

"Yeah, I felt a little bit like that today. It was really different."

"It's a good start."

"So what do they say it's like after you master meditation?"

"After you master it?" he smiled. "Then they say, *Mountains are just mountains, and rivers are just rivers again.*"

I laughed and he laughed with me. I wasn't really sure what was so funny, but somehow the whole idea of everything we'd done was summed up in that one saying.

DAY TWENTY-FIVE

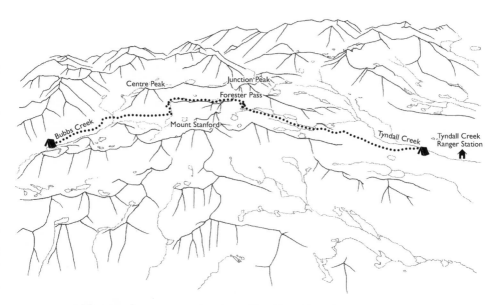

Bubbs Creek (10,480′) to Tyndall Creek (10,880′) via Forester Pass (13,110′)
10 miles—2,830 feet elevation gain; 2,430 feet elevation loss

S YD WAS SHAKING MY TENT, "Come on Gil, get up, we've got to get an early start today." It musta been four or five in the morning.

"Couldn't we do the JMT tomorrow?" I whined.

We ate huddled over our stoves, the overcast sky glowing like an old television set after you'd switched it on.

It'd drizzled on and off all night. We'd left our clothes hanging outside and they were still wet. Wringing mine out as best as I could, I squeezed them into a large sack. Only what I'd had on yesterday was still dry.

"No matter," assured Syd, "we can dry them out at Tyndall Creek when we get to camp."

My pack was seriously heavier 'cause of all the damp clothes, not to mention the wet tent. Shifting its weight around, I tried to make it sit comfortably. *Why had we done laundry yesterday? What were we thinking?* But it hadn't been anyone's fault—the sky was clear, who knew it would rain again?

The sun was below the mountains when we headed out. As we climbed, the trees began to thin, the landscape transforming into gray-brown rock shards and scattered boulders. High foreboding peaks loomed ahead below heavy gray clouds.

Beyond the tree line we came to the base of a tall ridge, its leftmost peak rising like a watchtower before the unearthly kingdom we were entering. There were no breaks in the wall of stone beyond. Could there really be a pass here?

Syd pointed at a tall peak to our right, "I believe that's Mount Stanford, which was first climbed and named by Bolton Brown."

"That must be over fourteen thousand feet!"

"Just under. Somewhere beyond it is Mount Ericsson, which Brown also named, and Lucy's Foot Pass, which he named for his wife."

A low rumble of thunder interrupted his narration.

"Are you sure the weather's gonna be OK?" I asked.

"I don't know, but so far it's holding."

Just beyond the watchtower, we entered the mouth of a large ravine. Walls of white-capped teeth jutted up on both sides, their tips scraping the shadowy gray clouds. At the far end rose a sheer granite face. A roll of thunder echoed off the walls, as if we were trespassers in some forbidden realm being warned back by the gods that dwelt there.

The trail was strangely empty. Normally we woulda seen at least one other hiker somewhere in the distance, but now there were none. *Were we the only ones foolish enough to attempt Forester today?* Except for Whitney, Forester was the highest pass on the JMT at over thirteen thousand feet. Even in good weather, I wasn't certain the two of us would make it. Biting my lip, I pressed on.

We crossed a narrow stream, the green sedge snaking down its banks the only color in this otherwise barren landscape.

Winding around rocks and boulders, we ascended into the ravine. There was still no sign of a gap or pass. It looked like we would have to scale the sheer cliff faces—my Spidey-sense was definitely tingling.

Wind echoed off the walls, wailing like the cry of ghosts. Heavy black clouds began gathering above. There was another roll of thunder, surprising me with a sudden violent explosion, but I saw no flash.

"Probably just little men playing nine pins," Syd shouted over the howling wind.

"Sounds more like Thor waging war at Ragnarök."

"Are you referring to Wagner's *Götterdämmerung, The Twilight of the Gods*?"

"No, to Thor—you know, the guy with the hammer in *The Avengers*."

Syd rolled his eyes.

We came to a solitary alpine lake. Blades of sedge grass poked up between the rock shards. The outflow becoming the narrow stream we'd crossed earlier. Beyond it the trail cut a long zigzag up the wall.

A violent gust whipped up, causing the straps of my pack to shake and vibrate. Then another roll of thunder echoed across the peaks.

We paused briefly to pump water and fill our bladders. Syd looked nervous. He was glancing repeatedly at the heavy clouds above. The wind grew stiffer, and it became increasingly hard to hear.

"If it starts to pour again, or we get lightning, we may have to turn back," he called above the wind. "But so far it looks OK. I'm hoping these clouds will blow over," he said, as if trying to make 'em go away through the power of proclamation.

We crossed the outflow and began climbing the long switchback, the trail just a narrow path through the jumbled gray rock shards. This was the back of the ridge with the watchtower and it looked like the trail would go straight up to the top.

As we climbed, the air grew thinner and my breathing deepened, the skin on my arms becoming prickly with goosebumps. We were definitely pretty high up. Syd was ahead. He seemed to be doing alright despite the rarefied air.

As we crested the ridge, the wind blasted us with renewed vigor—no longer restrained by the rock wall. The gusts shifted around, grappling with me like a Judo Master probing for a weakness in my stance. The trail ran straight along the exposed ridgetop, heading for the far wall of the ravine. Staying close behind Syd, I staggered on against the driving wind. Then it began to rain—a sideways icy windblown drizzle that stung my cheeks and arms.

We were still only wearing our thin hiking pants. Syd had on a long-sleeve buttondown, but I had only my sweaty cotton T-shirt and my hands and face were beginning to numb. The words, *cotton kills* echoed ominously through my head. The sound of Syd's teeth chattering reached me over the wind.

In silent synchronicity we dropped our packs, pulling out our stuff sacks full of clothing. Had we not done laundry, I could have worn a pair of socks over my hands like mittens, but everything was wet and useless. All I had was my yellow plastic poncho. Struggling against the howling wind, I unrolled it and drew it over my head, hoping the lightning bolt emblem of the Chargers would ward off, rather than attract, bolts. Its thin yellow plastic whipped and cracked, making a terrible din, but it was better than just my T-shirt.

"What the hell is that?!" shouted Syd after pulling on his own down jacket and fancy hooded raingear.

"It's my raingear," I shouted back over the wind and cracking poncho.

"*That's your raingear?!*" he scowled.

"You saw it before when we were under attack by mosquitos—"

"Yes, but I didn't know that was your only raingear. Where's the jacket I told you to bring?"

"I didn't take one. It was summer and all the jackets at REI cost a fortune. I figured my old Chargers poncho would be fine," I yelled, my face and hands burning in the icy rain.

He stood there flabbergasted, hand on hips, my yellow poncho flapping violently. Finally he hissed, "Let's hope it doesn't get any worse and we make it over the pass."

"Where *is* the pass?" I called back, hoping it was close.

"Somewhere up there," he shouted, indicating a narrow strip of gray stretched tightly between two peaks at the far end of the ravine. Squinting, I could just see bits of the trail winding up to it. We weren't even halfway yet.

"*Fuck!*" I spat.

"Yes, that pretty much sums it up." He pulled his pack on over his jacket and resumed hiking.

My own pack kept sliding around, making the poncho bunch up and threatening to tear its thin plastic. Fighting the pack straps and the wind, I cinched it tight, shifting it into a place where the belt and shoulder straps dug into me, but the pack sat firm. It was good enough. I hurried on after Syd.

The wind whipped and tore at my poncho, snapping it around like a flag in a hurricane. The sound drowning out even the crunching of the stone under my boots. The trail was a knife edge along the ridgetop. The wind threatened to blow us off either side. The icy drops of rain bit my face and ears. My hands were red and numb, the fingers frozen. Thunder repeatedly shook the mountains. Then it began to snow.

How the hell could it be snowing? It was the middle of fucking summer! Fuck—what was I doing here freezing my balls off up in the mountains when I could be playing volleyball down at Redondo Beach?

Somewhere ahead, I could just make out Syd's shadow plodding on through the snow. Even though we still had a long climb, we were too close to the pass to turn around. Following him, I clasped and unclasped my hands. *Why the fuck had I mailed my gloves home?*

Pushing on in slow motion against the wind, half blinded by gusts of driving snow, I reached the end of the ridge. Ahead the trail made a long traverse across the rockface before ascending again in a series of winding switchbacks, the gap above barely visible through the snow. Syd was already halfway across the traverse—at least he was ahead, how did he suddenly have so much energy?

Thunder rolled, but I pressed on. My poncho slowly becoming torn and useless in the wind. Icy water dribbled down my back, making me shiver. My face and ears burned, becoming so cold that I could barely feel the icy pellets beating against them. *Why the fuck hadn't I brought a jacket?*

The peaks shook, echoing through my frame like an immense subwoofer. Strobes of lightning lit up the driving snow. *Fuck!* Syd was up there somewhere. I couldn't see him anymore. Prodding myself on, I staggered up switchback after switchback. My hair frosting over. My hands ice. My eyes focused inches ahead on the trail—the only thing I could make out through the blinding sea of white.

Lumbering forward like a drunken zombie, like a frozen slushy, that song "Hombre Religioso" from *Nacho Libre* began playing in my head. Soon I was shouting the words above the howl of the wind, the crack of my poncho, and the blasts of thunder,

> Because you're there, when I awake
> and then you give, me a life so great
> Because the children, with you can play
> I think, I think I am . . .

The wind whipped my face. *Fuck it!* Singing for all I was worth—

> Cause when I speak, you're always there
> You even listen, what I can tell
> Cause you're my gospel, my daily bread
> That's why I think I am . . .

Getting to the chorus, I cried louder,

> I am I am, I am I am
> I think I am, I thank I am
> I'm glad I am, I'm proud I am
> A real religious man . . .

Like Popeye's spinach, the song gave me strength. Ascending turn after turn, plodding on against the rain, the sleet, and the snow, I called out—

> As I realized, you're my best friend
> Can separate, a chance from fate
> Cause you have all, I need to take
> That's why I think I am, I am, I am . . .

Lightning flashed, ice blasted my face, my poncho whipped and tore—I didn't care, bellowing,

> Cause I have prayed, I just behave
> Cause saints and sinners, aren't quite the same
> Cause it's my temple, the whole wide world
> That's why I think I am, I am . . .
> I am I am, I am I am.

Forgetting the rest, I just kept singing, "*I am I am, I am I am,*" over and over, struggling upwards against the gloom like some crazed mailman set on his appointed rounds.

The gods shook the mountains. Thunder bellowed. Lightning flashed. And then I saw the gap above, and Syd standing there waiting. Gathering up my strength, I ran in slow motion like *Rocky*, arms outstretched above me, my hands freezing in the snow, singing, "*I am I am, I am I am!*" cresting the summit in my shredded poncho.

The wind, the snow, and the cold whipped over me, but I was past caring. A brown metal sign declared, Forester Pass, Elevation 13,200 Feet. I danced around it in the wind. I'd made it to the top! Everything would be downhill from here.

"What's that you were singing?" called Syd, his hands cupped to my ear. His lips looked blue, and his arms were drawn way up inside his sleeves for warmth, but he seemed remarkably well given the cold and elevation.

"A song from a movie!" I shouted back.

"Oh, just like me," he cried into my ear, "as we climbed I kept reciting the first few verses from 'The Cloud,' you know," he recited,

> I sift the snow on the mountains below,
> And their great pines groan aghast;
> And all the night 'tis my pillow white,
> While I sleep in the arms of the blast.
> Sublime on the towers of my skiey bowers,
> Lightning my pilot sits;
> In a cavern under is fettered the thunder,
> It struggles and howls at fits . . .

"Who sang that?" I shouted, stamping my feet to keep warm in my wet clothes.

"No one—it's from Shelley."

"The poet?"

"Yes," he called into my ear, "it was better than Frost's

> The woods are lovely, dark and deep,
> But I have promises to keep,
> And miles to go before I sleep,
> And miles to go before I sleep.

—which is what I kept repeating to myself as we went over Mather."

I just let it go—this was no time for a lesson on poetry. We took a few quick photos of each of us in the snow at the pass, almost dancing to keep warm, then without a break or even dropping our packs, we started down the other side.

We wound down several steep twisty switchbacks. Then to my astonishment, the trail went right across a sheer granite face, running beneath a partially overhanging rock—gaining us a momentary respite from the wind.

Syd paused, pointing to some striations in the rock, "See these marks? This section of the trail had to be blasted out using dynamite. It was finished in 1932. Before that it ran over Junction and Shepard Passes, which are east of here. This was the only place on the whole JMT where a trail worker lost his life. An eighteen-year-old boy named Donald Downs had his arm crushed by falling rock. Despite getting a doctor up to the site to operate on him, he died later of infection."

"That's awful," I said, dancing while clasping and unclasping my hands to keep warm.

Forester Pass

"Yes, particularly given his age. There's supposed to be a plaque up here somewhere commemorating him, but we probably missed it in the snow."

I couldn't picture workers trudging up here each day with their hand tools and dynamite to cut trail at thirteen thousand feet. It was a miracle they'd only had one such accident.

"Who was Forester?" I asked rocking from leg to leg—the name vaguely recalling some British jungle explorer, or was it from an *Indiana Jones* flick?

"It was named for the U.S. Forest Service workers. It used to be called Foresters Pass, but they shortened it to Forester some years back."

It was really cold just standing here, my shirt was soaked, and I was shivering, so we moved on. The wind whipped around us, but the bulk of its force was blunted by the cliff face. To my relief, the thunder seemed to remain behind us over the pass. It was good to be heading down. As we descended, the snow began falling faster, sticking to the ground and turning everything white.

The trail made long sweeping switchbacks amidst jumbles of giant boulders. Even moving fast, I wasn't able to keep myself warm enough. Growing delirious, I started singing Bing Crosby's, "I'm Dreaming of a White Christmas," but then my teeth started chattering so much I gave up, just staggering forward.

We came to a plateau. Visibility was low, but the trail was the only smooth spot through the white jumbled rocks, so it was easy enough to follow. *What would we do if it really started piling up?* I didn't wanna think about it.

We had dropped considerably. Syd noticed my chattering teeth. "We'd better stop and eat something warm, it's nearly one o'clock, and you need to change."

Food? My stomach hurt, but I couldn't tell if it was from emptiness, the taut pack straps, or all the shivering. We hadn't had a bite since five this morning, but it was just too cold to think about eating.

Syd pointed at a pair of boulders and we trudged over. Huddling between them, we hunched down taking partial shelter from the wind and snow. Dropping my pack, I was immediately colder and began shivering uncontrollably.

"Strip off your shirt and pull on your long johns," Syd commanded.

"They're all wet," I protested, pulling the bag with my wet clothes from my pack and holding up my damp underwear up for him to see.

"Just put them on," he said, "They wick moisture and will dry quickly against your body."

"You could have told me that climbing up the pass!" I shouted, pulling off the shredded poncho and my cold wet T-shirt. My teeth chattered and my body shivered as I pulled the clammy black underwear top over my head and arms. But sure enough he was right, almost immediately I felt a bit warmer despite the dampness of the tight synthetic fabric against my skin.

Quickly removing my boots, I stripped off my wet pants, pulling on the damp long underwear bottoms. Then I replaced my soaked pants and boots as best I could—all the while balancing on one foot and then the other between the rocks, like some novice yoga practitioner.

"Here, take this," he said, handing me one of his large black trash bags.

"Whaddya want me to do with this, pick up litter?"

"No, it'll make a better raincoat than that shredded poncho."

He pulled out a small razor blade from his first-aid kit. Then, like an expert surgeon, he rapidly cut holes for my arms and head in the plastic bag as I held it stiff against the wind. Pulling it on over my long underwear, I felt immediately warmer and stopped shivering. I looked like a giant California Raisin, but it did a much better job of blocking the wet snow and wind than my flimsy poncho had.

Syd pulled out his stove and heated some water, bringing it rapidly to a boil. He made some of his tea, while I sipped hot cocoa—remembering how Ma used to make it for me as a kid after playing in the snow. Even my bars tasted better after the warm fluid. Now I knew how Solomons musta felt sheltered between two boulders up on Mount Goddard. Hiking in this weather was miserable, and I'd be glad when we could just put up our shelters, curl up inside our warm sleeping bags, and go to bed. I was right, I shouldn't have gotten up this morning—but at least we were over Forester.

Feeling a bit better, we packed up and headed on. We were like two polar explorers wandering over vast fields of arctic tundra, the first wrapped in his warm parka, the other vaguely raisinlike—with long arms and legs protruding from his wrinkled flapping body.

Eventually, we began descending again. Slowly the snow turned to rain, then the rain to mist, and finally we emerged into sparse trees and sunlight.

The trail wound through a forest. At about two in the afternoon, we encountered the first NOBOs we'd seen all day. A couple in their late forties were heading north toward Forester.

"You know it's snowing up there," Syd informed them after the usual greetings.

"We have our foul weather gear," they assured him, trying not to laugh at my large flapping garbage bag.

"It may be hard to make it over the top before sunset," Syd cautioned them.

"We're planning to camp near the base and summit in the morning," the woman replied.

"Well, good luck and stay dry," Syd offered. The couple headed north, while we continued south. I didn't envy them.

Gradually things warmed up and I was able to stop and take off my raisin suit. Finally, we reached Tyndall Creek, a lovely stream by a high alpine meadow. We made camp, stringing a long clothesline between two trees and hanging our damp clothes out in the sun to dry.

A young couple at a site about a hundred feet from ours was doing tandem yoga on a foam pad beneath the trees. The man was on his back and the woman suspended in the air above him, supported only by his arms and legs. It was surreal to watch their acrobatic dance of bending twisting poses, each dressed only in a thin black leotard, when just an hour ago we'd been stumbling through a raging snowstorm.

There was a ranger station close to camp. At around four the ranger came by to check our permit. She was a hearty looking blonde woman of about thirty. She asked if we'd seen anyone else coming over the pass.

"No," I said. "There's a couple headed north who are stopping at the base today, but other than that we didn't see anyone."

"You two were lucky," she informed us. "It's a total whiteout up there now and the snow's coming down fast."

Looking up, I couldn't even see the peaks—everything was blanketed in heavy white clouds, even though the sun was shining here.

"I was heading up to see if anyone had been caught by the storm, but if you're certain no one was behind you, then I guess it's alright."

We couldn't assure her that no one had followed us up to the pass. So just to make sure, she headed north to check things out. I didn't envy her job, but I was glad to know there woulda been someone looking out for us had we really run into trouble up there.

Syd and I ate an early dinner, the two of us sharing a cup of my warm cocoa. Afterward, we walked out into the meadow, sitting on a log to watch the gurgling stream. A small plump bluish-gray bird with a hint of chocolate on its head and shoulders was darting merrily about the bank, poking its head under the stones to search for insects.

"That's a water ouzel, also known as the American dipper," Syd smiled, "it was Muir's favorite bird."

We watched the cheery little guy playing in the streambed. When it flew off, Syd led me in another session of meditation. After the sun set, we returned to camp. My Bonfire bag had somehow managed to stay dry inside my pack. Steve had been wrong that first day— the toasty red-and-black synthetic snow-camping bag was exactly what I needed. Curling up inside it, I was soon fast asleep.

I dreamed I was playing volleyball with Kydoime at Redondo Beach—the bright LA sun shining down on her wild free hair. The restaurant at the pier was serving warm BLTs. It was heaven.

DAY TWENTY-SIX

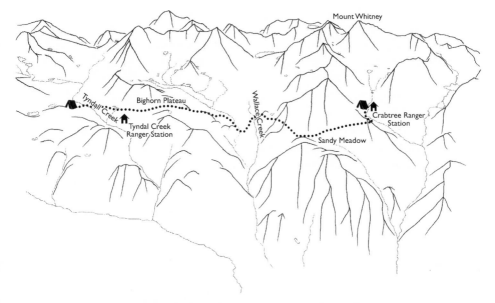

Tyndall Creek (10,880′) to Crabtree Meadows (10,640′)
7½ miles—1,160 feet elevation gain; 1,320 feet elevation loss

I N THE MORNING, we began climbing up toward the Bighorn Plateau. My legs were stiff, but it was more than made up for by having clean dry clothes. As always, Syd was ready with the details. "The plateau gets its name from the endangered Sierra Nevada bighorn sheep that live there. The sheep have massive curly horns, which they butt together during mating displays."

"Sounds like some guys I knew back in high school."

Ignoring my joke, he rambled on like the narrator of some TV nature show. I could almost picture him speaking with a British accent, *At dawn the first thing to touch the Savanna is the sun.* Why were all nature show narrators British? I couldn't recall even one that had an American accent.

Syd was looking at me expectantly. I musta missed whatever he'd just said. "How did they get here?" I asked, hoping he wouldn't notice my lapse.

It worked.

He continued, "The sheep are believed to have migrated here from Siberia during prehistoric times. There used to be thousands of them—in fact, there are ancient petroglyphs

315

depicting the sheep in many parts of Owen's Valley. But now only a few hundred remain in the wild, so it's unlikely we'll have a chance to see any. Actually, their true habitat is up on the slopes, not on the plateau, despite its name."

"What happened to all of them?"

"Some died because of trophy hunters, but most perished from diseases brought over with sheep imported from Europe. Remember, sheepherders used to graze their flocks up here before the Sierra Club helped pass legislation banning them."

"So diseases brought over by European people wiped out most of the Native Americans, and diseases from European sheep wiped out most of the native sheep?"

"You could say that," he looked down.

The plateau turned out to be a yellow-brown grassland. The surrounding peaks rose up on each horizon like granite teeth. Above us low-hanging clouds swept all the way back to Forester, making the vistas here even more dramatic.

Syd checked his map. "I believe that's Mount Tyndall," he said, pointing toward one of the distant bumps to the northeast.

Southeast of us a long range of sharp peaks ended in a broad-curving slope that rose gently to a point. It looked like the back of some great sleeping sea mammal. "What's that one?" I asked.

"That's Whitney."

"*That's Whitney?*" I croaked in surprise. "It's so close—"

"It's not as close as it looks," he dismissed, appearing somehow disquieted.

It was weird, here was Mount Whitney, our long-awaited goal. And yet his face was as ashen as Frodo's when he first saw Mount Doom.

"You don't look very excited about it."

"We still have a long way to go."

What was he talking about? Based on the map, we should be on the summit tomorrow. Was he worried about all the clouds? We had enough emergency food to hole up for an extra day or so if needed.

I changed the subject. "How could King have mistaken Tyndall for Whitney?"

The question seemed to perk him up. "King was the first surveyor to come here, and he had to navigate from the ground. There weren't any maps or trails for him to follow. He probably never stood where we are, where you can see both peaks at once." He glanced at me, "Imagine you were King, standing here without a map. Could you tell which of all these peaks is the highest?"

Glancing around, Whitney looked pretty tall, but it was also really close. Several of the more distant peaks seemed taller.

"If I had to guess, I'd pick that one," I offered, indicating a sharp solitary peak in roughly the direction of Forester.

He checked his map again. "That's Mount Ericsson, which Brown named. It's about a thousand feet lower than Whitney."

"How did King do it then?"

"By climbing up as high as he could get and sighting the various peaks. Then trying to judge, like you did, which one was the tallest. It isn't easy. Of course, he had a surveyor's level with him to measure the angles, but you can see how difficult it is—particularly for peaks of similar height where one is farther away. It was a problem all the early explorers and mapmakers faced."

"Then how did they ever get it right?"

"By triangulation. By climbing the actual peaks and measuring the angles between them. That's what LeConte spent so many summers in the Sierra doing."

"I see."

"As it turns out, there are only ten peaks in the Sierra over fourteen thousand feet tall, and Mount Tyndall is one of them. The fact that King was able to locate and climb one of these while traveling over uncharted territory is a tribute to his skill as an explorer, not his incompetence. Several years ago, the climber Daniel Arnold tried to reproduce a number of the early mountaineers' accomplishments, including King's. Taking just an old rope and what he dubbed a "hobo sack" of tied-up blankets, he discovered many of King's accounts to be more accurate than most historians give him credit for."

Syd pointed westward, "Do you see those red peaks in the distance? They're part of the Kaweah Range and the Great Western Divide. To get there you have to cross Kern Canyon, the longest linear glacially-sculpted valley in the world."

"Will we see that?"

"Not on this trip. Years ago, I hiked its length with my son. It's really quite spectacular. The High Sierra Trail runs through part of it."

"Is that another famous trail?"

"Many considered it the 'little brother' of the JMT. It was constructed around the same time and runs seventy-two miles east to west from the Giant Sequoias to Mount Whitney."

"A sorta mini-JMT?"

"You might call it that," he smiled, "it's actually a gorgeous and fairly challenging trail that can be completed in about a week. Unfortunately, it's also become quite crowded. I think the best way to see the Sierra is just to pick some lesser-known trails and make your own route. That's what your father and I used to do."

"Then why are we following the JMT?"

He didn't answer, glancing off in the direction of Whitney with a heavy look in his eyes.

As expected, we didn't see any sheep up on the plateau. Following a steep descent, we passed the junction with the High Sierra Trail just before Wallace Creek, which was wide but didn't look more than ankle deep. Stopping on the bank, we ate several of our remaining bars and filtered water. As we were relaxing several black and gray birds, which Syd had taught me were Clark's Nutcrackers, began cawing in alarm. Less than a minute later, a pair of tall well-tanned guys came jogging up. They had on spandex shorts, dirty sweat-stained T-shirts, and were carrying tiny backpacks. Their shoes were more like heavy sneakers than hiking boots. One had curly black hair, the other blond, their well-muscled legs were streaked with mud.

"How far to Crabtree?" the dark-haired guy gasped, pausing to catch his breath.

"About four miles," Syd answered.

"That's great," breathed the blond, who was bent forward with his hands on his knees, "we can make that in under an hour."

"Where are you coming from?" I asked.

"Yosemite," the guy with the dark hair said proudly. "This is our eighth day. We're running the whole trail. We've been averaging almost thirty miles a day," he panted, "but we're almost at the finish line now."

"Looks like we'll be able to make Guitar Lake before dark, catch the sunrise on Whitney, and jog out tomorrow," huffed the blond to his friend.

"Well, gotta run," the dark-haired guy exclaimed. The two strode across the creek, heading up the far bank at a fast clip. They were soon gone from sight.

Syd's face was all scrunched up in consternation. "I can't stand that," he scowled. "What's the point of hiking the trail if you never slow down enough to actually see anything? There's no goddamned *finish line* at Whitney. Why are people always so focused on arbitrary goals, instead of paying attention to where they are now?"

"What happened to *hike your own hike*?"

"True," he said, calming a bit. "But they're missing the whole point—everything will just whiz by in one big blur. They won't actually *see* anything. At that pace, they might as well be riding in a car. And when they get home, they'll brag to everyone about how *fast* they did it—when in fact the real prize, the intangible rewards, go to those who take it slowly."

"Maybe they find their own bliss through cross-country trail running?"

"Maybe, but hiking should be what Zhuangzi called, *carefree wandering*. You know there's an often-quoted passage reputed to have come from Muir," he said and then recited,

> People ought to saunter in the mountains—not hike! Do you know the origin of that word saunter? It's a beautiful word. Away back in the Middle Ages people used to go on pilgrimages to the Holy Land, and when people in the villages through which they passed asked where they were going, they would reply, "A la sainte terre," "To the Holy Land." And so they became known as sainte-terre-ers or saunterers. Now these mountains are our Holy Land, and we ought to saunter through them reverently, not "hike" through them.

"I agree with you—and Muir," I said. I was always impressed by his ability to quote whole passages like Pop had. "But you're not gonna get everyone to see the joy of slowing down. Nor do I think those guys will ever be able to show you why they love running so much."

"It doesn't matter," he said flatly. "That whole thing about sauntering—it's probably a fabrication anyway. It's from a short book by Reverend Albert W. Palmer, who was an early Sierra Club member and author of a number of spiritual texts. Palmer attributed the passage to Muir, but it's just as likely a rendition of Thoreau's speech 'Walking.' Even the etymology is questionable. Perhaps you're right. Perhaps running is how some people best enjoy the trail."

He sat and stewed a while. For some reason, the two trail runners had really irked him—or maybe something else was bothering him, it was hard to tell.

Of course there was no "right" way to enjoy the wilderness—everyone came here with their own needs and expectations. But I did agree that to really experience the trail, you had to stop and reflect along the way. Maybe his frustration was simply a universal compassion for everything the modern world had given up in its pursuit of speed. *You can't hurry up and relax*, Pop used to say. While walking out here time and consciousness expanded. There was something special about traveling on foot. It'd taken me weeks on the trail to see this, but the real value of wilderness lay in its expansiveness. In the space and solitude it afforded for reflection. It was a universal yardstick. A place to gauge our humanity and measure our very souls by. A space to reorientate ourselves and re-create our spirits.

Eventually Syd calmed down and asked, "Shall we go?"

We waded across the shallow water, then headed up the far bank, *a la sainte terre*. The trail climbed for about a mile, then wound its way around the edge of a high alpine meadow. Suddenly we both halted. Standing in the meadow not more than twenty yards away was a full-grown bear. It was staring straight at us.

We stood transfixed. Silently, I took the perfect photo—the sun behind the bear illuminating each raised hair with a golden-brown glow. The bear eyed us a while longer, then bolted.

"That was incredible," I gasped.

"Yes, and this time you didn't even scream."

"This time I wasn't afraid."

"I'm glad to hear it," he said, patting my shoulder.

We stood a while, catching our breath.

"Syd," I asked, "how come you didn't bring a camera or anything to take pictures with?"

"I used to own a really nice 35-millimeter camera," he said. "You know, the kind people used to use before digitals."

I nodded, recalling Ma's old Minolta.

"And I knew how to use it too. Back in the day, I took some spectacular outdoor photos. Did your father ever show you the one I made for him of some whitebark pines up on a bluff?"

"The one where the trees look like they're dancing?"

"I took that."

"Pop had it framed up on our living room wall. That's a beautiful photo. I always thought it was done by a professional."

"*It was!*" he said. "Or semiprofessional at least. For a time, I even developed my own prints. It was a hobby of mine."

"But if you're such a great photographer, why didn't you bring a camera? Is it because everything's gone digital?"

"It's not because of the digital thing—although they still haven't matched the magic of film. No, I own a digital camera, but I chose to leave it at home."

"Why?"

"One summer when I was about forty, I was up in the Yosemite backcountry taking photos as usual. When suddenly it dawned on me that I wasn't able to see *Yosemite* anymore. All I could see was how this meadow or that sunrise would look like in a photograph. I had lost all personal awareness of my true surroundings."

"You mean your lens was blinding you from seeing things through your own eyes?"

"Exactly. And not just seeing—*feeling*. From then on, I left my camera at home, except of course on family vacations, so that I could directly experience everything around me."

"That's a lot like slowing down when you're on the trail."

"Precisely."

"But what about me? I still wanna capture things like that bear to show others when I get back."

"There's nothing wrong with that. Just don't let it get in the way of experiencing things, like I did."

I nodded. We continued along the edge of the meadow, my senses heightened, experiencing the subtle shifts in the color and texture of the grass as the breeze caressed it. The smells of wood, earth, and meadow each filled my nose as the breeze shifted round. Even the texture of the soil felt different as we stepped over it. These were the subtle things you could only experience at foot speed. Syd was right—a camera could distract you from it all. Maybe even my boots were too much? Maybe like Caine in *Kung Fu*, I should tread barefoot through the wilderness, experiencing the feel of the earth under my feet? But the sharp rocks and pebbles dissuaded me from trying.

Syd looked at me as if he knew what I was thinking, "Edmond Hillary, the man who first climbed Everest said, *It is not the mountain we conquer, but ourselves.*"

We continued on, walking together in spiritual silence.

Maybe even our so-called knowledge and our attempts to filter the universe through our crude tools of words and language got in the way of direct experience? That bear probably experienced nature more directly than we ever could. Maybe that was the secret of walking in the woods and the meditation Syd was teaching me—directly experiencing, without language. Maybe all philosophical musings were just attempts to express with words what words never could express?

Growing along this section of trail were a number of strangely-shaped trees. Twisted like whitebark pines, but they were smaller with shorter denser needles. "What kinda trees are these?" I asked, pausing to examine them.

"They're foxtail pines, the kind Permi told us about."

"They do kinda look like foxtails—but not in the way I imagined."

"That's why a movie is never as good as a book—because it never perfectly fits our imagination. Just like everything I read about the trail hasn't been the same as hiking it. And even then, it won't be the same for everyone, or even every time."

"Do you think words and language also distract us from seeing our true surroundings?"

"I do."

"Kinda like what you said at the hot spring—*The Tao that can be told, is not the true Tao.*"

"That's right," he grinned, "that's exactly right."

For a moment it felt like I was his son, or he was Pop—that we were joined together by something beyond this world. I stared at the wise old trees. Most had stood here since before Muir's time. They'd witnessed everything from the construction of the trail to our presence now. To these venerable sages, even our foot speed would seem fast. What ancient memories and wisdom did these trees hold? What would they tell us if we could understand them? Maybe to them, we were the joggers who needed to slow down?

We hiked on. My feeling about Syd lingered. Was there some special connection between us? Something beyond what could be expressed with words?

Fresh clouds began rolling in, then it started to drizzle. By the time we reached Crabtree, it was raining and I was dressed in my plastic raisin suit again. Just before the campground, the trail split. One branch headed down to the ranger station, the other continued on to Whitney. Close to the intersection was a large bin. Syd went over to examine it.

"What's that for?" I asked.

"It looks like this is where we get our WAG bags."

"What's a WAG bag?" It sounded like something for dogs.

"It stands for *Waste Alleviation and Gelling.* Whitney's a pretty fragile environment. In the old days, there were pit toilets up there. But now there are too many hikers, so the Forest Service asks everyone to carry a WAG bag and pack out their own waste."

"*We've gotta shit in the bag?*"

"Once we're in the Whitney Zone, yes," he affirmed. "We'd better each take one."

"And what do we do once we fill up the bag?"

"We carry them out to the trailhead in our packs," he said flatly—as if carrying a bag full of shit, gelling powder or no, was an everyday thing to do—like packing a sandwich.

Still, we each took one bag. The whole idea grossed me out. Even my triple ziploc bags of used toilet tissue bothered me—but it was better than scattering California Whiteflower everywhere. My unstated plan was to take a really good dump in the morning, then hold my bowels until we reached the toilets at the parking lot. But I pocketed a WAG bag just in case.

The campground at Crabtree Meadows was deserted, maybe because of the weather, so we had our choice of spots. I'd been hoping we would catch up to Kydoime again, or at least one of the other people we'd met on trail. But it also seemed fitting for just the two of us to finish it together.

After setting up camp, we sat beneath the partial shelter of a pine. I ate my usual Backwoods meal, while Syd just sipped some of his tea saying he wasn't hungry yet.

"If the rain gets any worse," he said, "we might need to spend another night here because of the danger from lightning up at the summit."

Please let there be sun, I prayed. It's not that I wanted to leave the trail, I'd gotten used to things out here and was more nervous about going back. It's just that I didn't wanna eat any more Backwoods Buffet. There were three packets left in my canister and as far as I was concerned, when we got back *they* were going in the WAG bag!

Syd set his watch alarm for four-thirty, saying we'd need an early start. So after cleaning up, we tucked in. There wasn't much to do out in the drizzle anyway. Trying to sleep, I lay awake listening to the rain, then practiced my meditation. Eventually the soft pattering slowed and I drifted off, lulled by the music of the rain.

DAY TWENTY-SEVEN

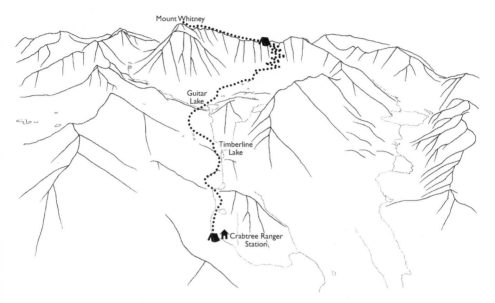

Crabtree Meadows (10,640′) to Whitney Summit (14,505′)

9¼ miles—3,800 feet elevation gain; 175 feet elevation loss

I'D SLEPT FITFULLY and was already awake when Syd's alarm went off.
The air smelled of rain. "How's the weather look?" I called over to his bivy.

"I think it's going to clear up," he called back.

Snapping on my headlamp, I began packing my gear.

A shadowy half-moon hung above us struggling to be free from the heavy clouds. Shivering in my long johns and T-shirt, I choked down my oatmeal while Syd finished packing. He was all layered up in his down jacket and raingear and I envied him. There was always the black plastic trash bag, but I really didn't want to be a giant California Raisin again.

"Aren't you gonna eat?"

"Later," he replied.

"What about the herbs Permi gave you?"

"I finished them yesterday with my tea. I think they helped."

That was good. I knew how he felt about eating—it was just too early for breakfast.

We walked in the dim moonlight, following the shadowy outline of the trail. We moved swiftly and silently, propelled by our need to keep warm. Sparse trees and rocks loomed like monsters in the morning mist, the distant mountains dark silhouettes against the cold gray sky.

"Did you notice that we're heading east now?" asked Syd trying to make conversation. "Most of the trail runs north to south. But here it turns eastward toward the great sawtooth divide that separates the Sierra Nevada from its drop-off into the desert at Owens Valley."

All I could do was nod and let him prattle on. It was too early for chitchat.

"The Whitney Range is composed of the tallest sharpest peaks in the continental United States. If this weather clears, we should be standing on the summit this afternoon. Otherwise, we may need to camp up around Guitar Lake. Over the years a number of hikers have been struck by lightning up on Whitney, so we'll just have to keep a sharp eye on the weather."

It was good he was being cautious. We climbed on, passing shadowy ponds and meadows. Slowly the glow over the eastern ridge brightened and the yellow sun crested the mountains, warming our bones and driving away the mist like fleeting ghosts. Before long the last lingering clouds dispersed and the sky became a clear blue, auguring well for our summit attempt.

By the time we reached Timberline Lake, the sun was well above the peaks and the air had become so warm we were forced to stop and strip off our morning layers. Removing my long underwear beside the trail I felt as comfortable as in my own bedroom, my body an extension of the natural world around me.

Pulling out one of my last granola bars, I chewed it slowly. Syd still ate nothing. My pack was noticeably lighter today, now that all of my clothes were dry and my bear canister was nearing empty. Soon we would have real food again!

Beyond the lake the trail became steeper, winding its way up through the foothills. Syd had begun to slow his pace a bit, which was understandable with the gain in elevation. Less than an hour later we crested a ridge and were looking down at Guitar Lake, easily recognizable by its shape. "Who named this one, Jimmy Hendricks?"

"Clarence King," he replied wiping his brow, It was getting pretty warm out.

The trail wound down to the lake, climbing back up the rocks on the other side. Yet another down then up that only served to add to the number of feet we would have to climb today. Somewhere in the guidebook I'd read that the total elevation gain heading SOBO on the JMT was forty-seven thousand feet 'cause of all the ups and downs. That worked out to about nine vertical miles, or two trips up Mount Everest from sea level. No wonder my legs were so buff.

Guitar Lake was the last reliable water source this side of Whitney, so we stopped to fill up. Even though camping is discouraged here, someone had pitched a small blue tent on the far side of the lake.

"Probably a PCT hiker or backpacker climbing Whitney for the sunrise, then packing out this afternoon," said Syd. "It's really hard to get a permit to climb Whitney from the eastside, so a lot of people hike around and climb it from here."

"Why's it so hard to get a permit?"

"Too many people want to say they've stood on the highest point in the continental U.S. and it's a very fragile environment up there. So there's a permit lottery, like there is for the JMT. The sad part is, many of those who get a permit aren't really prepared, or don't realize how difficult it is, and never make it to the summit—which wastes a space for someone who could. But fair is fair, and you've gotta give everyone a chance. I just wish they'd read up a bit more on what they're getting into. It's not a walk in the park. Many of them don't make it simply because they didn't train for it or didn't start their ascent early enough."

"You mean like getting up at four-thirty?"

"Exactly. The climb up Whitney from the eastside is twenty-two miles round trip, with a gain of over six thousand feet. The average day-hiker takes about twelve to sixteen hours to do it, so they need to start out at around three in the morning with headlamps to make the summit in daylight. And even so, they probably won't get back to their car until well after sunset. It's a grueling hike."

"Wait, I thought you said you've never been up Whitney."

"I haven't. And I wouldn't want to do it that way. If I were planning to climb it from the East side, I'd take a backpack and do it in stages—giving myself enough time to acclimate on the way up. You've seen how I do at altitude, going up to fourteen thousand feet in a day would be too much for me."

"What time do you think we'll reach the summit?"

"This side isn't as bad a climb, but we're carrying full packs. I'd expect we'll be on top sometime around two or three."

Two or three? It was only ten! How could the peak be that far above us?

Syd was pumping a lot of water, even for him.

"Do you think I have enough?" I asked.

"You have three liters, right?"

I nodded.

"That's plenty—but I want a bit extra today."

Syd filled his CamelBak, his water bottle, and even his extra four-liter collapsible pouch. *Why did he want so much?* At least if I needed water, I'd know where to find it.

Passing Guitar Lake the trail started to climb sharply, ascending rock shelves resembling titanic stairs. Finally we reached the base of a series of switchbacks up a very steep-looking slope. Breathing was already getting hard.

"How high up are we now?" I huffed.

"About twelve thousand feet."

That was the elevation of many of the so-called high passes we'd been over, but here we were only at the base. *Fuck.* "So we have over two thousand feet more to the top?"

"That's about the size of it."

"*Shit*, I thought Forester was bad—"

"At least it isn't snowing."

There was that.

We started up the first of the long switchbacks. Syd lagged behind, probably 'cause of all that water he was carrying. What was he trying to do? Set a record for hauling the most water up Whitney? At two pounds a liter, he was carrying at least sixteen extra pounds. Not as bad as a bear canister stuffed with food, but was he really gonna drink all that? Stopping, I munched on another granola bar while waiting for him to catch up.

He arrived shortly after I finished the bar and stood there catching his breath. Sweat was running down his brow and his lips had a tinge of blue, but it was nothing outta the ordinary. After almost a month of hiking together, we'd learned to read each other pretty well. When he was ready to go again, I followed to make certain he was OK.

The trail wound on and on up the rock face. Syd was stopping more and more often to catch his breath, making it hard for me to get into a rhythm. But each time he stopped I waited patiently. *We were gonna do this together.*

At the top of one of the long switchbacks he stumbled, teetering dangerously near the edge. Darting forward I caught him just before he tumbled over. His pack was clearly top heavy. He stood breathing rapidly as I steadied him, and we backed away from the edge. I helped him to remove his pack—the damn thing weighed a ton!

He curled up against the rock wall. "Too heavy," he gasped.

"It's all the water. *Why did you take so much?*"

"I'll explain later—"

"OK, take it easy. We can do this. Why don't I take some of this load for you?"

Dragging his pack over to the side, I pulled out the heavy bladder and brimming pouch. He tried to object, but I loaded them into my own pack, leaving him just the small bottle for the way up.

He muttered a brief, "Thanks."

When he was ready to go, I hoisted my pack on and followed. It felt like I was carrying a small hot tub the way my pack sloshed around with all the extra weight, but at least Syd seemed steadier and his pace a bit faster. Tightening my belt and trying to shift the new load into a more comfortable position, I continued up the long switchbacks.

Gradually my legs fell into their accustomed climbing rhythm, accompanied by my mantra—*And I'm climbing my staircase to Heaven*—looping over and over again in my head. This was it—our last stairway to Heaven.

My mind drifted across the rocks and scenery, mixed with thoughts of BLT sandwiches, but mostly it was blank. Climbing and meditation had blended. Even the "monkey mind" was too exhausted to pester me here.

The air grew progressively thinner. My breathing deepened, the weight of all that water pressed down on me, and my pace slowed. It was like climbing in slow motion. Syd was dragging too. Slowly it grew cooler, the temperature dropping the higher we went.

Step after step we trudged on. How many switchbacks was it now? I'd lost count. Slowly we gained on the ridge. Syd and I making our final ascent of the trail, together.

There were strange rock formations here. Curves and arches. Vertical orange pillars. They'd make great photographs—*fuck it*—it would take too much energy to pull my camera out and this pack was just too damn heavy. Time lost all meaning. Our only goal now was to reach the ridge. Then rounding one of the never-ending switchbacks, there was a gap in the rocks; a sorta flat camping area piled around with low stone walls. *Who the fuck would camp way up here?* Just beyond it was a small metal sign and a junction. *We'd made it—the ridge!*

The sign said it was 1.9 miles to the summit, and just 8.7 down to Whitney Portal and my BLT. This was the highest pass on the whole trail—some 13,600 feet above sea level. But before we could head down, we'd ascend an additional nine hundred feet up to the top of Whitney—the official end of the JMT.

To the right was a wide ledge. Syd dropped his pack, setting it down carefully against the wall. Dropping my own pack with a thud, I set it next to Syd's. We both collapsed in the shade of the wall catching our breath. A steady stream of day-hikers passed us, huffing and puffing on their way to the summit. Those returning had a look of relief and exultation on their brows. The top was less than two miles away now!

"Harder than I expected—" he said finally, "and no food—"

"Whaddya mean, no food?" I asked. "Did you run out? Why didn't you tell me? I've still got several bars left!" I reached for my pack.

"No, no," he said still laboring to breathe. "Don't want it. I've got food. I'm not eating. I'm fasting—"

"Fasting? Whaddya mean fasting?"

He caught his breath, took a long sip of water, coughed, then spoke haltingly, "I'm fasting today. Since yesterday. Just water. Didn't want to tell you. Didn't want to worry you. Gonna sit on the mountaintop tonight. And meditate. It's a vision quest."

"Vision quest? What the fuck are you talking about?"

"Native Americans. When they sought a vision. An answer. Would fast to purify their bodies. Then sit atop a sacred mountain. Waiting for a vision," he panted. "That's what I'm going to do. No tent. No bivy. I'm going to sit on the summit and pray. That's why I took all the water. I read somewhere Mount Whitney is sacred to the Paiutes. They call it, Tumanguya, the very old man. They believe the spirit watching over them resides here."

"What are you, nuts?" I lost it. "You haven't eaten in a day, you almost fell off the fucking mountain, and now you're planning to sit up all night freezing your ass off on a fourteen-thousand-foot peak searching for a message from *Tumanguya*—like Linus waiting for the *Great Fuckin' Pumpkin?* What if it rains? What if it snows? What if you freeze to death? Or get sick again? What if you get struck by lightning?"

"It's a clear day. I'm searching for a vision. An answer to the question I came out here with. It's important to me. If the weather changes, I'll take shelter, or come down. I promise."

"OK, *fuck it.* You're nuts, you know that right? But OK. I'll stay too. I'll stay with you and camp on the highest goddamn peak in America, just to make certain you're alright."

"No, Gil. After we summit, I want you to go down. I want you to wait for me at Trail Camp. It's the first campsite on the other side of this ridge. I have to do this alone. I'll be down in the morning. After dawn. I want you to wait for me below."

"No way! Not after all we've been through. We're a team now! If you stay on the summit then so am I. We're finishing this thing together!"

"No Gil. I know you want to do this for me, but this is my own thing, and I need to do it alone. Part of caring for someone is knowing when to let go—"

"Shit—do you know what you're asking after all we've been through? You're nuts. You know that right?"

"Perhaps, but wait for me below. If I'm not down by noon, come back up and find me."

"OK," I agreed reluctantly. He smiled, and that was that. There was nothing else to say.

He had me put the water back in his pack, then passed me his filter, "Here, you'll need this."

It didn't feel right, but this journey had been his dying wish, and he had to experience it in his own way. Taking the filter, I stuffed it into my pack.

He rested about fifteen minutes more, then declared, "Shall we go summit the highest peak in the contiguous United States?"

"Let's do it," I said, now more worried than excited.

Reaching for my pack, he stopped me, "You can leave that here and pick it up when you come down. Just bring some snacks, water, warm clothes, and any valuables. No one will touch your pack. And no one will carry it down for you," he chuckled.

Syd strained as he lifted his old green Kelty, weighed down again with all the water.

"At least let me carry that for you."

"No, I appreciate it, but this last part is something I must do myself."

He swung his pack on, the folding shovel swinging back and forth, reminding me again of a pendulum.

The walk from the trail junction wasn't easy. We had to scramble up and down over large rocks and boulders. Syd struggled visibly under the weight of his pack but refused all help. People with daypacks and much cleaner clothes were huffing up and down the trail in both directions. Many passed us, but others had to stop every few feet to catch their breath, reminding me of how we musta looked that second day on Donohue.

The way to the summit followed the ridge up a gentle arc, as if we were scaling the back of that great sea mammal I'd pictured from the Plateau. The way was lined with jutting orange rocks twisted into grotesque goblinlike statues.

After an hour, we reached a series of rocky fins with narrow openings between them. It was frightening peering down at the desert floor ten thousand feet below.

Passing these, we wound our way up a slope of broken rock slabs. Nearing the crest, we saw a small stone building with a gabled roof of corrugated sheet metal. It looked like a weather station, dotted with various meteorological instruments. Beyond it in every direction were rocks and sky. *It was the summit!*

The building was locked. A sign read, *Research station, no admittance. Severe lightning danger in storm.*

Syd dropped his pack, looking relieved. It was a bit chilly and a steady breeze was

Mount Whitney Summit Shelter

blowing, but nothing like Forester. Other hikers were standing on the rocks taking photos. Several were even wearing shorts.

"Why did they lock the doors?" I asked.

"Because a number of people have been killed by lightning while sheltering inside. Did you notice the metal roof?"

"A metal roof at the top of a mountain? Who designed this place, *Benjamin Franklin?*"

"No," he said, apparently taking me seriously. "It was built by Gustave F. Marsh, an engineer from Lone Pine. The Whitney trail and summit hut have an interesting history. Ever since Whitney was first summited, various researchers have come up here to conduct scientific experiments. They even planned to build an observatory once, but the project never really got off the ground."

"Ha, ha, ha," I said dryly—he couldn't be doing that badly if he was able to crack jokes and lecture on history.

He flushed, "Sorry, I didn't mean that to be a pun."

"Actually, the first trail from Guitar Lake to Lone Pine was a stock trail made by Buffalo Soldiers, who were sent to protect the park from loggers, poachers, and sheepherders. The work was carried out in 1903 under the command of Captain Charles Young, a graduate of West Point, and the first Black Superintendent of a National Park."

"In 1903?"

"Yes, there's a whole history of Buffalo Soldiers working in the National Parks that few seem to know about. And if not for racial prejudice, Young would likely have become the first Black American general."

"That's impressive." He nodded.

"Shortly after the stock trail went in, two prominent scientists met up here to discuss using the summit as a research station."

"Why'd they need it so high up?"

"One planned to measure solar radiation and the other was trying to detect whether water existed on Mars. Both decided Whitney would be ideal for minimalizing atmospheric interference. Under the direction of Marsh, the initial stock trail was improved for the transportation of scientific instruments up to the summit, and in 1909 the Smithsonian Institute Shelter was completed."

"So wait, this building is over a hundred years old?"

"Yes, although nowadays most people have forgotten its history and simply call it, The Mount Whitney Summit Shelter."

"Did their experiments work out?"

"I'm not sure any of them did. They were plagued with difficulties, like altitude sickness, getting their instruments up the trail, and electrical storms. In one report, the scientists described their hair standing on end and sparks jumping off the brass buttons of their coats."

"What did they expect with a metal roof?"

"In the end the shelter was abandoned. For a time, it became something of a dump, because hikers left trash and graffiti inside. Then following several fatalities involving lightning, the shelter was sealed."

"Are you sure you're going to be OK up here?"

"The sky is clear today. I should be fine. If it starts to cloud over, I'll come down."

He was right, the sky was a cloudless cobalt blue, and his breathing did seem better.

"Look," he pointed, indicating a heavy book with a sturdy metal cover fastened to the side of the building, "it's the summit register. We can add our names."

The last entry in the book looked like it was written in Chinese. "Can you read that?" I asked.

He examined it, then smiled. "Remember I told you about that famous poet Du Fu?"

"The one with the poem about the goose?"

"This entry was written by a Chinese hiker named Haihong who included two lines of another Du Fu poem. It's called, "Gazing at Mount Tai," which is the easternmost of the five sacred mountains of China."

"What does it say?"

"It literally reads, *If you reach the very top, all of the other peaks seem small.*" He became contemplative, then said, "Or perhaps it's better translated a bit more poetically as, *Climbing to this lofty height, all is dwarfed within my sight.*"

"Nice," I said, impressed by how fast he'd come up with a rhyming couplet. "It's certainly true—everything is far below us now, you really can see for miles."

We each wrote our name and the date in the register. Next to them Syd added, *We hiked the Muir Trail together from Tuolumne Meadows to Mt. Whitney.*

I wanted to add something about Syd having done the hike with terminal cancer, but in the end couldn't think of anything appropriate, not wanting to publicly announce his illness. So I added simply, *Happy to see my friend succeed!*

"Hey, do you think Kydoime, Permi, Rena, and everyone else will have signed the book too?"

We flipped back almost a week to find Permi and Dylan's entry. Dylan had simply written, *JMT× 4* next to his name, but Permi had added, *Syd, hope you get to record your name here. Peace! Your friend, Permi.*

Syd wiped away a tear. Then we began working back through all the entries. Two days after Permi and Dylan's entry, we found Rena and Kitty's. They'd summited together and had drawn cute pictures next to their names. Rena had drawn a bearlike anime Totoro, and Kitty, of course, had drawn a cat's face.

Two days before we got here we found Kydoime's entry. Even exiting at Onion Valley, she'd reached Whitney before us. All she'd added was, *Amazing views, amazing trail, amazing people!* Had she been thinking of me when she wrote it?

Those were all the people we knew that we could find in the register. We searched twice for Jay, Christie, Ken, and Azder, but couldn't find them.

"They were probably up here yesterday and skipped the summit because of the rain," suggested Syd.

Maybe tomorrow Lois and Clark would see our entries? They were probably a day behind us 'cause of the weather.

Closing the book and carefully fastening its metal cover, we strode together to the very top.

Climbing up the final rocks, we had a day-hiker take several pictures of us standing arm in arm at the edge of the precipice, the two of us together at the top of the world! The view was amazing, and we stood for some time looking down toward Owens Valley, then back over all the peaks we'd crossed. The view seemed to stretch on to eternity.

Finally, we headed back to the shelter. There was a metal plaque on one of the rocks that read, *National Park Service, U.S. Department of the Interior, Mount Whitney Elevation 14,496.811 feet, John Muir Trail—High Sierra Trail, September 5, 1930.*

"Wait, I thought you told me Whitney was 14,505 feet tall?"

"Actually, the official height has been revised many times. Clarence King first estimated it at over 15,000 feet, but remember, he liked to exaggerate things. Later barometric measurements put it at around 14,900 feet. Since then, the peak has been surveyed numerous times. Modern satellite measurements now have it at 14,505 feet, which I think is good enough—but who knows, maybe next year they'll change it again. Anyway, because this is a historic marker, they left it here. I believe there are a couple of others up here as well, all probably indicating different elevations from different surveys."

That made sense. There was a special area a little away from the hut where people had built up rock walls for camping. Syd brought his pack over and set out his air mattress. It didn't look like anyone else was crazy enough to camp up here, although obviously people had.

"Are you certain you want to do this? It's not too late to go back down."

"Yes, I'm certain," he replied, looking somewhat fatigued.

It had to be due to lack of food—fasting on a hike like this was nuts—but it could also be 'cause of his illness or the thin air. His lips weren't as blue as they'd been on previous passes, and his breathing sounded OK, so it was probably just the food.

"Are you sure you don't want me to stay?" I asked again. It was almost irresponsible of him to stay up here, but it was important to him, almost sacred, and having spent this much time together, I knew there was no way to change his mind.

"There's no one up here to help you out if you run into trouble. I could hike back down, grab my pack, and make it back here before sunset."

"I need to do this myself. Don't worry, I'll be fine."

"Are you really gonna sit outside all night? It'll be freezing—"

"I have my pack, my bivy, and my sleeping bag if it gets too cold. This isn't my first night on a mountain you know."

His eyes told me it was time to go. Giving him a long hug, I swallowed back my tears. *Was I really going to leave him here after everything we'd been through?*

Pulling on his jacket, he sat down cross-legged on his mattress and gave me a smile. Then he began his slow meditative breathing staring off at the distant sky. Waving silently, I turned and started down the trail, turning around twice more to see him sitting there in meditation. The third time I turned, the curve of the ridge blocked my view and I could no longer see him.

Torn, I continued on, fearful that this might be the last time I saw my friend and mentor. It felt like my not being there for Pop all over again.

We'd spent so many days on the trail together that it was strange to be alone now—like Caine in *Kung Fu* leaving the shelter of his beloved Shaolin Temple to head off for exile for America.

Time seemed to slow like in a dream. At least an hour passed, but it seemed like seconds later that I reached the junction with my pack. Just as Syd had promised, it lay unmolested against the rock.

Resting a while, I had some water and another bar. My heart tugged at me to go back, to camp with him, and make certain he was safe. But he had wanted me to wait below. Swallowing, I strapped my pack on and headed over the ridge.

DAY TWENTY-EIGHT

Whitney Summit (14,505′) to Whitney Portal (8,430′)
13 miles—50 feet elevation gain; 6,125 feet elevation loss

THE SUMMIT was draped in long cold shadows, a dull glow building on the horizon blotting out all but the brightest stars. Nothing stirred. A chill wind swept across the barren rocky landscape tasting of snow. Behind some rocks that'd been stacked up as a makeshift windbreak lay an unmoving figure curled up on a mat, partially wrapped in an old sleeping bag. Beside the body was a worn green pack and an old folding shovel lying askew.

There was a sound of crunching underfoot. "Syd!" I called out rushing toward the body. The figure stirred and moved. *He was alive!*

I ran over holding him upright, tears coming to my eyes. "You're OK!" I shouted.

"I must've slept—did I miss the dawn?"

"No, it's still early. We can watch it together."

"How did you get here? I thought you went down?"

"I was—I mean—I didn't. I got my pack and headed over the ridge, like you said, but then I just couldn't leave you. So I camped up by those rocks, you know, at that spot we passed yesterday, just before the sign. It was really blowing. I woke almost every hour imagining you up here alone. At around four-thirty, I packed up and came to find you."

"How did you know the time?"

"There's a clock in my camera—I checked it so many times the battery's gone."

"That was good thinking. What about water?"

"I had enough. After the Staircase, I always took at least three liters with me. What about you? Are you cold?"

"I'm alright, just a bit tired."

The glow grew brighter and then the sun crossed the horizon. A glowing ball of fire bathed the distant peaks in streaks of red then orange and brilliant yellow. It rose surprisingly fast, the sky warming to a radiant blue. Syd and I, the sole occupants of this great stone promontory witnessing the dawn of a new day!

Gradually the air warmed. Syd stood, stretching his stiff legs.

I'd left my pack back at the junction but using his stove I cooked us a breakfast of oatmeal and tea.

Syd swallowed hungrily as we watched the range of light come to life before us.

"I'm glad you came back and shared this with me."

"So what happened up here? Did you get your vision?"

He didn't respond. He just sipped his tea, staring out at the glowing spires illuminated by the sun.

Finally, he spoke, "Did I ever tell you the story about the seeker?"

"I don't think so."

He began, his voice raspy,

> There was once a seeker who traveled far and wide searching for life's true meaning. On one of his many journeys, he heard tell of a venerable old monk living on a remote mountain peak reputed to know the secret.
>
> The seeker traveled to this faraway land, undergoing all sorts of trials and tribulations, until finally reaching the snowcapped summit.
>
> There he found the venerable old monk sitting in profound yet serene meditation. When the time seemed auspicious, the seeker humbly petitioned him, "Master, I have journeyed far and wide seeking the meaning of life, please enlighten me with your wisdom."
>
> The monk opened his eyes and in a voice of ultimate tranquility intoned, "Life, my son, is a river."
>
> Upon hearing these words, the seeker's face flushed and he spat angrily, "*Life is a river? A river? I traveled all this way. Spent all this time, and all you can tell me is that life is a river?*"
>
> The venerable old monk looked shaken. A worried expression washed across his face. Staring at the seeker with eyes wide he begged, "*You mean it's not a river?*"

Syd looked at me expectantly.

"I don't get it."

He gave a sigh of frustration, "The monk didn't know the answer either. He was just repeating what someone else had told him."

"Oh," I intoned. "So what did *you* find?"

"Nothing," he said flatly. "I sat out on my sleeping pad. I meditated. I did yoga. I watched the stars spin round like a gigantic wheel. I saw meteors. I breathed. I listened. And I shivered. But I found nothing." He stared at the horizon in silence.

I couldn't understand why he was always searching for intellectual meaning in everything—wasn't it enough to just be sitting here enjoying the sunrise? I wondered if he was really as at peace with the world as he professed to be.

When it warmed up, I rinsed the pots and packed up his cooking gear, while he put together his other stuff. Finally, he nodded. Taking his pack for him, we headed down the trail together.

About an hour later we reached the junction and exchanged packs.

Passing the sign for Trail Crest, we began descending the eastern face. Far below, a line of day-hikers spread out along the trail, an antlike procession of pilgrims moving slowly up the mountain.

The trail wound back and forth, gradually making tighter and tighter turns. Someone said there were ninety-nine switchbacks down the face, but I lost count after the first few, trailing Syd down the steep descent.

Soon I could make out the colorful dots of tents perched among the rocks by a tiny lakelet below. That must be Trail Camp—a rocky outpost at twelve thousand feet where many spent the night before their final summit push.

Bacon, lettuce, and tomatoes on wheat toast filled my thoughts, as I contemplated what I would eat when we got down.

After a long while Syd spoke up, "Perhaps there isn't any real meaning. Perhaps that couple at the hot springs were right—that it's really just about raising a healthy family. I have two successful children, both with great spouses, and two wonderful grandsons. I've had a good life. Perhaps I should be content with that?"

"Do you know who you sound like now?"

"Who?"

"Dorothy, when she wakes from her dream at the end of *The Wizard of Oz*."

"Ah yes," he said, changing his voice to a falsetto Asian accent, "*but it was a dweam of extra-ordinary magnitude.*"

"Wait—*that isn't?*—are you quoting Mr. Han from *Enter the Dragon?*"

"No," he smiled, "Dr. Klahn, from *A Fistful of Yen.*"

"*The Bruce Lee parody? Seriously? You've seen that?*"

"It was one of Sean's favorites back when he was a teenager. That and *Big Trouble in Little China*."

"*Those are great!* You never said you liked martial arts films—"

"I'm not a big fan, but I never said I hadn't seen any."

This was so cool.

The trail leveled out and we passed Trail Camp, a ghost town of abandoned tents flapping in the wind.

"You know," I said turning to him, "about life's meaning and all. I've thought a lot about what Permi said back at the hot springs, and I think he was right."

"About the cosmic seedpods?"

"No—not the cosmic seedpods—well maybe—but that's not what I meant. I mean, maybe Permi was right about the trail being the *Tao.*"

He nodded in agreement, "Yes, you can say that."

"I don't mean that the words are the same, or that the trail is a kinda path, or way. I mean—well, let me try to explain—I've had a lot of time just thinking as we hiked, and especially last night up on the rocks—and I've found I really enjoy backpacking. Do you know why?"

"Why?"

" 'Cause when you're backpacking everything is simplified. You take only what you need, and that's what you've gotta make do with."

The trail wound around the side of some enormous boulders. A wide stream tumbled below us to our right.

"What you're saying is, out here in the woods you have no desire for any additional material items, because you'd have to carry them."

"Sorta," I struggled to make sense of my thoughts, "but it's more than that—the actual desire is gone too. Except maybe for better food and wishing I'd brought a jacket, I don't find myself thinking about things I wanna buy, or how to entertain myself. Out here there are no distractions."

"You're in the moment."

"Yeah. Back home there's always some message I need to answer. Some project I need to finish. Or some new place I wanna check out. And when I do get a few moments to myself, what do I do? I pick up my phone. I check my dating account. I read what friends have posted. *Anything* to keep from actually being present. I never just stop and reflect on where I am."

He nodded thoughtfully.

"But out here in the woods, it's different. You sleep, eat, pack, and walk. Except for the weather and maybe getting over a pass or something, there's nothing you need to worry about—no place you need to be other than where you are. You have all the time in the world to reflect and simply experience the present."

"Not everyone does. Remember those two trail runners who flew by us at Wallace Creek? They were in such a hurry to make their miles that they couldn't appreciate where they were. Even on the trail, there are many people who can't let go of their goal-orientated mentality. And it's sad, because it is precisely chasing after some arbitrary goal that prevents us from really experiencing the world. Like me with my photography."

The trail runners would probably have said differently. They probably found their own joy through pushing themselves to the edge—like I did when I used to swim competitively.

"But what about us?" I ventured. "We had a plan and a goal for each day. And finishing the trail is also a goal."

"Yes. But our hike has been open and flexible. We brought enough food and kept the mileage low enough that we could stop anywhere to enjoy a view or take a rest. There was never any hurry. We never had a particular date we needed to finish by. We were here to be on the trail and experience it, not to complete it according to some schedule."

"We were lucky that way. I think most people are constrained by a need to return to work. And we certainly didn't have enough food to linger forever. And then there was our reservation at MTR."

"I understand all that. But the key is flexibility. We got lucky in our timing at MTR, but if we had missed our reservation, then I would have let it go. If our food ran low, we could have found a workaround. *Hike your own hike* also means *make your own trail*. Living in the present doesn't mean abandoning all goals and directions—it's good to have some idea of where you're headed. But it's more important to be open and flexible enough to change direction when you need to."

"I've seen that in the way people walk the trail. Some people saunter, like you said Muir did. You can feel the relaxation in their bodies. They're fun to hang out with—like Permi and Dylan. But others are more rigid. They lean forward and hike with a purpose. They're the ones who end up alarming the birds."

"The same thing happens with people on vacation. I can't tell you how many times I've met people made miserable by their own inflexible schedules." He mimicked a British accent, *"We'll see the Eiffel Tower at nine, Notre Dame at eleven, and the Louvre at two-thirty—"*

"No room for change or to really enjoy something that catches your interest," I said. "You know, when I'm hiking, I get into a state that's very similar to that meditation you taught me. As I walk, I seem to work through my problems, and all the other distractions just melt away."

"I'm glad you've found that. Muir once wrote, *I only went out for a walk and finally concluded to stay out till sundown, for going out, I found, was really going in.*"

"That's exactly how I feel out here."

He smiled. A smooth lake rested on a forested granite shelf below us, the surrounding peaks reflected in its clear waters. The trail was wide enough now that we could walk side by side.

"I really see why Pop loved backpacking. It's amazing just walking through the woods, past lakes, over rocks, by rivers—seeing and absorbing everything around you. Our goal may be to reach some camp, but our real objective is to merge with everything around us."

I turned toward Syd, "Back in LA, when I'm pursuing some goal, like dating a woman, or buying a car, my whole life becomes focused on the future. All of my energy gets wrapped up in how good I'll feel later, and I simply can't enjoy where I am, like I do here."

"The Buddhists call such distractions *Samsara*, the world of false illusions. People chase these illusory desires, only to discover they're still unhappy."

"Like trying to hold on to those waves of pleasure you talked about."

"Exactly," he smiled, the sun reflecting momentarily off his eyes, "that's *Samsara*. The trick that endless goals and desires plays upon on our mind. True happiness is always found in the present."

"This spring when I lost my job, I was pretty upset. But now I see it and this whole trip as a gift from the Universe. A chance to reflect and re-create myself."

"That's a very healthy way of regarding it. Many people spend their present slaving away for some imagined future, when what they really should be doing is figuring out a way to do what they love right now."

"That's what Christie and Jay said. I have some savings—not as much as I'd like—but it's enough. You were right, I should go back to school. I wanna study journalism again, like I was doing before Pop's accident."

"That's quite wise, let me know if you need any help—but don't wait too long to ask."

"Just stop it!"

He halted.

"I've had enough of your fucked-up death humor. I know you're just trying to make light of it, and I'm sorry. But I've really come to care for you. You're like a second Pop to me. And while I know you're dying, it pains me every time you bring it up. I'm not trying to avoid it or anything. I mean, I was before. I was pushing it away like those waves of pain you talked about. But now I see that love also means loss—that you can't care for someone without risking something too. I'll always cherish this time we've had together. But please don't be in a rush to reach the end of it."

"I'm sorry," he said, and we embraced—like father and son.

"Syd," I said dropping my pack, "I wanna take the shovel."

"What do you mean?"

"I mean, you told me the shovel was for me, right? I wanna carry it, I wanna bear the burden. When you do come to die—and I hope it's years from now—I wanna come and help bury you with it. We can take you out to the woods or wherever you want. But I wanna be there to say goodbye, like I never got to do with Pop."

He nodded solemnly, removing his pack and passing me the shovel. It was heavier than it looked, and I strapped it onto the back of my pack. From now on I would keep it to remind me of Syd, to remind me that loving also means loss.

We started down the trail again, the pendular motion of the shovel keeping time as we walked.

"There's this old olive tree out on the farm," he said. "I used to sit under it and read when I was recovering. Cass knows the one. When I pass, I want you to bury me there."

"I will Syd."

There were more trees now. A gentle breeze caressed us with the scent of moist earth and pine. Soon we came to the lake, its waters reflecting the sunshine and helping me to gather my thoughts.

"What I was trying to say earlier—about Permi and the trail being the *Tao* and all—is that you said you found nothing when you sat up on the mountain last night. But I think it's 'cause you were trying too hard to find something. Isn't that a desire too?"

The trail wound its way through the dense trees.

"What I'm trying to say is, from the moment we're born, we're dying. Some faster than others," I glanced at him, hoping he wouldn't misinterpret me. "For example, those fox-tail pines we saw live thousands of years, we get about eighty, while a dog may get fifteen if it's lucky. But it's not about how long we live, it's *how* we live that matters. Walking the trail, I've realized I've been wasting my life. I don't like who I was before, and there's a lot I'm gonna change when we get back—not just school. I wanna find a partner I love and respect. I may even start a family. I'll continue my meditation. And I'll definitely do more backpacking. I hope we can even take another trip or two together—maybe a shorter one with some beers."

He smiled.

"But what I'm saying is, *This trail isn't a trail, it's our lives.* And we must constantly stay present, focused, and aware. It doesn't matter where the trail ends—all that matters is where we are now and how we choose to live in this moment."

He nodded in vigorous agreement, "I'm glad you see that."

"The thing is, we've been hiking together for what, twenty-eight days? And you've taught me a lot. This whole experience has. I don't mean to be critical, but what I've noticed about you, is that you can't seem to accept certain things from the heart. You want an intellectual explanation for everything. Like that experience you had at Woods Creek where you felt yourself becoming one with everything. You were as close to God, or the Universe, or the *Tao*, as one can be. And yet afterward, you started questioning it. You doubted whether the experience was real or not. So you had to starve yourself and sit up on a mountaintop to try again. For what? For confirmation? You already had a *genuine experience.* Why is it you can't accept what your heart is telling you?" His face looked pained, but I could see he was absorbing it. "Remember when we saw that bear just after Wallace Creek?"

"That was at Sandy Meadow."

"After we saw that bear, I started thinking, and I realized the thing that divides us from real experience is language. When we try to put things into words, we intellectualize. We slice up true experience with the blunt instruments of words and language, like a doctor trying to perform brain surgery with a hacksaw. It just doesn't work. True experiences can't be expressed in language, they must be felt, like poetry. Pop used to say that the beauty of poetry isn't in the words—it's in the space between them. Didn't Frost once say, *Poetry is what gets lost in translation?*"

"Your father was quite fond of that quote."

"It's the same with music. The beauty of music isn't in the actual notes—it's what's *between the notes* that matters. It's how it makes you feel. There's no language to describe it. The best we can do is metaphor. That's why I really love the meditation you taught me, 'cause it's direct—without words or thinking. Don't you see, you're asking whether that experience you had at Woods Creek is real is like that 'monkey mind' you taught me to let go of. It's your doubts and fears questioning what you already know with your heart."

We exited the trees at a small ridge. The view from here stretched on to the desert floor. Beyond it were new mountains.

"You see," I continued, "about life—it's like watching a show or a play. And death's the scary part. It's the villain, the monster lurking in the shadows. You told me when you were thirteen, you got into philosophy 'cause you were afraid of death. You wanted to know whether this play called life had a happy ending or not. And here you are dying, and you still don't know the answer. So you're panicking, 'cause you wanna know the outcome before the end of the show. To know if your hero's safe or not."

He swallowed and nodded, looking out toward the horizon.

"When I was a kid, there was this bully at school who picked on me. And I never got over it until I saw this episode of *Kung Fu* where Caine said, *Fear is like a seed that grows. When a fear becomes strong enough, it is like another being within you who fights to stay alive.* After that, I confronted him. I told him off. And you know what? We became friends. It turned out he was picking on me 'cause he was afraid of me too. I'll never forget that. Both of us had let our fear grow to the point where it was more real than each other. I did the same thing when Pop died. By trying to push away the pain, I let my fear of it grow."

We entered the trees again. Syd was listening intently.

"It's the same with you. You've let your fear of death became so large that you can no longer trust what your heart is telling you. There was another episode of *Kung Fu* where Caine said, *If a man lives, it is a certainty he will die. Therefore, it is foolish to think of death as if he were a foe to be vanquished. He will come when he will come.* The point of life, the point of a good play, is *not knowing the ending*. The point is to be present and live life to the fullest. To enjoy the play. Even when parts are painful or scary, they're part of the experience. The trail. The hike. Our lives. This is what it's all about. This is the meaning of life. To be present and not to chase some meaningless horizon. The trail is the *Tao*. The meaning of life is simply to be present during the journey. There is no goal, just the path."

Syd stopped walking, looking at me in profound silence while staring deeply into my eyes, "Thank you, Gil. In all my years of studying philosophy, I've never stopped to ask myself *why I was studying it.* I always thought it was obvious. That I wanted to learn what the great thinkers had to teach about life. But you're right, I was scared. I wanted to know what was behind the curtain. What was in that *undiscovered country* at the end of the play. You're right. Life. The *Tao*. The trail. It's really just where we are now that matters. I knew that in words—but somehow the words never really penetrated my being. Thank you." He was weeping. "Maybe Po really is the right trail name for you."

"Whaddya mean?"

"I'm not thinking of *Kung Fu Panda*. I'm thinking of your Master Po from *Kung Fu*. Maybe a teacher really does learn the most from his students. Maybe it is all a big circle. Your father was always trying to tell me the same things you have. That's why I valued his company so much. But I didn't listen—or at least my heart didn't. And now, like him, here you are at the end of my life, teaching me the lessons I should have learned years ago."

He gave me a long hug and I felt that special connection between us—something beyond father and son—something I couldn't put into words, but which I knew bound us together.

We hiked on. Listening to the birdsong. Breathing in the crisp pine scent. Feeling the warmth of the sun and the texture of the soft earth.

Suddenly the birds ahead fluttered up into the trees chirping in alarm. Sure enough, a group of four young guys came striding up the trail. They were wearing matching lime-green shirts proclaiming, "Whitney Hiking Team," with a sketch of the mountain's profile in white.

"How much further to Mirror Lake?" the leader called to us without breaking stride.

"I'm not sure," Syd replied.

"How's that?" grumbled the leader, not even bothering to stop as he passed. "Didn't you just come from there?"

Syd didn't answer.

The guy shouted back at us over his shoulder, "You know, you two could really use a bath!" His companions chuckled.

"What assholes," I whispered.

Syd turned to me saying, *"And you know what I think? O, wonder! How many goodly creatures are there here! How beauteous mankind is! O brave new world. That has such people in't!"*—It was exactly what Pop woulda said.

We continued, passed in both directions by a steady stream of hikers, either in a rush to get up, or get back down.

As we neared the bottom, we came upon two middle-aged women dressed in clean trail clothes with large black sunglasses. Both had new-looking backpacks, one with a tent strapped to the top. The two had stopped to take a breather. They were arguing in vaguely East Coast accents, "This is *way* harder than climbing Mount Washington," the older looking one was saying, "that was a four-thousand-foot climb, and this one is *six*, and then there's the altitude difference—"

"Well, it can't be harder than Mount Tai, that mountain your brother made us climb in China with a zillion steps!"

"This is going to be way harder than that," the older one insisted, her right hand on her hip.

The two looked up as we approached, taking in our grimy clothing, our worn boots, our unkempt beards, and dirty faces. The older one asked politely, but with some trepidation, "Did you guys just climb Whitney?"

"Yes," I said putting my arm around Syd's shoulder, "after walking two hundred miles in twenty-eight days from Yosemite."

The two women gaped, speechless.

I held back tears as Syd and I walked arm in arm down the rest of the trail.

When we reached the small café at the bottom, we shared a BLT.

EPILOGUE

ABOUT A WEEK after getting back to LA, I received a call from Syd. He was very excited and I could barely get him to slow down on the phone.

He said he'd seen his doctor up in San Francisco and his cancer was in remission. He was coming down to LA in a week to meet me, then we were both flying out to see Ma.

The doctors couldn't say if it was hiking the trail, calorie deprivation, the fresh air, Permi's greens, or any of a million other factors that caused his recovery. They didn't know how long he had—but then again who does?

I'd mounted his shovel up on my wall to remind me to live each day as if it were my last and cherish the time we have.

That night I drank a beer for him.

I'd also heard from Lois and Clark. They said the bulk of the storm we'd been in on Forester was centered over Kearsarge Pass. They'd been trapped by lightning in Onion Valley and finally had to return home 'cause of a schedule conflict at Lois's workplace. But they'd be back to finish the trail next summer. Both of them had me give my best to Syd.

As for me, after getting back, Syd and I spent a few days together on the farm. He'd insisted on my phoning up Northwestern and they'd agreed to let me return in the fall—I'd be studying journalism again.

I'd also lost about twenty pounds and my belly was all but gone. Maybe I should write a book called *The Muir Trail Diet—Lose twenty pounds in a month on America's most famous trail*. The time had come for some serious dating—*serious*, I mean. I might even take up swimming again.

I'd also heard something from Kydoime. She'd left a message asking me to call her and get together. Should I call her back, or leave what happened on the trail behind me? I had time to think about it.

There was this one strange moment that kept coming back to me. It was in Lone Pine, after Syd and I had finished the trail. We'd checked into a small motel and I'd gone out for a walk while Syd showered.

Going about a block, I came to an intersection with the main highway, which ran through the center of the small town. There was a traffic light. No one was coming the other way, but this whole line of sedans, compacts, trucks, and even a camper were all obediently stopped, just waiting at a red light. It was hot out, perhaps in the nineties, and through the rolled-down window of a car I could see the driver wearing what looked like a very uncomfortable suit and tie.

Sitting down on the warm sidewalk, I stared at the line of travelers, all waiting for a mechanical light at an empty intersection of life, and just wondered at it all.

Thank you for reading. If you've enjoyed this book, please consider leaving an honest review on your favorite store or book news website.

CONFESSION

THIS BOOK fits somewhere in the gray area between fiction and nonfiction. The story is based on a journey I took on the John Muir Trail at the age of 50 with my friend Joey and my wife Audrey. Joey hiked with me from Tuolumne Meadows to Le Conte Canyon. My wife rode in on horseback over Bishop Pass with our friend Tram. Joey and Tram then rode back out over the pass, while Audrey and I continued on foot to Mount Whitney.

All of the campsites and trails in this book are the ones we used on our journey, except for two, which I moved slightly in order to accommodate parts of the story.

Some of the characters are based on real people, others are composites or creations. Unless given specific permission, real names have been changed. Many of the incidents were taken from events that occurred on our JMT hike, or over the thirty or so years I've been backpacking.

Although my father has chronic lymphatic leukemia, which is now in remission thanks to chemotherapy, and my wife works in oncology, Syd's cancer is purely a story element. I would not espouse anyone hiking the JMT as a treatment for cancer. That said, were I diagnosed with terminal cancer and physically able, like Syd, I would rather spend my last days living in nature than dying in a hospital.

I want to say thank you to my wife and children for their patience with me while I was writing and rewriting this. To Faith Rumm, whose love for the wilderness is illuminated through her fantastic artwork. To Jeremy Ashcroft, whose maps and drawings bring the text to life and give the story that classic feel of the adventure novels I grew up with. To my fantastic editors: Alyssa Matesic, whose helpful comments, detailed discussion of various themes, and careful edits helped make this a better narrative; and Denise Botelho, whose eagle eyes and stylistic insights helped make this a much more readable text. To Mark Bergeron at PD&PS, whose fantastic job typesetting has made this book a pleasure on the eyes. To Elizabeth Wenk and Peter Hirst, whose close reading and comments helped with many of the factual details. To my sister Ruth and my friends Peter, Krishna, Wynne, and Xiaohong, whose helpful advice was invaluable in making this a better story. To Steve Roper, of whom I've always been a fan, thank you so much for agreeing to read my manuscript and for your kind words and helpful suggestions. To Lindsey, whose detailed editing of each chapter and comments were extremely helpful—I fully expect you to be a wilderness ranger one day! To Ryan, who schooled me on the intricacies of New Zealand accents and whose close reading was equally helpful. To my cousin Rachel, who has been busy summiting Adirondack peaks and hopefully one day will hike the JMT. To my best friend Jose. To my hiking buddies Joey, Roy, Pat, Corvin, and Hamid. To the folks of *CHAOS*—you know who you are. To Hikin' Jim—your many puns never failed to peak my interest. To Scott, Risa, Andrea, Brittany, Bob, Jeff, Laura, and all the others whom I met "on trail." To Phil and Mike, for your friendship at the gym. To Cuyler, for shuttling me to and from numerous wilderness trailheads over the years and always giving me a place to pitch my tent in Fresno. To the memory of Andrew Bradeen and Catherine Sothern. To everyone at VVR and MTR. To all the terrific backcountry rangers I've met helping to make the wilderness a better and safer place. To all of the fire crews and search and rescue workers keeping us safe out there. To the numerous trail crew volunteers and workers who help keep the JMT and other trails possible. To all of the great organizations working for the preservation and conservation of wilderness and specifically with regards to the JMT: The Yosemite Conservancy, Sierra Club, and Pacific Crest Trail Association. To all of the other wonderful people I've met in the wilderness over the years. And finally, to the memory of Bradley Dean, who first introduced me to Thoreau and *Walden*. All of your friendships and stories are what made this book possible.

I hope this book will inspire those of you who are able to strap on packs and venture out into the wilderness—if even for a day.

Hope to see you there!

—*Ethan Gallogly, aka "Po"*

FOR NEW HIKERS

A FTER THE PUBLICATION of *Wild* by Cheryl Strayed, the Pacific Crest Trail experienced what some termed *The Wild Effect*—a surge of inexperienced hikers applying for permits and setting out to hike the grueling 2,650-mile PCT. While some succeeded, most of these aspiring novices never made it more than a few days on trail. But they did create problems ranging from a lack of available permits, to an overwhelming number of unprepared hikers in both sensitive and potentially dangerous wilderness settings.

The John Muir Trail is a challenging and strenuous 220-mile long-distance hike that passes through the highest terrain in the Sierra. Every year hikers are seriously injured, need to be evacuated, or lose their lives due to falls, dangerous river crossings, and high-altitude mountain sickness—just to list a few of the more common hazards. And those who wish to start in Yosemite must enter a lottery to obtain one of the few precious permits available. It is not a trail for the typical first-time backpacker.

If you are a beginner, have been inspired by this book, and are longing to see firsthand some of the beauty of the Sierra, it is recommended you start with some shorter trips. Try to avoid heavily impacted areas, such as Yosemite Valley, Tuolumne Meadows, or Whitney Portal. Many great suggestions for exploring the less-traveled regions of the Sierra can be found in the resources *Sierra North* and *Sierra South* listed in the Recommended Reading section of this book.

Also consider visiting the Sierra Nevada foothills, which offer many gorgeous trails with beautiful wildflowers and easier approaches—making them excellent training grounds before venturing into the high country.

This book is not a backpacking guide. In fact, parts could be read as *what not to do while backpacking.* Many excellent guidebooks and online sites exist to help you prepare for a first backpacking trip. The best method is to go with an experienced friend, family member, or professional guide who can lend you equipment and instruct you in *leave no trace* (LNT) principles, proper food storage, packing, navigation, mountain safety, fire regulations, and help you obtain a wilderness permit.

In addition to backpacking, there are many amazing day-hikes that can be done in the Sierra, and a number of High Sierra Camps that offer beds, food, and shelter for those who don't wish to carry a heavy pack (a wilderness permit and reservation is required). A number of commercial outfitters and ranches also offer extended pack-animal supported treks. It is beyond the scope of this book to list all available options.

Finally, many novices seem unaware that mobile phones don't generally have reception up in the High Country. If you're heading out into the wilderness, please make a plan, share it with your friends and family, check the weather, and, if possible, carry one of the mobile emergency satellite devices now available for rent or purchase. If you do run into serious trouble, you'll have a way of getting help.

The Sierra Nevada is an amazing place, and I encourage everyone who can to take at least one journey into these mountains to witness firsthand what Muir called *The Range of Light*.

Happy Trails!

Follow *The Trail* at:

www.ethangallogly.com

BRIEF TIMELINE OF HISTORIC EVENTS

1823–1834: Scottish botanist David Douglas explores the West Coast of America and Hawaii, collecting botanical specimens and naming new species.

1848: Mexican cession of California to the United States.

1849: John Muir immigrates from Scotland to America with his family at age 11.

1851: Mariposa War against the Native Americans living in Yosemite Valley.

1850–1854: Scottish gardener John Jeffrey explores the Washington, Oregon, and California, collecting botanical specimens and naming new species.

1860–1868: California Geological Survey of the Sierra under Josiah Whitney. Members included William Brewer, James Cooper, William Gabb, Charles Hoffmann, Watson Goodyear, and Clarence King.

1861–1865: American Civil War.

1864: Clarence King and Richard Cotter climb Mt. Tyndall while aiming for Mt. Whitney; King makes a second attempt to climb Mt. Whitney but fails to find a route to the summit.

1864: President Lincoln signs the "Yosemite Grant" (the first instance of park land being set aside by the federal government); Yosemite Valley and Mariposa Grove become a California state park.

1867: Clarence King's third attempt at summiting Mt. Whitney results in his summiting of Mt. Langley.

1867–1868: John Muir embarks on a thousand-mile trek from Kentucky to Florida, then journeys to Yosemite.

1870: Geologist Joseph Le Conte (father to J.N. LeConte) meets with Muir in Yosemite and champions Muir's theory of the glacial sculpting of valleys and rock formations in the Sierra.

1872: John Muir makes the first ascent of Mt. Ritter.

1873: Clarence King finally summits Mt. Whitney, a month after its first ascent by Charles Begole, A. H. Johnson, and John Lucas, three residents of Lone Pine who want to name it Fisherman's Peak. Muir is the next to climb Mt. Whitney via what becomes known as *The Mountaineer's Route*.

1884: According to his 1940 account, Theodore Solomons at age 14 envisions a route across the crest of the Sierra that is later to become the John Muir Trail.

1890: J.N. LeConte at age 20 and three friends from Berkeley embark on a 652-mile trek through the Sierra.

1890: The land around Yosemite is made into a national park; Yosemite Valley and Mariposa grove remain a state park.

1892: Sierra Club founded to help protect the land in the Sierra Nevada. John Muir is elected its first president.

1892: Theodore Solomons' first expedition in search of a High Mountain Route along the crest of the Sierra with his cousin Sidney Peixotto. Together with J.N. LeConte, the three climb Mt. Ritter and return to Yosemite. Solomons then continues on his own, including taking the first photographs from the top of Mt. Ritter. That August, J.N. LeConte is appointed an Assistant Professor of Mechanical Engineering at Berkeley.

1893: J.N. LeConte's first integrated map of the Yosemite and Kings Canyon region is published in the *Sierra Club Bulletin*.

1894: Theodore Solomons' second expedition with Leigh Bierce. Following exploration of the Grand Canyon of the Tuolumne, the two flee the Sierra in a snowstorm near Seven Gables.

1895: Theodore Solomons' third expedition with Ernest Bonner, including spotting but not exploring Muir Pass, descending the Enchanted Gorge, and exploring the region around Tehipite Dome.

1895: Stanford Art Professor Bolton Brown at age 30 attempts Mt. Clarence King; then returning with a reluctant mule, travels up Cartridge Creek, sketches the Palisades region, and climbs Arrow Peak.

1896: Theodore Solomons, Walter Starr Sr. (the father of "Peter" Starr), and Alan Pickering set out on Solomons' fourth expedition. Solomons becomes ill and turns back. Starr and Pickering continue on, becoming the first to cross from Yosemite to Kings Canyon with pack animals, but over a lower route than Solomons envisioned.

1896: Bolton Brown and his bride Lucy spend their honeymoon exploring and sketching the regions around what is to become the southern part of the JMT. Brown summits Mt. Clarence King with a lasso.

1898: J.N. LeConte and Clarence Cory continue the search for a stock route between Yosemite and Kings Canyon across the higher elevation Goddard Divide region without success.

1899: Bolton Brown, his wife Lucy, and their two-year-old daughter Eleanor explore the southern Sierra, discovering with is now called Glenn Pass and Rae Lakes.

1901: San Francisco lawyer William Colby organizes the Sierra Club's first annual summer outing.

1902–1903: J.N. LeConte maps the Palisades, making a number of first ascents.

1903: Buffalo Soldiers under the command of Colonel Charles Young, the first Black superintendent of a National Park, construct most of a stock trail on Mount Whitney between Lone Pine and Guitar Lake. The last few miles of this trail were completed by the people of Lone Pine.

1903: John Muir guides President Theodore Roosevelt through the regions around Yosemite Valley, encouraging him to incorporate Yosemite Valley and Mariposa Grove into the larger national park surrounding them.

1904: J.N. LeConte returns with geologist Grove Gilbert to search for a stock route across the Goddard Divide, climbs what is to become Muir Pass, but turns back after staring down the "savage black gorges" on the other side.

1904: Gustave F. Marsh improves the Mount Whitney stock trail for the transportation of scientific instruments, extending the trail to the summit.

1906: Congress makes Yosemite Valley and Mariposa Grove part of Yosemite National Park.

1907: George R. Davis of the U.S. Geological Survey party makes the first crossing of Muir Pass with stock.

1908: J.N. LeConte, Duncan McDuffie, and James Hutchinson make the first thru-hike from Yosemite to Kings Canyon of the then proposed route for what is to eventually become the John Muir Trail.

1909: Gustave F. Marsh completes construction of the Smithsonian Institute Shelter on the summit of Mount Whitney.

1914–1918: World War I.

1914: Building of the High Mountain Route proposed and adopted on a Sierra Club Outing at Soda Springs.

1914: John Muir dies; it is decided that the proposed trail be named the "John Muir Trail" in his honor.

1915: Bill for the construction of the John Muir Trail passes the California State Senate.

1915–1917: J.N. LeConte becomes the second president of the Sierra Club.

1915: Official construction of the John Muir Trail begins under supervision of state engineer Wilbur McClure.

1917–1919: William Colby becomes the third president of the Sierra Club, continuing oversight of the construction of the John Muir Trail.

1923: Damming of Hetch Hetchy.

1928–1932: Construction of the High Sierra Trail, a route running perpendicular to the JMT from the Giant Sequoias to Mt. Whitney.

1929–1930: American Great Depression.

1931: Forester Pass completed (prior to this the route of the JMT ran east over Junction and Shepherd passes).

1932: Theodore Solomons returns to the Sierra in his sixties to hike the almost completed John Muir Trail.

1933: John Muir Hut completed on Muir Pass with dedication ceremony by the Sierra Club.

1933: "Peter" Starr (Walter Starr, Jr.) dies in a climbing accident in the Minarets, his body is located by the famous climber Norman Clyde.

1934: Walter Starr organizes and publishes his son's notes as, *Starr's Guide to the John Muir Trail and the High Sierra Region.*

1938: Work on the John Muir Trail is completed with the opening of the Golden Staircase (prior to its opening, JMT travelers detoured over Cartridge Pass or Granite Pass to continue the trail).

RECOMMENDED READING

INSPIRATIONAL WRITINGS

Abbey, Edward. 1968. *Desert Solitaire*. New York: Touchstone.

Abbey, Edward. 1975. *The Monkey Wrench Gang*. New York: Harper Perennial Modern Classics.

Blehm, Eric. 2006. *The Last Season*. New York: Harper Perennial.

Bryson, Bill. 1998. *A Walk in the Woods: Rediscovering America on the Appalachian Trail*. New York: Broadway Books.

Clyde, Norman. 1971. *Norman Clyde of the Sierra Nevada: Rambles Through the Range of Light*. San Francisco: Scrimshaw Press.

Diamond, Jared. 2005. *Collapse: How Societies Choose to Fail or Succeed*. New York: Penguin Books.

Feng, Gia-Fu, and Jane English, trans. 1972. *Lao Tsu: Tao Te Ching*. New York: Vintage Books. (Original Chinese from 6th Century BC [approx.].)

Feng, Gia-Fu, and Jane English, trans. 1974, *Chuang Tsu: Inner Chapters*. New York: Vintage Books. (Original Chinese from 4th Century BC [approx.].)

Fletcher, Colin. 1964. *The Thousand-Mile Summer*. New York: Vintage Books.

Fletcher, Colin. 1967. *The Man Who Walked Through Time*. New York: Vintage Books.

Hesse, Hermann. 1971. *Siddhartha*. Translated by Hilda Rosner. New York: Bantam Books. (Orig. pub. in German 1922.)

Kimmerer, Robin Wall. 2013. *Braiding Sweetgrass: Indigenous Wisdom, Scientific Knowledge, and the Teachings of Plants*. Canada: Milkweed Editions.

Mann, Barney Scout. 2020. *Journeys North: The Pacific Crest Trail*. Seattle, WA: Mountaineers Books.

Montgomery, Ben. 2014. *Grandma Gatewood's Walk: The Inspiring Story of the Woman Who Saved the Appalachian Trail*. Chicago, IL: Chicago Review Press.

Muir, John. 1911. *My First Summer in the Sierra*. Boston: Houghton Mifflin Company.

Muir, John. 1916. *The Mountains of California*. New York: Modern Library.

Schneider, Eric D., and Dorion Sagan. 2005. *Into the Cool: Energy Flow, Thermodynamics, and Life*. Chicago, IL: The University of Chicago Press.

Strayed, Cheryl. 2012. *Wild: From Lost to Found on the Pacific Crest Trail*. New York: Vintage Books.

Thoreau, Henry David. 1966. *Walden* and "Civil Disobedience" (A Norton Critical Edition). Edited by Owen Thomas. New York: W. W. Norton and Company. (*Walden* orig. pub. 1854; "Civil Disobedience" orig. pub 1849.)

Watts, Alan, with the collaboration of Al Chung-liang Huang. 1975. *Tao: The Watercourse Way*. Illustrated by Lee Chih-chang. New York: Pantheon Books.

Wohlleben, Peter. 2016. *The Hidden Life of Trees: What They Feel, How They*

Communicate—Discoveries from a Secret World. Translated by Jane Billinghurst. Berkeley: Greystone Books.

Xu, Yuanchong, trans. 2006. *300 Tang Poems (Classified by Theme).* Beijing: China Translation and Publishing Corporation. (Original Chinese from 618–907 AD.)

PHOTOGRAPHY AND ESSAYS

Adams, Ansel. 1936. *Sierra Nevada: The John Muir Trail.* New York: Little Brown and Company. (Reprinted 2006.)

Dittli, John (photos), and Mark A. Schlenz (text). 2009. *Walk the Sky: Following the John Muir Trail.* Bishop, CA: Companion Press. www.johndittli.com

Luong, QT. 2016. *Treasured Lands.* Petaluma, CA: Cameron Company.

Rowell, Galen. 2010. *Galen Rowell's Sierra Nevada.* San Francisco: Sierra Club Books.

HISTORICAL REFERENCES AND BIOGRAPHIES

Adams, Clinton. 1993. *Crayonstone: The Life and Works of Bolton Brown with a Catalogue of His Lithographs.* Albuquerque, NM: University of New Mexico Press.

Alsup, William. 2001. *Missing in the Minarets: The Search for Walter A. Starr, Jr.* El Portal, CA: Yosemite Conservancy.

Arnold, Daniel. 2009. *Early Days in the Range of Light: Encounters with Legendary Mountaineers.* Berkeley: Counterpoint.

Brewer, William H. 2003. *Up and Down California in 1860–1864: The Journal of William H. Brewer.* 4th ed. Edited by Francis P. Farquhar. Berkeley: University of California Press. (Orig. pub. 1966.)

Browning, Peter, ed. 2007. *Splendid Mountains: Early Explorations in the Sierra Nevada.* Lafayette, CA: Great West Books. (A collection of publications from the *Sierra Club Bulletin* and other sources dating from 1868 to 1921.)

Eldredge, Ward. 2003. *In the Summer of 1903: Colonel Charles Young and the Buffalo Soldiers in Sequoia National Park.* Three Rivers, CA: Sequoia Natural History Association.

Farquhar, Francis P. 2007. *History of the Sierra Nevada.* Revised and Updated. Berkeley: University of California Press. (Orig. pub. 1965.)

King, Clarence. 1997. *Mountaineering in the Sierra Nevada.* Edited and with a Preface by Francis P. Farquhar. Lincoln, NE: University of Nebraska Press. (Orig. pub. 1872.)

Roth, Hal. 1965. *Pathway in the Sky: The Story of the John Muir Trail.* Berkeley: Howell North.

Russell, Carl Parcher. 1932. *One Hundred Years in Yosemite: The Story of a Great Park and Its Friends.* Berkeley: University of California Press.

Sargent, Shirley. 1989. *Solomons of the Sierra: The Pioneer of the John Muir Trail.* Yosemite, CA: Flying Spur Press.

Wolfe, Linnie Marsh. 1945. *Son of Wilderness: The Life of John Muir.* Madison, WI: University of Wisconsin Press.

TRAIL MEMOIRS

Aksamit, Inga. 2018. *Highs and Lows on the John Muir Trail*. 2nd ed. Kenwood, CA: Pacific Adventures Press.

Foskett, Keith. 2018. *The Last Englishman: A 2,640-Mile Hiking Adventure on the Pacific Crest Trail*. London: CreateSpace Independent Publishing Platform.

Oliver-Tierney, Lori. 2019. *Trudge: A Midlife Crisis on the John Muir Trail*. Irvine, CA: Acorn Publishing.

Roberts, Suzanne. 2012. *Almost Somewhere: Twenty-Eight Days on the John Muir Trail*. Lincoln, NE: University of Nebraska Press.

TRAIL, HIKING, FOOD, AND FIELD GUIDES

Arno, Stephen F. 1973. *Discovering Sierra Trees*. Illustrated by Jane Gyer. Yosemite, CA: Yosemite Association and Sequoia Natural History Association in cooperation with the National Park Service.

Buscombe, Gary. 2015. *A Hiking Guide to the Theodore Solomons Trail*. 2nd ed. Edited by Jenna Tokoyama. Tulsa, OK: High Adventure Press. First printed in 1983.

Laws, John Muir. 2007. *The Laws Field Guide to the Sierra Nevada* (California Academy of Sciences). Berkeley: Heyday Books.

March, Laurie Ann. 2008. *A Fork in the Trail: Mouthwatering Meals and Tempting Treats for the Backcountry*. Birmingham, AL: Wilderness Press.

McDonnel, Jackie. 2018. *Yogi's Pacific Crest Trail Handbook: 2019 Edition*. Kennedy Meadows, CA: Yogi's Books.

Roper, Steve. 1997. *Sierra High Route: Traversing Timberline Country*. 2nd ed. Seattle, WA: Mountaineers Books.

Wenk, Elizabeth. 2014. *John Muir Trail. The Essential Guide to Hiking America's Most Famous Trail*. 5th ed. Birmingham, AL: Wilderness Press. (Orig. pub. 1978.)

Wenk, Elizabeth. 2015. *Wildflowers of the High Sierra and John Muir Trail*. Birmingham, AL: Wilderness Press.

Wenk, Elizabeth, and Mike White. 2021. *Sierra North: Backpacking Trips in California's Sierra Nevada*. 10th ed. Birmingham, AL: Wilderness Press. (Orig. pub. 1967.)

Wenk, Elizabeth, and Mike White. 2021. *Sierra South: Backpacking Trips in California's Sierra Nevada*. 9th ed. Birmingham, AL: Wilderness Press. (Orig. pub. 1968.)

Wenk, Elizabeth, and Jerry Schaffer. 2021. *Yosemite National Park: Your Complete Hiking Guide*. 6th ed. Birmingham, AL: Wilderness Press. (Orig. pub. 1978.)

FARMING AND FORAGING

Deur, Douglas. 2014. *Pacific Northwest Foraging, 120 Wild and Flavorful Edibles from Alaska Blueberries to Wild Hazelnuts*. Portland, OR: Timber Press.

Fukuoka, Masanobu. 1978. *The One-Straw Revolution: An Introduction to Natural Farming*. New York: New York Review Books.

Gibbons, Euell. 1962. *Stalking the Wild Asparagus*. Chambersburg, PA: Allan C. Hood & Company.

Kallas, John. 2010. *Edible Wild Plants: Wild Foods from Dirt to Plate*. Layton, UT: Gibbs Smith.

Mollison, Bill. 2002. *Introduction to Permaculture*. 2nd rev. ed. Tasmania, AU: Tagari Publications. (Orig. pub. 1991.)

Nyerges, Christopher. 2014. *Guide to Wild Foods and Useful Plants*. 2nd ed. Chicago, IL: Chicago Review Press.

Thayer, Samuel. 2006. *The Forager's Harvest: A Guide to Identifying, Harvesting, and Preparing Edible Wild Plants*. Bruce, WI: Forager's Harvest Press.

Thayer, Samuel. 2010. *Nature's Garden: A Guide to Identifying, Harvesting, and Preparing Edible Wild Plants*. Bruce, WI: Forager's Harvest Press.

WEBSITES

Because of their inevitable flux, some of these links may have changed since publication.

The John Muir Trail Wilderness Conservancy: https://jmtwilderness.org

Requiem for Hetch Hetchy: https://vault.sierraclub.org/ca/hetchhetchy/requiem_for_hetch_hetchy.html

Pacific Crest Trail Association: https://www.pcta.org/discover-the-trail/john-muir-trail/

Planning your Thru-Hike of the John Muir Trail: http://jmtbook.com

Inga's Adventures: http://ingasadventures.com

Ladies of the JMT: https://www.facebook.com/groups/LadiesOfTheJMT/

Here's What It Takes to Hike the John Muir Trail: https://www.outsideonline.com/2325726/john-muir-trail-backpacking-study

The Annual JMT Hiker Survey: https://www.facebook.com/JMTHikerSurvey

Yosemite National Park: https://www.nps.gov/yose/planyourvisit/jmtfaq.htm

FILM

Mile . . . Mile and a Half. 2013. Directed by Jason M. Fitzpatrick and Ric Serena. Written by Jason M. Fitzpatrick. 87 minutes.

WHERE TO START

The single most useful reference for someone considering a hike along all or part of the JMT is Elizabeth Wenk's excellent guide—the one Syd carries in The Trail:

Wenk, Elizabeth. 2014. *John Muir Trail: The Essential Guide to Hiking America's Most Famous Trail*. 5th ed. Birmingham, AL: Wilderness Press. (Orig. pub. 1978.)

Made in the USA
Middletown, DE
15 November 2022

14953926R00217